Pra

'No one can mix a deliciously classy cocktail of intrigue, passion and glamour like Tasmina Perry.'
Hello

'Takes you to the most glamorous corners of the globe while keeping you on the edge of your seat.' *Glamour*

'Another brilliant page-turner from the queen of the beach read.' *Red*

'Gripping from the off: sexy scandalous brilliance, this book is a genuine must-read' ***** *Heat*

'This glitzy, fast-paced mystery will hook you from the start…' *Prima*

'Tasmina Perry just gets better and better. Utter bliss.'
InStyle

Sunflower & Co is committed to the environment. This book was produced by print-on-demand technology as it is the best way to reduce waste. We have also launched The Sunflower Seed Project – for every print book we sell, we will plant a tree in a part of the world with high levels of poverty, to restore the forests and create employment opportunities. The sale of this book means a tree has been planted in Haiti.

This edition published by Sunflower & Co 2021

ISBN 978-1-911297-30-7

Also available by Tasmina Perry:
Daddy's Girls
Gold Diggers
Guilty Pleasures
Original Sin
Kiss Heaven Goodbye
Private Lives
Perfect Strangers
The Proposal
Deep Blue Sea
The Last Kiss Goodbye
The House on Sunset Lake
The Pool House
Friend of the Family

www.tasminaperry.com

The Yacht Party

Tasmina Perry

Sunflower & Co

Prologue

THE SEA STRETCHED out for miles in every direction, nothing but blue and green and glints of gold. Privacy. That's what money bought you. The bay was empty save for one solitary superyacht, her long white hull reflecting in the water; it might as well have been floating in space.

BOOM!

The walnut stock jerked against his shoulder.

BOOM!

'Another two there, I think,' he said, breaking the shotgun and watching the shells spin away into the water far below. The two men standing on the upper deck smiled as there was a sudden burst of applause from the cocktail lounge to the rear of the yacht.

'You're too kind!' called the grey haired man as three beautiful women in bikinis raised their cocktail glasses and whooped their approval.

'Sycophants,' he muttered to his companion.

'They merely appreciate a master at work,' smiled the younger man, raising his own gun. 'Pull!'

A uniformed crew member released the clays, arcing up over the starboard side of the yacht.

BOOM!

One clay shattered.

BOOM!

The other span across the horizon and dropped into the sea.

'Oh, bad luck.'

Except of course it wasn't. He'd missed the second clay deliberately. It was all part of the game. Let your opponent win, or at least think they have.

He looked down at the other guests watching this one-sided duel. The women in sarongs and sunglasses, the men all impeccably dressed in tailored shorts and shirts, despite the heat. Jermyn Street. Nantucket reds. Something discreet like a Breitling or a Chopard. Preppy, they called it in the States, but it was a uniform, a rigid dress code that spoke of history and privilege, a costume that declared their allegiance to capitalism and wealth. And above all, to continuity. Which was the real reason they were here. Not just shooting off guns for the fun of it.

He pulled two shells from a crystal bowl and slid them into the breech, cocking the gun with a satisfying click. When a gun cost more than a brand new Rolls Royce, you expected it to function perfectly and of course it did, just like everything else in this life. Almost everything.

'So your problem is sorted now?' he said, looking across to the grey haired man who nodded.

'Pull!'

The clays flew in a perfect parabola.

BOOM! – pause – BOOM!

'Yes, your man Schmitt was very good, as you

promised. You always do know the best people.'

'I'm here to help,' the younger man said graciously, swinging his gun up in an arc. 'Any problems and you can always come to me.'

'BOOM! BOOM!'

'You know I am grateful for our friendship.'

He put his gun down, ready to make his move. Outwardly he was calm, but inside, he knew how high the stakes were.

'Speaking of which, there is something you can do for me.'

He spoke smoothly, but this was a break with protocol. He never asked for help. He was the man who fixed other people's problems. But Schmitt couldn't sort this one. In fact the only man who could was standing right next to him. There was a moment's pause, then the grey-haired man raised a regal hand, signalling to yacht staff. The bloodsport was over, for now at least.

'I think this calls for a drink, don't you?'

Chapter One

LARA HAD EXPECTED the press, but she hadn't expected the crowds. She could hear them even before they got to the entrance, chanting some slogan she couldn't quite make out.

'Looks like the fan club has turned out, hmm?' said Gerald Rawles, the *Chronicle*'s barrister, as he led them through the high lobby of the law courts.

When Lara had first walked into the Royal Courts of Justice two weeks previously, she had been awed by its magnificence: the high Gothic exterior, the polished marble floor, statues and carved archways pressing in on either side, it was all designed to drown you in grandeur, to put you in your place. The great cathedrals worked on the same principle, to remind you that whatever your troubles, there were greater forces at work – God and the law. And in this building, they were one and the same. *Or they had been.*

Lara looked back at the grand staircase to her left, towards Court number three. Today the law had let Lara down, it had let them all down. Despite having evidence, despite *knowing* that they were absolutely right, her newspaper had lost their libel case against Felix Tait, a stronger, better connected opponent. And now this great open lobby felt claustrophobic and a little grubby.

As they reached the huge arched doors, the noise outside began to swell and suddenly a cheer went up.

'At least someone's having fun,' muttered Nicholas Avery, the Chairman of the *Chronicle*. He was a tall, aristocratic man, the kind for whom a Savile Row suit seemed part of his being rather than a style choice, a throwback to the old days of the 'inkies' when newspaper owners were Lords and journalism was a gentleman's career, but even Nicholas's upright bearing had sagged a little during the libel case. Not that the judgement against the paper had been a surprise – not really. In hindsight, who would have bet on the *Chronicle* beating a libel case against Felix Tait, one of the most wealthy and powerful men in the world? Yes, the *Chronicle* was a respected title with an international reputation for breaking news, but Felix Tait was, well, Felix Tait. If he didn't own something, he could just buy it up and shut it down. But now he didn't need to: he had crippled them.

'Sorry it didn't go our way,' said Gerald. 'But we did have rotten luck all the way through.'

Lara almost laughed at the understatement. Rotten luck didn't even begin to cover it.

The Chronicle's investigations team had caught tech tycoon Felix Tait visiting a high-class prostitute. They had sworn testimonies, photographs and phone records: they could prove it. But Tait had something up his sleeve. He had an alibi, dramatically entered into evidence at the last minute. It was flimsy to say the least, but the Judge had accepted it – and that had been it.

'Who needs bad luck when you have Judge Winters?' said Alex Ford, the deputy editor of the *Chronicle* and technically Lara's boss, not that he ever played that card. They were friends first, colleagues after. Gerald looked across, his expression sympathetic.

'The judge didn't help, I'll grant you that. But sometimes the game just doesn't go your way.'

'I'm not sure now is the time for blaming the system,' said Darius Allen, the *Chronicle*'s editor-in-chief. 'Instead, we need a full debrief on what went wrong. This has been a disaster for the paper and for the press as a whole.'

Lara glanced at him. *A disaster for you*, she thought. Darius had been bullish from the start, clearly imagining his speeches of personal victory on the evening news. As the trial had gone on and it had become obvious that The Chronicle might lose, Darius's rhetoric shifted to presenting himself as a crusader for free speech, crushed by judicial injustice when in fact, Felix Tait had simply out-played them.

As Gerald withdrew, Lara peered out through the doors of the court. There was an actual crowd out there, pushing against waist-high barriers; it was more like a One Direction reunion than a libel trial. Alex held up his phone and nodded towards the exit. 'Our car's here. Head straight for it.'

A roar went up as the doors opened and Lara flinched at the glare of the flashbulbs. The roar became a cheer as the assembled crowd recognised the *Chronicle* team. At least someone appreciated what they'd been doing.

'You were robbed!' shouted a man in a waistcoat. 'It's a bloody shame!'

'Vultures!' cried a woman, holding up a home-made banner with that same word scrawled across the middle. It wasn't clear who she thought the vultures were.

'Lara, this way,' shouted Alex, grabbing her hand. Two policemen were holding back a line of photographers and journalists, the car waiting at the far end.

'Lara! Lara, over here!' shouted a voice as they passed.

She looked up. Lara should have been used to this, of course, but her natural place was on the other side of the barriers.

'How do you feel about the verdict, Lara?'

Lara recognised the woman with the Dictaphone thrust out in front of her. Deborah Simmons from the *Examiner*, a sour smile on her face. Simmons was a mean girl writ large, using her column inches to bully and belittle. Lara stopped and leaned towards Deborah's tape machine.

'The verdict is bullshit,' she said sweetly. Lara took a moment to enjoy the look of shock on the woman's face, then added. 'You can quote me on that.'

She would have said more, but Alex was pulling on her arm, yanking her into the car then slamming the door shut behind them.

Lara slumped into the black leather seat trying to

draw breath. The quiet purr of the engine was a shock after the cacophony on the street.

'Don't engage with them,' said Alex firmly. He was angry, but Lara knew he was right. Alex was always right. He had been a close friend since their days as students on a postgraduate journalism course, and he had been a rock throughout the whole trial; as deputy editor he wasn't even named on the writ, but he had been there at the High Court whenever his schedule had allowed it, just to support her.

'Remember the day we graduated?' he said with a half-smile.

Despite herself, Lara gave a soft good-natured snort. They had raised a glass of cheap wine and had toasted 'our future adventures'.

'Not exactly what I had in mind,' said Lara, with a grim smile.

The driver was about to pull away when the front door opened and Nicholas slid into the passenger seat.

'Mind if I join you?' he said. Not a question.

'I thought you were doing the press conference,' said Lara.

Nicholas turned round to fix her with his disapproving gaze.

'Darius is making a short statement. The company will put out a press release later. We'll make sure it's more considered than your interchange with Deborah Simmons back there. 'Bullshit' indeed.'

'But it *is* bullshit!' snapped Lara, her patience finally giving way. 'If she had any sense Deborah Simmons would see that what's good for Felix Tait is bad for all the press.'

Nicholas tutted, the schoolmaster disappointed with his pupil.

'All Deborah Simmons cares about is tomorrow's headline. Something we could all learn from.'

Lara was about to snap back a reply, but felt an urgent squeeze of her hand from Alex.

'At least everyone knows what kind of man Tait is now, Lar,' said Alex.

'A noble sentiment,' said Nicholas. 'But it's not enough to *know* something. You also have to be able to prove it in court.'

That felt bit rich, coming from Nicholas Avery, a man who had made a fortune from splashing sensational headlines across the *Chronicle*'s front pages, relying on the supposition that most people wouldn't take it to court. But Felix Tait wasn't 'most people'. He had money and the hide of a rhino and despite the fact his alibi stank – his personal chef had sworn under oath that Tait had been with her at the time, discussing his nutritional requirements, and she had convinced the judge. And in the end, that was all that mattered.

She turned and looked out of the window as London slid past, petrol-grey and stagnant. A city on pause.

The *Chronicle* offices were in Victoria, but the car was creeping up through the streets of Mayfair. Nicholas leaned over to the driver. 'Could you drop us here, Michael?' The car slid to the kerb right outside Scott's, one of Nicholas's favourite lunch-spots.

'Alex, you head back to the office. Lara and I have

things to discuss. I'll see you later for a post-mortem.'

Alex glanced at Lara, then nodded. Nicholas was his boss too.

Lara was sorry to see her one ally go, but she knew she had to face this alone, just as she had as a teenager, summoned to Nicholas' study to discuss some transgression. While Nicholas Avery was Lara's boss, he was also her uncle. When her parents had died when Lara was eleven, she had been sent to live with Nicholas, his wife Olivia and her cousin Charlie. Nicholas had done his best to be a father figure, but he had still been a remote presence in her life, his ambition to make the *Chronicle* an even bigger media player taking up all his time and energy. They had never been the sort of family who played Monopoly. The only time she ever really spoke to him was when she was in trouble – just like now.

'So where does this leave us?' asked Lara when they were settled at the table.

'It leaves us screwed,' said Nicholas. 'Which was why Felix Tait sued us in the first place.'

'Tait has political ambitions. He sued us to protect his precious reputation,' said Lara.

Nicholas snorted.

'Felix Tait is far more strategic than that. He knew that if he won the libel judgement, we'd back away from anything else he did or said. And not just the *Chronicle*, but every paper in the country. He can do what he likes now.'

Lara disagreed. 'Surely not. Everyone's going to be looking at him all the more closely now.'

'Really?' said Nicholas. 'I think everyone's going to be looking at us. At you, in fact.'

'Me?'

'You were the lead writer, Lara,' said Nicholas patiently. 'You're also a shareholder in the *Chronicle*. Our detractors are going to make a point of that.'

His comment stung. Lara had inherited the shares from her father – Nicholas's brother – when he had passed away. She had never wanted or asked for a part of the company and had deliberately taken her mother's surname as a by-line to avoid accusations of nepotism.

Nicholas folded his arms in front of him, a look of weary disapproval on his face.

'I think you should take some time off,' he said.

'Time off?' said Lara, her heart beginning to race.

'I don't think we can have your by-line on anything for a while. Think of it as a sabbatical; time to consider what you want to do next.'

The full implication of what he was saying was beginning to sink in.

'Wait a minute. You're *firing* me?'

'Lara, you will always have a place at this company. But right now you don't have a position.'

'What do you mean?'

Nicholas met her gaze.

'We're closing the investigations department down.'

His bluntness was like a slap.

'Closing it down? You can't do that,' she said, struggling to get the words out.

‘I can and I have. The decision was made weeks ago and now this gives it more urgency. The verdict is a major blow for the *Chronicle* and we need to go into sack-and-ashes mode.’

‘So I’m a sacrificial lamb? A way to keep the advertisers happy?’

‘Partly, yes. This is a business, Lara and it’s a business you are a part of. I need you to behave like it.’

She glared at him. She fully understood the financial implications, but the *Chronicle* was more than just a balance sheet.

‘You’re just going to roll over and accept this? Let Felix Tait win the court case *and* dictate our editorial direction?’

He gave a bitter laugh.

‘Don’t be so naïve. I don’t need to tell you that circulation and advertising have fallen off a cliff. We certainly can’t afford to lose the million pounds we’re going to have to pay in damages and then legal fees. Besides, the data doesn’t back up this sort of expensive reporting.’

‘The *data*?’

Nicholas carefully re-folded his napkin.

‘Do you know how many people read the Tait exposé, compared to the latest online Kardashian item?’

‘That’s not news, it’s entertainment.’

‘It’s what sells newspapers, Lara.’

‘I get that. But newspapers aren’t just clickbait. We’re here to hold society to account. If we don’t then we’re just a bunch of children rehashing press releases, recycling other people's copy or writing titbits about reality TV stars.'

'Those *children* are generating thousands of stories in the time it takes your team to write one,' said Nicholas impatiently. 'Open your eyes Lara, seventy per cent of our revenue comes from the digital side of the business. We simply haven't got the time or the money for investigations. We need to have compulsive, fast-turnaround news, we need eyeballs on the page…'

'Now *that's* bullshit,' she spat.

Nicholas looked at her for a long moment.

'Then leave.'

Lara froze. Nicholas was her father's brother and sometimes it caught her by surprise how alike they were. Not in temperament, but the fierce blue eyes. And in their conviction that they were always right.

'Seriously, Lara,' he said. 'You really don't need the job. My brother left you enough money and investments that you could spend your days lying on a beach. Why don't you? At least for a few months.'

'I don't want a holiday, Nicholas. I want justice,' she said.

'Well good luck with that, darling,' he replied. 'Justice isn't part of our business model anymore.'

Chapter Two

ON ANY OTHER day, Lara would have been enjoying herself. The Engineer was a chic bar with warm lighting, cold wine and a congregation of hipsters with great bone structure. It was the sort of place she'd meet a group of friends on a Friday night, a staging post for an expedition into the West End or to one of a revolving line-up of restaurants or underground art happenings. But tonight everything seemed so hollow and pointless. Even the presence of her best friend couldn't lift her mood.

'Come on, Lara,' said Sandrine in her lilting accent. 'I know it's bad news about your job, but look around you. You're right at the centre of it all, in London, the second greatest city in world, and that very cute guy over there is looking at you.'

'Which guy?' said Lara, reluctantly lifting her gaze.

'The one in the dungarees.'

'You mean the rich kid pretending to be a painter? Sandrine, he's about ten years younger than me. Probably wondering what someone's mum is doing lowering the tone of his favourite bar.'

Sandrine gave a low laugh and Lara had to join in.

Her best friend lived in Paris – hence *second* best city – but she was in London on business. Lara's mood hadn't lifted since the Tait verdict the day before, in fact after her meeting with Nicholas, she seemed to have slumped into a deeper hole. The *Chronicle*'s investigations team had literally been disbanded overnight – all four reporters were being made redundant along with Lara's assistant Stella, who had the misfortune to be on a zero-hours contract. Lara felt the responsibility for their job losses keenly: hell, she *was* responsible. If she hadn't begun the investigation into Felix Tait, there was a good chance her team would still be gainfully employed.

Her friend reached over and squeezed Lara's hand, the bangles on her slim wrist jangling like a wind chime.

'Darling, there are plenty of fish in the sea, yes?' said Sandrine quietly.

'Him? I'm not interested in that idiot,' she said, nodding at Mr Dungarees.

'Not him, the job,' she smiled, topping up her wine glass. 'There will be other opportunities for someone as hot as you, Lara. We both know you could walk into a job in any media organisation tomorrow. The *Chronicle* is good, but it's not the only game in town.'

She was right, but there was another factor in play: Uncle Nicholas. A member of the Avery family working for News Corp, the *Telegraph* or *The Daily Mail*? He wouldn't let it happen and so Lara felt trapped: unwanted at the Chronicle Group but unable to go elsewhere.

'Thanks Drine,' she said, still grateful for her friend's reassurance. Sandrine had been Lara's first friend at LSE and they had been as close as sisters, guiding each other through life's highs and lows, ever since. Lara had chosen the London School of Economics mainly because of its location, sandwiched between the buzz of Covent Garden and the history of Fleet Street. Sandrine had done much the same thing, although her journey had been longer, from Ajaccio in Northern Corsica. As a wannabe reporter from a young age, Sandrine had considered London as the only choice for her studies, knowing that the world's top media was English-speaking. Ironically, she had still ended up working at *Le Figaro* in Paris, so they only saw each other a handful of times a year.

'Anyway, that's enough about me,' said Lara, tipping back her rosé. 'What about you? Why are you in town? It can't be just to see your favourite failure. Tell me everything: Paris, life, work. *Men?*'

Sandrine scooped her dark hair up and fastened it into a bun. 'When have we ever been the sort of women to obsess over men?' she smiled mysteriously.

'Obsess? You never tell me anything!' grinned Lara. 'Remember – you and Patric were living together by the time you even told me about him.'

Sandrine took a long drink and looked away.

'That was a long time ago,' she said.

Sandrine had met the handsome war reporter three months after she had started at *Le Figaro*. They were two fiercely independent people who fell deeply in love – and then Patric was killed in an explosion in

Aleppo. Lara knew Sandrine hated to talk about him and she could sympathise, having struggled with loss herself, but Lara believed that remembering people when they had gone was the only way to keep them alive.

'I see. Your love life is as barren as mine, then,' said Lara, trying to keep the tone light.

'I never said that,' replied her friend, not quite looking her in the eye.

'So there is someone!'

'Don't get too excited,' said Sandrine, waving a casual hand, but Lara couldn't miss the pink dots on her friend's cheeks.

'That's why you're here, isn't it?' said Lara, teasing. 'You said you were coming to London on Sunday, but you're in town early for a romantic tryst!'

'I'm in London for the Le Caché conference,' said Sandrine.

Lara paused, more serious. The Collective or *Le Caché* – 'The Hidden' – as they liked to call themselves, had been one of the media buzz stories of the past year. Frustrated at the rise of global media control and fake news, a group of investigative journalists had got together to share information, tips and sources with the intention of exposing stories which might otherwise go unreported. There had already been some major scoops including an international click fraud scandal and a money laundering scheme linked to prominent members of French society.

'The Le Caché conference?' said Lara, leaning forwards and lowering her voice. 'Are you involved with them?'

Sandrine nodded slowly.

'I am. And I think you should join us. Collectives are the future. You know better than anyone that proper investigations are being closed down and after Felix Tait, newspaper editors are going to be even more risk-averse. If we collaborate, we can put together every scrap of evidence and build a watertight case. We take away the doubt.'

Sandrine's passion was infectious and Lara had to admit she was intrigued by the romance of it all, like a cold war spy flying back and forth between Moscow, Madrid and New York, but Lara also knew what journalists were like. They were competitive and cut-throat. When it came to 'the truth' it was dog eat dog out there.

'Can I be honest?' said Lara. 'I'm not even sure I want to stay in journalism anymore.'

Sandrine looked at her wide-eyed and Lara could hardly blame her, but now the words were out of her mouth, Lara immediately felt better.

'I never thought I'd feel that way,' she continued. 'But the industry has changed, Sandrine. Everything is opinion not fact, so much is driven by personal agenda or the Twitter bullies. Those stories that we love breaking, the big, powerful, fact-driven exposés, where are they? How often do you see a Watergate or a Wikileaks on the front pages anymore? Could you even get something like that printed these days?'

'But that's exactly what we're fighting for, *ma chérie*,' said Sandrine. 'Just come to the conference on

Monday. Meet Eduardo. We might be able to change your mind.'

'Eduardo?'

'The founder.'

Her friend flushed again and Lara's mouth opened.

'Wait a minute. That's him, isn't it?' she said, pointing at Sandrine. '*Eduardo* is your mystery man!'

Sandrine was laughing now.

'Just come,' she smiled. 'You can meet him. He's pretty incredible.'

Lara had been telling the truth: the Felix Tait case had left her feeling battered and bruised, but she had to admit that she was intrigued how this collective, and Eduardo, had managed to win Sandrine's heart.

'So tempt me, what *are* you working on?'

Sandrine gave a casual shrug, her way of avoiding the subject.

'At least give me a clue,' pressed Lara. Sandrine hesitated, as Lara watched her eyes dart left and right. The Engineer wasn't a hack pub, but this was a well-connected part of London. For all she knew, the cute guy in the dungarees might be the son of a rival newspaper editor.

'Jonathon Meyer,' said Sandrine finally, her voice soft and low.

Lara knew the name – of course she did, Meyer's mysterious death had been the source of endless speculation a couple of weeks previously. A connected, multi-millionaire financier famous for throwing glamorous parties on his yacht in Monaco, Meyer had died after a violent mugging in the City. His death had triggered the usual conspiracy theories: claims he'd been mixed up with the mafia, the Russians, even the CIA. It was the sort of story that, in a slow news week, could have run and run, but it had coincided with a sex scandal connected to the England football team that had grabbed all the headlines, followed by a tell-all interview by the Queen's butler. Overnight, Jonathon Meyer had been forgotten.

'I didn't think there was any real story there,' said Lara. 'Was there?'

Sandrine raised a manicured brow.

'Let's just say I don't think he was killed by a random thug.'

It was Lara's turn to look surprised.

'You think he was murdered?'

Sandrine played with the shiny bird pendant around her neck, a gift from Lara many years earlier.

'He was not a good man, and he was not involved with good people,' she said finally. 'Anything is possible.'

Conspiracy theories were journalism's equivalent of explorers searching for El Dorado. The newsroom loved them, of course, but as Alex liked to say, 'ghosts don't print well,' meaning rumours and speculation were too flimsy for a headline and trying to pin them down in the absence of hard evidence was always a waste of time. But still, Lara had a sixth sense when it came to a story and she could tell her friend had something – and despite herself, she wanted to know what. It was one of the reasons she got into journalism in the first place: to know things other people didn't.

‘So what was Meyer involved in?’

Sandrine hesitated.

‘Trafficking,’ she said in a whisper.

‘Trafficking?’

Sandrine waved a hand, indicating that was all she was prepared to say.

‘You can’t tell me a highly connected financier was murdered because he was involved in trafficking and expect me to go to the bar to top up our olives. Come on, tell me. Is it drugs? Or people?’

Her friend paused and looked at her over the rim of her glass.

‘Look, I’m due to share the details with a few of the collective guys at the conference on Monday. Join us and you can find out.’

Lara shook her head smiling.

‘You’re a wily old bird, you know that.’

‘Less of the old…’

‘Okay, I’ll think about it,’ smiled Lara, deciding that it might be worth it if only to meet this Eduardo. Sandrine grinned and grasped Lara’s hand.

‘I do miss you, you know,’ she said.

Lara nodded, the feeling mutual. Lara had plenty of friends in London, and in her twenties she had considered them to be like a surrogate family. But lately, many of them had got married or had children. They had real families of their own, and were forging new lives with them in the suburbs. This year, Lara could count the number of nights out on one hand, and even then, you couldn’t get into deep conversations about love and life without friends glancing at their watches, saying they had to get back for bedtime stories or the last train from Waterloo.

'Maybe I'll just give up on all this and move out to Paris,' said Lara, sitting back.

'I'd love you to come,' sighed Sandrine. 'I'm just not sure you'd ever leave London.'

'Why wouldn't I?'

'Alex,' said Sandrine simply.

'Alex?' She laughed out loud at that one. Her first proper laugh since the whole Tait trial. Sandrine gave her a mischievous grin. Her friend had known Alex for almost at long as she had, and had always teased Lara about her relationship with Alex.

'How is the gorgeous man?'

'He's been a good friend throughout the trial.'

'*Just* good friends?'

'Come on, Drine. I thought you'd have finally given that a rest after fifteen years.'

'I'll give up when you finally admit you are in love with him.'

'I am not in love with Alex Ford and he's not in love with me. In fact he has a girlfriend now. A serious one.'

Sandrine shrugged as if that was a tiny detail. She was French, after all.

'So come to Paris then.'

Lara gave a soft sigh, imagined herself sipping a vin ordinaire at a pavement café, walking along the Seine or going to the cinema with some hot guy she'd met in the Shakespeare and Co book shop. Perhaps the Tait verdict had happened for a reason. Maybe Uncle

Nicholas was right that she needed to recharge, regroup.

'Perhaps it's time I made a move,' she said. 'We spend so much time looking for leads and chasing stories that we don't live a normal life like most people.'

Sandrine pointed at her.

'I'm not sure you *want* a normal life, Lara Stone.'

'Don't I?'

'No. You and I, we're writers. We don't live in the real world, we live in our stories.'

Sandrine lifted her glass and tapped it against Lara's with a 'ting'.

'And that is the only place we feel alive.'

Chapter Three

LARA STOOD IN the street, watching the brake lights of the cab flash then disappear around the corner. She looked down at the receipt in her hand and sighed. Getting home from the bar had been automatic: flag down a black cab, give the driver her Chelsea address, then say 'keep the change – and can you give me a receipt?'

But that was then, this was now. There *were* no expenses for the foreseeable future. Yesterday Lara had been a hot newspaper journalist who took cabs because she didn't have time for anything else – she needed to get across town or to the office or to the airport right away. Today she was… what? An ex-award-winning writer, an ex-mover and shaker. She was a *civilian*.

At least she'd had a great night out, she smiled to herself, shoving the receipt into her pocket. She'd loved seeing Sandrine, enjoyed their easy conversation, so much so that her idea to move to Paris for a few months had been growing in her head ever since Sandrine had mentioned it.

After all, if not now – when? She was single, solvent, and since the demise of the investigation department at the *Chronicle*, without responsibilities or commitments. Lara had always envied Alex's early career in journalism, bouncing from Berlin to Washington to Peshawar; in fact, in all the years she had known him, Alex had been happiest as a foreign correspondent. He too had asked Lara on a number of occasions, why she didn't come and work abroad, and the answer she had given was that she enjoyed living in London. Which had been true. The upheaval of her childhood – losing her parents, going to live with her uncle, shuttling between boarding school, the Averys' country house and their West London home, meant that deep down, Lara needed a steady base. But sometimes it was tempting to live a different life. A time like now.

She unlocked the gate to the marina, wincing as it creaked open and shut it with a clang behind her. She supposed now she'd actually have time to get it oiled.

People were always surprised when they heard that Lara lived on a houseboat at Cadogan Pier. 'Is it to avoid council tax?' they asked, perplexed. So Lara had long since given up mentioning it. She said she lived 'a stone's throw from Cheyne Walk' and left it at that, let peoples' prejudices about posh rich girls and their chichi SW3 flats fill in the blanks.

Lara walked down the boat's little gangway, down to the end of the dock. *This* is why I live here, she thought. The lights of Albert Bridge shimmered in the darkness, their reflection in the water like ribbons of gold. Sure, she could be in one of those fancy houses off the King's Road, but she wouldn't have a view, a feeling like this. The oil-black water rippling like muscle beneath skin, the constant movement, the sense of being in the embrace of a living thing.

She closed her eyes and drew a sharp breath in through her nose. Her parents had barely been 40 when they had died in a yachting accident off the Croatian coast. Eleven year-old Lara had been sent off to boarding school before she'd had chance to process it, but in the months that had followed, she had decided one thing; she was determined to stay close to the water. She learned to row and sail and swam freestyle for the county team; far from being a distressing reminder, water made her feel closer to her parents – or to the little of them she could remember. So when five years ago, the money left in trust had finally been released to her, Lara had snapped up *Misty*, this wide-beam narrow boat, a remodelled veteran of the Staffordshire canal, and called it home.

Unlocking the little fold-back door, Lara stepped inside, to be met by a happy 'Mewl'.

'Hey Dingo,' she said, reaching out to stroke her cat's black fur. Dingo arched his back and purred, following along behind as Lara walked into the living space.

'Have you missed me?'

Dingo answered by jumping onto the sofa.

'I'll take that as a yes,' she smiled, hanging her jacket on the back of a chair. Another thing that surprised people: *Misty* was lovely inside. A cool contemporary interior, all white clapboard, with a spacious lounge area at the front, two bedrooms and a full bathroom with clawfoot bath. There were bigger houseboats moored along the Thames but then she'd only gather more crap. As it was, Lara furnished it only with pieces that she loved. Framed original cinema posters for *Dr. No*, *To Catch A Thief* and *Vertigo*, reclaimed furniture and one-off design pieces – the desk that had come from a villa in Tuscany, a light-pendant that had once hung in a New York speakeasy, maps and books, things that reminded her where your imagination and a plane ticket could take you.

Lara went into the kitchen and clanked about in the cupboards to find Dingo's cat food, mulling over Sandrine's suggestion about joining Le Caché as she did so.

'Here Dings,' she said, putting down the plastic bowl. 'I'll leave this out for you.'

She leant back on the counter and pulled out her phone, flipping to Le Caché's home page, which trumpeted their latest scoop – exposing the connection between a Mexican drug cartel and one of the country's top political donors. It was fine reporting, but it was hard not to hear Uncle Nicholas's words: who would read this over an item about Meghan Markle or Kylie Jenner? People came to newspapers for entertainment and for an affirmation of their own beliefs. They came to comment below the line, to offload their own frustrations or add to the conversation – because *Look at me! My opinions matter and everyone wants to hear them.* In 18 months' time, Lara wasn't sure there would be an investigations team at *any* of the papers. It all made joining Le Caché seem a pointless exercise, a desperate swim against the tide. Still, if Sandrine was convinced, Lara wanted to know why.

She clicked on the 'About Us' section.

'Ah, that'll be why,' she smiled, as she saw Eduardo Ortega's black and white portrait. Sandrine hadn't been joking when she said Le Caché's founder and editor-in-chief was impressive. Handsome, connected and accomplished, Eduardo was only around forty and yet the Harvard and Georgetown graduate had worked for *El Pais*, *The Washington Post*, *CNN* and had found time to write half a dozen books on a range of subjects from the history of Myanmar to the civil war in Sri Lanka. He had founded Le Caché two years previously and while their main office was in Madrid, they had a long list of collaborators who worked for some of the biggest media players around the globe. Not really Sandrine's type though. She usually went for pretty boys with a dangerous streak, like Patric. Everyone grows up though, don't they?

Lara made a coffee and went back to the sofa. Opening her laptop, she went straight onto the main news websites. Lara's heart sank.

Newspaper Loses Libel Case

Felix Tait says court result 'a vindication'.

Justice done or a disaster for free speech?

Deborah Simmons reports.

But as she skimmed the text, Lara was surprised to

feel herself detached from the whole story. She was, after all, not part of it anymore and in truth, had felt that way for a while.

The Felix Tait thing *had* been a blow, but in reality, Lara had been growing increasingly frustrated at work for more than a year. Her promotion to Investigations Editor had, in theory, been a promotion, but had really been a backwards step, taking her away from the things she loved best – researching and writing. Darius Allen was an idiot, over-promoted and unbelievably pompous. Alex was Lara's friend, but as deputy editor, he still had to toe the line. The more senior you were in the management structure, the more office politics were involved and she knew Alex had to pick his battles. This one – folding the investigations team – had been unwinnable and she didn't hold that against him. No one was going to back a research team that had just lost the paper a million pounds, especially when the stories that got the most clicks were about reality TV stars.

Lara closed her computer and sat back, idly stroking Dingo, who had come to join her on the sofa. As she yawned and stretched, her eyes turned towards the coffee table where a photo of her father was in a frame on a pile of books. It was her favourite photo of her dad; standing next to his boat looking ridiculously pleased with himself. Lara thought of her dad all the time, but it was hard not to think of him this week in particular; it had been David Avery who had given Lara her love for the news and the desire to fight for the truth.

She remembered going into his study at their farmhouse on the family estate, a crackling fire of Scotch pine, always a source of calm wisdom, whatever her problem.

'What would *you* do, Dad?' she asked, looking at the photo.

He certainly wouldn't have rolled over and let his brother close investigations, that was for sure. David Avery was a scrapper, never afraid to get down in the dirt trading blows – he was old-school that way. Her father had worked during the swansong of Fleet Street when the *Chronicle* still had their offices within a stone's throw of St Bride's Church and newspapermen kept whisky in their bottom drawers. She wondered what he would have made of the modern media where a story could be broken by someone with a tweet and flash around the world before any of the official news channels had a chance to even comment. Lara didn't know for sure, but she guessed David Avery would have embraced it, taken it on board and used it to his advantage.

A buzzing sensation on her hip woke her up. It was a few moments before she realised she had fallen asleep on the sofa and that her mobile phone was ringing.

She blinked hard, pulled the phone out of her pocket and sat up, swinging her legs to the floor. She looked at the time; 2.30am. Phone calls in the middle of the night were rarely good news, even if it was the paper calling her in to work on a major breaking news story.

'Hello?' she murmured, her voice thick with sleep.

'Lara Stone?'

'Yes,' she said. 'Who is this?'

'Detective Sergeant Rob Monaghan. Met.'

The police. That set Lara even more on edge.

Lara rubbed a hand over her face to focus.

'How can I help you, Sergeant?'

'Do you know a Sandrine Legard, Ms. Stone?'

Now she was wide awake.

'Ms. Stone?'

'Yes, Sandrine's a friend,' said Lara, the air in the houseboat suddenly stale and overly warm.

'May I ask when you last saw her?' asked the policeman.

'I saw her tonight. What… what's this about, Sergeant?' she said, a sense of dread swelling. 'Is Sandrine okay?'

But she knew the answer even before the words were out and when the policeman paused before answering, it was all the confirmation she needed.

'A body has been found outside a building in Marylebone,' he said. Lara's heart was thudding now.

'A body? Where exactly? Are you telling me it's Sandrine?'

Her words poured out, not giving the policeman time to answer.

Panic filled her chest. 'Sergeant. Tell me, what's going on? Is Sandrine… dead?'

'Are you her next of kin?'

'I'm her best friend.'

Another pause.

‘We’re trying to trace Ms. Legard’s next of kin,’ said Monaghan.

Lara tried to swallow, decoding his words in her head. So they’d identified her, now they needed an official confirmation.

‘We retrieved your number from Ms. Legard’s mobile phone. Your number was the last she called.’

The last she called, Lara’s inner voice parroted. The last she *ever* called.

‘Ms. Stone? Can you tell us who is Sandrine’s next of kin?’

‘Her parents live in Corsica,’ stuttered Lara. ‘She works for *Le Figaro*, a newspaper. In Paris.’

‘I wonder if you’d mind coming down to…’

Lara was already reaching for her bag.

‘What’s the address? I’ll be there in fifteen minutes.’

HYDE PARK CORNER was empty as she gunned the bike’s engine, bending low over the tank and leaning into the bend, roaring up onto Park Lane, the darkness of the trees to her left, blurred lights to her right. Lara remembered meeting Sandrine for tea at The Dorchester when they had been students, giggling and a little squiffy, discussing running out on the bill they could ill-afford. Could she really be dead? Not Sandrine. Lara couldn’t make the idea compute. Drine was so full of life, so – vital. It had to be a mistake. *Had to.*

She dodged around Marble Arch, overtaking a lone

cab as she powered into Edgware Road, before crossing into the maze of Marylebone. Lara was a skilled and experienced motorcyclist; it was how she had got around London for years, but it was hard to concentrate and keep full control of the bike when her head was sweating beneath her helmet and her palms felt clammy in her leather gloves.

Sandrine had said very little about where she was staying during her trip to London. Her friend was never particularly loyal to one place, staying in whichever hotel *Le Figaro*'s travel agent had sorted out for her. When she came to London for pleasure rather than work, she often stayed with Lara on the houseboat, but Sandrine had turned her offer down this time, saying she wanted to be close to Paddington for the conference she was attending. Why? thought Lara, torturing herself as she twisted the throttle.

As Lara turned into Wallace Square, she could tell where Sandrine had been staying from the police van and an ambulance parked directly outside, their lights spinning blue and red in competition with each other, as a handful of rubberneckers were held back by fluttering tape and a bored-looking uniformed copper.

Lara kicked her bike onto its stand and ran across, pulling off her helmet as she announced herself to the young policeman. He frowned, then turned to shout for someone inside the building. 'Sarge?' he called without moving. 'Someone here for you.'

A tall man in a navy raincoat emerged, pulling off blue latex gloves as he approached her.

'Detective Sergeant Monaghan? I'm Lara Stone,

we spoke on the phone?' She fumbled for her driving licence and held it up, her hand still trembling. Monaghan tilted his head to read the card, then met Lara's gaze.

'You're a journalist.'

She was about to look at her ID again – her occupation wasn't on it last time she looked – before the penny dropped.

'You Googled me,' she said. Of course he had. He was a detective investigating a suspicious death.

A death. Lara tried to swallow, but found she couldn't.

'What happened?' she said quietly.

The detective caught the waver in her voice and his expression changed. 'A body was found behind the building. We believe she fell from the top floor balcony.'

'Is she alive?'

Monaghan shook his head.

'I'm sorry.'

'Can I see her?'

Monaghan looked at her for a long moment, then gave a curt nod.

'This way,' he said.

Sandrine's apartment was at the end of a long row of tall stuccoed terraced houses that faced the square. Lara followed Monaghan around the back of the building to an alleyway that had been taped off. The sky was beginning to lighten, but still it was dark, eerie in the narrow throughfare, thrown into sharp shadow by a white light where two paramedics were lifting something onto a stretcher. *Someone*. Lara's legs felt like dead weights as she followed the policeman and Monaghan noticed her hesitation.

'Are you okay to do this?'

Lara nodded, although she wasn't sure at all. She had been around bodies before – it was part of the job – but this was different. Very different. Taking a shallow breath, Lara approached the stretcher. She was still praying it was an error, some bizarre coincidence, mistaken identity.

Monaghan muttered something to the paramedic and he unzipped the body bag. There was no mistaking Sandrine's serene face, even in the low light. Her eyes were closed as if she had just fallen asleep on Lara's couch, and around her slim neck Lara could see her tiny gold bird necklace still glinting.

'Yes,' was all she could manage to say. 'That's Sandrine. Sandrine Legard.'

Lara's hand covered her mouth to stifle a sob, the tears beginning to flow. Rob Monaghan touched her shoulder, then gently led her back towards the street.

'It's fine,' said Monaghan. 'Take your time.'

There was a flash to their left and they both turned. A paparazzo was taking pictures from the other side of the tape. Lara knew how it worked. A lone wolf trawling the streets intercepting police calls and chatter, and within the hour the pictures would be offered to all the news outlets.

'Get away from her,' shouted Lara. 'Leave her alone!'

The photographer didn't flinch, his shutter still

whirring, and all of Lara's grief boiled up into a white-hot rage. She lunged at the man, hands like claws.

'Woah, steady there.'

She felt a firm hand of restraint on her arm and Lara turned.

'Fox…' said Lara, some of her anger draining away. Ian Fox was a chief inspector at Charing Cross police station. Ten years ago, when Lara had worked the news desk at the *Chronicle*, Fox had been one of the media-friendly officers in her phonebook, not exactly a friend but someone who knew how it worked. Journalists got tip-offs from the cops and that information was a two-way street if something came up in a reporter's investigation. Word on the street was that Fox had dated a journalist for a while, so he was generally sympathetic to the job.

Seeing Fox's familiar face gave her some comfort.

'Come on,' he said, leading her away from the police line. 'Assaulting a photographer isn't going to solve anything.' He looked up as the snapper disappeared into the dark. 'Much as I'd like to see it.'

Lara nodded wearily. 'She was my friend, Ian.'

'I know. Monaghan filled me in as soon as I arrived.'

They stood in the blue glow of the police van. Either Lara was dizzy or the lights were still whirling.

'Listen, I'm going to have to ask you some questions. Is that okay?'

'I'm not sure what I can tell you,' said Lara, staring at the ground.

'You saw Sandrine earlier tonight. How did she

seem?'

Lara expected him to get out his notebook, but he didn't. She was grateful for that at least.

'She was on good form,' sighed Lara. 'We went to a pub in Chelsea, The Engineer, had a fun night. We left at about 10:30 and I got a cab back to my house on Cadogan Pier. Sandrine said she was going back to… well, here. The next thing I know, I get a call from your detective.'

Fox nodded, absorbing the information.

'Was Sandrine drinking at the pub?'

'Not much. We each had a couple of glasses of wine.'

'How was her mood?'

'Mood?'

It was starting to dawn on her what the police thought had happened.

'You think her fall was deliberate?' she said.

'We don't know yet, Lara.'

She was about to reply when the paramedics pushed the stretcher past her. Lara had to look away; it was too painful. Just a few hours earlier they had been at The Engineer talking about the future.

'Can I go up there? To the apartment?'

Lara knew it was a big ask, even with her history with Fox.

'Please Ian. I just need to see.'

She watched as the policeman weighed up his options.

'Just so we're clear, no photos and no quotes.'

'Absolutely,' said Lara gratefully. Following Fox,

she walked inside the block and up five flights of stairs. The apartment occupied the eaves of the building, the door was open and they walked inside.

The flat was small. Just a bathroom, bedroom and an open-plan living space where two officers were bagging up various items they had found. The red jacket Sandrine had worn the night before was draped over the dining chair, her brown suede ankle boots were on the rug, one tipped on its side. She'd commented on how cool they were, asked Sandrine where she'd got them from. Lara squeezed her eyes shut. *Focus*, she told herself angrily. *Be professional. See what you can see.* Fox stopped to talk to one of the uniforms and Lara slid away, turning towards the French doors. They were open, letting a cool breeze into the room. Without glancing back, Lara stepped out onto the narrow terrace, where there was a rust-pocked bistro chair in one corner, a pot plant in the other.

Her heart was beating fast now, emotion choked her throat.

She tried to imagine Sandrine standing here just an hour earlier, tried to imagine what she was thinking.

'What did you do?' she whispered, bending to look at the waist-high wooden hand rail. Lara frowned when she saw four scrapes in the white paintwork.

'What are you *doing*?'

She spun round. Fox was standing at the French doors, glaring at her.

'Lara, get back in here,' he said. 'This is a bloody crime scene.'

He glanced across at the uniformed officers, then

lowered his voice. 'I thought we had an understanding.'

There was a moment's silence.

'Did you see the scratch-marks on the balustrade?' she said, glancing back to the terrace.

'Lara, this isn't a story,' said Fox, his voice tight. 'I let you in here as a favour.'

'I know and I owe you, but listen. You asked me about Sandrine's state of mind in the pub? Well she didn't go from sociable to suicidal in a few hours. Those scratch marks suggest she was trying to scramble back onto the balcony. This wasn't deliberate, Ian. She must have fallen.'

Fox pressed his lips together.

'Last time I looked Lara, *I* was the investigating officer.'

He didn't say it unkindly. He was too experienced to argue with a grieving friend, but he had a job to do.

'I just wanted to point it out,' said Lara, trying to hold herself together. Fox's phone started to ring and Rob Monaghan was hovering. 'Look,' said the chief inspector. 'You should go home and get some sleep. We'll take it from here, okay?'

'I want to help,' she said, eyes darting round the apartment, trying to take in every last detail before she was asked to leave.

'I know that, Lara. But we've got this,' said Fox. 'We'll find out what happened.'

She nodded.

'Sure Ian, thank you,' she said. But deep down she didn't believe him.

Chapter Four

ALEX TURNED HIS face into the needle-point shower jets. *That felt good*, he thought to himself, turning his broad back to take the full blast. It reminded Alex of the time he'd been to a Turkish bath house in Istanbul, where he'd been pummelled by a 20-stone dude with a moustache, but came out feeling fantastic. This bathroom had been one of the selling points for this apartment. Yes, it had been ridiculously expensive – a swanky modernist flat complex right on the Thames, it wasn't going to be cheap – but Alex could admit he had been completely seduced by the boy-toy mod-cons, especially when they helped you feel wide awake at 6am.

Having spent most of his twenties as a frontline foreign correspondent roughing it in roach-infested rooms in Delhi or bouncing in the back of a Jeep near Kandahar, it was a hoot to have a video intercom, motorised curtains and a kitchen like the bridge of the *Enterprise* from *Star Trek*. Alex had made an offer for the flat the same week he'd been promoted to Deputy at the *Chronicle*, justifying the eye-watering cost by telling himself he needed to be close to the office. The truth was, living here Alex felt like James Bond. The

Roger Moore version, obviously: ludicrous perhaps, but oh, so much fun.

He shut off the water and grabbed a towel from the rail, then pulled on his monogrammed robe, a Christmas present from his girlfriend Alicia. Alex still wasn't sure whether she was playing along with his ironic Hugh Hefner fantasy or whether she actually saw him as the sort of man who liked his initials stamped onto his clothes.

Surely she hadn't missed the shelves in the open-plan living room, filled with mementoes from his time living abroad and on the edge – a chunk of wall from Berlin, a Chesapeake oyster shell from DC, the head of a spear he'd had to smuggle back from Sudan. It was still how Alex thought of himself: flak jacket and combat pants, even if his shrapnel scar was now hidden by a crisp white shirt. He missed those days, but there was only so long you could stay on the front line, especially when your dream was to edit a national newspaper. So he had come back to London, his ambition propelling him from the foreign desk to head of news and then up to Deputy. Alex smiled as saw the monogram in the mirror: his journey from the son of a newsagent to a captain of the media industry was almost complete.

Still towelling his dark hair, Alex crossed to his desk, strategically placed against the tall windows to take full advantage of the view from the eighth floor. He'd been here well over a year now and that picture never got old. The apartment building hugged the river on the south side of Chelsea Bridge and at this time of the morning London was grey-blue and beautiful, the lights still twinkling on the water.

If he was totally honest, it wasn't just the gadgets and the parquet floors that had attracted him to this building, it was the view of the river. He'd spent countless evenings on Lara's houseboat and it had always been a sure-fire way to decompress after a hard day at the paper. His job was full-on, but a cold beer and the sight of the Thames from the deck of *Misty*? Nothing like it.

Snapping into work mode, Alex opened his laptop and began his morning routine, scanning through the news feeds. Alicia was always pushing to stay over at the flat more often, but on work days he liked to wake up alone. Alex had his morning routine down pat, catching up on any stories which had broken overnight, sifting through the speculation and PR spin, looking for anything they could use. Today there was a mud-slide in Argentina, a violent protest in Chicago and some B-list movie star in trouble over an outburst on social media: nothing out of the ordinary. Alex glanced at the time and scowled. He needed to get moving; he'd spent too long in the shower.

Alex was half out of his seat when he switched to the domestic news wires, just in case there had been a flood or crash: hard news could be a morbid business – people complained about the news cycle but no one wanted to read fluffy stories about rescued kittens, not really. He was just about to close the laptop when he saw it.

London, 4:30AM, French journalist falls to her death: W1. Met Police report.

It was the occupation of the victim that caught his eye. The media industry was a small world, and Alex knew most of the senior players. Clicking on the title, he sat back down, running a hand through his still damp hair.

'Oh no.'

Woman identified as Sandrine Legard, writer for Parisian newspaper Le Figaro. Neighbours alerted the emergency services, but Ms. Legard was declared dead at the scene.

He stared at the words, black on a white background, the cursor mindlessly blinking on, his heart thumping in time. And then he thought of Lara.

ALEX WINCED AT the 'bip-bip' as he locked the car. The road off the Embankment was residential and it was still early enough to wake... *to wake the dead*, his mind added. Alex took a deep breath, then walked briskly towards the wharf. He was dreading it, but he knew a friend should break the news about Sandrine's death to Lara and he needed to get to her before she checked the wires too. Alex had called a contact in the Met on the way over to check that the news agency hadn't got the name mixed up, but there was no doubt about it: the couple from the basement flat in Sandrine's block had found her and there had already been a positive ID.

Alex knew the code to get into the marina and as

he walked along the pier he tried to think of the right way to break it: 'Sorry, there's some bad news,' 'I think you'd better sit down…' There was no easy way to do it. In his days abroad, dredging human interest from the rubble of war zones, Alex had done plenty of doorstepping, informing parents that their beloved son or daughter had been blown in half. But this was different. Sandrine was his friend too.

He had met the beautiful Parisian within the first couple of weeks of starting at City University, where he and Lara had places on the prestigious newspaper journalism MA course. Sandrine was Lara's house-mate, her best friend from her undergraduate time at LSE, and somehow, after a big night out, they had all ended up at Lara and Sandrine's Fleet Street flat 'for cocktails', which had pretty much amounted to adding ice to vodka. Alex could remember that first night clearly, Sandrine seeming so sophisticated and worldly and so grown-up, already working as a stringer for *Le Figaro* at twenty-one. *Such a damn waste.*

Shaking his head, Alex walked up the gangplank onto the narrowboat, bending to knock on the door.

'Up front.'

Alex straightened and followed the sound of the voice. Lara was sitting on the deck at the front of the barge, watching the sun rise over the city. She had on a thick fisherman's jumper, her chin tucked into the funnel neck, knees drawn up to her chest. There was a glass of wine next to her, but it didn't look touched. It seemed very early for a drink, although Alex could hardly blame her: Lara had not only lost the libel case that week, but her investigations department and her job too. And now this.

'Hey,' said Lara softly, barely glancing up from the river. 'Making house calls now?'

Alex sat down on the wooden chair next to her and for a moment he was reminded of happier times – summer BBQs, the midnight gin sessions, fishing for trout from the deck and reeling in old boots instead. Right now, they all felt so far way.

'I needed to see you.'

She glanced down at her phone, glowing on the arm of the chair.

'6:30? I'm honoured.'

There was an edge to Lara's voice, none of her usual warmth. Alex swallowed: *cut to the chase.*

'Listen,' he said. 'I need to tell you something. I spotted something on the news wires when I got up, it's…'

'Sandrine,' said Lara.

Alex blinked.

'You know?'

'We went out together last night. The police called me first, my number was in her phone – last number she called. I went down to Marylebone and ID'd the body.'

He should have guessed – the positive ID would need to be someone who knew Sandrine well.

'I asked her to stay here, you know,' said Lara, looking back at him. Her complexion looked washed-out, her green eyes were lifeless and dull. Lara was always a magnetic presence, the brightest star in the sky, but today, she looked barely there, like a ghost.

'She said she wanted to stay nearer to Paddington, but I should have insisted. If I had insisted she would still be alive.'

He heard her voice catch as she spoke.

'Lara, none of this was your fault. If Sandrine had made up her mind she wanted to hurt herself, she would have done it wherever she was.'

'Hurt herself?' repeated Lara, turning to face him, those eyes suddenly fierce. 'You think she did this deliberately too?'

He saw her searching his face, desperate to hear a firm denial, but his police contact had told him that alcohol and anti-depressants had been found at the scene.

'We'll have to wait for the inquest to know for sure,' said Alex. 'And even then it will probably be an open verdict.'

'Verdict?' snapped Lara. 'This isn't another case, Alex. This is Sandrine and I know she wouldn't do a thing like that.'

Alex had worked long enough in news rooms to know that you never did truly know people or what they were thinking. He had interviewed the parents of terrorists and high school shooters, mothers and fathers who had zero idea their child had warped ideologies, until it was too late.

'She was fine last night Alex, happy, talking about the future. I saw scratch marks on the balcony too. Maybe she was trying to scramble back.'

Alex knew that didn't necessarily mean anything.

Suicidal jumpers often had a change of heart at the final moment. But he really didn't think now was the time to bring it up.

'You went out on the balcony?'

She nodded. 'Ian Fox was at the scene. He let me into the apartment.'

'What did you see?'

It was an instinctive question, but Alex immediately knew he'd over-stepped the mark. Lara turned on him, but Alex held up a hand.

'I've already told the news team not to run it, but you know I won't be able to do anything once Darius gets into the office – and we can't control the other papers.'

They both fell silent, just the gentle lap of river water against the hull of the boat filling the gap between them.

'I haven't offered you a coffee,' she said, suddenly standing up.

He grabbed her hand and stopped her.

'Stop, just come here,' he said, rising up out of his chair.

Face to face, he pulled Lara into a hug, resting his chin on the top of her head. Alex couldn't ever remember Lara crying, but he could feel her body against his chest, tight like a drum, as if she was holding it all back. They stood there for a long moment, the river moving beneath them.

'You know two days ago, I thought my world was going to end,' said Lara. 'Felix bloody Tait, some stupid argument about nothing.'

'It's okay,' he whispered, holding her. 'It'll be okay.' He knew the futility of the words, but what else was there to say?

Over the years they had been through so much together. Good times and bad. On their crazy nights out in their twenties they had laughed so much their bellies hurt. And the worst times too: when his mother had got sick and Alex had been stationed abroad, she had collected him from Heathrow, driven him home to Cumbria, saying all the right things on the longest journey of his life. Finally Lara pulled away.

'You know we had the talk about this at work?' said Lara, pulling away, wiping her moist eyes with the sleeve of her sweater. 'Appropriate contact between colleagues? I think even HR might allow this one,' he said, trying for a smile.

Alex wanted to stand there forever and pretend it wasn't happening, but he knew things needed to be done.

'Have you spoken to her parents yet?' he said.

Lara sighed.

'For the past hour I've just been running over and over in my head what I can say to them. But I just couldn't find the words. Not like me, huh?'

It truly wasn't. Lara was the smartest, bravest, most capable person he knew, she never hesitated. That's why it was so painful to see her this way, lost at sea.

'Let me sort out the arrangements,' said Alex.

'You don't have to do that.'

'No, let me. I met them at her flat in Montmartre that time we were all in Paris – they'll remember me.

I'll get them here if they need to come.'

Lara shoulders shrugged, a gesture of resignation.

'Thanks.'

She gave a small nod and turned away, looking back across the river. The sky was lighter now, with dusky apricot clouds blooming behind the distant high-rise blocks, far too cheery for the mood.

'You should go,' said Lara. 'You'll miss the morning conference. One of us has already been fired this week, we don't want to make it two.'

His eyes met hers.

'You know I'm always here for you, don't you?'

She nodded, then glanced away. Alex could hardly blame her for doubting him. There had been a time when Alex and Lara had been inseparable; best friends, if nothing else. But over the past eighteen months, since Alicia had arrived on the scene, they had hardly seen one another outside of a work setting. It was only now that Alex realised just how much he had missed her.

'Go on, go,' said Lara. 'Or I'll get Dingo to chase you off.'

He leaned forward and pressed his cheek against hers. Alex opened his mouth, but knew there was nothing more to say. He turned and walked back down the gangplank, wishing… what? That he could stay with her, protect her, hold her together as she fell apart? But somehow he knew Lara was made of tougher stuff. Somehow he knew Lara Stone would get through this.

He unlocked the car and slid his phone into the slot

on the dash, speed-dialling his PA.

'Celine? It's Alex. I need to get two people from Corsica.'

A pause. 'Yes. Today. Whatever it takes. This is a priority.'

He hung up and turned into traffic.

Chapter Five

SANDRINE'S FATHER STOOD upright and dignified, his silhouette stark against the hotel window. Jean Legard and Sandrine's mother Marion had flown in from Ajaccio to Heathrow via a connecting flight in Paris, several hours after Alex's assistant had begun making the arrangements. Woken by a call from the police, telling him about their daughter's death, then mere hours later, standing here in this stuffy hotel room, Jean had every right to look exhausted, but Lara thought there was something more in his expression. He was broken, even though he was trying to put on a brave face.

'I'm so sorry, Jean,' said Lara. 'I was with Sandrine last night. I just can't explain what happened.'

Jean gave a short shake of his head.

'Sandrine has suffered from depression for many years, Lara,' said Jean, his French accent strong. 'She was just very good at hiding it.'

Lara gaped at him. What he was saying just didn't make sense. She'd known Sandrine for almost twenty years and she had always brimmed with vibrancy and optimism.

'But she was fine,' said Lara, looking across to

Marion. 'How could she…'

Marion walked over and put a hand on Lara's arm, a mother still, doing her best to comfort her. Lara had spent enough time visiting Sandrine in Corsica in Uni holidays to consider Jean and Marion family and this was hurting her more than she could have anticipated. Seeing them so crumpled, yet holding themselves together – for her – was heartbreaking.

'Sometimes it came on very suddenly,' said Marion, her eyes damp. 'One moment Sandrine was fine, the next it was as if she was under a black cloud. She'd go to bed, sometimes for a week, sometimes longer.'

Lara looked back and forth between them.

'But depression? I…'

'C'est vrai,' said Jean quietly. 'It was why she had her gap year between high school and university.'

Lara frowned in bemusement.

'Her gap year? She went travelling,' she replied, remembering her friend's tales of Italian boys and sangria on the beach.

'Sandrine did not travel that year,' said Jean, shaking his head. 'She had – *comment se dit?* – a breakdown? She stayed in Corsica with us that year, healed herself the best she could. We wanted her to stay in Corsica to study but she was adamant she wanted to go to London.'

Lara felt as if the floor had fallen away beneath her. It was as if everything she had ever known about her best friend had been a lie. Jean seemed to see it and squeezed Lara's hand. She felt the callouses on his fingertips, rough, like bark. Sandrine's parents were both retired teachers, but Jean had always maintained that he'd have preferred to have been a carpenter. When Lara had gone to stay at their family home during university breaks, Jean was always in his lean-to workshop at the side of their farmhouse, turning wooden bowls and chair legs on his lathe. It was the sort of recollection you would end with 'happy days' – but they truly were. What Lara wouldn't give to somehow beam them all back there now in a time machine.

'But it did her good to go to London, especially when she found you, Lara,' said Marion. 'Remember when you came to visit us in the summer? We could see Sandrine was back to her old self, like a bright flame. But no one could be with her all the time. I think the sadness was always there in the shadows.'

Marion's voice caught and Jean put a hand on his wife's shoulder. Lara blinked at them. It was as if they were describing a stranger. If anything, Sandrine had been the one to pull Lara out of a funk about career or relationships, not the other way around. She remembered Sandrine in Paris, holding dinner parties in her apartment, surrounded by smoke and candles and a rag-tag assortment of artists and writers and aristocrats; she had *glowed*. How could she have never seen this? Why hadn't Sandrine ever told her? Lara was torn between disbelief and pain – what kind of friend was she to have missed it? What sort of friendship did they have that Sandrine couldn't confide in her?

It's not about you, Lara, she reminded herself. This is about Sandrine – and about Jean and Marion.

Whatever Lara's pain was, it was multiplied a dozen times in her parents.

'Did the police say if there was a note? An explanation?'

Lara had been down to the station earlier in the day. It was a question she'd asked Ian Fox but he'd been evasive.

Marion shook her head.

'The inspector said it is often the way. Not everyone leaves a note or their reasons why.'

They sat in silence for a while, listening to a distant siren. Lara felt as if she were intruding on the Legards' grief, but still wanted to do something to help.

'Would you like me to go to Paris?' she asked. Lara was a doer and she knew right now she had to do something, not just for Jean and Marion Legard, but for her own sanity. 'The apartment, I have a key. I could…' she shook her head. What *could* she do? Collect the mail? Water the plants? Sandrine was gone. Her old life was a shell, just ashes ready to blow away on the wind.

'That would be kind of you, Lara,' said Jean simply.

The room's phone rang, sudden and shrill, shattering the quiet intensity of the room. Lara quickly picked it up.

'Ms. Legard? This is Felicity in reception. I have a Mr. Eduardo Ortega in the lobby?'

Lara recognised the name immediately: Eduardo from Le Caché.

'Eduardo Ortega?' she said to Jean, covering the

receiver.

Jean nodded. 'Yes, send him up.'

Lara relayed the message and put down the phone.

'Sandrine's…friend?' said Lara. She wasn't sure if her parents knew but Marion nodded.

'Have you met him?' asked Lara.

'In Paris,' said Jean. 'He's very impressive.'

'That's what Sandrine told me.'

There was a knock at the door and Jean answered it. A tall, fortyish man embraced him, then crossed to take both of Marion's hands in a gesture that spoke of respect and familiarity. Eduardo Ortega was even more handsome that the profile picture she had seen on the Le Caché website. His pale blue shirt, expensive Italian shoes and swept-back dark hair gave him the look of European royalty – someone more at home in the lobby of the Paris Ritz than reporting from the field in Somalia or the Yemen.

He introduced himself, extended his condolences and some pleasantries. She'd met plenty of his type before, wealthy Europeans who'd had their accents rubbed away in British boarding schools and Ivy League colleges. He took Lara to one side and lowered his voice.

'I hate to ask, but would you mind giving us a few minutes? I want to say a few words to Sandrine's parents, but I would appreciate speaking to you too, Lara. Could you wait?'

Eduardo delivered the request as if Lara were doing him a favour, a trick many successful people managed to pull off. She would have said yes in any case – she was keen to talk to him too.

'There's a bar next to the lobby,' she said. 'I'll wait for you there.'

Giving Jean and Marion a final embrace, Lara left them talking quietly in French and took the lift down to the ground floor. The bar was more glamorous than the slightly faded hotel had suggested. Dark panelling with tall mirrors and a zinc-topped bar, it aped the Parisian haunts of the 1920s frequented by Toulouse Lautrec, almost getting there. Lara ordered coffee for both of them and was just sitting in a discreet corner when Eduardo arrived, already apologising.

Lara watched him as he took off his jacket and put it over the back of the chair. She knew that they were united in grief, that there should be a bond of solidarity between them. But still, it was hard not to view him with suspicion – to view everything with suspicion. The suicide, the hint about Jonathon Meyer, her new alliance with Le Caché, Eduardo's appearance on the scene. None of it seemed coincidental.

'So you're here for the conference,' she said, sipping her coffee.

'That's right.'

'I was going to come. Sandrine invited me along.'

'I know. I asked her to.'

Lara hid her surprise, filing that detail away for a later date.

'Are you still going ahead with it?'

'Yes. Sandrine, more than anyone, would want it to happen.'

Lara agreed with him on that.

'How did you know Jean and Marion were here?' asked Lara as casually as she could. Eduardo shrugged, as if it were obvious. 'When they heard the news, they called me.'

Lara waited for more explanation, but none was forthcoming.

'So how long were you together?' she asked, after a moment.

He looked down into his coffee before glancing back at Lara. 'Nine months. Not long enough,' he said looking away. 'We were supposed to see each other tomorrow. A walk in Regent's Park, lunch at some place along the canal. I told her there was so much to prepare for the conference. She told me that life was for living, not just working.'

He gave a soft, sad snort. His eyes were glittering now. Eduardo was either genuinely upset or a great actor. Both were possible; the truth was she knew nothing about this man or his relationship with Sandrine.

'The apartment in Marylebone,' said Lara. 'You weren't staying there.'

Eduardo shook his head.

'No. I'm in Kensington. When Sandrine was working, she preferred her own space. Besides, given my position at Le Caché, I wasn't sure how professional it would look to arrive together.'

Lara nodded. At least that made sense.

'So when did you see her last? How did she seem?'

'Two weeks ago. I came to Paris. She was fine. More than fine. She was sparkling.'

Lara had always said Sandrine had an indefinable stardust, she could light up a room just by walking into it. Eduardo looked into the distance.

'I guess we don't always know people, Lara. Even the people we love.'

'Did you know Sandrine was depressed?'

'No. But which woman would reveal such a thing so early in a relationship?'

She wasn't sure nine months was *that* early.

'Have you spoken to the police yet?'

'They called me this afternoon. I'm going down to the station after I have finished here.'

'Did they say why they wanted to speak to you?'

At her own interview, Ian Fox had asked about Sandrine's private life and she had told him about Eduardo and Le Caché. She had no idea if that was why the police wanted to talk to Eduardo now. Perhaps they knew something she didn't.

Lara did not consider herself a catastrophist, someone whose mind always went to the worst possible outcome, but as an investigative reporter, she was in the habit of considering every possibility of what *could* have happened.

And what she could imagine was a drunk and happy Sandrine inviting her handsome millionaire boyfriend round to her Marylebone flat after a night on the town. She could imagine her opening the French doors to let in the balmy summer night air. She could imagine an argument breaking out for any one of the thousand reasons couples quarrelled; a flash of anger, a hard push and that was all it could take for a tragedy.

Was that scenario more likely that Sandrine taking her own life? Lara thought it was.

'I'd better be going' said Eduardo, glancing at his watch. 'Hopefully the police will not ask me *quite* as many questions as you.'

He said it as a quip but Lara found herself bristling.

'I'm sorry, Eduardo, but I hadn't even heard of you until a few hours before Sandrine's death. And my best friend just died, so forgive me if I have a lot of questions.'

'That may be so,' said Eduardo crisply. 'But please try not to make them sound like accusations. You know, I cared for her too.'

'Did you?'

'What are you implying exactly?'

'Were you faithful?'

'Faithful? Yes, I was. How can you even ask me that?'

'Because she's *dead*, Eduardo!' said Lara, raising her voice. 'My best friend is dead and I want to know why. Is that so hard to understand?'

'I know you're upset,' he said sitting forward. 'But this isn't the time or place for this.'

'Isn't it? Because I thought we were both in the business of getting to the truth. Why be afraid of that?'

'I am not afraid of the truth, Lara,' said Eduardo, putting down his cup. 'But I'm aware that there are other people in this hotel who may not wish to listen to this.'

Lara looked up. He may have had a point; it seemed everyone else had stopped what they were doing and were looking over at Lara and Eduardo.

'Perhaps we could discuss this at a later date?' he said, standing. 'Right now I need to speak to the police. Perhaps they will have some insights into what happened and then you will know where to direct your anger.'

He tapped a finger on the table. 'But I assure you, Lara, it is not towards me.'

Chapter Six

L'ETRANGER CLUB WAS not what Lara had been expecting. Standing on the corner of a long terrace of whitewashed townhouses, the building was elegant, but there was an air of neglect that was entirely out of step with the club's reputation. L'Etranger had been one of *the* hang-outs in Sixties and Seventies London, the place Don McCullin and Francoise Demulder would carouse before grabbing their Pentaxes and heading off to the war zones. Back in the glory days of the inkies, L'Etranger had crackled with energy and intrigue, the famous 'long bar' attracting diplomats, attaches and thinly-disguised Cold War spies.

Right now, however, Lara thought it looked like a run-down residential hotel or a minor embassy. Marooned on a quiet side street off a major Paddington artery, the club had a polished brass plaque next to the front door, but it didn't exactly stand out from its neighbours. But then perhaps that was point: as the venue for the collective's annual conference, it was exclusive, but unobtrusive, anonymous without being actually underground. By reputation, Le Caché flew under the radar: they weren't going to hold a party at

Hakkasan and invite the paparazzi.

Lara walked slowly across the road. She knew she had to be here for Sandrine's sake, but she wasn't exactly looking forward to it, not after her fractious exchange with Eduardo at the hotel. Lara felt embarrassed by her outburst, but she still didn't trust him. So why come? Because she was intrigued. For someone who had grown up inside the media establishment, Le Caché was radical and exciting.

A blond man in a jacket with too many pockets was standing by the door, head bowed over his phone. He looked up as Lara approached.

'You're here for Le Caché?' he asked. She nodded and he pointed her to a desk where a woman handed Lara a lanyard. Clearly Eduardo hadn't blacklisted her. Not yet, anyway.

'First session is on the first floor,' said the woman, directing her up the stairs and into a tall open room rumbling with excited conversation, sixty or seventy people standing around drinking coffee and nibbling pastries, an air of anticipation even this early in the morning. Lara felt the energy too, but she also felt intimidated by some of the lined, sunburned faces: she saw Orla McGuinness, the celebrated Irish writer whose 'Tel Aviv Telegram' had influenced a generation of travellers, Avril Katz, the Canadian badass who'd gone undercover as a volunteer on the US campaign trail and learned first-hand just how cutthroat American politics could be. In the far corner, Lara recognised Francis Barbier, the legendary scribe who had walked through police lines in Berlin to get an interview with terrorist leader Karl Haas minutes before he blew himself to bits. Barbier was white-haired and craggy, but it was reassuring to see someone of his vintage there among the younger go-getters. Lara took a deep breath and sidled over.

'Amazing place,' she said. 'It's kind of off the beaten track though.'

'That's because of history. Back in the 1960s, the West London Air Terminal was just around the corner.'

'The West what?'

Francis laughed.

'Hard to believe now, but when Heathrow was built, air travel was so expensive, they assumed passengers would arrive with their chauffeur. So when ordinary people started flying in the 60s, there was no train or tube to the airport, so they'd check you in here, then bus everyone out to the runway.'

'So where is it?' said Lara, looking around as if she might see a baggage carousel.

'It's a supermarket now. But that's why the club was here: so people popping off to Aden or Saigon could leave it to the last minute.'

'Last minute – no change there then,' smiled Lara.

She could actually feel the history Francis had described, not just in the framed black and white photographs of unnamed conflicts on the walls or the famous oak bar at the far end of the room, but in the intent, that urge to get out there and find the news by seeing it happen, being first in, first out. She had spent the past few days feeling disappointed and angry with the world of journalism and yet, at L'Etranger, it was hard not to be swept back into the excitement and possibility of it all.

The good-looking blonde man from the street walked over to shake hands with Barbier, then turned to smile at Lara.

'You found us then,' he said, extending his hand towards Lara.

'I'm Stefan.'

He was around her age, with sharp blue eyes and dark blonde hair that looked as if it hadn't been brushed that morning. At first glance, he reminded her of Alex, the height and athletic physique, the careless stubble. But these days Alex looked ready for the boardroom while Stefan looked as though he had come straight from the Foreign Correspondents club in Phnom Penh.

'Lara Stone. Eduardo invited me.'

Stefan gave a nod. 'He told me; you're Sandrine's friend aren't you? I'm sorry for your loss.'

'Sandrine Legard?' said Barbier, perking up. 'That was tragic. She was so talented.'

Lara smiled. She knew that Sandrine would have been thrilled to get such a glowing assessment from someone she so respected. Stefan put a hand on Barbier's shoulder.

'It's about to start. You should probably grab a seat.'

He glanced over at Lara.

'We'll talk later?'

Up at the front, Stefan banged a coffee mug on the

bar to get everyone's attention and a large flatscreen came to life showing images from warzones, rioting, the G20, the front steps of the White House and Number Ten, all illuminated by flashbulbs. Then the pictures became more specific. The cities were less obvious: Copenhagen, Geneva, the locations office buildings or expensive private residences. Lara recognised some of the faces too, but not all of them. Bankers, Russian politicians. These were the stories Le Caché had worked on, not all of them familiar to Lara, but that made sense: even the most explosive exposé about government corruption in, say, Austria, would barely make the world news section of the *Chronicle* – but that didn't mean it wasn't vital to bring them to light. *No story too small, no lie too big.*

The images faded and Eduardo stepped up onto a low stage. A ripple of light applause ran around the room and he graciously nodded. Lara had to hand it to Sandrine: she had landed the most impressive man in a room full of pretty impressive individuals.

'Thank you for the welcome,' he said. 'And welcome to all of you: this conference is about all of us. The world press calls us a collective and that, at least, they get right.'

As a hum of amusement fluttered around the room, Lara could immediately see how good he was at this; how he instantly had the audience in the palm of his hand, how he could keep them quiet and captivated. The previous evening, Lara had done a deeper dive into the life of Eduardo Ortega and it was no wonder he was this slick and confident. Eduardo had family money and deep pockets. The grandson of Vincent Ortega, the Spanish industrialist worth over a billion euros, Eduardo hadn't followed his father and cousins into the family business. His French mother was a documentary film-maker and he seemed to have inherited her crusading zeal rather than the capitalistic instincts of the other Ortega family members. But he clearly had some of the same drive: Lara might question Le Caché's methods, but there was no denying it was 'getting shit done', as Alex always put it.

'We do this together,' continued Eduardo from the stage. 'Because it is the only way it can work. Working alone in our own little corners, the information is fractured and scattered, but come together and we make the picture whole. And that's what we stand for: telling the whole story, shining a spotlight into the darkness, making that which is hidden seen.'

He paused to look around the room, to make eye contact.

'We work together, because the stakes are too high to do anything else. This week we have seen just how high, with the tragic loss of one of our own.'

Eduardo's voice cracked on the final word and he looked down, composing himself, hiding his vulnerability. When he looked back towards the room, he raised his coffee mug. 'So here's to the work we have done and all the work we will do. Because we have to. Sandrine Legard. This conference is for you.'

As the crowd erupted into applause, Lara felt the depth of emotion for Sandrine in the room. It was a lovely thing and she knew her friend would have been pleased by that too.

The mood shifted into something more business-like as Stefan stood up to outline the activities for the morning: there was a lecture by a professor from the LSE and a panel discussion on interview technique. Lara chose a Q&A on global politics 'through a spy's eyes'. About twenty delegates crammed into a side room where a bald man with wire-rimmed glasses was already deep in discussion with a woman with wild hair, debating whether the paranoia of Hollywood and spy fiction was real. The discussion's title sounded lightweight, but Lara found it fascinating. Lara had been to a number of these things at literary festivals and they were usually either horribly dry or annoyingly thin. This however had the air of truth and authority about it, with the speakers beginning sentences with 'the Iranian ambassador told me…' or 'I was talking to the deputy director of the CIA…'. This was why Lara had always been attracted to this profession: she wanted to see what was really happening *behind* the news.

As the talk finished, everyone filed out of the room. Lara had already spoken to a handful of Le Caché journalists, dropping in Sandrine's name where she could, hoping she could tease information out of them, but few people seemed to know her well. For all the talk of collaboration, it seemed that the journalists only shared their work through servers and the occasional conference call.

Eduardo was standing at the door, shaking hands

and exchanging pleasantries like a vicar passing blessings to his congregation, which Lara supposed he was. Lara was bracing herself for an awkward encounter when Eduardo gave her a wry smile.

'You came,' he said simply.

'I did.'

'So, could I take you to lunch?' he asked.

'Now?' she said, glancing at her watch. It wasn't even noon, but Lara realised she was hungry. Since Sandrine's death she had barely eaten anything.

'Sure.'

They went out onto the street. It was working up to be a warm day and Lara knew she was going to be overdressed in a black trouser suit and white shirt. She took off her jacket as they walked.

'Your welcome address,' said Lara. 'They were nice words you said about Sandrine. I'm glad you did it.'

'Sandrine would have loved it here,' said Eduardo. 'You know she did the keynote speech at last year's conference?'

Lara hadn't known but she could certainly imagine her standing up on that stage, loving the atmosphere, loving being at the centre of all that. Lara glanced across at Eduardo.

'Look, I'm sorry about Saturday. I was upset, emotional, but I shouldn't have been so bloody rude.'

Eduardo nodded.

'I'm sorry too. As first meetings go, I'm not sure it was what Sandrine had in mind.'

'No. Probably not,' said Lara sadly.

They headed away from the rush of the main road, down a street of identical whitewashed terraces. 'The pub's just down here,' said Eduardo. 'It's a bit of a walk, but it does serve a very decent moules frites.'

'Could be my the first of the day,' smiled Lara.

'You like moules frites?' he said with a look of confusion.

'Yes. No, I meant I'm heading to Paris this afternoon. I'm checking on Sandrine's flat for Jean and Marion.'

'The flat?'

A look of concern crossed Eduardo's face, then it was gone.

'So Stefan is going to join us at the pub, I hope you don't mind?'

Before Lara could respond, Eduardo strode ahead and she had to trot to keep up.

'So Stefan's your right-hand man?' she said.

'He was the first journalist I invited to join Le Caché. I'd say he was more a co-founder rather than a deputy.'

'He's Dutch, right? So what brings the conference to London, rather than Holland or Spain?'

'Why is the City of London the number one global financial hub rather than Frankfurt or New York?' he said glancing across. 'It's because it's in the middle of the time zones and because English is the universal language and our journalists come from everywhere from Sydney to San Francisco. It would have been easier for me to have headquarters in Madrid, but not for anyone else. Which is why we're moving the main

Le Caché office to London, Shoreditch. I'm relocating here too.'

'I didn't know that,' said Lara. 'That's exciting.'

'Sandrine was excited about it too.' He said it with a sad smile.

Lara stopped.

'Sandrine was going to move to London?'

'We talked about it. But you know Sandrine. I'm not sure that was the level of commitment she was comfortable with.'

Over the years, many men had fallen in love with Sandrine but all of them, with the exception of Patric, had been very much one-sided affairs. She wondered if Eduardo and Sandrine's had been that way too. Perhaps he didn't even know.

Inside the pub, they ordered the moules then joined Stefan at a corner table.

'So what did you think of this morning? Are you going to join us?' Lara laughed at Stefan's bluntness. The truth was, Lara had enjoyed herself. Despite going in as a sceptic, she had loved the buzz of the conference and the excitement of being surrounded by like-minded people.

Stefan and Eduardo were passionate, smart and driven but handsome and charming too. It was a combination that took people places. She had seen the same thing happen with Alex Ford; she had known Alex would make it to the very top the very first day they had met.

'Look, this is all very flattering,' said Lara. 'But I'm not here to talk about joining Le Caché. I'm here to talk about Sandrine. She was going to discuss a new story she was working on at the conference.'

Eduardo nodded. 'That's right. But all I know is that there was a link to Jonathon Meyer, the financier who died recently.'

'Did you look into it?'

'A little. The problem is that Meyer's world is – was – so secretive. He lived in Monaco, had a fund for ultra-high-net worth investors and threw networking parties for billionaires on his yacht *Pandora*, but no one really knew anything beyond that. I thought it was a classic Vanity Fair-style investigation, a glimpse into the lurid world of the super-rich, but not the sort of thing Le Caché would get involved in.'

'Why not? Didn't you trust her to have found something more newsworthy?'

Eduardo met her gaze. 'I always trusted Sandrine.'

'So if Sandrine thought she had a great story then she did. Surely we owe it to her to complete her work.'

Stefan looked sympathetic but not entirely convinced.

'But where do we start? Sandrine didn't put her notes on the Le Caché server; we've asked a few colleagues and no-one seems to know anything about it.'

Lara looked at him.

'We're journalists, Stefan. Isn't that what we do? Dig?'

But as Lara spoke, a thought shifted; something Alex had said the morning on her houseboat. 'What did you see?'

It wasn't what Lara had seen in Sandrine's flat, it was what she *hadn't* seen. Her computer. Looking back, that was what was strange about that apartment, what felt missing. She looked up at Eduardo, debating whether to mention it. No. The truth was she still didn't trust him.

'So does this mean you're joining Le Caché?' said Eduardo.

'Maybe,' she replied. Perhaps it was a way to deal with the pain; it was certainly a way to honour her friend's life. 'I can't let Sandrine's work die with her.'

Eduardo raised a hand towards the waitress.

'Maybe is excellent news. How about we toast it with a glass of champagne?'

Lara nodded and smiled. *Sure*, she thought. *For now.*

Chapter Seven

STELLA HARRIS WIPED the counter, the latest battle in her endless war against coffee cup rings. It was, she estimated, the fiftieth time she had run a sponge over the faux-marble counter and still the stains wouldn't shift. She looked wearily back at the coffee machine, burping and hissing as if it was about to die: she shouldn't be surprised, everything in this café was peeling around the edges or falling apart.

Present company included, she thought, rinsing out her cloth.

Stella had signed up for as many hours as she could get at Starclucks coffee shop when she'd been 'let go' from the *Chronicle* the previous week. She hadn't exactly been the best paid member of the investigations team, but now even those modest cheques were gone, Stella's tiny place in Seven Sisters, a run-down flat she shared with other two girls and a lot of creeping mould, was a luxury she could barely afford.

She reached for a sack of coffee beans and began filling the hopper on top of the machine. The board outside the café boasted of artisan single-origin free trade beans, but Stella knew for a fact that the owner Jimmy got them in bulk from a bloke on the market, no questions asked.

Starclucks was an ironic pastiche of the more famous Seattle institution, although in reality, it was a standard greasy spoon café with stripped-pine chairs and a new logo painted on the front, the familiar green mermaid replaced by a chicken with a crown and a forked tail. It was owned by Jimmy Reeves, Stella's uncle. Not a real uncle, just an old friend of the family, a semi-criminal ducker-and-diver who owned a string of dodgy businesses in the North London corridor, but Stella couldn't really afford to be too picky about work right now and had been grateful for the offer of a position of barista-cum-cleaner. She looked down at her wrinkled hands, coffee grains under the nails. *Surely there had to be something better than this.*

At least the lunch rush was over; only one customer left sitting hunched over his long-gone cold cappuccino, a handsome forty-something sitting alone in a booth by the door. Stella pretended to clean the foam nozzle on the coffee machine while she used the mirror behind the bar to look at the lone patron. Now she thought about it, he'd been here quite a while. He was wearing a dark suit and reading the paper – the FT, which in Jimmy's café was like seeing a unicorn. A high-powered company director, perhaps? But this was the Holloway Road, not Mayfair. If you wanted a phone charger or a cheap haircut, London's main artery northwest was the place to be, but it wasn't exactly a hotbed of high finance. Stella's instincts for a story began to jangle. So why was he here? If he was just watching the world go by, he'd have been sitting in the window, not in a booth.

Curious, Stella walked across, picking up stray cups as she went.

'Can I get you anything else?' she asked.

'No, still got this,' said the man, lifting his cup.

'No problem, take your time,' said Stella.

'Oi, have you cleaned the machine?'

Glenda, Uncle Jimmy's eldest. walked out from the back. Jimmy had handed the café over to her to 'manage', which Glenda had interpreted as 'sitting in the back selling stuff on Ebay' and doing her best to push the staff around.

'I am doing it right now,' said Stella sweetly.

'Well, see that you do.'

Stella looked up as the door opened. An attractive forty-something woman. She didn't look up at the counter or the board behind listing the drinks, she looked around – then flashed a smile at the lone diner. Ah. He had been waiting for *her*. Stella watched in the mirror as the woman slid in opposite the FT-reader. A happy-to-see-you smile, but no kiss noted Stella. A first date? But then the woman glanced around and touched his hand. He had a wedding ring, she didn't.

An affair. Stella's instincts about a story were always right.

But look where it got me, thought Stella, wiping the nozzle again with increased vigour. Stella had not been given many breaks growing up in the Easterhouse district of Glasgow. Her father, a bitter, angry and abusive man, walked out when she was ten, her mother's alcohol problems ramping up from that standing start. Stella was told that she would never amount to anything – by her father, by the bullies at school, even by her mother, who lost herself in short-lived affairs. But Stella had ignored them all, worked hard at school, won a place at the city's University, where she'd found her passion – the student newspaper. At a time when her contemporaries were discovering social media and dreaming of becoming influencers, Stella had sold stories to the *Record* and *The Scotsman*, finally landing a job on the *Chronicle* investigations team. For a few short years, she'd found her groove, proved her detractors wrong, but even that had finally gone tits-up thanks to Darius Allen, Felix Tait and whole load of terrible luck. Or maybe cranking out caramel lattés and wiping the counter was her level after all.

The door opened; the cheating couple were on their way out, off to some hotel perhaps. Stella ducked under the counter, rummaging around for the floor cleaner. Might as well get on with it now while the café was a ghost town.

'Are you still serving?' said a voice.

'Just a minute madam, I'll be with you…' she said, bobbing up. 'Lara!'

She swung under the counter to embrace her old boss. 'What on earth are you doing here?'

'Who could resist a coffee shop called Starclucks?'

Stella pulled a face.

'Uncle Jimmy thinks it'll attract the hipster crowd'.

'More likely the attention of Seattle-based lawyers.'

'Yeah, well good luck with getting any money out of Uncle Jimmy.'

Lara looked around, taking in the empty tables.

'I can see it's a little slow.'

'What can I get you? Double caff Frappuccino with vanilla?'

Lara laughed.

'Just an espresso, Stel. Sorry – maybe you should give me a croissant or something too. I haven't been eating much lately.'

It was only then that Stella noticed the dark semi-circles under Lara's eyes and the pale skin. So much for being observant.

'I heard about your friend Sandrine. I'm so sorry.'

Lara gave a tight nod and looked away, so Stella gestured to the cakes under glass domes.

'Help yourself to whatever you fancy and take a seat. I'll crank up the machine and bring it across.'

Lara was waiting in the booth the affair couple had lately vacated. Despite the circumstances, Stella couldn't help but feel excited by her old boss's unannounced appearance. She had missed the excitement and the camaraderie. And she had missed Lara too.

'To what do I owe this honour?' she asked.

Lara pulled a thin smile.

'First I wanted to apologise.'

'What for?'

'All this,' she said, gesturing towards Stella's mop, propped up against the wall.

'Working in Jimmy's?' said Stella. 'It's not too

bad. He pays more than the minimum wage and lets me choose my hours.'

'Well, I'm sorry you're not working at the *Chronicle*.'

'Lara, I chose to join a profession that I knew was disappearing before our eyes. And everyone wants a cup of coffee. It's a win-win.'

She said it as a joke but Stella had been devastated when Oliver Wolf, the *Chronicle*'s managing editor had summoned her into his office on the day of the High Court verdict and told her to clear her desk. Being Lara Stone's assistant had been her dream job, right at the heart of one of the biggest newspapers in the country. But in ten short minutes, she was standing out in the street holding a box of files and all the staples she could carry. It was like it had never even happened.

'Forget making coffee, Stella,' said Lara. 'You belong in newspapers.'

Stella looked away. She'd thought that too until she'd emailed every news editor in town, only to be either ignored or told politely that she'd be 'put on file'.

'If you hear of anything, I'm available to start pretty much immediately,' said Stella, forcing a smile.

'Well that's good news, because how do you fancy coming to work for me?'

Stella felt her heart jump.

'Are you serious?'

It had always been Stella's dream to work for the great Lara Stone, the glamorous, fearless investigative reporter, ever since she had read a piece Lara had written about match fixing syndicates in European football leagues. It had been brave and funny and riveting and it was why Stella had turned down a news desk job at *The Scottish Herald* to move down to London for a zero-hours contract assistant's job – less of a sideways move, more a definite step back. But the job was Lara Stone's assistant and Stella would drop anything to work with her again: even working for Uncle Jimmy.

'Work with you *where*?' she asked. 'Hasn't the investigations team been disbanded?'

Lara downed her espresso. 'Not on a paper. Look, I'll lay my cards on the table here Stella. No one except me seems to care that my friend is dead, no one else seems interested in looking into why she died. If the situation was reversed, I'm pretty damn sure that Sandrine would be moving heaven and earth to find out what happened to me. So I'm going to Paris. Tonight. And I'd like you to come with me.'

Stella put down her cloth and started to laugh. Lara always made everything sound exciting, as if they were constantly in the middle of an adventure.

'Paris? Where are we going? Chanel? Dior?'

'We won't be going shopping,' said Lara. 'Call Jimmy. Tell him you won't be in for a couple of days and I'll fill you in on the way.'

Chapter Eight

SANDRINE LIVED ON the top floor of an apartment block at the very top of Montmartre, the famous hilltop arrondissement north-west of the Gare du Nord. Stella leaned on the bannister breathing heavily as she pulled off the red beret that she had bought from a tourist shop on the Boulevard de Magenta. After catching a late afternoon Eurostar from London, they had made the short journey from Gare du Nord to Pigalle by dented taxi, but Stella had wanted to climb the long stairway to the Sacre Coeur. She had been correct that it had offered an amazing view over the city, but she had underestimated the puff required, especially when they then had to climb five flights of stairs to the top of Sandrine's apartment building too. The sweat Stella had expended had left a pink line across her forehead.

'Why couldn't Sandrine have lived by the bloody river?' she panted, fanning herself with the beret as Lara unlocked the door to her friend's apartment.

'Step inside and you'll see why,' said Lara.

Sandrine's apartment occupied one corner of the top floor, with high moulded ceilings and a small balcony just big enough for two chairs. Lara crossed to the shutters and swung them open, filling the flat with lazy evening light.

'Okay, totally worth it,' sighed Stella.

The flat was just as Lara had remembered: cluttered and disorganised, but stylish, warm and artistic, a mishmash of thrift store and elegance. The apartment looked just like Sandrine: Parisian, chic and utterly individual.

'Look at that view,' said Stella, opening the door on the balcony.

The elevated vista over Paris was magnificent at any time, but it was never better than right now, just before sunset. The whole of the City of Lights, laid out flat and orderly like a model village, the horizon a blend of blue and pink, yellow streetlights just blinking awake like a holy procession.

'Amazing, isn't it?' said Lara.

Stella turned to look at Lara, a troubled expression on her face.

'What?' said Lara, sinking down on the sofa.

'I don't want to be morbid,' said Stella. 'But if Sandrine wanted to do what she did, why did she choose some anonymous London apartment?'

Lara had had the same thought. She could still hear her friend's words every time she opened the French windows to let in some night air. 'Careful,' she'd always say in her sing-song voice. 'Don't go too close to the edge. You don't want to fall.'

She closed her eyes, shaking her head. She had no answers and it had been a very long day. It was hard to believe that the Le Caché conference had only been that morning, and since then, she had been to Jimmy's café, over to Stella's flat to grab her passport and back to St. Pancras to catch the Eurostar. Add in that epic climb up to the Sacre Coeur, and Lara was exhausted.

'I don't know about you, but I need a drink,' said Stella, as ever attuned to Lara's thoughts.

'That's what Sandrine used to say every time we climbed those stairs,' said Lara. Dozens of happy images flashed in front of her: Sandrine holding carrier bags of vegetables they had picked up at the local supermarché, Sandrine, a foodie and brilliant cook, sipping deep red Cabernet as she made thick stews or gratins, sharing their stories, both personal and professional. And the laughter – oh, how they'd laughed. There were two bottles of wine on the kitchen side that Sandrine had been using as book ends for a wedge of letters.

'Do you think it's inappropriate to open one?' said Stella. Lara smiled.

'I'm pretty sure Sandrine would approve. She never liked to see a good bottle of Merlot to go to waste.'

She waited as Stella rummaged about for a corkscrew, then clinked glasses.

'Right, let's get to work. I'm going to make a start in Sandrine's study.'

Lara had already filled Stella in on what they needed to do. There were practical things, like closing up the flat – making sure that bills were being paid, that the premises were secure and the heating was off. Sandrine's things needed to be boxed away too, but Lara wasn't sure she was ready for that task just yet.

And there was another reason to be here too. The story. There *had* to be something here that would give them a clue as to what Sandrine had been working on.

On the face of it, Sandrine's study looked exactly as Lara remembered it: the messy, creative place of a messy, creative person. Lara had always thought of Sandrine's brain as a buzzing fly – Restless, inquisitive – and it seemed to work at twice the speed of everyone else's. But still…something was off.

'You should take a look at this letter,' said Stella, walking through.

Lara held up a hand, stopping Stella in the doorway.

'Someone has been here.'

Back when Lara was a junior reporter, working the London crime beat for the *Chronicle* news desk, Lara had become friends with a Chief Inspector named Ray Banner, one of the friendly coppers at Paddington Green. Ray had been pushing sixty and heading for retirement, but she'd loved listening to his stories of being a detective during the gritty Seventies and Eighties, when old school hunches and dogged trawling was the staple of police work before the luxury of databases. Ray had drilled into Lara the importance of stepping back to look at the scene as a whole.

'What's on the pinboard?' asked Lara.

Stella looked at it. 'Well, pictures of you and Sandrine,' she said, pointing to a photobooth strip that had been taken in their student days. There were a few other notes – the number of her dentist and the local pharmacist, some old theatre ticket stubs and a list of birthdays. 'But apart from that, not much.'

'Exactly,' said Lara, leaning closer, running her fingertips over the cork. There were dozens of tiny holes in it where pins had been stuck in – and removed.

'Sandrine used to write everything down – I mean everything,' said Lara, thinking out loud. 'This pinboard was always covered with stuff and she'd stick Post-it notes all over the wall too. When we lived together, I used to joke that she should buy shares in the company, because she used so many of them.'

'That was a long time ago, Lara. Maybe she's changed her ways. You know, put things on her computer?'

Lara shook her head. She'd been here before Christmas and there had been so many yellow Post-it notes that Lara had said her study looked like a canary's wing.

'Okay, so where are her notes? And where is her computer?'

She'd already spoken to Ian Fox and Jean Legard and neither of them seemed to know anything about Sandrine's laptop.

'Lara, this letter,' repeated Stella, handing it to her. 'It's from HR at *Le Figaro* inviting Sandrine to an *entretien préalable au licenciement*, which according to Google is a preliminary meeting to discuss a potential severance. If you're here to find a reason for Sandrine's death, then this could be it. You said Sandrine was devoted to her job. If she was depressed and lost the thing she most cared about…?'

But Lara knew – just knew – that something else was at work here.

'Someone has searched the apartment,' she said decisively. 'Can't you see?'

Stella walked around the room silently considering it. Five minutes earlier, Lara might have agreed that Sandrine's job being in jeopardy might have explained a lot of things. But now it seemed obvious to her: the desk wasn't just messy and the books, the magazines, the papers, they had all been shuffled, upended, examined.

'So what are we going to do?'

Lara smiled gratefully. She loved how Stella trusted her judgement. Plenty would have dismissed it as clutching at straws.

'Okay, you take the living room and kitchen. I'll look in the bedroom, study and bathroom. We're looking for anything that will help us build a picture of Sandrine's final few weeks.'

She searched her bedroom first, looking through the drawers and cupboards. She found handbags full of mints and make-up, a file of expense receipts, a box of old letters and photos from her time in London. Lara paused to smile at a picture of herself and Alex at Glastonbury, their faces painted with glitter, another of Sandrine on her graduation day – happy and proud in her black gown.

Looking in Sandrine's wardrobe, Lara fished metro and bus tickets from her coat pockets, but nothing felt significant and she moved to the bathroom. There was a toothbrush sat in a bamboo cup on the sink, just waiting for its owner to return. There were headache pills in the cabinet and lotions and potions in the shower. Nothing out of the ordinary. Lara picked up the laundry basket and tipped the contents on the floor, picking out a pair of grey jeans. She pushed her hands into the pockets. A train ticket dated four weeks previously and a crumpled piece of yellow paper. Lara felt her heart leap at the sight of one of Sandrine's beloved Post-it notes.

She unfolded it and immediately recognised Sandrine's swirly Gallic handwriting. Three words in black ink, stacked on top of one another.

Helen
Michael
Jonathon.

Stella was standing at the bathroom door.

'Found anything?' she asked.

Lara held out the note.

What does it mean?' asked Stella.

'I don't know,' said Lara. 'But we're sure as hell going to find out.'

Chapter Nine

THE TROUBLE WITH newspaper people was that they never switched off. Alex stood in the garden of Nicholas Avery's Holland Park home clutching a glass of warm champagne and listened as Darius held forth about global media, seemingly oblivious to the fact that they were supposed to be at a party. Nicholas certainly seemed to have glazed over, while his son Charlie was knocking back the Krug to dull the pain.

'Of course the Gulf War was the best thing to happen to American media,' said Darius. 'It really put them back on the map.'

'Back on the map?' asked Nicholas, tilting his head in a way that Alex recognised. It was Nicholas's way of saying 'I disagree, but do keep digging yourself into a hole.' Darius missed the cue and ploughed on regardless. 'The way I see it is, America was this grey superpower then BAM! There's CNN with the rockets and the hi-tech drone strikes. Suddenly America looks sexy again.'

'The glamorization of war, you mean?' said Charlie.

Alex knew Charlie was just baiting Darius, but all the same he had to step in.

‘I think what Darius means, is that the US media coverage set the tone for the way war looks on screen. They used Hollywood techniques to engage the folks at home so they could understand foreign policy and see the brutality of conflict.’

Darius nodded enthusiastically, as if that had been his point all along. Darius could be pompous, but Alex knew that his editor would be in a foul mood tomorrow if Charlie humiliated him in front of the big boss.

‘Yes, things have changed, haven’t they?’ said Nicholas, diplomatically steering the subject around to the recent revamp of the *Chronicle*’s news app. The irony of course was that this party was to celebrate the 100th anniversary of the Avery Media Group and yet, here in the London media bubble, nothing much *had* changed. A century of headlines had kept the Avery family at the heart of politics and power. Back through the open French windows, Alex could see that Nicholas’s beautiful house, well-known as one of the finest private homes in Central London, was packed with the wealthy, the connected and the influential. Ministers rubbed shoulders with models, columnists chatted with bankers, just as they had back when the Averys had launched the *Chronicle*. In spite of the seemingly revolutionary changes in digital media, the Averys were still here, still at the controls.

Excusing himself, Alex walked down a curving stone staircase from the terrace and into the depths of garden. The house had almost an acre of grounds, and right now it looked like a luxury circus had come to town. In the centre of the lawn was a huge illuminated, circular bar, model-grade waiters flitting about with champagne and canapes. There were fire-dancers and even a sleight-of-hand magician. Alex gave a quiet chuckle. It was all a long way from his Cumbrian upbringing, where a party meant a lock-in in the local pub and maybe a plate of grated cheese sandwiches. But that was the point, wasn't it? It *was* a long way. And tonight Alex felt part of it.

'Marks out of ten?' said a husky voice behind him.

He turned around to see Nicholas's wife Olivia smiling at him.

'Ten and a half. I think it's absolutely sensational. The party, the house, all of it.'

Olivia Avery was wearing a beautiful blue silk gown and a smile of genuine pleasure. Perhaps Olivia wasn't used to people complimenting her Holland Park bolthole. In which case, she was inviting the wrong people to her parties.

'I'm glad you like it,' she said modestly. 'I've spent six months organising the damn thing and it's not easy when you're dealing with such a limited space. Nicholas wanted to have the party at the Foxhills estate, but I managed to convince him there was no way we'd get this lot further than five miles from the Garrick Club.'

Not for the first time, he tried to suppress a smile. He had known Olivia Avery for years and she was everything you'd imagine the grande dame of a media dynasty to be. Her icy beauty could be intimidating, but if Olivia thought you might be useful or fun, she would draw you in with a joke or an indiscreet nugget of gossip. 'The rich are different from you and me,' that was what Scott Fitzgerald had once said to Hemingway, but on nights like this he knew it wasn't just the money. It was about confidence.

'Well it definitely makes it more special having the party here rather than at some hotel in London.'

'That's what Nicky thought, although we did have to put all the art work into storage.'

'We wouldn't want a hand going through that Bridget Riley in the kitchen.'

Olivia nodded in agreement, missing Alex's ironic tone.

'So where is the lovely Alicia?' asked Olivia.

Alex had arrived with his girlfriend a couple of hours earlier and he had barely seen her since. She had been thrilled to find herself surrounded with so many influential people and had immediately disappeared to take full advantage of it.

'She's almost certainly inside, talking to the Home Secretary, of course.'

Olivia raised a surprised eyebrow. 'Of course?'

'Alicia has an amazing ability to seek out the most important person in any room.'

'A valuable skill,' said Olivia, touching his arm meaningfully. 'You should hold onto that one.'

Hold onto her, don't let her go. That's what everyone had started saying lately, and of course it made sense. Alicia was sexy, elegant and ambitious, a political lobbyist going places, and with Alex well on his way to media glory, they'd make a fine power couple. Alex took a gulp of his wine; so what was stopping him? He wasn't sure that *power* was up there on his wish-list when it came to finding a soul-mate.

'Have you seen Lara?' he asked after a moment. 'Is she coming?'

Olivia gave him a sideways look.

'You never know with Lara. I called her this afternoon as she hadn't RSVP'd. Apparently she was in Paris.'

'Paris?'

Olivia's lips tightened.

'You've heard about Sandrine? I begged her to come and stay with us at Foxhills, but she wanted to help the parents by sorting out Sandrine's apartment. Such a tragedy. Sandrine was a very positive influence for Lara, the sister she never had. And now, I fear, she is going to feel so alone.'

'She's not alone. She has you, Olivia. She has me. And Lara's tough.'

'Not as tough as she'd like you to think,' said Olivia, fixing Alex with one of her searching looks.

'Is everything alright between you two?'

Alex frowned.

'Sure. Why shouldn't it be?'

'I just hear you two don't see each other as much these days.'

'She said that?'

'Not in so many words, she didn't have to darling. For so long you were as thick as thieves. It was Alex, this, Alex that. I have to admit, I was cynical. I've seen *When Harry Met Sally*. Can men and women ever be friends? But I thought you two were the real deal. Then again, I suppose it's difficult when someone else comes onto the scene. When you fall in love.' She said it with a mischievous smile. 'I'll leave you to it, hmm?'

She walked off towards the bar and Alex was still mulling over what she meant when he felt a slim arm snake around his waist.

'Alicia,' he said turning round.

'Who did you think it was? Darius?'

She laughed at her own joke as she snaked her arm through his.

'So what were you and Olivia talking about?'

'Nothing much. She likes you. I didn't know you'd met.'

Alicia couldn't hide her pleasure that the great, influential Olivia Avery had given her approval.

'You know me,' said Alicia, gesturing towards the house with her Champagne. 'I do like to mingle. And talking of which, how have you been getting on with Nicholas?'

'Fine. I told him my best knock-knock jokes.'

'Jesus, Alex,' she said, stepping away from him.

'I'm joking,' he smiled.

'You do know this isn't *just* a party, Alex,' she said, stroking a twist of honey-coloured hair over her shoulder.

'It's the ideal time to get closer to Nicholas, dazzle him with your brilliance now Darius…' she glanced around and lowered her voice. 'Well, now he's on the way out.'

Alicia was convinced that after the Tait disaster,

Darius's tenure as editor was coming to an end – very plausible, Alex had to concede – and was constantly urging him to 'make an impression' on Avery senior.

'You do realise I was part of the team that ran the Tait story?' said Alex. 'Darius didn't do it on his own.'

'Exactly why you need to distance yourself from that whole mess – and anything like it. You don't want to win a Pulitzer prize, Alex. You want the editor's job. It's not in your interests to champion contentious stories that no-one gives a shit about.'

Alex didn't respond, because Alicia was wrong. He *did* want to win a Pulitzer prize. He always had done, ever since he'd gone to see Bob Woodward give a lecture on Watergate. He smiled: he'd been with Lara and Sandrine that night and afterwards they gone to the American Bar at the Savoy and bet a round of whiskey sours that one day, one of them would win journalism's most prestigious award. His money had always been on Sandrine.

'Alex, you are the best person on that executive team by a mile,' said Alicia, running a hand down his arm. 'These are not easy times for the media. They need the very best people at the top, otherwise an entire industry is going to be destroyed. They need people like you.'

Alex had to admit that there was a lot of sense in what she was saying. The entire senior *Chronicle* team was staffed by old-school newspaper people who were great at what they did, but they were still playing catch up with social media, a race they would never win. Alex had tried to encourage Charlie and Darius to recruit more widely – from the tech giants and the music industry – but they hadn't listened to him, and as Deputy Editor, he only had a limited influence. Quietly, Alex had been educating himself, trying to stay ahead of the curve and his bedtime reading these days were Harvard Business School case studies, but did he have all the answers to revive the Chronicle's fortunes? He wasn't sure he did.

'Find Nicholas and charm him, okay?'

He gave a quiet laugh.

'You're very bossy, you know that?'

Alicia laughed.

'What do they say? A man with dreams needs a woman with vision.'

'Right now I need a woman with something to eat. Shall we head up to the buffet? Apparently Olivia's got her own pastry chef.'

Alicia pirouetted away from him. 'I'd love to stay and feed you macaroons, but I must go and speak to Penny Burling, she's just back from Koh Samui. I'll pump her for tips.'

Tips. Recently Alicia had been slipping exotic destinations into conversation, places Alex knew he was supposed to decode as fitting places for a romantic long-haul holiday – or even possible proposal spots. Perhaps she had a point. Alex worked hard, barely left the office, lived and breathed the news. If Nicholas Avery hadn't seen his 'brilliance' by now, then he was doomed anyway. Maybe stepping off the treadmill for a while would be a good idea.

Alex was just turning back towards the terrace

when he saw her. Lara always stood out in a crowd, but particularly tonight. In the sea of silk and crepe she was wearing jeans and a red t-shirt, her dark hair tied back in a simple ponytail. She looked fantastic, but Alex was even more impressed that Lara never felt the need to dress up. She walked over, smiling.

'You're looking good tonight, Mr. Ford,' said Lara, nodding towards his classic black suit. 'You look as if you're about to present an Oscar.'

'Not sure about that. Two people have already asked me where the cloakroom is.'

A moment's silence hung between them.

'I popped round to the boat last night,' he said. 'You weren't there.'

Lara shrugged.

'No, I wasn't.'

'Olivia said you were in Paris. Doing what?'

Lara rolled her eyes.

'Alex, you're sounding like a needy boyfriend.'

He held up his hands.

'I'm just asking. I'm your friend. When you don't reply to my calls, I get concerned.'

'Scared I might do something stupid too?'

Alex felt the challenge of her gaze and saw the pain behind it.

'I'm sorry,' she said quietly. 'Look. Maybe we can do something this weekend? Every day is a weekend for me now, so you say when.'

Alex pulled a face.

'I'm in Monaco this weekend.'

'Romantic mini-break?'

'Work: Grand Prix weekend. Buttering up the advertisers.'

'I thought that sort of thing was right up Alicia's street. Networking is her idea of fun, isn't it?'

Alex knew Lara was pushing his buttons, but there was something reassuring about the banter, the way they knew each other so well. Olivia had been right, there had been a time when they had been inseparable. So why was there so much silence between them?

'Apparently there's a Henry Moore sculpture around here somewhere.'

'It's over there,' said Lara pointing. 'Want to see?'

It was in a hidden pocket of the garden away from the house, the chatter and laughter from the party fading as they went to find it. The bronze was a fluid contortion vaguely in the shape of a reclining woman.

'That's how I feel most days,' said Lara.

There was a bench opposite the sculpture and they sat side-by-side.

'What were you really doing in Paris, Lar?' asked Alex, still looking at the sculpture.

'I went to Sandrine's flat.'

'What for?

'Just sorting stuff.'

Alex glanced sideways.

'*Just* sorting stuff?'

She didn't look at him. He knew her well enough to detect her tells.

'Do you remember Vinnie Hero?' asked Lara.

Alex nodded. It was a story they'd worked on just after he'd arrived at the *Chronicle*. Vinnie had been in a minor boy band in the noughties, who'd turned to selling tricks and blow when the spotlight waned. One dark weekend, Vinnie had been found with his wrists cut in a trashed hotel room. The world shrugged its shoulders: just another tragic case of the music biz eating its young. But by chance, Lara had met Vinnie a few weeks before his death, working in a motorcycle repair shop.

'It didn't add up with Vinnie, remember? He had a job, a flat, he'd been getting his life back together, he was settled.'

And it had turned out that Lara's hunch had been correct. Part of Vinnie's turnaround had been due to a new relationship with a married politician who, in a fit of drunken self-loathing, had killed Vinnie, then staged the suicide to cover up the crime. It was the story that had really made her reputation at the *Chronicle*.

'When I saw Sandrine on Friday night she told me she was working on a story,' Lara continued. 'A story about Jonathon Meyer and trafficking.'

Alex glanced at her, his curiosity piqued. They'd run a story on Meyer's death when it happened. At the time there had been plenty of speculation about his involvement with billionaire yacht parties and Russian mafia king-pins, but nothing had held up, so the story had fizzled out.

'What was her angle?'

'She didn't give me any details. Apparently she was going to unveil something this week at the Le Caché conference. She was excited about the story. Perhaps a little scared too.'

Lara turned and looked at him, her eyes shining in the low light.

'Someone has been into her apartment, Alex. Searched it, taken things from it. There were no notebooks, no computers, not a trace of anything to do with any of her work.'

'And who do you think searched the flat?'

'I don't know yet.'

'It sure wasn't Jonathon Meyer,' said Alex.

'No,' said Lara, looking back at him. 'Coincidence, though, isn't it? Another violent death.'

Alex knew what she was thinking. That there was some connection between Sandrine and Meyer. Alex had lost friends in the line of duty – a photojournalist who'd been shot in Homs, a Mexican writer named Alejandro who'd been killed by a drug cartel. He knew the dangers of their job, but still, he wasn't convinced.

'The number of journalists killed chasing a story is tiny, Lar.'

'Tiny isn't never. And we both know it happens.'

'In war zones, the third world, not Marylebone.'

'Sandrine didn't take her own life, Alex.'

He looked away, feeling conflicted. Lara was grieving and he knew she was looking for meaning in Sandrine's senseless death. On the other hand, Alex had always subscribed to the maxim of 'chase the hunch'. And now Lara had a hunch. He pulled out his phone and quickly tapped out a text. There was a pause, then Lara's phone chirped.

'What did you just send me?'

'Frank Benson's mobile, in case you don't have it.

I also sent him a text telling him you were going to be in touch.'

'Frank on the *Chronicle* news desk?'

Alex nodded. 'When the Meyer story blew up, I got Frank to speak to Jonathon's brother Simon. He's a lawyer, somewhere out in Surrey, I think. Frank will give you his contacts.'

Lara's face lit up. Alex knew that look – she had the scent.

'Don't get too excited, Sherlock,' he said with a laugh. 'Simon didn't have much to say, that's why we didn't run the interview.'

'But it's a start.'

Alex put his hand on hers.

'48 hours, Lar,' he said seriously. 'That's what I'd give you as an editor. Find the story or let it go.'

Lara turned and kissed him on the cheek.

'Thank you,' she said, then jumped up and strode off down the garden. Alex just sat there, watching her go, two fingers touching the place her lips had just been.

Chapter Ten

LARA ZOOMED DOWN the A3 out of London, the long undulating stretch of road disappearing underneath her front wheel. Lara enjoyed having such a powerful bike, but sometimes the Triumph seemed hellbent on killing her, especially on a day like today when the roads were slick with a summer shower, the sunshine making the tarmac shimmer like a jeweller's window. Still, it was good to get out into the light, especially after the morning's gloom. It hadn't been necessary for anyone to attend Sandrine's pre-inquest review, but when Jean and Marion had said they were going to go before their return to Corsica, Lara had felt duty-bound to join them. The hearing had been short and formal, the room claustrophobic and dry, but it had been worth going along to catch up on Marion's arrangements for the funeral, scheduled to take place in three weeks' time once Sandrine's body had been flown back to France. There was a family plot at the local church in their village and the wake was to be held at Sandrine's favourite restaurant, a place by the beach where a teenage Sandrine had waitressed barefoot in the summer. It seemed fitting; an untamed spirit being remembered and celebrated in the place she had felt most carefree.

Lara downshifted and eased off the throttle as she saw the sign announcing her arrival in Cobham, the well-heeled Surrey village just beyond the outer limits of London. To her left, willows dipped their long fingers into the river Mole, a scene straight from Constable's sketchbook, but on the right was a new-build gated estate and a car showroom specialising in high-sheen Range Rovers. Cobham was wealthy, but it wasn't Monte Carlo. Neither was Simon Meyer his brother.

Whilst Jonathon held parties on his giant yacht in the Med, Simon Meyer was a solicitor working from an office on Cobham's high street, doing the humdrum work of a local lawyer, writing wills and handling the conveyancing for house sales. According to Stella's research, his most racy client was a supplier of school uniforms. It was hard to imagine someone more distant from the life of Ferraris and penthouses of Jonathon Meyer, and Lara wondered how two boys with the same start in life could end up so far apart. For a moment she thought of her cousin Charlie. He was a year younger than her and they'd been brought up like siblings after she had been sent to live with Nicholas and Olivia after the death of her parents. Like the Meyer boys, you'd think they'd landed at different ends of the scale. Charlie worked in the Avery publishing business but had a reputation as a spoilt playboy living on the family dollar, while Lara was driven and committed to her work. The swot and the waster – it fit the cliché, but Lara knew Charlie's image was just that, an affectation. He wore flash suits and favoured fine wine, but it was a way to disarm and ingratiate himself with potential advertisers and brand partners. Charlie hid his light under a bushel. She wondered how different the Meyer brothers really were.

Lara pulled into a parking space next to the Cobham branch of Waitrose and headed towards the office of Meyer and Birch on the high street. She pushed through the glass door and was rewarded by the tinkling of a bell. The office had that air of dustiness and age that was both rare and reassuring. Lots of dark wood furniture, a worn green carpet, framed certificates on the walls: in an age when high street banks had been updated with cartoon characters and bright plastic mouldings, there was something solid and decent about Simon Meyer's workplace.

'Miss Stone?' said a tall man in a shirt and sober tie, walking out from a back office. Simon Meyer looked like a slightly faded actor playing the role rather than the real thing. Lara could see the resemblance to the pictures she had seen of Jonathon, but it was more his bearing that made him stand out. He looked as solid as the office.

'Thank you for seeing me,' said Lara, shaking his hand.

'You've saved me from filing some Land Registry charges,' he smiled as he led her back to his private office and closed the door. Simon was friendly and polite, chatting as he sat down behind his wooden desk. Lara felt herself being assessed, which was fine, she was used to it. Everyone was suspicious of journalists; it came with the territory.

'So you're from the *Chronicle*?'

'That's right.'

She didn't think it was the time or the place to describe her employment instability.

'I was surprised when Frank Benson called. I read the piece about Jonathon in the paper and saw my interview had been cut. I apologise if I wasn't particularly interesting. When someone calls the day you find out your brother has died, I'm sure you'd forgive me for not being articulate.'

'I'm sorry about your loss,' said Lara. She'd had so many people say those words to her over the past few days, it was almost a relief to say them to someone else. 'It must have been a shock.'

'I don't know about a shock,' said Simon.

He pushed his chair away from his desk and loosened his tie.

'Did I expect to get a call saying my brother had been killed in a violent mugging? No,' he said, shaking his head. 'But did I dread the day when I'd hear that something awful had happened to him? To that I'd have to say yes.'

He looked at her evenly. 'Why are you here, Miss Stone?' he asked.

'Because I lost someone too, last week. My best friend. The police think it was suicide. But I'm not so sure.'

She watched his face, trying to gauge Simon's mood. She saw sympathy, but no reaction. As a solicitor, Simon was presumably used to listening without judgement as people arranged a divorce or wrote loved ones out of their will.

'I think my brother's death was suspicious too,' said Simon simply. 'Jon died from hitting his head against the pavement. Pushed over in a violent mugging, they say. The police put out an appeal for witnesses, but nobody came forward. My suspicion is they never will.'

'Why do you say that?'

'I'm a high street lawyer, Lara. I deal with wills, probate and suburban house sales. I'm not a detective, but I'm old enough, experienced enough in the ways of the world, to know when something feels off.'

He pushed up his shirt sleeves and leaned forward. 'Jon's attack happened in a dark street in the City on a Sunday night and despite there being 600,000 CCTV cameras in London, Jonathon had the misfortune to be mugged in one of the blind spots. Perhaps he was unlucky. Or perhaps it's not a coincidence.'

Lara didn't comment. She knew that Alex would have some pithy aphorism for this: coincidence is not conspiracy, or something equally trite.

'What was your brother doing in the City?'

'Jon lived in Monaco most of the time, but he was often in London on business. He was staying at a hotel in Mayfair. He liked that part of town. He told me once that he never went to the City unless he could help it. So to answer your question, I've no idea what he was doing there, especially late at night on a Sunday.'

'Are you suggesting that it wasn't a random attack?'

Simon shook his head, his expression sad.

'I don't know what happened to Jon, but I know that he had a lot of friends – and a lot of enemies. And they were definitely the sort of people who had the connections and cash to get rid of him if they wanted to.'

Lara nodded. She'd researched the *Pandora's* yacht parties and Jonathon Meyer's fund, but she had hit a brick wall. The people with that level of wealth actually employed PRs and lawyers to keep them out of the public eye, but you could easily speculate that these investments involved huge profits – and huge losses.

'Was Jonathon a risk-taker?'

Simon Meyer smiled.

'Always. Jon lived on the edge. Bet big, win big,' he said with a nostalgic smile, as if he was repeating back something his brother had once said. 'Jon was younger than me by a year. Always getting into trouble, always trying to pull off some scam or other. I'd fight his corner, try to ensure he didn't bite off more than he could chew. But he always did.'

Simon shook his head. 'Jon was quite brilliant in lots of ways. He had a huge brain, but he was left-field, had a unique way of looking at things. He found the conventional tedious, school work was boring. People called Jonathon a financial genius but I'm convinced he was an *actual* genius. It's hard to contain people like that. It made him as rebellious as he was smart. You know he got into Cambridge to do maths, but left after a year? Too easy he said, but then he got a foothold in banking and that's when he really started to fly.'

Simon sighed. 'Possibly too high. He was Icarus. He flew too close to the Sun.'

'You mention enemies? Have you any idea who they might be?'

Now she looked more closely, Lara could see Simon looked tired; the lines on his face were deep.

'Jon never talked business with me. We had supper together a couple of days before he died. He came out to Cobham for the first time in years. He said he envied my life. First time he had ever said that. Maybe it was the first time he ever thought it.'

'Did he seem worried about anything?"

'Jon never showed weakness. I suppose it was why he was so successful. But looking back, he didn't seem as bullish about business as usual.'

Lara nodded, thinking about the Post-it note she'd found at Sandrine's flat.

'Does the name Helen Michael mean anything to you?'

Simon shook his head.

'Is she a friend of Jonathon's?'

'I don't know yet.'

He smiled.

'I don't think it will be long before you do.'

Lara was grateful for the confidence. For a moment, she felt as if she had someone on her side, even if it was a solicitor in leafy Surrey. As she rose to leave, Simon leaned forward and scribbled a number on a Post-it note.

'You might want to speak to Tom Ramsay,' he said, handing it over. 'Tom is the man who runs the *Pandora*.'

'Jonathon's yacht?' she said in surprise.

'You want to know about Jon's life and are wondering where to start? That's the place. Go and see the *Pandora*. Because everything starts with the yacht.'

Chapter Eleven

LARA SANK BACK into the seat as the taxi swung along the Nice-Monaco coast road, past the blue shimmer of the Baie de Laurent to their right and the elegant houses and palm trees of Saint Antoine on the left. The sun glinted off the passing traffic – high end lime-green street machines hub-to-hub with rust-patched Citroens – and the bougainvillea shone pink against the bleached stone walls: everything was lurid like neon, even in the middle of the day.

Lara had flown into Nice and grabbed the first cab she had seen outside the terminal. Arriving in town with nothing but an overnight bag, she felt a little of the old energy flowing back through her, even if this was an unofficial visit, given she no longer worked for the *Chronicle*. Maybe she should start calling herself a freelancer, she mused, as she looked out of the window. That sounded better than unemployed. Or 'private investigator' – even more glamorous. But she was back on the hunt and that was what Lara Stone was good at. Sandrine had been right: it was what made her feel alive, especially when she was in her favourite corner of France.

Lara remembered her first trip to the Côte d'Azur,

on a mini-break holiday with a long-gone boyfriend, Carl. All six-pack and no brains. How old had she been? Twenty-one? Twenty-two? Carl had moaned; he had wanted to go to Ibiza, but Lara had loved the sights and smells of the Riviera, swinging through Juan Les Pins, blagging their way onto the terrace at Belles Rives hotel, drinking a bank-breaking martini where Zelda and Scott Fitzgerald had sat, then back to some flea-bitten pension up near the train station. Carl hadn't seen the romance in it. In fact, he'd sulked so much, he had refused to go into the Picasso museum and when Lara had come out, she'd found Carl chatting up a couple of pretty Spanish tourists. She smiled to herself, shaking her head. Carl, Carl… he had been good-looking though.

'Madame? Nous sommes ici. Le port.'

Lara sat up as a tangle of masts appeared through the window. Yachts, crammed together in orderly lines, millions, possibly billions of Euros just bobbing gently side by side in the afternoon sun.

This was Cap d'Ail, the smaller, slightly less glamorous cousin to Monaco's Port Hercules, just around the headland, perhaps ten minutes by speed-boat, but it still glittered with summer magic.

She got out of the car and walked towards the port, along the boardwalk, passing the smaller sailing boats, sleek and wind-powered crafts that sacrificed living space for speed and sea-worthiness. Not cheap by any means, but they had an adventurous air about them that Lara loved; they reminded her of her father who had loved boats and the sea. Sailors with frayed shorts and bare feet moved across their narrow decks. They wore designer sunglasses, sure, but at least these guys knew a few knots.

But as she looked further on, out to where the big yachts were moored, it was a different world entirely. Exclusive in the purest sense: only open to the very select few and excluding everyone else. What was it John Cleese put in his advert for Fawlty Towers? 'No riff-raff'? That sign might well have been posted at the entrance to the marina.

A noise from inside her bag made her stop. She scrabbled her phone from her tote, the ringing sounding unnaturally loud out here on the wharf. Two or three faces on the boats had turned to look at her curiously.

'Stella,' said Lara, picking up the call.

'Boss, where are you?' asked her assistant.

'Cap d'Ail, the port. I think you'd appreciate the view,' she said, as one of the more handsome sailors smiled at her.

'I'm glad you're having a lovely time,' said Stella, her voice tinny down the line. 'I'm outside a greasy spoon talking to cabbies.'

Lara had asked Stella to stay in London and try to untangle the timeline of Sandrine's movements leading up to her death. They simply didn't know what Sandrine had been doing, where she had been, or crucially, who she had spoken to in the days before she had gone to The Engineer to meet Lara.

'I found the driver who took Sandrine home that night,' said Stella. 'He remembered her being… hang on.'

Lara pictured Stella flipping open her notebook. '…Like one of those Victoria's Secret models. All long hair and legs.'

Lara gave a soft snort. 'She'd have liked that.'

'More importantly, the driver said she was in good spirits, joking with him about the French football team. Apparently she said they're not as good-looking as they once were. She definitely didn't sound suicidal.'

'Good stuff. Any luck with the neighbours?'

'Not so much, no. I spoke to everyone in the building and an old girl across the road. The tenants in the basement flat found Sandrine's body when they were coming home from a night out. But other than that, no one saw or heard anything before the police showed up and no one had even noticed Sandrine beforehand either. No real surprise to be honest, it's an Airbnb rental with a separate entrance on a side street.'

Lara nodded to herself. She'd guessed as much. This was Central London. Not exactly an engaged community.

'I did manage to speak to the couple who owned Sandrine's flat,' Stella continued. 'Both lawyers, property bought as an investment. Sandrine booked it six weeks ago, but they had no dealings with her beyond a few emails. She arrived the day before she met you at The Engineer. She picked the key up from a lock-box.'

A dead end, in other words, thought Lara, mindful she couldn't sound too disappointed to Stella. 'This is good work,' she said. 'Keep on it.

Someone will know something. They always do.'

Lara wished she was as confident as she sounded. Right now, Lara felt as if she was flying blind. All she had was a name. Or rather two names: Jonathon Meyer and the *Pandora*.

She walked along the jetty, reading the names on the hulls. Jonathon's yacht was at the very end: of course, it was the biggest one in the harbour, a three-level vessel with twin jet-skis flanking the gang-plank, the millionaire equivalent of strapping a mountain bike to your estate car, she supposed.

'Hello?' she called, taking a tentative step onto the gently swaying walkway. 'Anyone at home?'

'I think you mean "ahoy there".' A tall man in his early thirties stepped out from the dark interior, smiling.

'Lara?' he asked, offering her a hand as she tottered across onto the boat. 'I'm Tom. Tom Ramsay. When Simon said you were going to drop in, I didn't realise he meant so soon.'

Tom was deeply bronzed and gym-toned, emphasised by his uniform of tight white shorts and matching polo shirt with a Pandora logo on the breast: a woman with flowing hair looking down into a glowing box.

'Shoes off,' he said cheerfully. 'Don't want any slips while I'm giving you the tour.'

Tom led her inside the boat, through a comfortable lounge and down some tightly-furled stairs, towards the living quarters and galley, telling her his own story as they went: Tom was a Dorset boy who had grown up watching the boats in Poole Harbour, starting to work on yachts straight out of school as a steward, working his way up to first officer, clocking up sea miles, gaining qualifications along the way. He was looking for a captain's position next, once *Pandora* had been sold or put up for charter.

'I live on a houseboat back in London and it's nothing like this,' smiled Lara as they passed the 'cocktail area' on the middle deck, complete with white leather seating and a full wet bar overlooking the compact pool.

'No doubt your boat is an actual home,' said Tom kindly. 'These places are all about entertaining: *Pandora* can accommodate 100 people for stationery parties at the harbour and Jonathon's special guests got to travel: three, four day trips to Ibiza, St Tropez or Porto Cervo.

He gestured towards the modernist art on the walls.

'This is how serious money impresses serious money.'

Lara could see the logic. You could step into an office building in London or New York and barely notice your surroundings, but here? You couldn't help being bowled over by the sheer wealth being dangled before your eyes.

'Of course the *Pandora* is on the subtle side of things. Our neighbours in Port Hercules were much more flamboyant, shall we say?'

Lara laughed.

'So it used to be moored in Monte Carlo?'

'Until last week.'

'Why did you move?'

'Executor's orders,' said Tom, with a shrug that told Lara he wasn't happy with the relocation.

'Simon is looking after Jonathon's estate. He thought it was a waste using the berths in Port Hercules especially during Grand Prix week when the rental price goes through the roof. So we've sub-let our spot and moved here. At least the beer is cheaper,' he grinned, nodding towards a harbourside bar.

'So Jonathon did his entertaining on the yacht?' she asked.

'Yes, Jonathon had an apartment in Fontvieille, but he practically lived on the *Pandora*. He used the top stateroom as his office and when he wasn't working, there was a rolling guest list that came for lunch, cocktails, dinner.'

'Can I see?' Lara said it casually, but it was the one part of the yacht she most wanted to look at. Where Meyer actually lived, his inner sanctum.

'Sure,' said Tom, but Lara saw his smile dim slightly.

The master cabin occupied the entire top deck, beginning with another open-air lounge area. The sky above was an intense blue and Lara felt the sun beating down on her shoulders. She tried to imagine Jonathon Meyer up here, hands on hips, head-to-toe in designer clothes, Swiss watch on his wrist, watching as his superyacht slid into yet another exclusive port.

The bi-fold doors leading to the suite itself were slightly ajar and Lara craned her neck to peer inside. A huge desk was by the window and the biggest bed she had ever seen was at the far end of the room: a place for work and play. Lara felt a prickle of excitement, a feeling that answers were finally drifting within reach, until Tom walked over and gently closed the doors, moving in front of her to block her view.

'Why are you here, Lara?' he said.

'I've come because Simon Meyer asked me to come.'

It wasn't strictly true, but Tom didn't need to know that.

'Are you police?'

'No. I'm a journalist.'

He gestured towards the stairs.

'I think it's time for you to leave.'

Lara stood her ground.

'Simon wanted me to come because he thinks Jonathon might have been murdered.'

That got his attention.

'Murdered?' Despite the tan, Tom had visibly paled.

'Please Tom, just let me into his office. Answer a few questions.'

Tom gave a firm shake of the head.

'I was recruited through a company that has a reputation for absolute discretion and loyalty. Just because Jonathon's dead doesn't mean I can betray that confidence.'

She knew he was thinking about his own position. His next first officer's job or captaincy. She didn't blame him but she knew she had to push back. There was more at stake here than Tom's career.

'Are you saying there are things that happened on

Pandora that would require you to be discreet and loyal?'

'I'm saying that rich, powerful people pay a premium for their privacy. I'm their employee. I have to honour that.'

'What happens on the yacht, stays on the yacht, right? Even if it's illegal?'

He flashed a look of anger.

'Illegal? No. These were networking parties. Rich men drinking champagne and doing deals. That's all.'

Lara hadn't expected Tom to give her chapter and verse – he had far too much to lose and very little to gain – but she still needed to find a way through his armour.

'But if these yacht parties were just like a golf club social, why were they so popular?'

'They were the best,' said Tom matter-of-factly. 'That's why people came. There are bigger yachts in this part of the world, but the *Pandora* had the best of everything. The best wine, the best food, he'd get DJs in from Ibiza and girls from central casting. Jonathon knew what made people tick – put a smile on their faces and then they'd do the deal. Which is what this is all about in the end.'

'What about drugs?'

Sandrine had connected Meyer with trafficking. Her friend hadn't been specific about what sort of trafficking but Lara knew what went on in this part of the world. How boats took illegal cargo from the North African and Turkish coastline – drugs that had travelled through the Asian and African trafficking routes to Mediterranean ports for onwards smuggling into Europe. Meyer's parties must have cost him a fortune; perhaps he had worked out a way to pay for them.

'Drugs?' Tom shook his head with irritation. 'I never saw them and I had no part in providing them, if that's what you're suggesting.'

'You didn't see anything?' She wasn't convinced.

He snorted, his face stony.

'I'm paid to not see things.'

Lara could see that Tom wasn't going to give her anything else. She had let Sandrine down.

'I'm sorry I can't be more help,' said Tom in a gentler tone. 'But you must understand my position. I said the same thing to the other woman.'

'Which other woman?'

'French. Dark hair. Attractive.'

Lara grabbed her phone and scrolled to a selfie that she and Sandrine had taken of themselves at The Engineer.

'She came here? Before Jonathon died?'

'Yes. When we were still moored in Port Hercules. I refused to let her on the boat, but she accosted Mr Meyer on his way out.'

'What did they talk about?'

'Perhaps you should ask her.'

'She's dead,' said Lara quietly.

'Oh,' said Tom, looking shocked. 'I'm sorry.'

Lara held up the photo again.

'Tom, this was my best friend Sandrine. Her death was as strange and random as Jonathon's. If you know anything, please tell me.'

Tom looked out to sea where the sun shone in platinum ribbons on the water.

'Look, maybe you should speak to Melissa Gelman. She arranged Mr Meyer's party guests: the girls anyway. She might have seen something, heard something. Melissa always has her ear to the ground. It's Grand Prix weekend so she'll be busy, but you can try her.'

He took a pen out of his pocket and wrote her number on the back of his business card.

'Thank you, Tom,' she said, stepping forward and kissing him on the cheek.

'I hope you find what you're looking for,' he said.

'Me too,' she said. 'I really do.'

Chapter Twelve

SCHMOOZING THE ADVERTISERS, that's what he was supposed to be doing. Alex looked around the Fairmont Hotel's rooftop pool, packed with people in designer sunglasses and unbuttoned Armani shirts, lanyards and laminates catching the afternoon sun, over-loud music clanging like a fire drill. How anyone was supposed to sweet-talk anyone out here, Alex couldn't imagine. It was hard enough to get the bar-staff to hear your order. Still, a free weekend at the Monaco Grand Prix was a free weekend. The sun was out and, for a while at least, Alex didn't have to worry about tomorrow's front page.

He watched Charlie Avery weave his way through the crowd, somehow looking fresh and tanned. Charlie found this stuff effortless; something to do with being the boss's son, perhaps. Charlie was born to do it. But then so was I, thought Alex with an ironic smile. Alex's father had been a newsagent and Alex had learned about the news sitting on the bales in the back room, reading headlines about a 'Missile Crisis' or a 'Stripping Vicar', his eyes wide.

'Alex, come and meet Anton Cuovo,' said Charlie, gripping him on the shoulder and steering him towards a roped-off seating area.

'Anton's the VP for Volcan rum. We could do with getting them onboard, so be nice.'

'Aren't I always?' said Alex, taking a glass of champagne.

As Deputy Editor, it wasn't usually his job to come to corporate events like this. It was Darius who was parachuted in to drink the free cocktails, press the flesh and build relationships with advertisers. But today the editor had been called to Chequers to interview the PM, a last-minute date-shuffle, meaning Alex had to do his bidding in Monaco instead.

Anton was wearing a bright red Ferrari cap and was leaning over the balcony when Charlie introduced them.

'So this is where the race takes place on Sunday?' shouted Anton, above the music.

'All through these streets,' said Charlie, waving a vague hand around the principality. 'We're going to be right on top of the action!'

The Fairmont wasn't the most beautiful hotel in Monaco – a modernist structure that reminded Alex of an airport terminal – but it was one of the in-demand places to stay during the Grand Prix for the simple reason that it had the best view, right on a hairpin bend. It was costing the *Chronicle* a fortune but Charlie had insisted it was money well spent.

'What celebrities are going to be here this weekend,' said Anton, still shouting, as two screaming models jumped into the pool behind them.

'Loads of them,' said Alex, forcing a smile as he

felt spray all down the back of his chinos. His phone was vibrating in his pocket. He pulled a regretful face at the rum VP. 'Sorry, got to take this,' he shouted. 'News never sleeps.'

Anton looked at him. 'Has something happened? Is it big?'

'Yeah, could be very big.' He glanced around, then leaned close to Anton. 'Beyoncé,' he said. 'I'll come and find you later, tell you all about it.' Anton gave him a big thumbs-up and Alex knew right then that Volcan rum would be committing to a hefty ad spend.

He pressed the phone hard against his ear. Alex immediately recognised Lara's voice.

'Hey. How are you?' He moved to a quieter corner of the pool.

'Bloody hell. Where are you? I thought there were no races on today?' she shouted.

'Pool party, which means I still need ear-plugs. Do you want me to call you later?'

'I can go one better than that. How about we meet?' He could hear the smile in her voice. 'I'm in Monaco.'

'You're in Monaco?'

'Couldn't bear to be away from you,' said Lara, deadpan.

Of course he was pleased she was in town. He'd much rather be sitting with a drink in Casino Square, people-watching with his old friend, but it only took him a split second to realise what she was doing here. Jonathon Meyer had a yacht in Monte Carlo. It was surely no coincidence.

'There's some big advertiser party tonight I have to show my face at, but how about you come along? Charlie will be there but we can lose him and escape to the casino.'

There was a hesitation, then: 'Sure, why not?'

'Don't get too excited,' laughed Alex, although he'd expected some resistance. 'It's only the hottest party of Grand Prix weekend and therefore the entire year.'

'No, I'll come. It will be fun.'

Alex found himself smiling down at his phone.

'Alex Ford, you dark horse. What are you looking so pleased with yourself for?'

He turned and saw his old friend Dominic Parker. Dom was an old colleague from his early days at the *Chronicle*. Short and stocky, he was wearing a dark pinstripe suit with a purple tie so loud it hurt the eyes: Dom was an ad man through and through.

'Just glad to see you,' said Alex, embracing him. 'Apart from the tie, obviously. What are you doing here?'

'Same as you, I imagine. Advertiser love-bomb. Half of media and finance London is in a one-mile radius of this spot.'

Dom had started at the *Chronicle* on the same day as Alex and the pair of them had hit it off on their induction course. They'd lived a mile apart in Finsbury Park, and played five-a side soccer together on Sunday mornings. Their friendship had been short-lived when Alex was posted overseas within twelve months, but they'd stayed in touch, even though Dom hadn't stayed long at the *Chronicle*, bouncing from job to job at an ad agency, a music publisher, a TV station, then back to an ad agency, each time climbing several rungs of the ladder, each time gaining more experience in different areas of the media. Dom was self-interested and ambitious, but he was sharp and wasn't frightened about trying new things. Alex thought that Dom was exactly the sort of MD they needed at the *Chronicle*.

'So how's things in the cul-de-sac of print media?' he asked.

'Pretty good. I'm Deputy Editor, now.'

'I heard – I rang you to congratulate you,' he frowned. 'Or didn't I?'

'Maybe,' grinned Alex. 'Possibly got lost in the haze of flowers and whisky.'

They spent a few minutes catching up on their news. It was good to speak to someone in the business without worrying about the politics. Back when Alex worked on the news desk, he would sometimes take Dominic along to parties and junkets. Dom's smooth patter in the hotel bar was always an icebreaker with sources, attachés or celebrities. Dom could get anyone to tell them their story; he'd have made a fine reporter.

'So what are you up to Dom? I heard you've left the agency.'

'The rumours are true. I've got a start-up.'

It was something Alex heard a lot these days. His profession seemed to split into two camps. Those who were just clinging on, hoping to make it to retirement, or those taking leaps: over the past year he'd heard of dozens of journalists and executives retraining as life coaches, landscape gardeners and teachers. It was no big surprise that Dom was joining the exodus.

'So what's the big idea?'

Dom shrugged, as if it was obvious. 'Smart news. It's an "on your phone" news portal called *The Filter*. Podcasts, digital, TV, non-fiction books. Think of us as a club, not a newspaper. All tailored to your tastes, interests and beliefs. There's a studio arm too, gathering stories from around the world and packaging them up as IP to the streamers.'

Alex nodded, impressed. The bespoke aspect seemed smart and he knew that the demand for intellectual property – ideas for film, TV and games – was voracious.

'Sounds good. Have you got backing?'

'There's some seed funding in place, but I need to recruit someone to run the editorial side before we go out for further investment.'

'Well, there's plenty of good people looking for work at the moment. The *Herald* just laid off twenty members of the senior team.'

Dom clapped him on the shoulder. 'Why would I want them when I have the world's greatest newsman right here?'

'Me?'

'Al, you're the best.'

'I'm flattered Dom, but…'

Dominic gave an impatient shake of the head.

'Does print news still excite you?' he asked bluntly.

Alex still loved his job, but he had to admit that

newspapers were falling behind. At the last two elections, the *Chronicle's* headline the next morning had read 'Polls Too Close To Call', when everyone in the country already knew the result. It looked unprofessional, sure, but it also looked out of touch, which was unforgivable for a news source.

'Traditional media still has power, Dom,' he said, feeling the need to defend his position.

'But aren't you sick of working for someone else? With this, you'd own the company. In at the ground floor, full equity partner. You'd be calling the shots – but you'd get to live a life too.'

Alex knew Dom had a point, but it had always been his dream to be the editor of a national newspaper. It all went back to his local paper growing up: *The Cumbrian*. When Alex had been 14, a child had gone missing in the hills and Doug Bannen, editor of *The Cumbrian*, had gone into crusading overdrive. Usually a weekly paper, *The Cumbrian* had pumped out a mini-edition every day, lambasting the police, praising the mountain rescue, mobilising the community to 'search every hedge and hayloft'. Given he lived above the newsagents, Alex had felt right at the heart of it; he had seen the excitement in the punters' faces as they queued to buy the new issue. Six days in, the girl was discovered on the Isle of Man, having been snatched by her estranged father – and *The Cumbrian* had gone back to being a sleepy rag discussing council plans for a new bus stop. But what a week it had been. It had taught Alex that the news had power to excite, to enthral and to motivate – he couldn't turn his back on it now. Not when he still hadn't realised his dream of being an editor.

'How long have you been with the *Chronicle*?' asked Dominic. 'Fifteen years, is it? You know yourself you're not going to be the sexy appointment for the editor's job when it comes up. But stepping away for a couple of years might be a smart play.'

That was the trouble with old friends. They seemed to know what you were thinking. Alex's climb up the *Chronicle's* editorial ladder had been slow and steady. And Dominic was right, when they were looking for a new face to head up their flagship, the Avery execs were going to be looking for someone who could bring a new energy or experience to the paper. They weren't going to be excited by someone they passed every day in the corridor.

Across the pool, Alex could see Charlie waving at him.

'You go,' said Dom squeezing his friend's arm. 'Go and drink some free cocktails and think about it. The offer's there, but it won't be forever.'

Chapter Thirteen

LARA HAD NEVER been to Monte Carlo before, but it looked exactly as she had imagined. As a teenager, she spent most summers in Scotland at the Averys' Highlands estate, but one glorious week in the Easter holidays she had been to Epcot in Disneyland, which had miniature versions of world destinations: Paris, Kyoto, Marrakesh– or at least fantasy versions of them.

Monte Carlo was like that, a billionaire's version of the Belle Époque Riviera, the Casino and the Hotel de Paris facing a formal square designed for Victorian promenading, now used as a mini racetrack for expensive performance cars driving at five miles an hour: being seen was much more important than getting there.

Lara had grown up around wealthy people, she had been to a boarding school boasting one princess and two countesses, but this world, the world of the billionaire party-goer, was on a whole different scale. The Averys' wealth was old and quiet, this was flashy and loud, like a performance engine revving in the street with the sole purpose of drawing admiring looks.

There were designer boutiques and jewellers everywhere too, but Lara was looking at the real spectacle: the couples. Barrel-chested Eastern Europeans in open-necked shirts and dinner-plate watches that cost more than a house. The women were leggy and groomed, wearing anything floaty and short, strappy high shoes, perhaps an ostrich Birkin.

Lara paused for a moment, idly looking for a dress for that night's party. No Monaco designer store would stoop to putting the prices in the displays, but Lara had to assume they would all be ruinously expensive. Anyway it was the company she was looking forward to. Hopefully tonight Alex could get that corporate stick out of his backside and go back to being the unpredictable fun-loving goof she used to know. Hope springs eternal, thought Lara as she walked back up towards the Hôtel Hermitage with its elegant balconies and queue of expensive vehicles parked outside. Lara saw a Porsche and a Bentley and a shiny 4x4 all queued up behind a Fiat van with rakes and brushes poking out the back – the driver leaning out of the window, smoking a Gauloise. The one drawback to being a billionaire, thought Lara. Even supercars get stuck in traffic.

Lara strode into the Hermitage, smiling at the doormen. Lara turned at the stairs past potted palms and went out to the terrace restaurant at the side of the hotel with a sweeping view of the principality. Lara didn't usually go to fancy places, she preferred dive bars with loud music, but the setting here was stunning. Sometimes it *was* worth the money.

Lara spotted Melissa before she stood. Unlike

many of the other tourists, she had curves, with a natural beauty that made her stand out.

'Melissa? I am Lara.'

'I'm very pleased to meet you, Lara.'

Another surprise: a cut-glass English accent. Lara immediately imagined Melissa wafting around Pony Clubs before sidling off to the hayloft with an Argentinian polo player: or perhaps she had read too many Jilly Cooper novels as a teenager.

'I ordered tea and cake, I hope that's alright?' said Melissa as she poured Darjeeling from a bone china pot.

'You're a friend of Tom's, I understand?' she asked, passing Lara a cup and saucer. Lara nodded, hoping not to give too much away.

'Tom's fabulous,' said Lara smoothly.

Melissa would not be a pushover, not in her business. Even if Tom hadn't filled her in, Lara knew that the woman would have already Googled 'Lara Stone' and would know she was a journalist. And yet she had still agreed to meet. That told her something – that Melissa had something she wanted to say.

'Did Tom mention why I wanted to talk to you?' asked Lara.

The other woman shook her head. 'Something about the *Pandora*?'

'Yes. Sex trafficking,' said Lara.

There were many tools in a journalist's tool-box. Sometimes you had to chip away with a source for weeks, months, sometimes years, persuading them to talk. Other times you just had to go for the throat in the hope of catching them off-guard. She watched Melissa's face. She had expected outrage and denial, but the woman simply threw her head back and laughed. Full and fruity, a laugh of genuine pleasure.

'Well, I appreciate you getting straight to the point,' she smiled. 'I spend far too much time being achingly polite, so it's refreshing to meet someone who cuts the crap.'

Even the word 'crap' sounded pretty coming from Melissa's lips. She was a class act.

'So I'll return the favour and do my best to speed things up,' said Melissa. 'The answer is no.'

'No?'

'No sex trafficking. Not on the *Pandora* or any other yacht in Monte Carlo that I am aware of.'

Lara frowned. She hadn't expected a tearful confession of orgies with women groomed for the ordeal, but she had anticipated evasion. This flat denial was a surprise. Melissa looked at Lara over the rim of her cup.

'You think I'm a madam, don't you?'

Lara shook her head.

'I don't want to make assumptions.'

'You shouldn't.' For the first time Lara saw the steel under Melissa's polish. Just a flash, then it was gone.

'Let me make some important distinctions,' said Melissa, her perfectly buffed nails toying with a silver fork. 'A madam provides sex workers. I do not. I run a companion service, an escort agency if you prefer. They are not prostitutes, they are more like extras in a movie. They are paid to fill out party scenes, chat to the party goers, laugh at their jokes.' She spread her hands. 'That's it.'

'No sex at all?' Lara could hear the disbelief in her own voice but Melissa was polite enough to ignore it.

'If there is sex, the girls do it on their own time. It's not part of the job.'

'But why did Jonathon want to pay for female company? Why did he have to? Surely they'd jump at the chance to meet rich men.'

'Because the last thing a rich man at a party wants is someone looking to be his wife.'

She sipped her tea and put it back on the table.

'These are bold claims, Lara. Why are you making them?'

'A friend told me that Jonathon was involved in trafficking.'

'A friend? Well, Jonathon was my friend, so forgive me if I find your accusations hurtful and offensive.'

In that moment, Lara could see how fond Melissa was of Jonathon.

'I'm sorry Melissa, but I have to ask. I'm sure you know I'm a journalist.'

'Indeed,' she said crisply.

'I'm looking into the trafficking claims, but also the theory that Jonathon was murdered.'

'Murdered?' said Melissa. Her expression was sceptical.

'I think Jonathon might have been deliberately targeted. Can you think of anyone who wanted to harm him?'

Melissa shook her head slowly. 'The high-finance world is tough, ruthless even. But they're not murderers.'

'His brother Simon thought he might be worried about his business.'

It was a slight exaggeration, but Lara was convinced that Melissa knew something.

'I have no knowledge of his business affairs, although there was one thing…'

'Go on,' pressed Lara.

Melissa hesitated before she spoke again.

'I've worked with Jonathon for nearly ten years and he always paid promptly, but his last two invoices are still outstanding.'

'Jonathon didn't pay you?'

She waved it away.

'Look, financiers have cashflow problems like anyone. Besides, I owed him. Jon helped me out over the years, so I was prepared to cut him some slack.'

'How much did he owe you?'

Melissa told her a six-figure sum. Not for the first time, Lara wondered if she was in the wrong business.

'That's a lot of money.'

'He was a good friend.'

Lara looked at her directly.

'If you did care for him, help me out here, Melissa.'

'Help you fuel a wild conspiracy?' she said, shaking her head.

She put her hand on the table, her dark red polished

nails like spots of blood on the starched white linens.

'Lara, rich men die every day. They may have more money in the bank than you or I, but they bleed the same blood, succumb to the same illnesses. I'm not sure theories involving murders and trafficking are helpful.'

Lara knew Melissa was talking about Jonathon, but she had unwittingly touched a nerve. Lara had been young when her parents had died, but she wasn't too small to hear the whispers – from adults and the bullies at boarding school.

'Have you seen something, Melissa? Heard something?'

'There is someone who might help you,' she said finally. 'A guest.'

She lowered her voice. 'Jago Bain, he's some sort of PR guy, lobbyist. There was a party on *Pandora* a few weeks ago for Jon's inner circle.'

'His inner circle?'

'A select group of close friends. Jon's A-list of finance and business people, the really big hitters. Anyway, he took them on a jaunt to St Tropez. Jago was invited but he got into some sort of argument with Jonathon and was asked to leave.'

'Were you there?

Melissa shook her head.

'I wasn't, but my friend Willem, one of the stewards, had to escort him off the boat by tender and get him to shore.'

'What was the argument about?'

'I don't know. But apparently Bain didn't go quietly. It was a big loss of face for him. You know that phrase "if looks could kill?" Willem said that was how Jago Bain was looking at Jon as the security guys led him away.'

She paused. 'And that's all I can tell you.'

She shrugged as if it was nothing, but Lara had a feeling that it was important. Very important indeed.

Chapter Fourteen

'WHAT THE HELL is Lara doing in Monaco anyway?' said Charlie irritably. He had a cigarette clamped between his teeth as he used both hands to adjust his tie. Hermes, thought Alex. And a Tom Ford suit – that was definite, as Charlie had repeatedly mentioned that the designer had 'insisted' on sending it over during London Fashion Week.

'I know she's got that wretched bike, but I didn't think the Grand Prix would be her thing.'

They were standing on the promenade between the road and the Port Hercules marina, a discreet distance from the yacht *Goliath*, venue for the most prestigious party of the weekend in honour of designer Christian LeFey. Charlie was keen to get onboard and 'get stuck into the fizz' and was annoyed that Lara was keeping them waiting.

'My guess is that she needed to get out of London,' said Alex, not wanting to mention Lara's investigation into Sandrine's death. 'Do you blame her after the week she's had?'

Charlie shrugged, clearly unmoved. 'I suppose. But I hope she realises there's a dress code. Did you see how she turned up at the party last week? Mother was not pleased.'

Alex tried to bite his tongue. For all his posh-boy posturing, most of the time Charlie was fun company, but occasionally he was just a prat.

Alex looked down as his phone beeped.

Running late. Go in. I'll busk it. Lx

'You're in luck,' said Alex. 'Lara says she'll see us in there.'

Charlie rolled his eyes, 'Wonderful, she's given us permission,' he said, flicking his cigarette into the water and heading for the yacht.

As they walked up the gangway, it was obvious that the *Goliath* lived up to its name.

'It's bloody huge,' muttered Charlie admiringly. The superyacht was also surprisingly chic,. with smooth art deco lines in cream, walnut and gold. The floors looked like real marble: they probably were. The wealth in Monaco was staggering – and it was supposed to be. These yachts were shining castles on mountain tops, blaring declarations of power and imperviousness, a carving over the gate that read 'only the truly privileged may enter here'. The 10,000 euro-a-day moorings functioned as an exclusive club and a shop window that implied further riches for those who could get onboard.

Alex could see why Christian LeFey, the Parisian priest of high fashion, had chosen the *Goliath* as the venue for his show-stopper party. In a marina packed with gigantic yachts, the *Goliath* was the biggest, and in Monaco, where restraint was seen as weakness, that made Christian's party the most important. Fashion was a conjuring trick and this party was the equivalent of a Las Vegas magician firing rockets into the sky.

'Is that thingy, the actress?' whispered Alex, as they walked up a softly lit staircase onto the main deck, which seemed to have been designed as a high-class recreation of the Cotton Club, all crisp white tablecloths and over-sized Lalique sculptures.

'Yes, it's Julianne George. Calm down, it's like you've never seen a celebrity before.'

They both took a glass of champagne, fittingly served in vintage amber-coloured coupes. Alex had been to a lot of parties since he'd risen to the executive team, but this was on another level. Yes, Charlie was connected, but it was still testament to his world-class hustling skills that he had secured invitations to this most glittering bash.

'This suits you,' said Charlie, lifting his glass to Alex in salute.

'Between you and me, it's a blessing in disguise that Darius had to go to brown-nose the PM. Although one shivers to think of what Darius is saying to the poor man. Hopefully none of that stuff he was spouting about the Gulf War at the anniversary party.'

Alex glanced at Charlie.

'What do you think about that by the way?

He hadn't really had chance to discuss it with him.

'About the trial?' sniffed Charlie. 'It was a cluster-fuck.'

'No, I mean the way it all played out. I was there from the start. We had photos and documents, sworn statements, expert witnesses. And it all fell apart.'

Charlie shrugged. 'Tait's a bastard, no question, but he's smart. And you have to say his barrister was good.'

'I think we should appeal.' Alex knew Charlie would be against it, but he had to try.

'Pointless,' said Charlie, draining his glass and accepting a refill from a waiter. 'We went through this with the Jimmy Redfern case, remember? You need to present additional evidence or arguments to trigger an appeal.' He looked at Alex meaningfully. 'And I imagine if we'd had those, we'd have used them at the time.'

Alex bristled. He knew there was an implied criticism there, but he needed to keep Charlie onside.

'I'll find it. More evidence, better arguments.'

What Alex had hated about the trial was how everyone had known what Felix Tait was up to, yet seemed happy to let him off on the basis of a blatant lie. But more than that, Alex had hated to see what the trial had done to Lara. She had put a brave face on it, but he could see, day by day, how it had rattled her, frustrated her and, in the end, undermined her faith in not just the law, but in the importance of journalism too. Perhaps an appeal might restore some of that faith; because if Lara Stone couldn't believe in the righteousness of the press, there was no hope for any of them.

'Listen Alex, sit tight,' said Charlie distractedly. 'Don't go poking the hornet's nest.'

'What hornet's nest?'

'Don't be naïve. The Avery Media Group owns the *Chronicle*, but the Group is publicly owned. My father might be the controlling shareholder, but there are other investors, big City investors, who don't want any drama. So smile, nod your head. Wait and see.'

'Wait and see? What does that mean?'

Charlie turned to face him. 'Look, if it was up to me you would already be in that editor's chair. You're good at all this.' He waved his glass to indicate the yacht.

'But?'

Charlie opened his hands and made a hopeless gesture.

'Pops was best pals with Dickie Allen at school.'

Alex swallowed, a growing feeling of dread in his stomach.

'Who's Dickie Allen?'

'Darius's father. You didn't know?'

Alex was plugged into the media grapevine, but was hopeless when it came to the who's who of society. Alicia was always berating him for it.

'I suppose they keep it quiet,' said Charlie. 'It's bad enough Lara was a department head, family connections and all that. They don't want to hear the editor is a family friend as well.'

'So you're saying Nicholas will never fire Darius?'

'The time will come. One day. In the meantime, why rock the boat?'

Charlie disappeared to talk to Christian LeFey, a big bear of a man in a white suit. Alex stayed where he was. He felt as though he'd been hit by a falling rock.

He'd been working his backside off, every hour, never taking a holiday – and there had never been a chance of promotion. Never. Alex drew in a ragged breath, trying to slow his pounding heart.

He wasn't even angry at Nicholas; he was angry at himself for not seeing it. And to think, he'd felt guilty talking to Dominic about the possibility of joining his start-up.

Alex looked for a quiet spot on the aft, his eyes scanning the crowds for Lara.

'Looking for me?'

Alex turned; Lara was standing there in a drop-dead gorgeous off-the-shoulder emerald coloured dress. Her dark hair was piled up on her head, and there was a diamond-drop pendant around her neck. His career was forgotten for a moment; he was just glad to see her.

'What?' she said defensively.

'You scrub up well.'

She hit him on the arm.

'Okay, ouch. You look fantastic. Like a glamorous mermaid.'

It was true; he could barely remember seeing Lara in anything but jeans. He was shocked and a little unsettled.

'Comes at a price. I could tell you, but it'd be too upsetting. Monte Carlo isn't big on affordable evening wear.'

'Whatever it costs, it's worth it.'

Lara rewarded him with a smile and joined Alex at the rail. She clicked her glass against his and they stood in silence watching the rich and influential moving below them. He wanted to tell Lara about Charlie's revelation that his career had stalled and about Dominic's offer too. He certainly wanted to hear her take on it all, he trusted her opinion more than anyone else's. But Lara had enough of her own work problems to worry about without adding Alex's precarious career situation to. Keep it light, he thought.

'I spy with my little eye, something beginning with C.'

'Conspicuous consumption,' she said, giving him a sideways smile. Alex shook his head.

'That's two 'C's.'

'Okay… Cartier?'

'One point to Mademoiselle Stone. I would have also accepted Chihuahua or crocodile Birkin.'

They both laughed, her tanned, bare arm bumping again the sleeve of his jacket. It was fun sharing all this with someone on his wavelength, someone who could appreciate the absurdity. Unlike Alicia, who Alex knew would be enjoying the party for entirely different reasons. In fact, she would probably already have cornered the president of Bolivia by now.

'So let me play another guessing game,' said Alex. 'Why has Lara Stone come to Monte Carlo?'

'Do you want to guess or do you want me to lie?'

'Or you could just tell me.'

Lara blew her cheeks out.

'I've been on Jonathon Meyer's yacht,' she said.

'It's here? In the harbour?' said Alex, looking out into the darkness.

'In Cap d'Ail down the coast. I spoke to the first officer.'

Alex was already getting a bad feeling about this.

'And what did he tell you?'

'Not much, but he put me in touch with a woman called Melissa who supplied girls to Meyer's parties.'

'Girls? Like prostitutes?'

'She says not. Seems like a grey area. But she did say there's a guy named Jago Bain who was thrown off Meyer's yacht and might have an axe to grind. I called Eduardo from Le Caché earlier and it turns out he knows him. He's going to set up a meeting.'

There was another long pause.

'What?' said Lara, her eyes challenging.

'Look, I'm not judging, but it doesn't sound like you know much more than when I spoke to you at Nicholas's party.'

Alex saw her face darken. He had been trying to help, trying to gently point out that Lara was chasing a ghost. He'd seen it happen to friends on the paper or in the police again and again. Eaten up by frustration and disappointment when they couldn't solve a case or a story. Alex wanted to stop her pain, but clearly Lara didn't see it that way.

'Sandrine was my best friend, Alex. I won't stop until I find out what happened to her.'

'She was my friend too, and...well, I think we know what happened to her.'

He paused a moment, wondering if he should just keep quiet. But he couldn't. Lara deserved to hear the truth.

'Lara, I spoke to Superintendent Wilson at Charing Cross two days ago. There were no fingerprints of anyone else at the Wallace Square apartment. They've spoken to neighbours, but no-one heard or saw anything unusual and the police found alcohol and anti-depressants in Sandrine's blood stream.'

'I know all this,' said Lara, her lips tight.

'Okay, but I also spoke to a detective in Bishopsgate – the place where Jonathon Meyer was killed? It was the third mugging in that area in six weeks. Meyer's watch and wallet were stolen, the wallet was found ditched a few streets away with the money and credit cards removed. A classic opportunistic snatch according to the copper. He reckoned the muggers were just waiting for some rich guy to come out of the bar alone. He was just unlucky that he smashed his head when he went down.'

'Simon Meyer thinks it's suspicious too.'

Lara's face was pale. Alex waited, unsure whether to proceed.

'You encouraged me to look into it, remember?' said Lara, tension evident in her voice.

'Yes, I said give it 48 hours and if you haven't found anything by then, give it up.'

Lara stared out to sea, refusing to meet Alex's eye.

'You want to know what I think?' he said as gently as he could. 'I think Meyer was killed by a random mugger and I think Sandrine was a brilliant, complex person who was struggling with depression. Are there loose ends and inconsistencies? Yes, of course. But were they both murdered over some trafficking story we have zero evidence about? I don't think so.'

'That's what you think, is it?' she said, a look of contempt in her eyes.

'Simon Meyer is grieving. You are grieving. You've both lost someone you love and we all need to make sense of that. But I care about you too Lara, and I think you need to step back from this. You need to let her go.'

Alex felt a stinging slap on his cheek. He jerked back, one hand cradling his smarting face.

'How dare you tell me how to feel?' she yelled. Her eyes were wild and Alex took a step away, fearing another slap. 'You really believe Sandrine killed herself? Bullshit, Alex! Bullshit!'

Alex wanted to respond, but he could see Lara was out of control. Alex had spent hours at her side during the Felix Tait trial when she had been under intense pressure. Through all the lies, frustrations and a vicious cross-examination by Tait's barrister, Lara had stayed calm, composed – totally in control. But this had sent her over the edge.

'When did you become one of them, Alex?' she hissed, jabbing a finger down towards the lower deck. 'You used to be so strong, so bloody committed. When you were stationed in Beirut and Aleppo, you would go anywhere – across minefields, under wire – anywhere to get to the truth, to tell the stories those bastards down there didn't want told.'

Alex glanced across at the partygoers staring at them.

'Lara, stop,' he said.

'No Alex, I will not stop. This is our *friend.* I will not stop until I find out exactly who hurt her. Then I will hang them out to dry. What are you going to do, Alex? Are you going to do anything, or are you just going to forget all about her?'

'Just listen to me,' he said, as calmly as he could. 'People can spend a lifetime searching for answers to a tragedy and they never find them. It never brings a person back. All that happens is that they get more hurt. I don't want that to happen to you.'

Lara's eyes narrowed.

'Do you ever stop and look at what's happened to you, Alex? Who you've become? There was a time when you'd never give up on a story. Now you and Darius spike more stories than you print. Why? Because they involve a friend or an advertiser.'

'Lara, that's not true.'

'Isn't it? And now you want me to stop chasing this story down. Because it's hard. Because you're not getting enough answers fast enough. Because you just don't care enough.'

'I don't have to listen to this,' snapped Alex, finally losing his temper.

'Then don't,' she said, turning away. 'Because I'm sick of trying to persuade you to be on my side.'

'I AM on your bloody side!' he shouted.

Lara strode back across the deck and, knowing he'd gone too far, he ran to catch up with her.

'Lar, stay,' he said, catching hold of her arm, but she flinched and pulled away from him.

'Lara, please!'

Alex ran after her, only to see her jump into a taxi. He punched her number into his phone. It rang and rang but she didn't pick up. Exhausted, he turned back towards the boat, desperate for a drink. To his dismay, Charlie was standing at the foot of the gangway smoking a cigarette. Alex had the uncomfortable feeling that he – and the rest of the party – had heard every word of their exchange.

'Lovers' tiff?' smirked Charlie, grinding his butt out before he sauntered back onto the yacht.

Chapter Fifteen

AS HER EYES fluttered open, Lara had to immediately squeeze them shut again. Despite the half-slanted shutters, the room in her Roquebrune pension was far too bright. She pressed a hand against her forehead but that only made her feel worse. Reaching for her phone to check the time, she knocked something to the floorboards with a clatter. *Damn.* One of the miniatures. *I'm too old for this*, she thought, peeling her eyes open again. Hangovers used to be a breeze, but lately they had become an ordeal of nausea and recrimination. 'Never again,' she whispered. *The whole mini-bar*, she thought, shuddering at the cost. Brandy, vodka, even those weird crispy nut things: the bright orange dye was still coating her tongue.

The previous evening, the hotel mini-bar had seemed like the answer to her problems. The trial, Nicholas dropping the axe, Sandrine's death – each event had stripped layer after layer from her usually tough hide and now she just felt raw. Her argument with Alex had been the last straw, the exhaustion of the week feeding into her frustration.

Limping to the bathroom, she ran a cold flannel over her face, filled a tooth-glass with water and returned to perch on the edge of the bed.

'Four o'clock?' she muttered, her mind clearing enough to register what she had just seen on her phone screen. Had she really slept for eighteen hours straight?

Her phone delivered another blow of disappointment. No messages from Alex. She didn't know what she was expecting, but still, it made her feel even worse.

She lay back on the white sheets, staring up at the ceiling. She shouldn't have hit him, but she had meant every word she'd said on the *Goliath*.

There had been a time when Lara and Alex had been completely on the same page, sharing ideals and dreams, even sharing the same room on mini-breaks to Rome and Istanbul, but lately Alex had changed. The suits, the playboy apartment, the way he seemed to care more about 'the business' than the actual truth.

The bedside phone rang.

'Miss Lara? It is reception. I have visitors for you.'

Her heart jumped. *Alex.* She couldn't remember telling him where she was staying, but perhaps he was feeling guilty and had tracked her down. She glanced in the mirror and grimaced: she looked like death.

'Visiteurs?' she asked. Plural? Her pleasure faded; he must have brought Charlie with him.

'Oui, Mademoiselle, deux. Eduardo Ortega et Monsieur Stefan Melberg.'

'WHAT ON EARTH are you two doing here?'

They were sitting in the courtyard garden under a pergola twisted with honeysuckle, radiating a sweet, heady and floral scent. Lara felt far from fragrant. She'd had the world's quickest shower and tied her still-damp hair up into a bun, but even a slick of red lipstick couldn't disguise her crumpled clothes – or her crumpled face, come to that.

'Pleased to see us, then?' said Stefan, rising to give her a double-kiss.

'It's a long way from Shoreditch.' said Lara. 'How the hell did you get here? Gulfstream?'

It was meant to be a joke – as a member of the Ortega family, she was sure he was used to flying private, but Eduardo just shrugged.

'Easyjet,' he replied.

Eduardo smiled gratefully as an elderly man with a tray brought them a jug of ice tea, jingling with ice.

'After you rang me yesterday to tell us about Jago Bain, I made a few calls myself,' said Eduardo, as he poured the tea. 'Turns out he is in Monaco this weekend. I've arranged a meeting.'

'Bain's here?'

She was impressed. Lara liked can-do people, but Ortega was on another level.

Lara sat forward eagerly. Perhaps it was the aspirin she had dry-swallowed, but the moment Eduardo mentioned the meeting, she felt her headache ease; this was what she needed. Energy and forward motion.

'So what do we know about him?'

'Bain is an operator. Always on the lookout for business and feathering his contacts with the press.'

'No wonder he's in Monaco this weekend,' noted Stefan.

Eduardo continued. 'He runs his own corporate PR firm, but he functions more like an old-school lobbyist, a middle man between politicians and finance. Lately he's moved heavily into reputation management.'

Lara hadn't heard of Jago Bain before the previous night, but reputation management was something she knew all about. She'd seen Felix Tait's spin doctor go into action during the trial, portraying him as a virtuous philanthropist, sending out press releases emphasising his charity work, making sure he was photographed at the right sort of events – benefits and gala dinners. It was the same all over the corporate sector. The energy company liable for a disastrous oil-spill had careful strategies to rehabilitate its image, the billionaire who had made his money in arms threw lavish parties to launder his reputation – all of them had teams of strategists, lawyers and publicists to deflect, distract and in some cases, punish journalists who sought to reveal the truth.

'Do you know him personally?' asked Lara, the sweet, cold tea soothing her gravelly throat.

'We are slightly acquainted,' said Eduardo, with a hint of discomfort. 'But I can tell you that Bain has a reputation for getting results. And a reputation for being something of a hedonist.'

'To put it politely,' said Stefan.

'Hedonist?'

'Party boy. Word around town is that Jago has an escalating drug problem.'

'Is that why he was kicked off Jonathon Meyer's boat? Bad behaviour?'

Eduardo sat back in his chair and looked at Lara.

'Perhaps you can ask him that tonight.'

Lara tipped her sunglasses forward.

'I see,' she smiled. 'So that's my role? To sweet-talk Jago Bain?'

Stefan laughed.

'Lara, your reputation precedes you. You're the best at getting answers from reluctant subjects.'

'I'm flattered,' she said sceptically, searching their faces. 'And what if he won't speak to me?.'

Stefan looked at Eduardo, who shrugged.

'Then we're screwed.'

AS HER TAXI rolled down through the hills and out onto the coast road, Lara turned her face towards the open window, feeling the rush of sea air, a faint tang of salt and sand and cut grass; she was at least feeling human again. She was sorry to leave Roquebrune behind. After Eduardo and Stefan had left, she had gone for a walk around the old town, a rambling hill settlement of steps, cobbled squares and red slate roofs. In the local coffee shop, someone had told her how Coco Chanel had once lived in the village, and pointed out an olive tree that was over a thousand years old. Lara had taken a seat beneath its branches and read a pulpy novel she'd found in the little post office. It felt like the first time since leaving the Law Courts that she had actually allowed herself to relax. Even her argument with Alex seemed to have faded into the distant past, a mere irritation.

Now the car was slipping through the back streets of Monte Carlo, down past gated dwellings, neon-lit cafes and endless lines of parked scooters, finally reaching the Buddha-Bar, the restaurant/nightclub where a bottle of champagne could set you back 10,000 euros. No big surprise that someone like Jago Bain had chosen it for their meeting.

Walking up the grand steps to the building, Lara suddenly felt exposed in her green dress. This was the playground of the super-rich and she suspected there weren't many people who were wearing what they'd had on the night before. Even so, the receptionist-cum-host took Lara's name and told her that her party was already here, leading her into a magical Eastern-style indigo-lit space, heaving with the glamorous crowd. She crossed the floor towards Eduardo's table.

It was still early in Monaco terms but already the place was rammed; refugees from the casino next door, middle-aged men with slightly too-small shirts and willowy women in slinky dresses. And then she saw him coming into the bar: Jago Bain. He was forty-something, good-looking although slightly going to seed, with a heavy tan, swept-back, thinning hair and a blue shirt beneath a light grey suit. Bain spotted them and walked over.

'Heyyy, Eduardo, looking good,' he cried, faking a punch.

Eduardo actually flinched, but he did his best to

cover it up. 'Join us Jago, please.'

'You've met?' asked Lara.

'Only once,' smirked Bain, raising an eyebrow at Eduardo. 'Your brother's 40th at Annabel's, wasn't it? What a night that was.'

Lara couldn't picture Eduardo strutting around one of the smartest members' clubs in London. She imagined that sitting at home reading leather-bound books or watching heavyweight documentaries was more his speed. Jago squeezed himself in next to Lara, both arms spread along the booth behind. He clicked his fingers at a waitress, mouthing the word 'Krug' and pointing to Eduardo's table.

'So you're the famous Lara Stone, hmm?' he said, greedily looking her up and down.

'Famous?' said Lara, refusing to react.

'I don't think anyone could have missed all that Felix Tait nonsense. I know your cousin Charlie too.'

'Of course.'

The champagne arrived and Stefan made a toast. 'To money.'

It was meant to be ironic, even mocking perhaps, but Bain grinned. 'Very apt,' he said, knocking back the fizz like it was Evian and reaching for the bottle.

'So what can I do for you folks?' he said, filling his own glass.

'I hear you were a friend of Jonathon Meyer's.'

Bain shook his head.

'Ah Jonathon, that was awful. We had our differences, but still sad. Very sad.'

'What happened with you and him?' asked Lara, as

casually as she could.

'What do you mean?' said Jago, sniffing his champagne glass before taking a sip.

'I heard you were thrown off his boat last month.'

Jago pointed a finger at her, then looked at Eduardo and Stefan.

'She's good, this one. Keep hold of her.'

He shrugged and tipped back his champagne. 'I got a bit too boisterous. Went a little too heavy on the bubbles.'

'So who was on the boat? Who was Jonathon trying to impress?' asked Eduardo. Lara saw Jago flinch and she flashed Stefan a look. To her relief, Stefan understood immediately: Lara needed to get Jago on his own. Stefan pretended to look at his phone, then tapped Eduardo on the knee. 'Apologies, Jago,' he said, getting up. 'Eduardo and I have to go and make a quick work call.'

'We do?' said Eduardo.

'Can we leave you with Lara for five?'

'Take all the time you need,' he said wolfishly. 'Lara's in safe hands.'

I'm not entirely sure about that, thought Lara, sliding a little further down the booth.

'We're better off without Eduardo anyway,' said Jago, when they'd gone. 'Bit of a stiff, that one. Nothing like his brother Felipe.'

Lara was intrigued and would have loved to quiz him for more insights into the Euro elite, but she knew she needed to stick to the plan.

'Why are you here, Jago?' she asked.

He shrugged. 'When an Ortega rings, you take the call. If I do him a favour, I can call one in later down the line. It's how the world works, sweetheart.'

'Okay, so do me the favour and tell me about Meyer,' said Lara. 'Why was he so popular? Surely there are lots of generous hosts in this part of the world.'

'Correct. Anyone can throw a party but people went to the *Pandora* because of what Jonathon could do for them,' said Jago with a touch of contempt.

'Do?' said Lara, topping up his glass. 'What did he do?'

'You don't know? Jonathon was a fixer, a fluffer. Okay, sure, he was a fund manager too, but Meyer's gift was connecting people. You needed investment? He knew where to send you. Got a problem? Jon had a man who could fix it. Jon was smart. Brilliant, really. They came for the advice, not for the party.'

Lara watched Bain's face as he spoke. She had no reason to believe he was lying. Yet.

Jago pushed himself up and held out a hand.

'Talking of which, come on, let's dance.'

Lara gave a nervous laugh.

'Dance?'

'Dance. It's party time. Indulge your old Uncle Jago.'

Reluctantly, Lara allowed herself to be led to the small dancefloor at the far end of the bar. There was one other couple dancing cheek-to-cheek, but that didn't seem to deter Jago. He threw out a hand and whirled Lara around. As he dropped her into a dip, Bain's mouth came close to the side of Lara's face.

'Because I have morals,' he said into her ear.

'*What?*'

'That's why they threw me off the boat,' he said, with a smile. 'I know, right? The irony.'

He was making a joke of it, but Bain wasn't an idiot. He knew she was a journalist and he wanted this information to get out into the world. She took his hand and led him outside onto a terrace, away from the crowds, but with enough bass-thump to ensure they wouldn't be overheard.

'Who are *they*, Jago? You said "they" threw you off the yacht.'

'Jon's inner circle.'

'Inner circle?'

Melissa had also mentioned them.

'Jon had a circle of mates. They had an insiders-only syndicate, sunk their own personal cash into sure-fire growth investments.'

'Why did they invite you, Jago?'

He shrugged. 'Advisory capacity. I'd worked with Jon and a couple of his inner-circle guys before. They liked me. Or rather they liked what I could do for them.'

'And what did they want you to do for them this time?'

'They wanted me to "rehabilitate" one of their investments.'

Lara felt the hairs on her bare arms raise; she knew this was important.

'Which investment?'

'A cobalt mine in the Congo,' said Bain, looking

away, his bullishness having disappeared. 'They bought it three or four years ago; it's doubled in value since then. Apparently, cobalt's important in electric cars, so suddenly everyone wants it.'

Lara didn't know anything about cobalt, but she did know that mining in the DRC – Democratic Republic of Congo – was a political mess, with accusations of environmental violations and health hazards for the miners.

'And you didn't want to work with them on it because…?'

Bain pursed his lips.

'A rare attack of conscience.'

Jago looked less sure of himself now, the cockiness gone. Lara didn't want to lose him. She stepped closer.

'Jago, let me help you. I can tell you think what they are doing is wrong.'

She met his eyes. 'What is it?'

He exhaled loudly.

'Look, I don't have many standards, but I do believe you should leave children out of it.'

'Children?'

He pulled a face.

'They use kids in the mine. Some as young as seven working in the tunnels. Terrible injuries, deaths, parents quietly paid off, but it starts to leak out just as an American automobile giant shows interest in buying the mine. So Jon and his mates wanted me to clean up its reputation; come up with a bunch of bullshit initiatives aimed at making the mine look good. Holiday camps for the kiddies, all that crap.'

'Where is the mine, Jago?'

He closed his eyes and shook his head.

'I've already told you enough,' he said, turning back towards the bar. Lara took his arm.

'Jago, please. Tell me.'

Bain opened his mouth to speak, then both of them saw Eduardo approach them. Coming to check on her presumably, which was sweet, but terrible timing.

'You want the name of the mine, pay me,' said Bain, his bravado coming back. 'You can both afford it.'

Lara caught Eduardo's eye and shook her head.

'I thought you said you had a conscience, Jago.'

'And I also need to make a living.'

'Those guys humiliated you, Jago, because you're a better person than they are. Or at least you want to be, otherwise why did you come here tonight?'

He didn't speak for a few seconds.

'The Kanjomo mine,' he said quietly. 'It's owned by an off-shore company belonging to the inner circle. You'll have to find it yourself. The people on the *Pandora* that night were Richard Stewart, Donald Van Leder, Bernard Gander, Philippe Marsaud, Eugene Dre and Jonathon Meyer – you'll have to remember all that, because I won't be repeating it and, in fact, I never said it in the first place.'

His eyes met Lara's and he waved his empty glass.

'Now if you don't mind, I have some champagne to drink. Tell Eduardo he will be covering my tab.'

He turned and walked back towards the thumping music of the bar.

'Jago,' called Lara, but he just raised a hand as if he were flapping a fly away.

'Thank you, Jago,' she said to his back. 'Thank you.'

Chapter Sixteen

MONACO WAS BUZZING. The Place du Casino was packed, well-dressed tourists rubbing elbows with the ultra-rich, high-rollers with rubber-neckers. Race weekend was Monte Carlo's biggest weekend of the year and there was a carnival atmosphere in the air; lights and laughter and couples walking arm in arm, some women's heels so high they could barely walk any other way.

Lara and Stefan stood by the Hôtel de Paris watching Eduardo ascend the wide steps and push through the revolving doors. No one had been particularly surprised when Eduardo had cried off after they'd left the Buddha Bar: Monte Carlo clearly wasn't his kind of town.

Lara, on the other hand, was beginning to love its energy and spectacle. And the company wasn't too bad either.

'So you're not at the De Paris?' she asked Stefan as they turned away from the hotel.

Stefan shook his head.

'I was amazed Eduardo managed to get a room at such short notice, but his magic and my bank account didn't stretch to two of them. So I'm in an Airbnb in

Menton.'

'I'm not in Monaco either,' replied Lara. 'I'm in Roquebrune. It's going to be murder getting a taxi home.'

'Then we'll have to sit it out until it quietens down.'

'How about we go to the casino and put everything on red.'

'Hmm, one problem with that…'

Stefan mimed pulling out his pocket linings to reveal empty hands.

He was flirting with her, but she didn't mind. It had been a long time since Lara had had a boyfriend, and sometimes she thought she'd forgotten how to flirt back. But there was a charge between them that wasn't just the Grand Prix buzz.

'Why don't we just walk,' she said, inhaling the soft, sugary evening air.

They walked down the steep avenue towards the port, the pavements choked with idling pedestrians, the bumper-to-bumper traffic on the road barely moving any faster.

'I love how F1 cars go at 200mph, but in Monte Carlo, no one gets out of first gear,' said Lara. It was a petrol-head's version of an evening stroll, dozens of super-sleek supercars crawling at 5mph then – if they tipped enough – briefly pulling into a rare parking space in front of one of the hotels where they could loiter and soak up the admiring glances from the passing tourists.

'Those things cost $500,000 new,' said Stefan,

nodding towards a Lamborghini in a vivid lime green. 'Do you think the reward is worth the cost? Half a million for a few guys going 'wow, nice car'?'

'I'm more of a 'two wheels' kind of girl.'

AS THEY APPROACHED the port, Lara could feel the deep bass thump from parties on board the yachts positioned all along the front. This was the Yacht Party phenomenon in microcosm: she and Stefan strolled past each gangplank, craning their necks to look inside. Lara didn't have any great desire to be part of this crowd, but she was still curious, and it was hard not to wonder if she was missing out on some amazing experience behind the velvet ropes. That psychology was why Jonathon Meyer had bought the *Pandora*, why he held those networking parties on a boat. Yes, they were expensive and glamorous, but so were nightclubs like Jimmyz or the Buddha Bar, why not hold his parties there? Because only the chosen few had been allowed onto the *Pandora:* only la crème de la crème. The very size of a boat limited the guestlist so even the *Goliath* was small when compared to somewhere like the Buddha Bar. It was exclusive in every sense.

Lara nudged Stefan. 'Check out this guy.'

A banana yellow supercar drew up at the walkway to a three-tier yacht named *Neptune's Daughter*. The gullwing door flipped up and a young man stepped out wearing wraparound sunglasses and a loud patterned shirt open to the waist. He didn't even look as a valet jumped inside his car and whisked it away. Half a mill gone in exchange for a ticket stub.

'What do you think's going on inside?' said Lara.

'The best party in the history of the world,' said Stefan. 'Although if that guy's on the guestlist, I'm not sure I want to go.'

'You're only saying that because you're a socialist,' smiled Lara. 'Oh, and you're not invited.'

'Exactly,' agreed Stefan. 'If only Tsar Nicholas had allowed the peasants into his parties, there would have been no Russian revolution.'

He was about to say more, but Lara was distracted. She had spotted a familiar figure walking down the dockside towards them.

'Alex.'

'Oh. Hi,' he said awkwardly, walking over. She watched Alex glance towards Stefan, assessing him, weighing him up; they were like two cats passing in an alleyway.

'Alex Ford, this is Stefan Melberg. Stefan meet Alex. He is – was – my colleague at the *Chronicle*.'

Colleague. Ouch. Lara almost winced at her own coldness, but then she was still cross with him after last night.

'Alex, of course,' said Stefan, putting out his hand. 'I followed your work in Syria. Powerful stuff.'

'Thanks,' said Alex, but all his attention was on Lara. As she met his gaze, her mood towards him softened, but now wasn't the time to talk about their argument on the *Goliath* and how he'd made her feel.

'Off partying again?'

It was meant to sound light-hearted, but it came out

like an accusation.

'I'm working, Lara,' said Alex crisply. 'I have to meet the advertisers.'

'Of course. Which ones?'

'Emirates have their America's Cup boat down the far end of the marina and McLaren are toasting their pole position at the yacht club.' He glanced at his watch. 'Actually, I had better be off.'

'Sure,' said Lara quickly. 'Don't let us keep you from your free cocktails.'

Alex gave a curt nod towards Stefan and a lingering look to Lara, then moved off.

'I see you two have history,' said Stefan, watching Alex go.

'Alex is one of my oldest friends,' she said. 'It just gets awkward sometimes. We went to college together and now he's my boss. Plus we had a bit of a ding-dong last night. I think I might have accused him of being a terrible corporate yes-man.'

'Might?'

Lara grimaced.

'Ah. That *is* awkward.'

Despite the encounter with Alex, Lara was glad she had come out. Stefan was easy to talk to and didn't judge anything she said. It was such a simple thing, but it felt liberating to talk to someone who had no expectations and no knowledge of her baggage. They walked on, the line-up of yachts seemingly endless. Some were huge, others were relatively modest motor yachts and cabin cruisers – relatively, this was Monaco, nothing less than 50 feet. They bought two bottles of water from a Tabac and stopped at a bench, looking out over the blue-black water, the thrum of a dozen parties still audible.

'I live on a boat,' said Lara, glancing at Stefan with a half-smile.

'Really? That's glamorous.'

She laughed.

'Not when it pours down.'

She looked at him.

'So where is home for you?'

'I've just found a place in Shoreditch for when we open the London Le Caché office. Until a few weeks ago I was based in Amsterdam. De Pijp. Do you know it?'

She did. It was a cool, creative part of the city. It was no surprise that Stefan lived there.

'Is that where you grew up?'

'I was born in Amsterdam, but when I was little we moved to Texel, one of the Frisian Islands.'

'Frisian as in cows?'

He grinned. 'I think that's where they originated, yes. But Texel is mainly a tourist place now. White beaches, an old lighthouse. My parents had a café right on the sands.'

'Sounds idyllic.'

'I guess it was. As a kid there was a lot of hunting for oysters and pearls, pirate booty and washed-up bottles.'

Lara looked at him with new eyes. He seemed so urbane and sophisticated, she hadn't imagined Stefan barefoot and poking about in rockpools.

'Although there's a limit to how much nature anyone can stand,' he smiled. 'By the time I was 18, I was itching to get out and see the world. I moved back to Amsterdam to study, then I went to Georgetown University in Washington for postgrad study. It was where I met Eduardo.'

He swigged his water bottle then looked at her.

'So what about you, Lara? Was it all pony rides and garden fetes.'

Of course, she thought sadly. He had researched her, he knew all about her – the headline version of Lara Stone, anyway. A privileged, silver spoon socialite, part of the glittering Avery dynasty. If only real life worked so well.

'Not quite,' she said. 'My childhood wasn't quite so simple.'

She nodded towards the smaller yachts ahead. 'My parents died when I was eleven. They were sailing something very like that in Croatia.'

'What happened?'

She didn't mention her parents often and when she did, most people made a few platitudes, then moved the conversation swiftly on. But she was glad Stefan was honest enough to ask the question everyone thought.

'Every summer my parents took a sailing trip together. My father loved boats. I would go to my granny's house and they would travel to Majorca, the South of France, Greece, any one of the summer sailing hubs. That year they went to Split. They wanted to sail to Hvar and the outlying islands. The next thing we knew, there was an explosion. A defective diesel pump, maybe the stove in the galley. There was an investigation, helicopters, diving crews, a British team went out to the Balkans, but nothing was found except wreckage of the boat.'

'Your parents were never found?'

She shook her head. 'It's still a mystery,' said Lara. 'The Adriatic is bigger than it looks.'

'I'm sorry. It must have been a very difficult time.'

'There were lots of unpleasant rumours. That didn't make it any easier.'

That was an understatement. There had been an affair, a secret child, the whispers had said. And of course the most poisonous story had been the one which had stuck: David Avery had killed his beautiful, but difficult wife and then set fire to the boat – the lack of evidence was merely proof of a cover-up by the powerful Avery family.

'My grandfather tried his best to find out what really happened but he never did. A year later he was dead too. He had a heart attack. I still think he died of a broken heart.'

'Haven't you ever been tempted to look into it yourself?' asked Stefan.

It was the obvious question. She was an investigative reporter, one of the best. Who better to dig out the truth?

'No. Because whatever I do, they're still gone. My fantasy mum and dad are the ones I carry around in my head and as it stands, they can be perfect, until the day I die.'

And they were perfect in her mind. Her beautiful mother Ramona with her bright green eyes and waist-length black hair. And David Avery, her beloved father. A handsome, rugged man with dark hair and a wide smile standing at the tiller of his boat, his eyes fixed on the horizon. Lara knew that cherished image might be a figment of her imagination, or even a scene from a half-remembered movie. None of her memories were very reliable. But they were hers and she didn't want to spoil them by digging too deeply into David and Ramona's deaths. Perhaps Stefan might find that strange given her determination to investigate Sandrine's apparent suicide. But it was how she felt.

'Come on,' she said, standing up. 'Race you to the top.'

Stefan looked up in surprise, then alarm. 'To the top of the rock?'

'What, are you scared that a girl will beat you?'

He looked up towards the Prince's Palace towering high above them.

'What are you waiting for?' she grinned, hitching up her dress, then turning to sprint off towards the steps.

The Rock of Monaco was a geographical slab that had been the original fortified settlement; the old town was up there, so was the Cathedral. Lara knew that much, but she had no idea how many steps there were to the top. She was already thinking she had bitten off more than she could chew when she heard Stefan's footsteps behind her. OMG! He was actually doing it!

'I'm coming!' he shouted. Lara started laughing

even as she increased her pace. 'Never catch me!' she called back.

She bolted across a road – mercifully clear – and then onto another set of steps. Stefan was gaining, which for some reason made her giggles worse.

'Ah, crap,' she panted, collapsing on the stone steps near the summit. Not as fit as she thought. Or maybe it was her shoes – her Grecian sandals weren't exactly trainers made for running. Stefan caught up and dropped down next to her, his chest heaving from exertion, but also from laughter. Lara had underestimated how many steps there were.

'You… are…crazy…' he managed, before dissolving into guffaws.

Without thinking, Lara rolled over and grabbed him, kissing Stefan hard on the lips. After a moment's hesitation, Stefan kissed her back, pulling her closer.

'We're going to get caught by the Monaco Guard,' she laughed into his ear.

The palace was barely two hundred yards away and in the darkness she could see a glimpse of white uniform.

'We'd better keep out of sight then,' he whispered.

He took her hand and pulled her through the grand *porte* to the old town.

'Just look at that,' she said, taking a moment to look at the Palace, gloriously illuminated.

'I'd rather look at you,' he said, leaning over to kiss her neck.

They crossed to the other side of the square. There were few tourists up here despite the busyness of the weekend.

They found a bench in a quiet corner; it was dark and secluded but overlooked Port Fontvieille, Monaco's second harbour down below, just pin-pricks of light in the dark.

'How are we going to get back to your apartment?' she asked between kisses. If she was being forward, she didn't care.

'We're not. Not yet,' he said.

She loved the taste of him, champagne, toothpaste and sweet tea.

'Come here. Come closer,' he said, positioning himself so that she could straddle him.

He held her face as they kissed again. As she tipped her head back, he pushed the fabric of her dress down from her shoulders. Lara wasn't wearing a bra. Her breasts sprang free and her nipples hardened as soon as they were exposed to the fresh air.

When Stefan kissed each one in turn, she couldn't wait a moment longer.

Rising up from his lap, she unbuckled his trousers and rolled her dress up over her thighs.

He was hard, and as he guided himself into her, she moaned with delight.

She didn't care who was watching, a tourist, a local, the Monaco guard, she just wanted to feel her desire build. And it did. They rocked in time, and as he held her hips, she arched her back so he could pusher deeper into her.

'Yes, yes, yes,' she groaned, clenching herself around him, shivering as she crescendoed into a tight pulse of delirious pleasure before she crashed over the edge, every nerve ending on fire as he withdrew from her.

She closed her eyes, and tried to catch her breath, sweat trickling between her breasts. When she opened her eyes again, she smiled at Stefan, blushing, not quite able to believe she had just done that.

There was a brief moment of tension between them.

'Does that mean I'm in pole position,' said Stefan and they both started to laugh.

'I don't know, let's try and get back to one of our hotel rooms, and we can do that all over again to find out.'

Chapter Seventeen

THE TRAIN FROM Gatwick wasn't exactly the Orient Express, but still, Lara liked to travel by rail. She loved the way it cut straight through the landscape giving an unparalleled insight into people's real lives.

She'd flown in from Monaco via Nice and Lara supposed it was fitting that the last leg home should bring her closer to real life. From the air you saw cloud, from the road, you saw the façade, but trains let you see people's washing, their discarded junk and their open curtains. An unguarded reality of barbeques, trampolines and toppled football nets: details of lives lived or imagined. From the train you saw how people really were, not what they wanted you to see. Lara rested her head against the window, her cheek pressing against the cool glass, as her mind circled back to Jonathon Meyer. What was true of the back yards of Surrey was true of the yachts of Monaco. Everyone had a public face and a real, slightly less palatable one. Everyone had secrets, things they'd rather you didn't ever see. But had Jonathon's secrets been enough to get him killed? Had he, like Jago Bain, said 'no' to his Inner Circle?

Lara was rattled from her daydream by her phone

buzzing on the table in front of her.

Number unknown.

She found herself smiling, a fluttering in her stomach. *Stefan?* She wondered, picking it up. And if it was, how should she play it? They had ended up back at her Roquebrune pension after their tryst on the Rock of Monaco. Lara still blushed when she thought about it. Their morning in bed together, and then meeting up with Eduardo at the Hotel de Paris to discuss their meeting with Jago Bain, trying to pretend they hadn't been up most of the night having sex.

She tapped the green button.

'Hi there.'

'Lara Stone?'

Not Stefan. A female voice, American.

'Yes,' said Lara, immediately on alert. 'Who is this?'

There was a second's pause.

'I'm a friend of Melissa's. Melissa Gelman. She suggested I speak to you about Jonathon.'

The voice was young, nervous. Lara's eyes darted around the carriage. Maybe she had reason to be anxious. In eyeshot she could see a group of backpackers, a young couple, and a man wearing headphones looking engrossed in his phone. It was doubtful she was being watched, but still, Lara didn't feel as if this was the place to talk.

'Where are you?'

'London.'

'Can you meet today?'

There was a hesitation at the other end of the line and Lara held her breath. *Say yes.* She had a sense that things were finally starting to move – and she wanted to keep pushing.

'How about seven o'clock?' said the voice. *Crap.* Seven was when Alex's birthday meal was due to start. Drinks at some fancy riverside restaurant followed by an even fancier supper. Alicia had invited her a couple of weeks earlier; it was meant to be a surprise, although she knew how much Alex hated surprises. She made some mental calculations. If she took the bike, she could probably make it in time for the starter. Main course at the very least.

'Okay, seven. Where?'

'Do you know St. Martin-In-The-Fields? On the steps of the church.'

THE CHURCH WAS closed, the black gates already locked. Lara walked to the bottom of the wide stone steps and checked her watch again. It was already ten past seven and no sign of the mystery caller. Not that she had much idea of what – or who – she was looking for. A young American woman: great. Across the road was Trafalgar Square; at this time of year, central London was teeming with tourists – there wasn't a lot to go on.

Lara looked up at the mottled sky, fading into grey as the evening light waned. There had been a high white quilt of cloud over London all day – Lara wouldn't normally have noticed, but it had been in such stark contrast to the heat and sunshine of Monaco. She shivered, not entirely because of the cool. The girl on the phone had sounded scared. Should Lara be frightened too? When money was no object, everything was disposable. Jago Bain and Jonathon Meyer both specialised in making things disappear for the ultra-wealthy: tax bills, bad PR, who knew what else? If you had enough money, anything could be swept under the carpet. *Including people.*

'Lara?'

Jumping at the voice, Lara turned. A pretty girl in her early twenties was standing there.

'Sorry, I was watching to make sure you were alone,' she said. 'I'm Josie. Josie Bourne.'

At second glance, the girl was striking; fine-boned and smooth-skinned. She didn't have a scrap of make-up on and loose black clothes disguised her willowy figure, but Lara could immediately see that this girl was more at home at the Hôtel Hermitage than a busy London street.

'Shall we walk?' said Lara, nodding towards the square. Clearly Josie had chosen the location for the 'safety in crowds' factor. Lara wasn't entirely convinced that was foolproof, but she wanted the girl to feel comfortable.

'So you knew Jonathon?' she asked, as they crossed the road.

'We were in a relationship,' she said simply.

Meyer had been pushing fifty. Josie looked barely 21. Despite Melissa and Tom's glowing testimonies about their boss it seemed like another black mark against him.

'I didn't know,' said Lara. 'That he had been seeing anyone I mean.'

'Not many people did,' said Josie. 'But we'd been together almost a year.'

She explained that she was from a small town near Toronto – Canadian not American – and had come to Europe to model the previous year.

'As a model, you get invited to lots of parties. I met Jonathon at one of them.'

'In London?'

Josie shook her head.

'In Monaco. I went out there in September to do a job at the Yacht Show.'

'What's that?'

'A festival for superyachts. If you want to buy or charter one, you go there. If you want people to think you might be buying one, you go there. It's easy to get caught up in all that glamour.'

She smiled sadly. 'I went to Monte Carlo for three days and stayed three weeks.'

Lara glanced at her.

'You stayed because of Jonathon?'

She nodded. 'I met Melissa on the night I arrived and she invited me to a party on board *Pandora*. Then Jonathon invited me out for dinner. That was it.'

'But you didn't move to Monaco full-time?'

'No. Jonathon liked his space. I knew from the start that he wasn't going to ask me to move onto the *Pandora*. It was his workplace.'

As Josie talked, Lara quickly realised that, despite being his girlfriend, Josie hadn't spent much time with Jonathon Meyer. In October, the yachting season in the Mediterranean ports wound down with the charter boat crowd and the party scene that came with it moving on to the Caribbean and the Indian Ocean. Meyer used the time for business trips to New York, Singapore and Beijing, only meeting up with Josie when he flew into London. The remote nature of Meyer's relationship didn't surprise Lara – for men like Jonathon Meyer it was about following the money, not your heart. They stopped near the stone lions beneath Nelson's column.

'Why did you want to see me, Josie?' asked Lara.

'Melissa called me. She said you'd spoken and that you thought Jonathon's death was suspicious.'

'I told her that was one theory I was investigating.'

A group of Spanish students jostled past them, shouting and laughing, and Lara saw Josie flinch, glancing around.

'I think I might be in danger too,' said Josie.

'Why do you say that?'

The girl seemed to be looking at something over Lara's shoulder. She turned: a middle-aged man wearing an overcoat was striding towards them. As Lara watched, the man took a selfie with the fountains in the background, checked it, then apparently satisfied, walked off towards the National Gallery. Josie shivered. She was skittish, something had clearly rattled her.

'Look,' said Lara, pointing to a brightly lit cafe on the other side of the square. 'Why don't we get out of these crowds? We can sit down and talk more easily.'

The girl looked dubious, as if being cornered was worse than being attacked in the open.

'Please, Josie,' said Lara. 'I want to help you.'

The girl reluctantly nodded and followed Lara across the road into the cafe. Once they were settled at a table, Lara jumped straight into the question that had been on her lips.

'Jonathon had an inner circle of friends. Did you ever meet them?'

She told her the names of his investment syndicate that Jago had mentioned.

'I met lots of people in passing,' said Josie. 'But Jonathon tended to keep his business associates to himself.'

'Josie, you're scared,' said Lara quietly. 'Tell me why.'

Josie paused, looking away as if she wasn't sure whether to say it.

'Jon had an apartment in town but we mostly stayed on the yacht. His stateroom was on the top deck which was out of bounds during parties. There was a passcode to get in but I had it.'

She paused before she continued.

'A few weeks ago Jon threw a party to kick-off the yachting season. I flew in for it the day before. I hadn't been feeling well all week, but by the night of the party, I felt terrible, pounding head and aching body. I kept smiling, drinking, hoping I would feel better, but small talk is exhausting when you're ill. By ten o'clock, I ducked out and went to Jonathon's cabin. No one was going to miss me.'

Josie looked down at her hands and Lara saw that her fingernails were chewed to the quick.

'So I was lying in the dark and the window was open: I heard Jon outside talking to another man. It sounded like business chat, like they'd come up to get some privacy away from the party. But then they started talking about a woman. The other guy? He told Jon he needed to get rid of her.'

'Get rid of her? In what context?'

'At first, I assumed they were talking about someone who was underperforming at work. But then the other guy said we need to "shut her up". Like, once and for all. And he wanted Jon's help to do it.'

Lara looked at her, her heart thumping. Was it Sandrine they had been talking about?

'Did they say what this woman had done?'

'No. It sounded like something they both already knew about, something they'd been discussing before.'

'So what did Jonathon say?'

'I couldn't hear everything. I could still hear the music from the party. But I could tell Jon didn't want to do whatever it was. The other guy kept pushing; he said, "You owe me, Jon. You owe me for everything."'

'Owed him for what?'

'He didn't say – but it must have been a big favour because finally Jon said he would arrange it. He wasn't happy, but he agreed.'

Lara leant forward.

'Who was this other man?'

'The blinds were closed so I didn't see him. I

didn't recognise his voice either. But I heard a name.'

Lara waited, breath held.

'Jonathon call him Mike.'

'And the woman they wanted to get rid of? Did she have a name?'

Lara's heart was in her mouth. She had no idea how long Sandrine had been working on her story, but if these powerful men had heard about her investigation, it was more than possible they might arrange to make that particular problem go away.

'Was it Sandrine? Sandrine Legard?'

Josie shook her head.

'No. The woman was called Helen.'

It was a name Lara immediately recognised. Could it be Helen from Sandrine's Post-it note? *Helen... Michael... Jonathon.* All in a rush, it started to connect.

*Jonathon...Michael...Helen...Sandrine...*This 'Mike' was the link between two people, Jonathon and Sandrine, who had met violent ends.

'Do you think I'm in danger too?'

Josie seemed to be reading Lara's face.

'You do, don't you?' said the girl in a panic.

Lara reached out to touch Josie's hand, to reassure her, but the girl kicked her chair back and grabbed her bag.

'I should go,' she said. 'I'm sorry.'

'Josie, please...'

But then she was gone, running out into the square before she was lost in the dark.

Chapter Eighteen

ALEX TOOK A deep breath and blew. The candles fluttered, then blinked out.

'HAP-py BIRTH-day!'

A huge cheer went up and Alex winced as a host of party-poppers fired and a dozen hands threw streamers in the air. Family, friends and colleagues gathered around to clasp his shoulder and slap him on the back and Alex found that, despite his embarrassment at all the fuss, he was having actual fun.

'Speech!' shouted a voice he recognised from the *Chronicle* contingent. Reluctantly Alex stood up and raised his hands for quiet.

'Thank you all for coming to my birthday party at…' he looked around. 'Where am I?'

There was a big laugh.

'The Bankside Cafe, darling,' whispered Alicia. Alex was joking of course; his post-Monaco hangover was bad, but not that bad. The Bankside was a classic venue for a media power lunch and Alex adored the parmesan linguine, their signature dish.

'Thanks for coming to my favourite restaurant in the world and I'm so happy to be here to share it with all of you. I have no idea how Alicia did it in complete and utter secrecy.'

More laughter from those who knew Alicia and how super-organised she was. More still from those who knew that Alicia had consulted Alex at every stage of the 'surprise' from venue to cake to guest list. 'There's no point in wasting time or money on people you dislike,' she had said crisply, during one of their planning meetings. She had even insisted on holding the party on a Monday night: the Tuesday edition was always slow. No point in letting festivities get in the way of your career.

But Alex had to admit the end result had been worth it all. It was a perfect evening, from the blood orange Negronis at the drinks reception to the petit fours, it had all been thought through and perfectly executed. There was only one thing missing, but Alex knew he only had himself to blame for that.

Speech over, Alex shrugged off a final round of applause and made his way over to Alicia.

'Hey you,' he whispered into her ear, snaking a hand around her waist and kissing her neck. She smelt great. Even better than she looked. And Alicia always looked terrific.

'It was just perfect Alicia, thank you.'

She smiled modestly.

'You're very welcome. I love to see you smile.'

'Meaning I don't usually?'

She laughed.

'Meaning I don't see it enough.'

Alex nodded, feeling a pang of guilt, because she was right. He had met Alicia at a Christmas party just a week after he'd been promoted to Deputy Editor, so to Alicia his 15-hour working days were normal. But they weren't, he knew that.

'I'll work on that smile with you,' he said. 'But first I should go and talk to my dad,' he said, noticing Terry Ford leaving the dining room.

'And thanks for bringing him down. Now that *was* a surprise.'

'Always like to keep you guessing,' she said, throwing a grin over her shoulder as she went to mingle. Alex followed his father out through double doors into a small courtyard garden filled with flowers and potted ferns. It was good to get out into the fresh air, even if he was closed in on all sides by other parts of the restaurant.

'Great speech, lad,' said his father as Alex approached. 'Great party too.'

'I'm glad you're here,' said Alex, as he embraced the old man. Terry felt small, thinner, more brittle, but Alex held on, enjoying the feeling. It had been six months since he'd last seen his father and it was only now that he realised just how much he had missed him.

'So you're coming back to mine tonight?'

'No, Alicia's put me up in Claridge's.'

Alex couldn't hide his surprise.

'*Claridge's?*' he said.

'I know,' grinned Terry. 'I was as gobsmacked as you. Not that I'm complaining. Twenty-four hour room service, everything laid on. Been a long time since I was so pampered.'

Alex examined his father's face: was that a comment about his mum? Since she had passed away five years before, Terry had been fending for himself, juggling his newsagent's shop in the village with domestic life. The shop had closed the previous year – his father had tried to keep it going as long as he could, selling loo roll, baked beans and tea bags alongside a dwindling stock of magazines and papers, but had finally flipped the 'closed' sign for the last time, calling it early retirement rather than pointing out the real cause: newspapers just weren't selling anymore. Still, even though Terry had less to worry about now, Alex wasn't sure how well his father was coping. He was the kind of man who liked to stay active.

'Next time I'll do the pampering,' said Alex. 'And we should definitely do this more. We don't see enough of each other.'

Terry squeezed his shoulder.

'You have a big newspaper to run, son. You're busy.'

'But I could come up more. I don't want you thinking I don't want to see you.'

Terry was shaking his head, an amused smile on his face.

'That genuinely never crossed my mind,' he said. 'Seriously Alex, I'm your dad, all I want is for you to go out into the world and succeed at whatever you do. And…' he gestured towards the sumptuous surroundings. '…it definitely looks like you're succeeding. It's a long way from the White Lion, that's for sure.'

Alex smiled, thinking about his 18th party at the local pub. Wilted cheese and pickle sandwiches and thirty quid behind the bar.

'So how's things back home?'

'I saw Gaz Dickenson the other day. He was down the pub with that other reprobate, Jacko. Same old, same old. Drinking, singing, arguing about football. They said to say hello.'

There had been a time – around that 18th birthday in fact – when Alex had wanted nothing more than to get the hell away from the Lake District village where he had grown up. It was too small, too claustrophobic and Alex needed to get out into the world, find action and adventure, get his boots dusty in far-flung hot-spots. Now? Now he was looking at Gaz and Jacko through rose-tinted spectacles. Maybe they were the ones who'd got it right, surrounded by friends and good tunes on the jukebox. Alex looked back at the private dining room. Plenty of friends, sure. But would they join in if he started singing 'Wonderwall'?

'So where's Lara tonight?' asked Terry.

'I'm not sure. You know how it is, Dad, always running off chasing some story. You can't always schedule social arrangements around the news.'

Lara had sent a bland 'happy birthday' text earlier in the day, but it wasn't the same as seeing her in person. Clearly she hadn't forgotten their disagreement in Monte Carlo.

'Alicia's really done you proud though, hasn't she?'

He was sure his dad hadn't meant it to sound like a consolation prize, but that's how it felt.

'You know, I wasn't sure about her at first,' said

Terry, lowering his voice. 'But she's won me round. She's a good 'un.'

Alex was surprised to hear him say it. The first time he had taken his new girlfriend up to visit, there had been a definite frostiness. It wasn't for any lack of effort on Alicia's part; she had taken a Single Malt Whisky and was polite and attentive, but Terry hadn't warmed to her. Too posh, too southern, Alex had thought at the time, but actually it wasn't that. Lara was pretty posh but Terry and Diane Ford had treated her like a daughter they'd never had. Terry felt around inside his jacket and pulled something out. He thrust a black velvet pouch towards Alex.

'I thought you might want this.'

Frowning, Alex opened the bag and there, flat on his palm, was his mother's engagement ring.

'You've been together for a while now, so I thought I'd give it to you just in case you're having thoughts about something more permanent. If Alicia's special to you, I know your mum would want her to have it.'

Alex looked down at the ring. It was simple, a single small diamond on a plain gold band. Unbidden, a memory flashed in: his mum's hand lying on the white sheets of the hospital bed, Alex squeezing her fingers and feeling this ring press into his skin.

'It's a lovely thought,' said Alex. And it was, especially as Alex knew how hard it would have been for Terry to part with the ring, but Alex also knew something else: he knew that Alicia would hate it. Alicia would want some giant rock with a brand name like Cartier or DeBeers, something she could flash at her envious girlfriends. Alicia wasn't entirely hard-hearted – she would appreciate the sentiment of Terry's gesture – there was just no way she would actually wear the ring. But Alex wasn't about to say any of this to his dad; not the time, not the place. Instead he hugged Terry tightly.

'Thanks Dad,' he said. 'But don't hold your breath, eh?'

'No rush lad. Whenever you're ready. Although I get the distinct feeling your good lady is more than ready.'

He glanced across at Alicia who was standing by the door. It wasn't as if it hadn't crossed Alex's mind either. Alex slipped the ring into his pocket and patted it. 'I'll keep it safe Dad, don't you worry.'

Terry winked at him and squeezed his arm.

'I know you will, son.'

Weaving through the guests, Alex crossed to Alicia.

'There you are,' she said. 'I've been looking for you. Guess who's here?'

'Here's the birthday boy,' said a deep voice. *Ah crap.* It was Darius. Alex had, of course, invited his editor – office politics demanded it – but he hadn't actually expected him to come. Darius was the kind of man who would treat a no-show at a party as a power-play.

'Hey Darius, glad you could come,' said Alex, as warmly as he could. 'Shame you missed the meal. It was an awesome Beef en croute, wasn't it Alicia?'

'Yes, I had the beef when I was here with Jonathon and Olivia last week,' said Darius. Of course he had. And in one seemingly innocuous sentence, Darius had reminded him of the pecking order and the fact that he had the ear of the company power couple. Nice.

Sensing a captive audience, Darius launched into a retread of the Felix Tait affair with himself as the crusading hero of the piece, blind-sided by a blinkered judiciary.

Alex was still nodding and making sympathetic noises to Darius when he saw Lara walk in, holding her bike helmet and looking nervous. A smile immediately spread across his face. Leaving Darius with Alicia, Alex strode across.

'You came,' he said.

'I did,' Lara replied shyly. 'Oh, and happy birthday. I'm so sorry I missed it, I was interviewing someone. I thought I might make it in time for pudding, but… sorry, I…'

'It's fine,' he said, cutting her off. 'I'm just glad you're here'.

'Looks like you've come up in the world, Ford,' said Lara, gesturing towards the restaurant. 'I'll have to remember that next time I throw you a bash.'

For his birthday two years ago – pre-Alicia – Lara had hosted an impromptu barbeque on *Misty*, inviting as many of their City University friends as she could round up in twenty-four hours and the spontaneity had added to the fun. Sandrine had been in town and had come along too. The thought stopped him: Alex realised that was the last time he had properly spoken to Sandrine.

'I've got you something,' she said, pulling a slim package from her rucksack. 'I hope it makes up for my tardiness.'

'A present? Can I open it now?'

'How do you know I haven't got you something embarrassing?' she said in a stage whisper.

Alex looked up. 'Like a sex toy?'

'No, like a thesaurus.'

Alex laughed, but he knew Lara well. She used jokes to cover her nerves; perhaps the present really was something private.

'Listen, I just wanted to show my face, but I have to shoot off again.'

'Really? Where are you going?'

'You mean what is an unemployed journalist doing at this time of night?'

She leaned forward to kiss his cheek before he could answer.

'Happy birthday, Alex. Have a great evening.'

He watched her leave then, unable to resist, began to tear the paper, gasping when he saw what was inside. It was a scarf. But not just any scarf, it was a Shemagh, the traditional Arab head cover that doubled as a mask against sand and flies in the desert. Nothing very unusual about that, but this one was very distinctive, woven in black and white with the linked 'GG' of Gucci. And looking at it made Alex's pulse race.

'I don't believe it.'

He ran out of the restaurant, catching up with Lara in the car park, just as she was about to put her bike helmet on.

'Where the hell did you find it?' he said, waving the scarf.

Lara leant back against her bike and tried to hide a smile. If he didn't know her better he would have sworn she was blushing.

'I didn't find it,' said Lara, her eyes twinkling. 'I had someone make it for me. I had to rely on my memory – I hope it's alright.'

'Alright? It's amazing.'

And it was. It was a near-perfect reproduction of a scarf Alex had bought in a market on the West Bank while on assignment years ago. The Gucci logo was something of an ironic joke. Alex wasn't exactly a designer-label kind of guy; hadn't been then, anyway. Still, the Shemagh had served its purpose, saving him from heatstroke and sandstorms and in Iraq and Afghanistan it'd become a lucky talisman. Then on a night out with Lara when he was stationed in Berlin, the scarf had been lost. They had retraced their steps bar-by-bar, but it had disappeared into the night.

'I can't believe you remembered,' said Alex, examining the fabric.

Lara gave a slow grin. 'Don't worry, it's just as crappy as the original.'

It was in stark contrast to all the carefully chosen and tasteful presents Alicia had given him that morning along with breakfast in bed. The Dunhill cufflinks, the expensive camera lens, the first edition of a Bukowski novel. Thoughtful, expensive gifts, but the Shemagh? That was something you couldn't compete with. A breeze, soft and briny, blew in off the Thames.

'I'm sorry if I upset you in Monaco,' said Alex. 'I really didn't mean to.'

Lara shrugged it off.

'So what happened? Did you find anything else?'

Lara pulled a face.

'No, nothing. As you said, it's probably a wild goose chase anyway.'

'Hey, I didn't say that.'

She looked away, down the river. Alex didn't want to pick a fight. Not tonight.

'So that guy Stefan? He's from Le Caché, right?'

He said it as casually as he could, although Alex had Googled him as soon as he'd got back to his room at the Fairmont. He was Dutch, forthright, worthy. A bit too good-looking, in Alex's opinion. A bit smug.

'Stefan? Yes, he's the co-founder.'

'I see,' said Alex, pressing his lips together unconsciously. He'd been shocked when he'd seen them together, by the harbour laughing, not quite holding hands but their intimacy had put him on edge. Alex and Lara stood there awkwardly, both knowing they had stepped into a minefield, but neither really knowing how to back out.

'Well, I'm glad you like the scarf,' said Lara.

'I love it,' he replied, remembering that trip to Berlin, how excited he'd been when Lara had flown out to see him. He wanted to tell her, to remind her how close they had been, to talk about all the memories they'd shared, but his phone was ringing. It was almost certainly Alicia asking him where he was.

'Sorry,' he said, pulling his mobile out of his pocket to reject the call. In his haste, something else flew out and tinkled to the floor. Lara bent down and picked it up.

She held it between finger and thumb for a moment, before she held it out to him.

'A ring,' she said.

He hesitated.

'It was my mum's.'

Lara raised an eyebrow.

'Tonight's the night, then?'

'For what?'

'The proposal, you idiot,' she said, with a hint of amusement in her voice.

'No, my Dad gave it to me just now. You know, for when I'm ready.'

He took the ring and put it back in his pocket.

'And are you ready?'

He looked away from her. 'I don't know Lar, are you ever ready for something like that?'

Lara just snorted and threw a leg over her bike.

'What, don't you think I should?' asked Alex.

Lara met his gaze.

'When have you ever listened to anything I say, Alex Ford?'

'You didn't answer the question.'

She shrugged her shoulders. They'd only met a handful of times, but Alex suspected that Lara and Alicia weren't overly fond of each other. Too different. Lara looked as though she was about to say something, but his phone began to ring again.

'She'll be wondering where you are,' said Lara, pulling on her helmet, then firing up her engine with a roar.

'I'm not proposing to her,' he said, raising his voice. He didn't know why it was so important to tell her, but it was.

Her face was covered and Alex couldn't tell if Lara had even heard him. She turned the bike back towards the road and, wiggling her fingers in an ironic good-bye, tore off, leaving a trail of rubber behind her.

Chapter Nineteen

LARA WAS IN a foul mood. Stella could sense it even from a distance. As she walked up Brick Lane, it was like her boss had a pitch-black cloud over her head. Lightning and everything.

Stella was glad she had brought gifts: strong tea and bacon sandwiches. That would cheer anyone up first thing in the morning.

'Do you know how hard it is to find a proper caff around here?' said Stella, filling in the silence as they met at the corner of Bethnal Green Road. 'This is supposed to be the East End, fergawd's sake.'

'Hipsters don't do grease,' said Lara, taking the bag and peeking inside. She grimaced. 'Too early for me. Maybe Eduardo will want one.'

They crossed the road, heading into the arty enclave of Shoreditch.

'You alright boss?' said Stella, trying to lift Lara's mood. 'Teeny bit hungover?'

'Why do you say that?' Lara could do froideur when she wanted to and she was giving off icy vibes right now.

'Wasn't it Alex's birthday party last night?'

Lara glanced at her as if she was surprised she had

remembered.

'I only popped in,' she said in a way that suggested the subject was closed. Perhaps they'd had a ding-dong – shame. Alex Ford was the best-looking bloke at the *Chronicle* and the Deputy Editor to boot, something of a catch by anyone's standards. Certainly, everyone in the office fancied him, even the married ones. Gayle in Features had been in dedicated pursuit of Alex for at least a year, even joining his gym, although Stella wasn't sure Alex was even aware of Gayle's feelings. There were rumours of a girlfriend – Alice, Alicia? – but no one had ever seen her. Besides, it was so obvious that he liked Lara, although Stella wasn't sure it was mutual. After all, if it was, wouldn't something have happened by now? Stella had always been curious to know but now was not the time to start digging. Lara was all business this morning, updating Stella on the events in Monte Carlo, particularly the 'Inner Circle' names Jago Bain had given them. She clearly wasn't in the mood to speculate on Alex's romantic status.

Instead Stella updated Lara on her family drama. Her mother had gone 'batshit' when she had heard that Stella had 'left poor Glenda in the lurch' by walking out of Jimmy's café. She'd ranted about gift horses and Jimmy's golden heart until Stella had finally snapped and told her how much salary Lara was paying her.

'You said I was giving you *how* much? Does she think I'm a billionaire?'

'Yeah, she does,' said Stella apologetically. 'Sorry boss, it was the only way I could shut her up.'

They stopped outside a tall, narrow building with ancient brickwork. It had once been some sort of mill or workshop as there was a pulley system and access doors on the second floor. It had, however, all been sandblasted and repointed, with only a little of the grittiness deliberately retained.

'Looks like your friend Eduardo's come down in the world,' said Stella, grinning at the thought of a regal Spaniard in a hipster flat.

'Eduardo doesn't actually live here,' said Lara. 'I think he's got a place in Kensington. This is just the collective's new office.'

The door buzzed and they stepped inside. The building's interior had also been stripped and buffed, with exposed brickwork and iron joists painted tasteful shades of green and grey. Even the entrance door was slick, a single sheet of glass with 'Le Caché' artfully etched down the side. It all said, 'We're edgy, but we're serious,' which Stella supposed was the whole idea. Whatever, it was cool. And… OMG.

Stella's heart fluttered as she caught sight of the Le Caché guys.

When Stella first came down to London, she had a romantic idea – that all journalists would look like Robert Redford in All The Presidents Men, or at the very least, like Johnny Depp in Fear and Loathing. They did not. Journalists were generally pudgy, pasty and losing their hair; they didn't even dress well, seeming to favour the colour beige. Stella had once even seen someone wear a cardigan.

But Stefan and Eduardo were exactly as she had

imagined writers to be. Eduardo was tall, dark and had hair like a Spanish prince – in fact, wasn't he *actually* a Spanish prince? Whatever – he was hot, even if he looked like the sort of man who owned a suede brush. And Stefan had those continental cheekbones and Euro-chic thing going on.

Stefan introduced himself to Stella, then his eyes flicked across to Lara's and she mouthed 'hi', accompanied by a bashful smile. Stella caught the blush on Lara's cheeks and her instinct tingled; they'd either had sex or would do very soon.

'Come in, come in,' said Stefan, leading them into a high open-plan space lit by long windows. 'Sorry about the chaos. We only got the furniture yesterday.'

It was unruly, certainly, with boxes stacked here and there, some of them open and half-unpacked, but there was a sense of purpose here.

'I've brought breakfast,' said Stella, holding up the tray.

'So kind of you,' said Eduardo, graciously taking the offerings through to a little bar area to one side of the room. There was already a huge silver coffee machine sitting on the counter, but Eduardo still fussed around putting the sandwiches on plates, flattering Stella for her thoughtfulness. Briefly she entertained the idea of her and Eduardo, even picturing asking him back to her house-share with T-shirts on the floor and damp on the walls. *Could happen.* Unlikely, yes. *But never say never.*

'So shall we discuss the Inner Circle?' said Eduardo, leading them over to the brand new designer sofas which were soft and white and still had a showroom smell. To Stella, there was something miraculous about a new sofa. Growing up in a rented house where the sofa had been used by the six previous tenants did that to you.

Eduardo had propped up a series of whiteboards on easels, each with a name written at the top.

'Richard Stewart (US/Miami)', 'Donald Van Leder (S. Africa)', 'Bernard Gander (London), 'Philippe Marsaud (Geneva), 'Eugene Dre (Caymans).'

They had neat notes beneath each name with print-outs attached to the boards with little magnets.

'This is Le Caché in action,' he said, with a hint of pride. 'We have members and contacts in each of these guys' home territories, so we have been able to connect them all together. Stella was impressed. In less than 48 hours they had names, places and connections. The collective was like Interpol for investigative journalism.

'So where does the trafficking come in?' she asked.

Eduardo gave her a nod, which Stella took as a good sign. It was better than a laugh, anyway.

'When you say trafficking, people think of drugs or the sex trade. But human trafficking is getting an illicit workforce and exploiting them, which is what is happening here, getting children to work in the cobalt mine. Modern slavery by any other name.'

Stella thought about her own childhood in the schemes: there'd been violence, deprivation, it'd been a place where school dinners had been the only meal many kids would get all day. It had been tough, sure, but nobody had to dig with their bare hands. There had been a chance.

Next Lara recounted her conversation with Josie Bourne. Stella felt a flush of pride as she watched her speak: Lara was assured, concise, impressive. Since the *Chronicle* had dispensed with her services, Stella had seriously begun to question her career choices. Her friend Minnie was making five figures a month on Instagram, while Stella had to go to the corner shop to pre-pay her electric. But this reminded her of why she was here, why she had come down to London: she had come to learn. And who better to learn from than Lara Stone?

'Do you know who this Mike is?' asked Eduardo, when Lara had finished.

Lara shook her head.

'No, but look at this.'

Lara reached into her bag and pulled out the Post-it note that they had found in Sandrine's apartment.

Helen
Michael
Jonathon

'At first I read it as 'Helen Michael' – one name – but we couldn't find anyone by that name linked to Jonathon Meyer. Now I think these are three separate names.'

'"Get rid of her" – that's what this guy said?' said Eduardo. 'And this Josie thought he meant "kill her"?'

'Josie wasn't sure,' admitted Lara. 'This was at a party, the music was loud…'

'So it could have been anything,' said Eduardo.

Eduardo had a bluntness Stella had seen in many newsroom editors and execs. From the outside it seemed rude, but there was a method in it too: each detail had to be examined from every angle or 'tested to destruction' as Alex used to put it. However, Stella could smell something more here: the first whiff of a power struggle.

'Are there any Mikes or Michaels in the inner circle?' said Stella, doing her best to support Lara's thesis.

'Not that we know of,' said Eduardo, shaking his head decisively.

'Look, I think the Kanjomo mine is the strongest lead we have. It's an actual link from Meyer to trafficking and that's what Sandrine said the story was about.'

Stella saw Lara's eyes narrow, but even she had to agree that Eduardo had a point. Stella spoke up again.

'If Sandrine had the story of trafficking in the Kanjomo mine, I see how that might put her in danger, but why kill Meyer? He co-owned the mine – and he threw Jago off the boat because he wouldn't help with it.'

Eduardo let out a frustrated sigh.

'One, we don't know for sure that Jonathon Meyer had invested in the mine and two, we don't know for sure that he was murdered.'

'We don't know anything for sure, Eduardo,' said Lara, her own frustration plain. 'That doesn't mean we shouldn't do anything.'

Eduardo looked at her.

'We're not doing nothing, Lara,' he said. 'There's a flight to Kinshasa via Brussels leaving this afternoon and I'm booked onto it.'

'You're going to the *Congo*?' said Lara in surprise.

Eduardo nodded. 'A Le Caché member based in Nairobi is flying out to meet me. He's a photojournalist. We need photographic evidence of what is going on at the mine.'

Stella looked at Lara. If she had been in a bad mood this morning, this definitely wasn't going to help; Eduardo seemed to be sidelining Lara's efforts.

'And I'm going to Geneva,' said Stefan, with a hint of apology. 'We have a contact there who knows Philippe Marsaud.'

Lara looked at them both, then nodded to herself.

'Well, it looks like you've both got it all in hand,' she said, picking up her bag. The tension was so high, Stella could almost hear a hum.

Eduardo took a step towards Lara. 'Are you…?' he began but Lara silenced him with a shake of her head.

'I don't care who does what or who goes where,' she said. 'So long as we find out what's going on. We should all remember that this is about Sandrine, not about anyone else.'

She looked at Eduardo, then down at her watch.

'Anyway, I've got to go. I have lunch with Simon Meyer. Let's see if he knows anything for sure.' She looked at Eduardo as she said it, emphasising the last two words, then walked out, leaving the room in silence.

Chapter Twenty

LARA WALKED QUICKLY, turning corners left and right. *Where the hell is it?* She had parked her bike on a side street off Brick Lane and for the life of her, Lara couldn't remember which one. They all looked the same; narrow stone terraces with the same doorsteps and cast iron drainpipes. She stopped on a corner and took a deep breath, trying to calm her whirring mind. Eduardo had wound her up with his superior attitude, but actually, Lara had meant what she said. If Eduardo's thread had a better chance of getting to the bottom of Sandrine's death, then she was happy for him to go ahead. Even so, she still believed Meyer's yacht was the key to it all – and she was determined to prove it.

She turned as she heard urgent footsteps behind her.

'Stefan? What's up?'

'You walk fast,' he gasped, out of breath. 'I didn't think you were going to leave so soon.'

Lara shrugged.

'I have a thirty-minute window with Simon Meyer so I've got to shoot. He's fitting me in before seeing a client in Mayfair.'

'Great, sure. I just wanted to check you were okay.'

Lara gave a half-smile. Even with pink cheeks, she couldn't deny how good he looked. The Monaco tan brought out the blue in his eyes; he looked more like an off-duty surfer than an investigative reporter, even with a pencil tucked in the top pocket of his shirt. Which, now she noticed it, was adorable. Geeky, but adorable.

'I called you last night,' said Stefan. Lara nodded. She'd got his message but hadn't been in the mood to speak to him. Alex and the ring had unsettled her. Another friend gone.

'I'm sorry, Stefan,' she said quickly. 'I went to meet Josie, then I had to go to my friend's birthday thing… I just went home and flopped.'

He nodded, like he understood.

'And the meeting,' he pointed his chin back in the direction of the office. 'I'm sorry if Eduardo sounded harsh. He gets like that.'

'Seriously, Stefan, I understand. I'm a big girl; it's not the first time I've had a tricky editorial meeting.'

'So come to Geneva with me,' he said suddenly.

'Geneva?' she laughed. 'Why?'

'Why not?'

'Because I'm sure you've got the whole thing covered. You don't need me.'

'It's not a matter of need, it's a matter of want,' he smiled. 'The hotel I've booked isn't fancy but the lake is beautiful at this time of year and I know this great bistro…'

Lara gave a soft laugh. There was a time when she would have jumped at the chance to go to Geneva with a sexy, talented and adorable Dutchman. In fact, she wouldn't have thought twice about it. So why was she hesitating now? Was it because she liked Stefan more than she wanted to admit? If she went off on a romantic mini-break to Switzerland, they might well come back as a couple. And then where would she be? Happy?

'Lara, when was the last time you had fun?'

'Saturday night,' she said, without having to think about it.

Stefan grinned back.

'So…?'

She put her hands on her hips.

'Look, Stefan. We're in the middle of a story and we're working together. What would Eduardo say if he knew about us.'

'Eduardo guessed.'

That stopped her. She felt strangely uncomfortable, like hearing that your dad knew you were sleeping around.

'Alright, so no Geneva. How about I take you for dinner when I get back? Is that okay?'

'Okay then,' she said quietly. 'That would be nice. How long do you think you'll be away for?'

'I don't know. But I will be hurrying back.'

He stepped forward and kissed her tenderly. Lara thought of the engagement ring at her feet the night before, then put her hand on the back of Stefan's neck, losing herself in his soft lips. Then she pulled away.

‘It’s a date,’ she said. She could feel his eyes on her all the way down the street.

GREYS WAS A Mayfair dining institution, at least if you were the sort of person who wore a three-piece suit and believed Eton had been the best days of your life. The décor certainly reminded Lara of the headmistress’s study at her boarding school, all dark wood panelling and gilt-framed portraits; in Greys they were of its most famous patrons, most with drooping moustaches and stiff collars. Still, the little booths with their red leather banquettes and crisp linens did look tempting and Lara was now wishing she hadn’t turned down Stella’s bacon sandwich earlier that morning. But she wasn’t here to eat, she was here to speak to Simon Meyer. This was business.

Lara had contacted him at his Cobham office, but Simon had sent her a message saying he was in London and could squeeze her in for a drink. He was perched on a stool by the bar nursing a glass of something she suspected was gin.

‘My client gets here at one o’clock, but he’s always late,’ said Simon, standing to greet her with a formal handshake.

‘Snack?’ he asked, noticing Lara’s eyes following a passing waitress with a bread basket. ‘The olives are also very good.’

Lara had once been embedded with The Royal Marines, who had taught her that in the field, the rule was 'eat when you can' because you never knew when you'd get another chance. Lara was unlikely to find herself pinned down in a foxhole, but the principle was sound. She helped herself to the silver bowl in front of her.

'So how was Monaco?' asked Simon.

'Useful. Thanks for connecting me to Tom. I also spoke to Jonathon's girlfriend Josie.'

'Jon had a girlfriend?' said Simon, sipping his gin. 'I didn't think commitment was his thing. Does she live in Monaco?'

'No, she's Canadian. A model. I don't think it was serious. Or at least, I didn't get the feeling Jonathon had been treating it that way.'

'Ah,' he said, as if it was no surprise.

Lara leant forward.

'Simon, I need to pick your brains. Do you know any of Jonathon's friends or clients called Mike or Michael?'

Simon shook his head slowly.

'As I've said to you, we weren't close. Our lives were very different and I didn't know Jon's social circle. And of course, he kept his client base closely under wraps.'

'As executor of his estate, do you think you could find out?'

Simon sighed.

'I suppose I could, yes.'

'But you don't want to?'

He rubbed his face wearily.

'Look, as you can imagine, the thought of administering Jon's affairs is terrifying. Like going into a bear cave, you never know what you'll find there. There's his apartment to sort out, the sale of the yacht, winding up his businesses – God, the paperwork.'

'I suppose it will be worthwhile, though?' said Lara, wiping her oily fingers on a napkin.

Simon raised an eyebrow. 'Is that your way of asking if I am his main beneficiary?'

Lara waited.

'Yes, I am. But I strongly suspect it will be something of a poisoned chalice. Not only will I be tied up in legal disputes with his investors for years to come, there's a damn good chance we will end up with a deficit.'

'As in there will be no money left?'

'Lara, you've seen *Pandora*. It's a flash yacht moored in one of the most expensive marinas on earth. Does that look like the purchase of a man who carefully plans his finances?'

Lara chuckled.

'No, I suppose not.'

Simon exhaled loudly.

'Jon was an all-on-red kind of guy. I would be surprised if there is a single penny left at the end of it.'

Lara smiled, but she thought it a strange thing to say. After all, the media had referred to Jonathon Meyer as a multi-millionaire. Some had even referred to him as a billionaire. There had to be something left, even if it was only the yacht.

Simon signalled to the barman for another drink.

'So who is this Michael?' he asked.

'That's what we need to find out. Josie – the girlfriend – overheard a conversation between Jon and this guy "Mike". She said they seemed to know each other well. Perhaps they were old friends?'

Simon took a sip of his gin and looked thoughtful.

'Our father's best friend was called Mike but he must be over eighty now, if he's still alive. It's a popular name…'

Lara leaned forward.

'This Mike was asking Jonathon for a favour: a big favour. He thought Jon would do it as he owed him. Apparently, he said Jon owed him everything.'

Simon Meyer looked at her.

'Then I wonder if it was Michael Sachs.'

Lara felt her back stiffen.

'Michael Sachs? Who's he?'

'Big-time financier. Something of a socialite and philanthropist; Michael and his wife Victoria are always in the party pages of society magazines – a very impressive man. And in the early days, Michael Sachs was a mentor to Jon.'

Lara tried to contain her growing excitement.

'So how did Jonathon get to know him?

'Through Sachs's son, actually. After Jon left Cambridge he moved to West London and did odd jobs to get by. Being a maths guy, it's no surprise he fell into tutoring and did some for Michael Sachs's little kid. Jon used to tell me how much he liked going round to their house – some stucco pile in Kensington.'

Simon smiled fondly.

'Apparently, Jon turned the boy's maths around in

three months – typical, really. The family were so grateful, Mr. Sachs got Jon a job at one of the banks. Jonathon didn't stay long with them, but it was how he got his break, how he got into finance.'

Lara had assumed that the 'Mike' from the *Pandora* was a current business associate; she hadn't considered it might be someone from his past. In fact, if the whole thing hinged on 'you owe me', then a debt from the start of Meyer's career would make perfect sense.

'What was the favour? Do you know?'

Lara looked down at the empty olive bowl.

'I don't know. Not yet.'

Simon looked at her with cynical grey eyes.

'Nothing?'

Lara didn't want to tell him – didn't want to be the one to undermine Simon's memory of his brother – but if she stood any chance of getting Simon's help in going through Jonathon's paperwork, he needed to know what was going on. Slowly, she began to tell him about the Inner Circle syndicate and the allegation about the Kanjomo mine. Simon's face clouded.

'You're suggesting that Jon was trying to cover up child labour?'

'No, I'm saying that someone may have asked him to. As far as we know, Jonathon is entirely innocent.'

'As far as we know', repeated Simon, his face beginning to colour. 'And yet you are already insinuating some wrong-doing here, based on a barely-heard conversation.'

Immediately, Lara knew she had made a mistake

telling him so much.

'Simon, I'm just trying to help you.'

'No Lara, you are not,' he replied. 'You are helping yourself. You are trying to write a headline-grabbing story.'

'Story? I don't even work for the *Chronicle* anymore.'

'Even so, your approach is to put together a narrative, is it not? Good guys, bad guys, heroes and villains. And my brother is being cast as a villain.'

She began to object, but Simon put up his hand like a stop-sign.

'I said I would help you look into Jonathon's death in good faith. If his mugging wasn't a random attack, I want to know that too – perhaps even look for justice. But not at any price. Not if it means my brother's reputation is destroyed in the process.'

'Even if the allegations are true?'

Simon Meyer fell quiet, then looked at his watch.

'I think you'd better go,' he said finally. 'My client should be here any minute.'

'Simon, I didn't mean to upset you.'

He looked at her with an even gaze.

'And yet, Miss Stone, that is exactly what you have done.'

Standing out in Dover Street, Lara pulled out her phone and tapped Michael Sachs into the search bar. Her eyes opened wide: Sachs was a handsome, silver-haired man with a wide smile that oozed confidence. Lara scanned the headlines:

'New York philanthropist opens arts centre'

'Sachs donate dialysis machine to children's hospital'

'Queen of the fundraisers pays tribute to her husband'

She clicked onto the business sites:

'Sachs Capital invests in green energy site'

'Michael Sachs in merger talks with Johnstone Fund'

Michael Sachs wasn't exactly hiding in the shadows, was he? But Lara felt the tingle. She had the scent. There was something here, she was sure of it. She flipped over to her contacts and dialled up Stella's number.

'I have Michael.'

She could almost hear Stella's mouth drop open.

'*The* Michael?'

'His name's Michael Sachs.' Lara smiled into the phone. 'And he could just be our man.'

Chapter Twenty-One

STELLA WAS COASTING downhill, but she kept pedalling anyway, increasing her speed, enjoying the rush of wind in her face.

Who knew that cycling could offer such fun? She zipped through an amber light and left a sooty red bus standing. In fact, who knew that the Capital was so hilly? It was only by travelling by bicycle that you got a sense of the ups and downs of the city. When you were encased in steel and glass or shooting along underground, it all felt like it was flat, but London was a bowl, everything heading down towards the river.

Not everything, she thought, standing on the pedals to get up an incline and around the roundabout at Sloane Square. Seeing a snarl-up at the entrance to the King's Road, she jinked left in front of the tube, rolling down through the millionaires' terraces towards Royal Hospital Road.

Stella put in another burst, her excitement rising in anticipation of getting to Lara's houseboat. Because Stella had news: big news. She had found Helen. The Helen from the Post-it note Lara had pulled from Sandrine's pocket in Paris: the Helen that connected Sandrine and Michael Sachs.

She dismounted the bike at the wharf, clattered through the gate, bumping it up *Misty*'s gang-plank and propping it against the side of the boat. Through a porthole window she could see Lara in the living space, on her laptop sipping a cup of tea.

She rapped on the window and Lara came to open the door.

'Sorry, Boss,' panted Stella. 'Boris bike… all the way… from Islington…'

'Islington? What were you doing there?'

Stella took a deep breath, then blew it out.

'I found Helen,' she said.

Lara beckoned with both hands. Inside, she clattered around the kitchen making the tea while Stella caught her breath and gave her the run-down of what she had found out.

'We want to connect a Helen with Michael Sachs, right?' said Stella. 'So I had a root around Sachs Capital, put the company into a networking site and found Helen Driver. Her CV says she spent two years as PA to Michael Sachs. I called the offices who told me Helen left a couple of months ago. So, another little dig around on the electoral roll and I find her in Islington, so I popped up there and knocked on the door. She was at home.'

Lara listened in silence, but Stella could see she was pleased.

'She was happy to talk to you?' asked Lara.

'No, not at all,' said Stella. 'In fact, she was quite freaked out if I'm honest.'

Never come back without the story. That had been

Lara's first piece of advice when Stella had started working with her, so Stella had flashed one of her old *Chronicle* business cards and told Helen she was doing a piece entitled 'His Girl Friday', profiling PAs to top businessmen.

'Quick thinking,' said Lara. 'Very tabloid.'

Stella could tell this was meant to be a compliment. She beamed.

'Anyway, I let Helen waffle on about how vital she was to Michael Sachs, but as she spoke, I got the distinct feeling that Helen didn't have much of a clue what Sachs did. He was a decent boss and the pay was good, but he spent a lot of time abroad so she didn't even see him every day.'

Helen could feel Lara's scepticism growing.

'Why did she leave?' Lara asked.

Stella pulled a face.

'New job which starts next month. She's on gardening leave.'

She watched Lara mull it over. Stella knew how badly her boss wanted a breakthrough. Over the past seven days they had seemed to find so many pieces of the jigsaw, but none of them seemed to want to form into a recognisable picture.

'Did you ask her if Sandrine had tried to contact Michael?'

'I did,' said Stella. 'But she hadn't heard of Sandrine Legard.'

Lara looked disappointed – as well she might.

'I did find out one thing though,' said Stella. 'Michael was having an affair.'

Lara looked up.

'Did Helen tell you that?'

'Not in so many words. She said Michael was a brilliant businessman but you wouldn't want to be his wife.'

'Why not?'

Stella sipped her tea.

'She wouldn't be pushed much more on it but she did say that Victoria Sachs, the wife, was a lovely, elegant woman but it didn't stop him getting "distracted."'

Lara was quiet for a few moments, then stood up and wiped her hands on her jeans.

'It's not her,' she said finally. 'Much as I want it to be, Helen Driver isn't the Helen from the note.'

Stella felt her shoulders sag with disappointment. Lara was right. She'd been so excited to find a Helen with such a close link to Michael Sachs it had blinded her to the fact that she hadn't revealed much.

'I'm sorry' said Stella. 'It wasn't much use, was it?'

'Don't be sorry,' said Lara, her expression softening. 'You got a stranger to talk. That's no small thing – and someone whose loyalties were to her boss too,'

Stella shrugged off the compliment. She knew that talking to people was her superpower; she'd always found it easy. As an only child, it was a skill you had to cultivate and as a teenager, when her mum used to give her a fiver to stay out of the flat because she had a boyfriend round, Stella had developed a wide circle of loyal friends and neighbours who kept her off the streets – literally. But she'd also known that Helen Driver would be happy to talk without too much persuasion. On the surface a PA was a loyal and sometimes fierce guard-dog, but Stella instinctively knew that loyalties only ran so deep when you spent your days booking private jets, luxury hotels or ordering bottles of wine that cost more than your annual wage.

Lara opened a drawer and handed Stella a wedge of takeaway menus. 'Choose anything,' she said. 'The pizza's good.'

Stella looked down at the glossy brochures, feeling even more dispirited. She didn't want to say she couldn't afford a gourmet calzone and she didn't want to assume that Lara would pay for it either. Lara was already paying Stella's wages from her own pocket with little prospect of making anything back from the investigation.

'I'm not that hungry,' said Stella.

'I'm getting one and it's two-for-one night,' she said.

Stella had the unsettling feeling that Lara saw right through her.

'You sure?'

Lara nodded.

'Then I'll try the hoi sin duck pizza. I've never had duck on a pizza before.'

Lara laughed and picked up the phone to make the order. When she'd finished, she beckoned Stella into the next room.

'While we're waiting for the food, come and look

at this.'

Stella followed her to the spare room.

'Wow', she gasped, 'You've been busy.'

One wall was covered with photos, maps, and print-outs of news items. It was a visual guide joining all of the threads of the case together. In a Hollywood movie, there would be surveillance pictures taken with a long lens, mugshots from the FBI files and the huge map of New York or Los Angeles with each crime scene joined together by a latticework of bright red thread. Lara had made do with smudged pictures from her ancient ink-jet printer and words – 'Meyer', 'Yacht', 'Inner Circle?' – scrawled on lurid yellow and pink sticky notes.

It was all a bit ad hoc but it certainly worked as a summary of the evidence they had gathered so far. More than anything, it showed how committed Lara was to the project. This was hours, days' worth of effort, especially considering Lara had been to Paris and Monte Carlo in the interim.

'Impressive,' said Stella. 'It's not quite *Mission Impossible*, but it does cover what we know.'

'Which isn't much,' said Lara, sounding glum. 'You know, looking at this, maybe Eduardo's right. Perhaps chasing Helen and Michael is a bum steer. After all, it was just one Post-it note in Sandrine's pocket. Maybe it was nothing.'

Stella gave Lara a sideways glance. Her boss looked exhausted, which wasn't surprising given she had clearly sacrificed sleep to work on the story, but Stella knew she needed to rally her.

'Remember that piece of advice you gave me when I started at the *Chronicle*?'

Lara smiled.

'Which bit? Don't drink at lunch? Always use spell-check?'

'You told me to listen,' said Stella firmly. 'You said most journos write a list of questions and stick rigidly to them, then wonder why they don't get good answers. It's the same here: we need to stop and listen to what the evidence is actually saying.' Stella nodded towards the wall chart. 'The answer is up there.'

Lara folded her arms and looked at the wall, deep in thought.

'What do rich men fear the most?' she mused.

'Losing everything,' replied Stella.

Lara grabbed her computer and sat down on the bed. Stella grinned, glad to see her boss back in the game.

'We need to make a list,' she said, tapping away. 'All of the business interests Meyer and Sachs were involved with. See if we can find any that were going under or in danger of a takeover.'

Stella opened her own computer, smiling to herself: this was her chance to shine. She could admit she sometimes felt out of her depth with investigations but this was the one place she felt confident. Lara's training had been old school: you read the cuttings, you phoned people up, you went and knocked on their door, but Stella was a digital native and for her, the answer to every question had always been a click away. It was just a matter of negotiating your way through the dark maze of the Net. It could be a rabbit warren of dead ends and distractions, but Stella felt it was the width of information that the internet could provide that gave twenty-first century reporters the edge.

They worked in silence, even after the pizza arrived. Stella had headphones on, picking at a slice of garlic bread as she scrolled through the data. It quickly became clear that the world of high finance – funds and money management – was quite secretive. There was very little detail about Meyer's investment business other than it was super-exclusive and invitation-only. Sachs's business was less opaque – but only just. There were more column inches given over to his philanthropic work – it seemed that everything Sachs touched turned to gold.

'Either Michael Sachs's hands are completely clean, or he's very good at hiding the fingerprints,' said Lara, without looking up.

Stella nodded, looking more closely at the picture of Michael Sachs that happened to be up on her screen, his arm around his wife Victoria, elegant in her Chanel and pearls. Stella read the caption:

ImpactAid benefit dinner, The Pierre hotel,
New York. Victoria Sachs, founder.

Stella pulled up the ImpactAid website. According to the 'About Us' section, the charity was founded by Michael and Victoria Sachs twenty years earlier, although Michael was no longer listed as a board member or trustee. Stella scanned the charity's good works: they had built clinics, dug wells and worked on literary programmes in Africa, then after the earthquake in Haiti, ImpactAid switched their focus to recovery efforts there.

Intrigued, Stella began researching the charity. To her surprise, Stella discovered that relief efforts in Haiti had been attracting a certain amount of flak in the press. Despite billions in foreign aid being poured into the country, many Haitians were still living in shanty towns with no running water, the implication being that misuse of funds, poor governance and political turmoil was widespread. ImpactAid hadn't specifically been singled out, but Stella found it sad that so little progress had been made to help the Haitian people. Suddenly she stopped, fingers frozen on the keyboard.

'British Aid Worker Killed.'

'Lara, look at this,' she said, swivelling her screen around.

'Check out this news piece. An ImpactAid worker was killed in Haiti in a hit and run. Look at the name of the dead girl…'

'Helen,' said Lara.

Stella could feel her heart bumping. Something was telling her this was significant. She was already typing, searching up more stories relating to the girl's death. *Helen Groves… hit by a car while walking back to the ImpactAid bunkhouse…*

Lara was back on her own computer and called out as she found another online news item.

Grieving Parents Blast Charity

The parents of an aid worker killed in Port-au-Prince have hit out at the lack of answers from police about their daughter's death. 'Nothing can bring our Helen back,' said Ian Groves, father of the 22-year old Scot, killed in a hit-and-run incident. 'But we want justice to be served.'

'Charities such as ImpactAid are happy to have young people fly over to work for them, but when something goes wrong, they must help us find answers.'

Helen was hit by a car and died at the scene. Police were unable to trace the driver.

'No one wants to listen. It's like they just want to forget Helen ever existed.'

Lara looked at Stella.

'What's the date? When did Helen die?'

Stella scrolled to the top of the news item.

'Two weeks before Sandrine died.'

Their eyes met.

'We have to speak to her parents.'

'They're in Edinburgh,' said Stella, who had already found them online. 'I can look up their number.'

Lara looked at her watch. Then she strode over to a cupboard and grabbed her spare helmet.

'Do it on the way,' she said, shoving the helmet at Stella. 'If we hurry, we can just make the sleeper train.'

Chapter Twenty-Two

AT TEN TO seven in the morning, Edinburgh felt deserted. The sleeper train had delivered them like magic into the centre of the Scottish capital and as Lara and Stella rode up the escalators onto Princes Street, it had the air of a place which had yet to wake up. Lara could sympathise. A combination of their spontaneous dash up to Euston, the excitement of being in an actual cabin with an actual shower cubicle – and the whisky selection in the dining car had meant that they had stayed up far too late. Lara squinted in the grey light and raised a hand to cover her eyes. Stella had, with her customary efficiency, arranged to have a hire car delivered to the Balmoral Hotel right next to the station and the moment she had the keys, Lara slid gratefully into the driver's seat and flipped the sun-visor down.

She was running on empty, drained physically and emotionally; Lara knew she was close to the edge. Her skin felt thin, her eyes raw, but even through it all, Lara was struck by the bleak beauty of the city, the sun shining off the grey granite, all the buildings tall and thin, crowded together, spooky burrows in between.

They drove the hire car out towards Merchiston, a

suburb to the south west of the city. It was made up of large stone houses, affluent and respectable.

'This is the place,' said Stella, checking the map. As they pulled up, Lara caught a face at the window, pale, fleeting, before it pulled back.

'D'you think we'll get a warm welcome?' asked Stella, catching the movement. It wasn't something they'd really had time to consider before they'd bought their tickets.

'Too late to back out now,' whispered Lara, taking a breath, reminded of her early days as a reporter doorstepping. Hammering on doors, trying to get exclusive interviews – it was grim, unpleasant work, but it was a rite of passage when you were a young journalist trying to impress the editor and win your spurs. Lara knew she'd been sent out onto the streets more than most, however. They were testing her mettle, seeing if Nicholas Avery's niece was up to the job. Hoping she would fail.

The door opened as they walked along the path. A woman stood there, early fifties, shoulder-length beige hair, flecked with grey. She looked as tired as Lara felt.

'Lara?' she asked.

'Yes,' said Lara, showing her press card. 'Mrs. Groves? This is my colleague Stella. Thank you for seeing us.'

A man appeared at her shoulder. He was tall and lean, older than the woman, but not by much. His was a more genial face. In happier times, Lara supposed you'd find him at Wimbledon, a panama on his head and a Pimm's in his hand.

'Come in, come in,' he said with more warmth than his wife, 'I'm Ian, this is Callie.'

They were ushered into a pin-neat living room. Lara found herself picturing a teenage Helen sitting on the sofa, flicking through a magazine or her phone, wishing she were miles away from here.

'So you said on the phone that you were looking into Helen's…' Mrs. Groves stumbled on the word, then recovered. '…Her passing?'

Lara nodded. 'I was wondering if you could tell me what happened?'

'You don't know?' said the woman, glancing at her husband.

'We assumed you had some information for us,' said Ian, jumping in.

'I am investigating the circumstances of Helen's accident. It's part of a bigger piece about the dangers of young women abroad, but yes, we'd also like to find out more about what happened to your daughter specifically.'

While Helen's mother went through to the kitchen to make them tea, Ian Groves told them how he'd flown out to Port-au-Prince within hours of a policeman turning up at their door to tell them about Helen's tragic accident. He described the frustrations of the delays and the countless meetings he'd had with the Haitian police and Embassy officials.

'Helen had died instantly at the scene,' he said, glancing towards the kitchen door. 'I went to the place where it happened. It was a quiet part of town. It was no wonder there were no witnesses. I know none of this will bring Helen back, but I just want to ask whoever it was: How could you do that and drive away?'

Callie Groves came in holding a tray. A cup was rattling against the teapot. Best china for the guests. They were grieving, suffering and yet they still needed to keep up appearances.

'Why was Helen in Haiti in the first place?' asked Lara.

Callie was concentrating, pouring the tea, but she looked up, her dark eyes fierce.

'Rebecca Robertson,' she said tersely. 'If it hadn't been for that girl…'

Her husband's gentle hand reached out to touch his wife's wrist.

'Rebecca is – was – Helen's best friend,' said Ian. 'Ever since middle school. Inseparable, they were. Whatever the latest fad was, whatever the fashion, they'd be dressing up together. They egged each other on.'

'And it was Rebecca's idea to go to Haiti?'

'Rebecca announced she was having a gap year after university. So Helen decided she wanted one too. She liked causes, you see, causes and marches. Always raising money or signing a petition. Her dream was to be a human rights lawyer. So before we knew it, they were both off to Haiti to work as volunteers for ImpactAid.'

Lara saw Callie shake her head in disgust. Lara could see the split here. The mother hating the cause that had taken her baby away, the father who wanted

Helen's death to have some meaning. Neither of them were going to find an easy peace.

'Was Helen happy there?'

'Oh yes. She sent emails when she could,' said Ian, smiling softly. 'She was proud to be helping people. But she was also pleased to be coming home.'

'Oh?' said Lara. 'I didn't know she was due to come back.'

Ian took out his phone, then fished out his reading glasses from his top pocket.

'Now what did she say?' he muttered to himself, scrolling through his messages.

He paused as if he were about to read it out but then handed over his phone.

'Her last message,' he said. Lara read the text quickly and then slowed down to take it in once more. Not just reading the words but trying to imagine what Helen was thinking when she wrote it.

Hello from Haiti! Still having a ball, although I could do with less of the heat. And the mozzies! And I'm yearning for a glass of milk, it's one thing no one ever has out here. Becky has a boyfriend (not sure it's serious!) MY big news…drum roll…I'm coming home. Things have got a little complicated recently. I think my time is done here.

Anyway, I will let you know when I've got flights and stuff. Can't wait to see you all. SOON!

Love ya, Hxxxxx

'When was this sent?' asked Lara.

'The week before the accident.'

'"*Things have got a little complicated.*" Have you any clue what that means?'

'I've no idea,' said Ian. 'We spoke to her a week before the email. She sounded a little distracted but didn't indicate anything was wrong.'

'Did you show the police?'

'Of course, but they didn't think it was significant. And obviously, no one in the Edinburgh police wanted to know – why would they? It happened on the other side of the world, not on Princes Street.'

'Was Rebecca still in Haiti at the time?'

'Yes, she was,' said Callie.

'And was she with Helen at the time of the accident?'

'No. She was out with her boyfriend.' The woman snorted, as if this was some deliberate oversight.

'Rebecca was very shaken up by it, obviously,' said Ian. 'She left Haiti within the week and came home.'

Out of the corner of her eye, she could see Stella glance at her.

'I'd like to speak to Rebecca if I could. Does she live in Edinburgh?'

'She did,' said Ian. 'But I don't think she's here now.'

'Why do you say that?'

'Because she didn't come to the funeral,' said Callie, her voice still terse.

'Do you have a contact number for her?'

'You won't get through. We tried to call her before the funeral, but the number appears to be disconnected. Her parents said Becky had gone up north and wanted some alone time.'

Lara saw Ian look across at his wife.

'If you think it would be helpful to speak to her, I think I know where she is,' he said.

'Ian, please.'

Mr Groves turned towards her, a flash of anger finally showing through. 'No, Callie. I've checked up on Miss Stone. She's a good journalist, fair. I think she can help us.'

Callie stood up and clattered the tea things onto the tray. They all sat in silence until she carried it out to the kitchen. The tension felt so out of place in this neat, homely space.

Undeterred, Ian went to a desk at the far end of the room and took an envelope from a drawer. When he returned he handed it to Lara.

'Becky sent a card. It's got an Ullapool postmark.'

Lara looked up.

'You think that's where she is?'

Ian Groves nodded.

'Becky's aunt has a rental cottage up there. The girls went a couple of summers ago.'

'Do you have the address?'

'Got a phone number, but I can't guarantee she'll be there. Or if she'll talk to you.'

Lara stood up and tried to give him a smile.

'I think it's worth the risk, don't you?'

Chapter Twenty-Three

ULLAPOOL WAS A long way in the rain. It was a long way whatever the weather – the hire car's sat-nav had reckoned over four hours non-stop driving on a good day – but it seemed even further with the grey clouds sitting right on top of the road. The drizzle leaving Edinburgh had been steady up until the Cairngorms, then it had really started coming down. The windscreen wipers had been on 'full' since Aviemore and they had been crawling along, terrified of meeting a tractor coming at them around a blind bend. That, or finding a herd of shaggy Highland cattle sitting in the middle of the road. But then every half an hour or so, the rain would stop as if someone had flipped a switch and the wind would lift the fog away and they would find themselves descending into a gorgeous valley rich with heather, or travelling along the edge of a gorse-trimmed loch. Lara would slam on the brakes and they would gaze in genuine wonder, feeling tiny in the midst of such beauty – then all too soon, Mother Nature would drop the blinds and they would be back in the murk, the windscreen thick with rain.

'Have you got any signal?' asked Stella. Every

now and then a bar would pop onto a phone and they would scrabble to send or receive a message.

'Nothing,' said Lara. 'Not since I heard from Marion.' Sandrine's parents had returned to Corsica, but had kept Lara up to date on the plans for the funeral. They were being kind, of course, keeping Lara involved, but with each missive it became more real. One day soon, she was going to have to accept the idea that Sandrine wasn't coming back. But not yet.

'Are you sure we're close?' said Lara. She was sitting so far forward over the steering wheel, her forehead was practically touching the glass.

'That's what my phone's saying,' said Stella. 'Mind you, I've got zero signal, so we could have passed Ullapool hours ago.'

'There!' She pointed at a sign emerging from the sea mist.

Ullapool Harbour, it read. *Ferry vehicle check-in.*

'We'd better park,' said Lara, swinging into a space by the dock. 'Otherwise we might drive off the edge of the world.'

She yanked on the handbrake and they clambered out, stretching and groaning, the cold air clean and sharp after the over-heated fug of the car. Lara turned her face up towards the sky. The weather was definitely easing off. Maybe.

'Would you just smell that, though?' said Stella, inhaling deeply.

'The sea?'

Stella grinned and pointed to a café behind them.

'No, fish and chips.'

It was already gone two o'clock and they both agreed that they were starving. Stella went into the shop and came out with two white bags. They sat on the stone wall that framed the crescent of pebbly beach. Lara unwrapped the paper and picked off the crispy batter just as a blast of wind whipped along the front and pushed the cloud back. Suddenly they could see the other side of the bay, then, like a giant hand was pulling back a curtain, the snow-capped mountains beyond.

'Now that's special,' said Lara, eyes wide. 'Almost worth the drive.'

'Almost,' said Stella, dipping a chip into a pool of ketchup.

'So have you been here before?'

Stella shook her head.

'Nah. We didn't really go on holiday when I was a kid. And if we had, we'd have got the hell out of Scotland and gone somewhere bloody warm. What about you?'

'I spent nearly every summer in Scotland but never came this far north.'

MOAAA-RRRGH

'What the…?'

MOOAW-WARR

A ghostly shape emerged from behind the harbour buildings, like a moving office block.

'Is that the ferry?'

'It's huge. How many passengers are they expecting?'

Although it was late spring, the town looked deserted. Lara wondered what had brought a young woman like Rebecca out here.

'Why do you think Rebecca didn't go to Helen's funeral?' said Stella, as if she were reading her thoughts. 'It seems strange given they were such close friends.'

Lara tried to imagine herself not attending Sandrine's funeral but she couldn't, no matter how painful her grief.

'I'm not sure. But we're going to find out,' she said, crunching her wrapper into a ball and tossing it into a bin.

Rebecca's aunt hadn't returned Lara's call, but it hadn't taken Stella too long to find out the address of her Ullapool property. When you had a name and an approximate geographical area, it wasn't difficult in the twenty-first century. They drove up the hill away from the water into a residential area of squat houses. Pebble-dashed and simple, they were designed with the sole purpose of standing up to wind, rain and snow. Practical, yes, but welcoming they were not. Flipping up her collar – their flimsy London coats entirely unsuitable for the north – Lara strode up the path and rang the doorbell. Nothing. She tried again: they could hear the buzzer inside, but no lights, no movement. No one home.

Lara peered through the front window into a living space. She could see a copy of *Grazia* magazine, a can of coke on the coffee table and a pair of Converse by the sofa. Lara got back in the car.

'No-one's home but I don't think they'll be long,'

she said, turning up the heater.

'Not long is too long,' said Stella. 'I'm freezing. I might go back to the chippy to get a pie.'

Lara silenced her as she adjusted the rear-view mirror to watch an approaching figure. A young woman with blonde hair pulled back into a pony tail.

'Is that her?' said Stella, but Lara was already out of the car.

'Rebecca Robertson?' she called, crossing the road to cut her off before she could reach the house. Fear crossed the girl's face. 'Who are you?'

'My name is Lara Stone. This is Stella Harris, we're journalists. Ian Groves suggested we speak to you.'

'About what?' she said, her body language guarded.

'About your friend Helen and what happened in Haiti.'

Rebecca shook her head and dodged around Lara.

'I don't want to talk about it,' she said. 'You shouldn't have come.'

'Rebecca, please. This is important.'

The young woman flashed her a look of anger.

'Who for? You?'

In her rush, the girl dropped her keys trying to get them in the door, swearing under her breath.

'Listen, Becky,' said Lara quickly. 'My friend was killed too and I'm pretty sure her death is linked to Helen's.'

Rebecca straightened up and looked at Lara, then across to Stella, who nodded.

'Let's walk,' she said.

She skirted around the house, passing the backs of narrow gardens, then down a grassy bank towards the loch. She walked briskly, with Lara and Stella having to pick up their pace to catch up.

'I bet this feels very different to Haiti,' said Lara, drawing level with her.

'Sometimes the real world can feel very far away in this part of the Highlands. Haiti is busy, chaotic sometimes, but it can still feel alien. So I guess the two places aren't so different.'

'Down here,' she said, passing through a gap in the breakwater and down onto the stony beach. Rebecca sat down on a rock in the shelter of a beached sailing boat, its pea-green paint peeling like shavings of bark.

'So?' said Rebecca, finally looking directly at Lara. 'What do you want?'

'We don't want you to feel frightened, that's the first thing,' said Lara.

'It's a little late for that,' she said, curling her lip. 'Jumping out at me in the middle of the bloody road. I can't believe Helen's dad told you to come.'

'You're hiding, aren't you?'

Rebecca gave a sarcastic laugh. 'You think I'd come to live up here out of choice?'

'What happened in Haiti, Becky?'

Rebecca glared at Lara. 'Nothing good.'

Then she seemed to lose all her fight and her shoulders slumped.

'Look, we were having a good time, at the start anyway. Helen loved it, she was so taken with the whole thing.'

'Just Helen? Not you?'

'I just wanted to travel. I'd never been out of Europe, so I was up for the experience, meeting new people, eating weird food. I wanted a buzz, you know? I knew Haiti would be gritty, but honestly, it was too gritty for me. Helen loved it though. She was really into the cause, she was properly passionate about helping people.'

Rebecca threw a stone into the water. 'I guess that's what got her into trouble.'

'What trouble, Rebecca?'

The young woman didn't reply.

'I know you know something, Becky,' pressed Lara. 'And the more people you tell, the safer you'll be.'

The young woman's eyes were glittering.

It was a few seconds before she spoke again.

'Helen saw something,' she said. 'Trafficking.'

It was just one word, but it made their whole investigation come together. Lara wanted to let out a whoop, but it wasn't the time or place. Besides, they were a long way from proving anything.

'Helen loved photography,' continued Rebecca. 'As soon as she got to Haiti she started a project photographing the people; she wanted to show the beauty of the country as well as the poverty. She had some idea about putting on an exhibition once we got back to Scotland. So she used to wander about on her own taking photos.'

Lara gave a sad smile, imagining Helen's adventurous spirit.

'On one of the photography trips, Helen saw a man put a young Haitian woman into a pick-up truck. Helen recognised her. Her name was Esther. Barely sixteen and until recently she had lived in one of the orphanages in Port-au-Prince. The following day Helen tried to find Esther to see if she was okay, but she had disappeared.'

'Helen thought she'd been trafficked away from the area?' said Lara.

Rebecca nodded.

'Helen asked around and found out that over the past few months, fifteen young women had gone missing from the Cité Soleil slums alone.'

'Did Helen tell anyone? The police or one of the charities?'

Rebecca gave a cynical smile.

'The man with Esther, the one who put her in the truck? His name was Nils. He worked for ImpactAid.'

Lara looked at her in disbelief. 'Seriously?'

'Yep. Helen told Diego, our manager, showed him the photos she'd taken of Esther and the pick-up truck. Like that,' – Becky clicked her fingers – 'Nils disappeared too and we thought he'd been arrested or something. But no, one of our friends saw him a few days later up in Port-de-Paix on the other side of the peninsula.' Rebecca jabbed a finger for emphasis. 'He was still working for the charity.'

'Wow,' said Stella and Rebecca nodded. She seemed calmer now, almost relieved to be finally telling her story.

‘Helen was furious. She said she was going to go straight to the top because it turns out that Victoria Sachs, the founder of ImpactAid, was coming into town for some photo-story for one of the big American papers.’

Stella was standing closer now, fascinated by the story.

‘Did she see her?’

‘Oh yeah, Helen was ballsy. She went to Victoria’s hotel, showed her the photos and told her how many girls had disappeared. How she believed Nils was involved in the trafficking. How she thought his role was to use his knowledge of the locals via his ImpactAid work to identify vulnerable girls.’

‘Because they’d trust Nils,’ said Lara grimly.

Rebecca nodded. ‘Victoria was outraged, said she’d launch an immediate inquiry.’

‘And did she?’

Rebecca looked at Lara, her eyes glistening.

‘I don’t know. Helen didn’t seem to think so. She was so angry she contacted some journalist at *Le Figaro* to tip them off about the scandal. The next thing I know, Helen was dead.’

Chapter Twenty-Four

'NICE PLACE,' WHISPERED Alex, leaning across the restaurant table to Dominic. 'How the hell did you manage to book this?'

The Corinth was a throwback to the days before the credit crunch, a converted bank in Threadneedle Street, which made the most of the opulent ground floor; the reception-cum-bar was housed in an airy circular room surrounded with white pillars, lit from above by a domed glass ceiling. It was certainly a fitting setting for Dom's dinner. The private banqueting rooms were so sought after that solid-gold connections and a hefty bribe to the maître d' were required. Alex had to hand it to Dom; he knew how to impress.

'Well here they are,' said Dom, standing to greet the other guests as they walked in. 'This is David and Paul. They've already slung in some seed capital, you'll like them. Sean's a big City player too, he'd be really useful down the line.'

Alex smiled and shook hands, but he had to admit he was on edge. He'd called Dom to suggest that they meet to discuss *The Filter* project in more detail. Alex wasn't seriously considering jumping ship – not yet – but it was definitely worth exploring, especially after

Charlie's revelations that Darius wasn't going anywhere anytime soon. Dom had jumped at the chance, and Alex had expected a convivial supper to discuss Dom's vision for the company, but this? This didn't feel like recruitment. It felt like an episode of Dragon's Den.

'Dom tells me you're the George Best on the pitch,' said David, as the conversation turned to football, not long after the main course had been cleared away.

Alex usually found banker-types hard work, but Becker was down-to-earth with a dry sense of humour – he didn't take himself too seriously and they'd bonded within the first five minutes over a shared love of running and soccer. In another life, Alex could see himself being friends with someone like Becker, jogging together or going out for a drink.

'I'm not sure if that's a compliment,' smiled Alex. 'Is he calling me an alcoholic womaniser?'

'I think he said you have a "sweet right foot", but yes, I suppose he could have been alluding to the "talented but failed to reach his potential" part of it.'

Alex looked at him with surprise, but Becker laughed.

'Alex, I'm an investor in *The Filter* and I'll be putting more money in the pot once we've found an Editorial Director. You can't blame me for doing my due diligence. I know you've stalled at Avery Media and I know you're smart enough and ambitious enough to see that this is a good move for you.' He see-sawed a hand. 'Although I can also see that it might feel like a risk too.'

Alex looked at the man with interest. He'd done his homework too: Becker had made a fortune selling his mail-order beauty company and now was considered one of the most astute investors in the City.

'I thought the purpose of this meeting was to convince me that *The Filter* is the right career move for me. Not to insult me.'

He smiled; he said the words light-heartedly but he meant it.

David didn't take it personally.

'Look Alex, the others…' he nodded across to the other members of the investment syndicate currently deep in conversation with Dominic. 'They're young, they're flash and they love media investments like this: they sound impressive when they're boasting about their portfolio poolside in Ibiza.'

Alex laughed.

'And you're not an Ibiza kind of guy, am I right?'

'No, I'm not.'

'So why have you committed to *The Filter*?' asked Alex. 'I mean, I think Dom's idea is a strong one, but you must have been offered dozens of media investments, why this one?'

Becker looked straight at him.

'Because of Dom. And if you sign on the dotted line, Alex, I'll be happier making a further investment.'

'Me?'

'The idea is good, sure, but what I like to do is invest in *people*,' said Becker. I ask myself "can this guy, this team, do what they're saying?" Dom's full of energy and can charm the birds from the trees, but he needs an editorial magician and I think that person is you.'

Alex nodded. It had been a long time since he'd been talked about as an asset.

'You really think I should do it?' he asked Becker. He was flattered, but he was also genuinely interested. Sometimes you needed to see things – yourself – through someone else's eyes.

'I'm not sure you should be asking me for advice,' said Becker. 'My money's already in, remember? But yes. I think you're wasted at the *Chronicle*. You have an impressive CV and a rock-solid reputation, but I really think you can do more, Alex. Newspapers were cutting edge in Queen Victoria's time. The world's moved on.'

Throughout the rest of the meal, Alex found himself mulling Becker's words – and more importantly, watching the other men around the table.

David, Paul and Sean were all sharp, energetic men who approached life as if everything was possible.

'Listen Alex,' said David quietly. 'I've laid my cards on the table and I genuinely think this project would be a good fit for you, but can I ask you what your hesitation is?'

'Honestly? I love print, I always have. My dad was a newsagent, I grew up with ink on my fingers. And print still has authority. People believe what they read in papers, they trust us to tell them the truth. There's power in that.'

David nodded, sipping his wine.

'Very true. But is truth enough? You asked me earlier why I chose this project over the others I've been offered? I liked this one because it's focused on what the reader actually wants. You'd be amazed how rare that is. There was one other media start-up I was tempted by: LiveNews – have you heard of it? I think the guy pitched it as TED Talks meets *The Economist*.'

Alex laughed. 'Actually that does sound pretty good.'

'Yeah, but it was so worthy,' said Becker. 'So serious. Why can't anything have a personality anymore?'

Alex nodded. It was something he had to fight against all the time. Corporate entities valued data and spreadsheets and they resisted anything which couldn't be quantified like 'fun'.

'I think you nailed it earlier,' said Alex. 'It's all about the people running things. New media launches are often run by City guys and entrepreneurs. They don't have anyone on board who really understands how to connect with the news.'

David put his glass down.

'Actually this one did. He's a senior editor at that Dutch paper, *De Telegraaf*, the one that keeps winning awards? He was impressive but… who wants to be lectured to all the time?'

Alex was intrigued. It was always interesting to know who in their little world was making moves.

'I worked in Europe for a little while. Who was this guy?'

Becker hesitated.

'Come on,' said Alex, topping up his glass. 'I won't tell.'

'Stefan Melberg? Do you know him?'

Stefan? Lara's Stefan?

He missed David's glass and wine dribbled onto the tablecloth.

'We've got mutual friends,' said Alex, as casually as he could. 'Actually Stefan's involved with Le Caché, the journalism collective. Was this LiveNews an extension of the collective?'

'No, this was something new.'

Alex wanted to ask more, but just then the waitress brought the bill and someone suggested pushing on to a private members' club. Alex wasn't in the mood to party and besides, he needed a clear head.

He said goodbye to David, looked across at Dominic and tapped a finger on his watch. 'Got to go,' he mouthed and before his friend could object, he slipped out of the door, thinking of Lara and thinking of Stefan Melberg. Right now he had his own due diligence to do.

Chapter Twenty-Five

INVERNESS LOOKED GRIM, or perhaps it was just Lara's mood. Driving into the city, the cloud seemed to be sitting oppressively low, the windscreen speckled with drizzle, their hatchback pushed sideways on the exposed brown hilltops. Stella had booked the return journey home from Inverness rather than Edinburgh because it cut out three hours of driving time – and they wanted to board the train home as soon as they could.

They dropped off the hire car, and with an hour to kill in Inverness, they walked up to the castle, which to Lara looked more like a prison. She was sure that it was usually lovely, but clearly Rebecca's paranoia had been infectious. Lara knew they should be excited and energised – Becky's revelations were a big breakthrough in the story – but it had come with a huge side-order of reality. This wasn't a game. Rebecca had been terrified.

By the time they had settled on the sleeper train and it had departed for its journey south, it was almost ten o'clock. The long nights this far north meant that there was still some watery light in the sky outside. Lara closed the window blind to shut it out.

'Do you ever get scared?' said Stella, from her position on the top bunk.

'Scared of what?' said Lara climbing under the duvet of her own berth.

'The job. Did you see Rebecca's face? She was terrified because of what she knew, because she knew that information made her vulnerable.'

'Sometimes, sure,' said Lara honestly. 'When you have a byline printed next to the story, you're putting your head above the parapet. But generally you don't get anything more threatening than a snotty legal letter,' she said, deciding not to mention the odd death threat and crank letter that occasionally appeared in her in-tray. 'I certainly don't get as scared as the people getting trafficked in Haiti.'

Stella muttered a vague noise of approval. On the drive from Ullapool they'd speculated what had happened to Helen's friend Esther. None of the options had happy endings. Most likely, she'd been smuggled over the border into the Dominican Republic where Esther and everyone else tricked into that pick-up truck would end up in forced prostitution. Lara had recounted how in India, she'd heard of children deliberately crippled and blinded in order to make them more effective beggars, and even in Eastern Europe, young men had their organs trafficked: a kidney could raise $20,000 on the black market.

'We can't let them get away with it,' said Stella.

'No, we can't.'

Lara had thought she was hardened to the evils of the world, but putting Esther's name to those abstract statistics had made it real, had made *her* real.

The click-clack and sway of the train was a soundtrack to her thoughts, and the soft rhythm helped soothe her mood.

'I mean, I know it wasn't the most uplifting trip,' said Stella, clambering under her own sheet. 'But I have to say, travelling this way is romantic.'

Lara smiled as she reached over to flick off the light.

'Yes, when we were in the dining car, I could imagine Cary Grant and Eva Marie Saint sitting down to join us.'

There was a pause.

'Who?'

'Eva Marie Saint. Cary Grant,' said Lara. 'In *North By Northwest*?'

'Him from *Four Weddings And A Funeral*, right?'

'Not Hugh Grant, *Cary* Grant. Jesus, Stella.'

She cut herself off as she realised Stella was teasing her. Lara tried throwing a complimentary shortcake biscuit at her.

'Can I ask you a question?' said Stella finally.

'Another one?'

'Why have you never got together with Alex?'

Lara laughed.

'Seriously,' pressed Stella.

'I liked him once,' she said, after another moment.

She surprised herself when the words fell out of her mouth. Lara hadn't admitted it to anyone, not even Sandrine. *Especially* Sandrine. But the darkness of the cabin made it easier to talk openly, and besides, it was good to finally get it off her chest.

'The first time I ever saw Alex was a thunderbolt moment. For about nine months, most of the way through our City course actually, I was convinced he was The One. But there were so many nights when we went out and I waited and waited. And…'

'And?'

'And nothing ever happened. And so I moved on. And now he's getting married.'

She felt Stella stir.

'To Alice?

'Alicia.'

'Eww!'

Lara laughed. 'Stella, you've never even met Alicia.'

'But you two are perfect together,' said Stella urgently. 'You haven't had a boyfriend since I've known you and you're so beautiful, that it doesn't make *any* sense – unless, deep down, you love Alex.'

'I do love him, Stel, but not in the way you mean. Not anymore. That was all a long time ago.'

Lara blinked in the darkness. But was it? She thought of the engagement ring, how she had felt when she had seen it fall from Alex's pocket. Scared, was the truth. For fifteen years, Sandrine and Alex had been constants in her life. It didn't matter that she saw them less, Lara had always known that her two best friends would be there for her no matter what. With Sandrine gone and Alex set to pair off, Lara could no longer pretend she had anything, or anyone, to rely on.

But was there another reason why she had felt so

unsettled to see the winking gold band? She didn't want to dwell on it.

'What have you always told me about the job, boss?' Stella's voice was soft, but insistent.

Lara smiled. She immediately knew what Stella meant.

'Listen to your gut,' she said. 'Because your gut always knows.'

'My gut is telling me that it's time to get some sleep,' said Lara, rolling over, determined to forget that they had even had the conversation.

LARA WOKE WITH a start, hands twisted in her thin quilt, her whole body sweating. In her dream, she had been locked in the back of a truck. The oven-hot metal walls were closing in on her and she was scrabbling at the lock, trying to call out, but no words were forming, no one could hear her. Trapped, hammering at the door with her fists.

And then, in the way of dreams, Lara was no longer Lara: she had somehow become Sandrine, her knuckles scraping against bare wood, the unfinished lid of a coffin. It was a moment before Lara realised there was no van, no door. She was on the sleeper train and the knocking was coming from the corridor.

'London Euston ten minutes,' said a voice.

She inhaled deeply, the fear still hanging over her like fog. *Only the train*, she thought. Lara sat up slowly, swinging her legs out to the side of the bunk and put her feet on the floor. Breathing deeply, she took a minute to place which city she was in. London? It was hard to tell she had been to so many in the past week. Lara flinched as the door swung inwards. Stella's beaming face peeked in, holding up a takeaway coffee like a trophy.

'Shake a leg, boss. This will perk you up,' she said cheerfully. 'Didn't want to disturb you until the last moment. Thought you needed your beauty sleep.'

'Thanks,' said Lara sarcastically. 'I'm not that decrepit.'

She peered at her reflection in the mirror above the sink. *Or then again…*

Her face was creased with pillow marks, puffy dark circles hung beneath pink-shot eyes. She splashed cold water on her cheeks and did her best to make herself look human, then bundled all her stuff into her tote as the train pulled into the station. With one last fond look towards their cabin, Lara followed Stella onto the platform and up the ramp into Euston, already humming with the buzz of hundreds of commuters.

'So what are we doing now?' asked Stella with unflagging enthusiasm. 'Have you heard from Stef and Eddie?'

Lara laughed, despite herself.

'You make them sound like an 80s comedy duo.'

'Comedians they ain't,' smiled Stella.

'Look, you go home and we'll meet later,' said Lara. 'I'm going to see my cousin.'

'Charlie? Why?'

Lara took a breath.

'I think we need to start working with the paper.'

Stella looked at her incredulously.

'With the *Chronicle*? No! This is our scoop, Lara – they got rid us of us, remember? We can't just do all the donkey work and hand it to them on a plate.'

Lara could understand her reaction. She knew she would have felt the same way if their positions had been reversed, and she didn't like it either, but they needed more firepower. And she had to admit she was feeling vulnerable, out here on their own.

'We do have to place the story somewhere,' said Lara. 'Not even Le Caché publishes their own scoops.'

'I thought this was for Sandrine, not a headline.'

'I know, and it is. But if we can get Charlie onside and get him excited about a huge scoop, we might have a chance of getting the investigations team reinstated.'

Stella frowned.

'But isn't Charlie an idiot?'

Lara gave a lopsided smile.

'Maybe. We'll see.'

As Stella disappeared into the Underground, Lara grabbed a taxi and directed the driver to Primrose Hill. She hadn't been entirely honest with Stella when she said she wanted to try and get the investigations team reinstated. Of course she loved the buzz of her old department. Those late nights, firing off suggestions and ideas around the table, pizza boxes stacked high and too many black coffees – they'd been glorious times. But there was something else too. She'd told Rebecca Robertson the more people who knew, the safer she would be, and that stood for Lara and Stella too. If Helen and Sandrine had been murdered, that put them at risk. She hadn't wanted to frighten Stella, but Lara was experienced enough to know that their only real protection was to get the story out there – and fast. It didn't have to be perfect or comprehensive, just done – and soon.

Traffic was slow through Camden: Friday morning, people were hurrying to work, shopkeepers pulling up shutters or setting out fruit, plus the inevitable roadworks cunningly timed to cause the maximum disruption. Muttering to himself, the cabbie veered off into the leafy, village-like atmosphere of Primrose Hill. Here the passers-by changed too: glamorous brunettes in expensive-looking gym gear, young nannies pushing buggies worth more than their monthly wage, it was a world as alien to Lara as the hill tribes in Laos.

Lara glanced at her watch. Right now, most senior members of the *Chronicle* would already be at their desks, sipping strong coffee and steeling themselves for the daily conference where the contents of the next day's paper would be decided. But not her cousin. Most days Charlie sloped into the office at nine o'clock and right now, Charlie would almost certainly still be at home, if not in bed.

Lara leaned forward to guide the taxi through the tangle of pastel terraces, stopping short of Charlie's place: a pale blue townhouse in a prime position. Lara took a deep breath. This was going to be tricky. She wasn't particularly close to Charlie, but she still considered him an ally.

The summer that Lara had gone to live with Uncle

Nicholas following the death of her parents, Lara had found solace in the great outdoors. Charlie was a year younger than her, and as another only child, he had been Lara's constant companion in those sad, summer weeks. To distract herself from her grief, she'd taught her cousin how to dive into the pool at Foxhills, helped him to climb trees too big for him and liberated treats from the pantry, forbidden by Aunt Olivia, for picnics in the meadows and riverbanks around the estate. They had been, if not actually brother and sister, close enough for friends, and although they had grown up to be very different people, Lara felt there was still a bond.

She paid the driver and got out of the cab, waiting on the pavement as it drove off.

Lara knew it was polite to call Charlie first, but then again, it would be just like Charlie to fob her off and she didn't want to give him the chance.

She was about to cross the road when the door to Charlie's house opened and he stepped out, slipping on his jacket and laughing. Some instinct made Lara pull back into the shadow of an overhanging tree. She watched a honeyed blonde woman follow Charlie out, and as she bent to whisper something in his ear, a smile spread across his face. His arm snaked around his companion's waist and he pulled her close, kissing her passionately right there on the doorstep. A gust of wind blew across the street and the woman brushed her hair back off her face. It was then that Lara could clearly see the woman that Charlie was kissing, as plain as day. Alicia. The woman was Alicia.

Chapter Twenty-Six

THE NEWS ROOM was in uproar. Shouts going back and forth across the desks. A screwed up ball of paper bounced off the side of a head. Abuse, ringing phones, music, a sudden burst of laughter.

Alex grinned to himself as he walked through. Just another day in paradise.

'Hey Alex, I just heard that the *Mail* has a story about a talking horse. You should get on that,' shouted a voice.

'On the horse, or on the story?' said another.

This was what he had always loved about working on a paper; the energy, the chaos, the camaraderie. The noise was huge, swelling like waves hitting the beach in a storm. Stories coming in, raw information, people shouting out soundbites: 'Get this: front runner for the next Olympics is Cairo'; 'Hey, some professor says women are actually over-paid – and she's a woman.' Everything was up for discussion, everything was a news item until proven otherwise.

To get into tomorrow's issue, they'd have to elbow out today's hot items: a footballer caught taking bribes from a betting syndicate, a leaked government proposal about free school meals or a story about a rival paper being sued for printing unfounded allegations about a Hollywood actor's sexual preferences. But Alex was working on something bigger – potentially much bigger, at least for the *Chronicle*.

Alex walked down the corridor, the noise receding behind him, and into a small office with a piece of paper taped to the door marked 'Spy Shit. Please knock.' The room was usually used by researchers who needed peace and quiet, but it was also used – as now – when someone was working on a story they wanted to keep under the radar.

Alex put his head around the door.

'Any news?'

Louis Brand looked up. One of the news team, Louis was an up-and-coming star with a talent for finding big stories. He nodded to Alex.

'I think she'll talk.'

'She will? My God.'

Louis had heard a whisper that Christie Spencer, Felix Tait's personal chef, the woman who had given him his dramatic alibi in court, had a story to tell: she had lied. Christie had given Tait a false alibi because she had been head over heels in love with him, but now Tait was off the hook, the chef had been dispensed with. Christie was furious and looking to get even.

'Did you talk her through the legal problems?' asked Alex.

'I did. She's so angry right now she says she'll take the consequences.'

Alex nodded, trying to keep his excitement in

check. While the woman's testimony would certainly be enough to trigger a High Court appeal, it was also highly risky. Christie would have to admit to perjury, an offence that potentially carried a jail sentence. And what if she suddenly changed her mind again? What if Tait managed to sweet-talk her, declare his undying love?

'Okay, run it all past the lawyers,' said Alex decisively. 'If they give the thumbs up, get her on the record and we'll take it from there.'

He pointed a finger at Louis. 'Good work. But it goes without saying, don't breathe this to a soul.'

Louis gave him a mock salute. 'Understood.'

Alex walked back to his office and grabbed his jacket from his chair. He needed to get out into the sunshine, breathe some clean air – or at least as clean as you could get in London. As he pushed through the revolving doors, his phone chirped.

Can you get out of work early?

He smiled. Lara.

Not a problem. Is this the birthday night out you promised me?

Something like that. The Mermaid?

How about 6pm? And mine's a Guinness.

His mood lifted. He couldn't wait to tell Lara about the developments on Felix Tait; he could trust her to keep it to herself and she would love the opportunity to take the fight back to her nemesis. The fact that Lara had chosen The Mermaid was also a good sign. The old pub had become Alex and Lara's refuge from work, close enough to the office that they could get there and back within a lunch hour, but not so close that there was any chance of seeing anyone else from the office.

Lara was sitting at a picnic table up against the whitewashed wall of the pub, her face tipped up towards the early evening sun.

'Not wearing your scarf?' she said, squinting up at him as he slid in opposite her.

'Doesn't really go with the suit,' he replied, taking a grateful sip of his waiting pint.

'How long have you been here?' He looked down at her G&T, which was down to the ice.

She waved a vague hand. 'Time means nothing to me these days. I'm retired, remember?'

'You should get together with my dad,' said Alex. 'He stayed at Claridge's after my birthday dinner. He loved it. I think he's got a taste for the high life.'

'What can I say? Terry and I live a life of leisure.'

Alex raised a finger.

'Maybe not for long.'

He told her about the revelations about Felix Tait and the possibility of an appeal. She nodded, but barely cracked a smile. Odd.

'We need you back, Lara.'

She looked down, swirling the ice around in her glass.

'Actually I went to see Charlie this morning – to talk to him about coming back.'

He looked at her over his pint. 'Why?'

'The Meyer story.'

Alex tried to hide his disappointment. He thought they were here to celebrate his birthday. He thought they could have a few drinks, maybe see a movie at the Curzon or the Prince Charles in Leicester Square. He'd already had a look to see what was on. But apparently, she was here to talk about work.

As he listened to Lara outline a story about Jonathon Meyer, his girlfriend Josie, a billionaire investor and an aid-worker called Helen, he perked up.

'Wow,' said Alex, sitting back in his chair. What Lara had just told him was the reason he'd got into journalism in the first place. A tale of greed, scandal and the pitch-dark side of capitalism. More than that, it was a conspiracy which, like an oil slick, had spread so far that it had touched their lives.

'You really think this Michael Sachs got Jonathon Meyer to kill Helen the whistleblower?'

She nodded.

'And if Sachs was ruthless enough to get rid of Helen to keep the story quiet, what's one more?'

Sandrine. Their lost friend was where all this had started and if Lara was right – and she almost always was – this was a sensational story. But only if they could prove it. *If.*

Back when he was a junior reporter, his then boss, Barry Levin used to take him out for lunch to this very pub. He'd spend an hour talking about the 'old days' – life in Fleet Street in the Seventies and Eighties, then he'd spend the last five minutes tearing Alex's latest story apart and explaining why it didn't hold up. Barry was gone now, like so many hacks who'd lived on Bell's and Silk Cut, but Alex realised he was Barry now; it was his job to point out the flaws in her story.

Certainly, Lara's theory meant that Helen and Sandrine's deaths were professional hits, which were big accusations to direct at one of the country's top financiers. If Felix Tait had taught them anything, they needed cast-iron proof of everything if there was any hope of running the story or bringing someone to any sort of justice.

'So what did Charlie say about coming back in?'

Lara paused, running a fingernail along the grain of the table.

'I didn't get to speak to Charlie. That's why I wanted to talk to you.'

Alex rolled his eyes.

'Is he being difficult? No surprise there, Charlie doesn't exactly have much editorial vision.'

Lara put out a hand.

'No, it's not that.'

She looked away again. She seemed nervous, jumpy.

'Lar, what's wrong?'

She had always been so open with her feelings, it was one of the things he loved about her. Lara Stone didn't play games. Finally, she looked up at him.

'Remember the other day when you asked me if you should propose to Alicia?'

He nodded, feeling his pulse start to beat faster.

'*Don't*,' she said.

One word and Alex was immediately transported back to a night years ago, back to when they were both students at City. They'd been at a party and Lara had met some pretty boy, all fancy hair and triceps. Alex had stewed all night, watching them dance around each other, until their faces were inches apart. Then when Lara had come over to tell him she was going home with this bozo, Alex had whispered that one word in her ear: 'Don't'.

Their eyes had met, the music swirling around them. 'Don't go with him,' he had said. 'Come home with me.'

Even now he could feel the tight anticipation he had felt when he had said it. He'd spent weeks, months, wondering how he could bare his soul to Lara and finally admit his feelings for her, and when it had come, his words had been clumsy. But it hadn't even mattered, for at that moment, the pretty boy had sidled up behind her and slid an arm around Lara's waist.

'Let's go,' he had murmured. And she had gone, acting as if she hadn't even heard what Alex had said.

He could still feel the sting of that rejection even now, as Lara repeated the word back to him, a code that joined them together and held them apart.

'Why not?' he said, looking back at her.

Did he want Lara to tell him that she loved him, that she always had done? To finally hear the words *I love you.* Or was it really too late? Alex had emotionally moved on from Lara years ago. At least that's what he had always told himself.

'Alex, I took a cab to Charlie's place in Primrose

Hill this morning,' said Lara, her soft green eyes on his. 'I'd just got out of the car when I saw Charlie come out of the house. He was with Alicia.'

Alex felt his world contract.

'What do you mean, *with*?'

She looked down at the table again.

'I saw them kissing. I'm pretty sure she had stayed at Charlie's overnight.'

'What are you saying, Lara?'

The words came out automatically, but of course he knew what she was saying. He'd been at dinner with Dom and then had gone back to his place alone. Business as usual for a Thursday night with work the next day.

'Did Alicia say where she was?'

'I don't check up on her every move,' he said, with irritation. But she had said something, hadn't she? A night out with friends; standard procedure for Alicia. Parties, openings, networking events were all part of her job and Alicia spent less time in her tiny apartment than Alex spent in his. He'd once told her that she was like a pre-credit crunch New Yorker and Alicia had grinned, taking it as a huge compliment.

Lara pushed her phone across the table towards him.

'What's this?' he frowned.

'I took a picture.'

Alex looked at her incredulously.

'You *photographed* them? What the hell for?'

'Proof.'

His mouth practically dropped open. Was everything a story to her?

Alex didn't want to look, but his eyes betrayed him. He gulped hard. There was no mistaking the intimate way Charlie was touching the small of Alicia's back or the fact that their lips where connecting and Alicia's mouth was smiling as they kissed.

'So I guess that answers the question of whether I should propose,' he said, pushing it away. He could hear the bitterness in his own voice, the cynical inevitably of it all. But that wasn't true, was it? He hadn't expected it, hadn't suspected a thing. If there had been signs, Alex had missed them all. He'd deluded himself that Alicia loved him for who he was, not for who he could be moulded into. But really, it was obvious. If he resigned from the *Chronicle* and moved back to the Lakes, would she come? Of course not.

'Alex, she's not worth it. She wasn't right for you.'

He drained the last of the Guinness and banged it down on the table.

'Is that what you think? Well, perhaps you could have said something before you caught her shagging my boss.'

'Alicia's an operator, Alex. She's too ambitious, too aspirational. Charlie's an idiot, but he's a very rich idiot. That's what she wants.'

Alex gave a sour smile.

'Well, there's a lot of that about.'

He knew it was unfair, knew he was lashing out, but the Guinness, swiftly drunk, had loosened his tongue. He hadn't planned to tell Lara what David

Becker had told him, not until he knew more, but right now it all seemed far too similar. Lara was beautiful and smart and funny. And she was rich, as rich as Charlie, and that made her vulnerable.

'Are you seeing Stefan Melberg?'

'Why?' she asked, with a defensiveness in her voice. 'Alex, what is it?'

'I was out with some investment guys yesterday. One of them told me that Stefan is seeking finance for a media start-up.'

She looked confused, suspicious.

'So? Le Caché costs money. Eduardo can't be expected to keep paying for it all. It would be unusual if they haven't looked for outside investment after this length of time.'

'The money wasn't for Le Caché, Lara. It was a solo venture for Stefan.'

'Wait,' she gasped. 'You think Stefan's dating me for some ulterior motive? You think he wants money from me?'

Dating. The situation was worse than he thought.

'It's not what I think, Lar. What do you think? Seems a little coincidental that he's appeared in your life at the time he needs cash.'

The more he spoke, the more Alex knew he was right. He had met so many of Stefan's type before. Sanctimonious hypocrites in geek-chic glasses and expensive trainers. They made a big deal about seeking 'the truth', sneering at established media, whispering about hidden agendas, but they almost always had an agenda of their own. Le Caché was a fine example, alluding to some global cabal of industrialists conspiring to protect their own interests, but the vast majority of Le Caché journalists worked for the big newspapers in their own countries. It was hypocrisy dressed up in radical clothing.

'Why don't you just admit you don't like him, Alex?' she said, as if she was reading his thoughts. 'Admit that you are just jealous of Le Caché and people like Stefan. Real journalists, finding real stories that matter.'

Alex shook his head.

'Lara, I'm just saying be careful. I don't want you to get hurt.'

'Really?' said Lara. 'Because it sounds the exact opposite'.

She grabbed her bag and stood up. 'You know, just because your girlfriend is screwing around, you don't have to make me feel shitty about my love life.'

He got up to follow, but Lara was already striding off down the street.

'Lara, wait!' he called.

But she was already gone.

Chapter Twenty-Seven

ALEX HESITATED BEFORE he rang the bell. He looked up at the blue door and he could just see the narrow staircase through the frosted glass panel. Alicia had the smallest apartment on one the best streets in Notting Hill, a quiet mews street with pastel coloured houses just waiting for a rom-com film crew to roll up with Hugh Grant and a rain machine.

'It's all about the postcode.' That's what Alicia had said the first time she had brought him here and Alex had always admired that about her: she always knew exactly what she wanted. Alex wished he felt the same. He had no idea what he wanted from coming here: an explanation? Some logical justification for Alicia being on Charlie's doorstep first thing in the morning? The picture on Lara's phone had seemed fairly conclusive. But then perhaps Alicia had a paper-round as a sideline and Charlie had been uncommonly grateful for the service. He smiled sadly to himself: gallows humour.

He pressed the doorbell and saw Alicia's slim form running down the stairs, distorted, refracted. Maybe Lara was right, perhaps he hadn't ever seen Alicia clearly. The door opened.

'Hey there you,' she said, darting forward for a kiss. 'I wasn't sure you'd be coming tonight. I've actually eaten but I can whip up a bowl of pasta for you if you'd like.'

'I'm not hungry.'

He said it to her back as she had already gone upstairs.

Her flat was on the first floor, up a dark set of stairs. The door led straight onto the living space. The room was lit by a lamp in the corner and a little sodium from the streetlight outside the window.

The bed was on a mezzanine platform reached by a steep set of stairs, a small kitchen ran along the back wall. It was still warm from the heat of the day and a candle in a ceramic pot dispensed a sweet, herbal scent that made him feel as if he was in the waiting room for the sort of deluxe spa that Alicia liked to go to.

As he watched her fluid movements, her elegant posture, Alex recognised that he was still attracted to Alicia. Had been from the minute he'd seen her. She had a delicate small-boned beauty that was in complete contrast to her steely personality. The teenage Alex would have run a mile from someone like Alicia Croft, but the grown-up Alex had fallen in love with her, and he still thought she was hot, no matter what she had done.

'Drink?' she asked, heading through the narrow apartment to the kitchen.

She fiddled with her iPad, settling on an Adele song before turning to the fridge and pulling out a bottle of wine.

'I'm not staying.'

She turned, frowning.

'Not staying?'

He stood awkwardly by the front door, as if poised on the edge of a cliff.

'I met Lara after work,' he said.

'Again?' she said distractedly, uncorking the bottle.

He ignored the jibe. Alex hardly ever met Lara after work these days; what little free time he had was given over to Alicia. Which was how it was supposed to be when you were serious about someone.

'Lara went to Charlie's place early this morning, around eight,' he continued, determined to get it out. 'Some urgent business to discuss.'

'Could it not wait for the office?' said Alicia, pouring the wine. 'Oh of course not, she's *suspended.*'

Alex almost smiled: a pre-emptive strike on Lara, a feint to distract him, draw his fire in another direction. Oh, she was good. Alex had always known that Alicia was an operator and up until this point he'd seen it as a positive. She worked hard at everything, yet it seemed that deceit was just another skill in her arsenal to get her what she wanted. Tonight, however, it wasn't going to work.

'Lara saw you with him,' said Alex. 'Coming out of the house just after eight AM.'

Alicia blinked at him.

'Charlie Avery's place?'

Alex closed his eyes. So it was true. It felt like a door slamming shut. An innocent person would have immediately replied, 'But I've never been to Charlie's house.' Or 'At eight o'clock, I was on my way to work.' Alicia was playing for time, sipping her wine, presumably thinking of a strategy, a way out. Alex wasn't in the mood for playing games, but he was curious to see where Alicia would run with this.

'Alex, I have no idea why Lara would say something like that,' she said finally. 'I do know she is in a dark place right now. She's been fired, she's grieving over the death of her best friend. Those sort of emotions can do odd things to people. Make them behave in strange ways.'

'So you weren't at Charlie's this morning?'

She paused a beat.

'No,' she said, meeting his gaze. 'If Lara saw someone, it certainly wasn't me.'

Alex nodded.

'She has a photo of the two of you together,' he said. 'You were wearing that blue jacket I bought you.'

Alicia's eyes flashed.

'What the fuck was she doing taking photos?'

And there it was – all the confirmation he needed. The innocent Alicia would have been furious with *him* for believing such crap and demanded to see the photos. Instead she was angry with Lara for catching her out.

There was a long silence. The scented candle flickered and sent long shapes up the wall. The sense of an ending was palpable in the room. Despite everything, Alex felt a wave of sadness, that he would not come to the small, neat, sweet-smelling space again. He'd been happy here. A version of it, anyway.

'It's over, Alicia,' said Alex. 'Why don't you just tell me the truth?'

She didn't speak for a second, then looked at him, her expression hard.

'You want the truth, Alex? We've been together for nearly two years and I'm sick of there being no forward motion. I'm sick of never seeing you. Sick of being an afterthought in your life.'

'Alicia, you knew about the demands of my job when we met. I need to put in long hours in the office. That's just how it is at a newspaper.'

'Yeah? Well Charlie is managing director of that very same newspaper and he doesn't feel the need to put in half the hours you do.'

He looked at her.

'And how would you know that?'

The room fell quiet.

'How long has it being going on, Alicia?'

She looked away and took a long drink of her wine.

'It doesn't matter,' she said, not even bothering to deny it anymore.

'It matters to me.' And it did. Even though the relationship was over, even though knowing the details would not change the outcome, Alex still wanted to know.

'How long?' he repeated.

He wondered if they had met at the *Chronicle's* 100th anniversary party, but Charlie's name had been absent from Alicia's guest list for Alex's birthday dinner compiled two weeks earlier. At the time, he thought it had been a thoughtful omission. He knew that Alicia's default position would be to invite the glamorous people, the useful people but instead of including Charlie Avery she had asked Alex's dad and Chris and Harry from the subs department, colleagues he actually liked. He had loved her for that, but now he realised that she simply hadn't wanted Charlie there, fearful that either of them might give away their affair.

'A couple of months,' she said finally. 'We've been seeing each other a couple of months. Happy now?'

Alex tried to think back that far. What had he been doing? What had *they* been doing? But it was futile: they went to the same parties, moved in the same circles. It could have been going on the whole time and Alex would never have known.

Alicia was staring at him now, her eyes hard and defiant.

'You can't blame me, Alex,' she snapped. 'Admit it, you weren't even thinking about any sort of commitment.'

'You could have been more patient.'

'Would it have made any difference?'

Alex thought about his mother's ring. How it felt in his hand. How he had felt seeing it in Lara's hand.

It wasn't true that he hadn't thought about commitment. But she didn't need to know that. He suddenly felt weary, all the anger replaced by sadness.

'It's her, you know,' said Alicia, as he turned to leave.

'Lara. She's the reason why it would have never

worked between us. Do you think it's any coincidence that Lara was the one who told you about this?'

Alicia saw that hit home, her mouth a twisted smile of triumph.

'Things might be better for everyone if you two just admitted you are in love with each other.'

'In love?' said Alex, incredulously. 'Alicia, Lara is my friend. There's no need to feel jealous of her.'

She stopped him with a harsh laugh.

'I'm not jealous of Lara Stone, Alex. A washed-up hack with an inflated sense of her own importance? I don't think so.'

'Alicia, all Lara did was catch you in your lie, you don't need to go on the attack, she hasn't done anything wrong.'

'See?' she said, tossing her hair back. 'Always defending poor Lara. Poor Lara born with a silver spoon in her mouth, poor Lara with her trust fund and her pretend down-to-earth canal barge. Poor little rich girl.'

He was about to point out that she had hardly chosen Charlie for his street cred, but he decided not to rise to the bait.

'Alicia, I came here because you have been cheating on me – don't make it about Lara.'

'But it is, Alex,' she said, with a fierce blink. 'It has always been about her. Have you ever thought for one moment how it feels for me to see you together, to listen to your in-jokes, to see that stupid scarf she bought you or those trinkets around your flat that I know are from places you have been to with her? I feel like the other woman, not your girlfriend, Alex. I can't get past your history with Lara and I don't want to keep trying.'

He'd genuinely never considered that a girlfriend might find his friendship with Lara threatening. Perhaps there was something in it, perhaps he could have been more considerate. But then his eyes strayed towards Alicia's mezzanine bedroom, picturing her leading Charlie up there by the hand, imagining them kissing and whispering and plotting before they pressed their hard bodies against one another.

'Goodbye Alicia,' he said. And he turned and walked back down the stairs.

Chapter Twenty-Eight

LARA WALKED HOME from The Mermaid. On warm days like today, she loved threading through the back streets of Chelsea, gorgeous little terraces with black railings and white pillars, steps running up to their grand doorways, miniature mansions with delusions of grandeur. Usually a long stroll along these wisteria-clad lanes would clear her head and give her perspective from her immediate problems, but today, her mind was a tangled knot. *Alex.* The look of utter dejection on his face when she had told him about Alicia and Charlie. Lara hadn't expected him to turn cartwheels, but neither had she thought she would see him crumble. She had completely underestimated his depth of feeling for his girlfriend: such idiocy. Only days before, Alex had been waving around an engagement ring and talking about proposing; why on earth did Lara think he would just shrug his shoulders and mutter, 'c'est la vie'?

But then what else could she have done? Should she have kept quiet about what she had seen? On the one hand, it was none of her business, but if Alex really was about to propose, to commit to one woman for the rest of his life, then he deserved that woman to be someone who loved him right back with all her heart.

'What a mess,' she whispered, feeling the weight of it all at once.

She still hadn't been home since arriving into Euston that morning and her bag was beginning to feel heavy. She turned into a narrow walk, trying not to glance over her shoulder. Lara had done her best to shake off the paranoia she had felt in the Highlands, but she wasn't entirely sure it was working. This part of London had always felt like home to Lara, all the hidden alleyways you couldn't even see on Google Maps. Judge's Walk was a particular favourite, with its shoulder-width passageway and peeling sign advertising a pub which had never existed. No one could follow you down there if they tried. But still… As she turned the corner into Cheyne Walk, a gust of wind blew a swirl of dust and grit into her eyes and Lara felt a chill, a shift in the atmosphere as she hurried across Embankment, the houseboats lined up down to her left.

She knew something was wrong before she even stepped into the boatyard, the squeaky gate squealing. Lara ran up the jetty, seeing with a lurch that the narrowboat's door was slightly ajar, the frame splintered. She took the gangway in two strides and ducked inside.

'No… no, no.'

The boat had been trashed. Someone had torn it apart: crockery smashed, papers strewn about, cushions slashed. It was like a wrecking ball had passed through it. Lara's hand pressed to her mouth in horror. This was her home, part of her. The place she felt safe. *No, not anymore.*

Anything that had been on a surface now lay on the floor. Books, notepads, plants, cups, and worst of all, her favourite picture of her father, the one where he was standing proudly by his boat. She bent down to pick it up and saw that the frame's glass was shattered in a fractured crescent: the same shape as a heel of a boot.

Taking a deep breath to steady herself, Lara propped the picture back up on the table, then went to the spare room, where the mess was even more frenzied. The photos, notes and newspaper cuttings on the wall had been torn down, the book case had been upturned, her grandfather's collection of leather-bound books face-down, pages deliberately torn out, spines broken: what kind of burglar would do that?

Instinctively Lara knew it was linked to her investigation into Sandrine, Meyer and Helen Groves. She had done plenty of investigations into dangerous people before: an Albanian drug gang, even an expose that had sent an East End crime lord to jail. She'd been threatened, once even physically, but never before had her work spilled over into her private life in this way.

She pushed through into her bedroom: ransacked. The duvet was leaking fluff, her wardrobe door and drawers were open, the arms and legs of jeans and shirts strewn like broken limbs across the floor.

Don't just stand there, said a voice in her head. *Don't let them win.*

She pulled out her phone with trembling fingers.

Her first instinct was to call Alex, but she doubted he'd take her call right now: she could hardly blame him. Instead she scrolled to Stella's number and was greeted with a blast of noise as her assistant answered.

'Boss? Is that you?' Music and chatter and laughter in the background.

'Where are you?' asked Lara, struggling to get the words out.

'At The Glasshouse with Karen and Rosie. What's up?'

Lara closed her eyes, imagining her young assistant somewhere fun and fabulous, enjoying life with her friends. She knew that if she told her what had happened, Stella would immediately swing into action, rush over and sort everything out. But this wasn't her fight and her assistant deserved a life away from work. At the very least after losing her job at the *Chronicle*, Stella could do with a good night out.

'Nothing, it's fine,' she said quietly, sinking down onto the arm of the sofa.

'Sorry, what d'you say, boss?'

The line was breaking up. Lara raised her voice.

'I said have a drink on me and I'll give you a call tomorrow.'

Lara hung up and looked down at her phone. If not Stella, then who? She scrolled through her numbers, considering various names and rejecting them one by one. This was what happened when your work was your life – and your two best friends were… unavailable.

She walked back through the boat towards the

kitchen, desperate for a drink. She knew she had a bottle of gin in the fridge – maybe, if they hadn't smashed that too – although alcohol probably wasn't the answer right now. Strong tea, then she'd call the police, even though Lara had little hope they'd do much. Burglaries in London had a tiny clean-up rate and as far as she could see, nothing had been taken.

She could see slate grey clouds through the skylight and before she could even think 'storm', she felt the thrum of heavy rain against the roof and the low boom of distant thunder.

Lara flicked on the kitchen light – on, off, on – nothing. *Dammit,* she thought, edging forward through the gloom, feeling her way down to the cupboard where she kept the lightbulbs. Finding the fridge, she opened the door for the light and immediately saw a dark shape on the floor.

'Oh God, no.'

Poking out from beneath a torn curtain, there was a single white paw. Dingo.

Dingo was dead.

His neck twisted, his body was limp, casually discarded alongside a crushed cereal box. Emotion caught in her throat and tears began to fall. Sobbing now, Lara fell to her knees. 'Dingo, no, no,' she whispered, resting a hand on his little head. 'I'm so, so sorry.'

Desperate to get out, Lara stumbled for the door, blindly pushing out onto the deck, her shoulders and hair immediately soaked by the downpour. She bent over, gulping in air, her throat rasping, her hands gripping the rail. If she didn't hold on, she knew she would fall down. Her world was tilting, threatening to tip her over the edge in every sense. First *Misty*, then her cat. You're next. That was the message, loud and clear. *You're next.*

Lara looked down at the phone still in her hand. And she knew there was only one person left to call.

Chapter Twenty-Nine

Detective Chief Inspector Fox said he'd be there within the hour, but he arrived in less thirty minutes. Lara met him at the gate. She wasn't sure if she had been more pleased to see someone in her life.

'Thanks for coming,' she said formally, trying to keep her voice even. Lara was embarrassed that Fox was seeing her like this; she was usually so together, so competent, but right now her face was red and tender, her eyes barely two slits. If Fox noticed, he was good enough not to mention it.

'I was on my way home,' he said, as Lara nodded with gratitude.

'Shall we take a look?' he asked, pointing towards the boat with his chin. Lara led him to the gangplank, but let him go ahead. Fox stopped to briefly examine the splintered door, then stepped inside. Lara waited on the dock. She didn't want to watch him poking around in her things, it already felt tainted enough inside there. Fox was a senior detective and he was here to help, but even so, this wasn't a social call. When she thought she'd given him long enough to see the damage, she followed him back down the steps.

'Bloody hell,' he said, looking around, then rubbing his chin.

Lara nodded dumbly.

'They killed my cat, Ian.'

It sounded faintly ridiculous as she said it out loud. As if it was a punchline in some absurd comedy.

Fox looked at her, then gave a sad nod.

'Where is he?'

She motioned towards the kitchen.

'He's still in there. I was going to move him, but thought I should wait until you came.' The tears started to fall again. 'Sorry, I'm not usually like this, I couldn't…'

Ian Fox put an awkward arm around her and they stood like that for a minute or two. Lara supposed this was all part of the job for Fox, plus he was a decent man.

'Do you have a box? A blanket would be good too.'

She nodded and went down to the bedroom, coming back with an old wicker basket and a fleece throw.

'You stay here. I can deal with this,' said Fox, disappearing into the kitchen.

Out of the corner of her eye she could see him crouch down over Dingo's body. Not wanting to watch, she crossed over to the window, letting her gaze settle across the dark waters of the Thames.

Lara pressed her thumb and forefinger into her eyes. She had to stop crying. She already looked a sight.

After a few minutes Ian came back into the room.

'What do you think?'

'It's not a standard break-in,' he said, still looking about. 'Burglars are in and out. They grab high-value items and are gone – you have a nice TV on the wall there and they didn't touch it.'

It was the answer she had expected, but it wasn't what she'd wanted to hear. Lara had harboured a slim hope that Fox would say, 'Oh, it's just some kids messing about. We've had a spate of these over the past few weeks.' But Lara had known in her heart it wasn't kids or opportunistic thieves. Which meant it was something much more dangerous.

'Have you pissed anyone off?'

'All the time,' she said, with a snotty smile.

Fox took a tissue out of his pocket and handed it to her.

'Feels personal, doesn't it,' he said, nodding towards the slashed cushions. 'They were either looking for something or they're being vindictive, deliberately destructive. Possibly both.'

He paused. 'What stories are you working on at the moment?'

'I think you know the answer to that one.'

'Your friend. Sandrine?'

Fox inhaled sharply.

'Could this be connected?'

Lara snorted.

'You're the detective, Ian. Dead girl, dead cat, trashed boat. Are you seriously wondering if it's not?'

'It's possible.'

Lara knew it was time to stop tip-toeing around the edges of their conversation.

'This isn't a break-in,' she said, hearing the desperation in her voice. 'It was a warning to stop working on my story. Killing Dingo, they were telling me what they could do to me.'

'Lara, who are they?'

She was hardly listening to him. Her head was spinning. The air on the houseboat felt thick and stale. She was suddenly aware that there was water under her home and she could feel the fluidity of the river through the soles of her feet. She put her hand out to stop herself from falling but Ian caught her.

'I think you'd better sit down,' he said.

Lara sank into the sofa, perching on the cushion, like a nervous swimmer on the edge of a pool.

Ian sat down beside her as she tried to control her breath.

She wanted to tell him everything, her belief that Michael Sachs had ordered the killings of Sandrine, Helen Groves, perhaps even Jonathon Meyer, but in this state he wouldn't believe a word she said.

Ian looked across at her.

'Look, I'm back in work on Monday. Why don't we arrange an appointment and you can tell me what you know. What you think has happened here.'

'Thanks Ian,' she said, although Monday seemed a very long way off. 'What else are you going to do police-wise?'

'I can sort out your door. We have a guy who can come out and secure it…'

She waited for him to say something else, panic swelling in her belly.

'My door? That's it?' she said, hearing the hysteria in her voice.

'And I've got a couple of lads on their way over to see if there's any CCTV footage, make some local inquiries.'

It didn't feel like much.

'There's got to be something else you can do.'

She was grateful that he had come but it all felt thin.

'Lara, what do you expect?' he said, exasperated. 'There's been a break-in. But no-one has threatened you, nothing has apparently been stolen.'

Her hand clenched into a fist. 'Fox, there are two dead bodies. Three if you add Dingo – which I do. You'd better hope there aren't any more on your conscience.'

He paused, considering.

'Do you have anywhere you can stay?'

Lara had a cottage on the Avery estate in Oxfordshire, but with Friday night traffic it could take two hours to get there.

'Do you know The Pengelly?' he said, when Lara didn't reply to his question.

She looked at him.

'That hotel off Sloane Square, where all the celebrities stay?'

Fox nodded.

'They don't just go for the pillow menu, they go because it's safe. A mate of mine runs security there, it's a tight ship, a vetted staff, that's why the big stars love it. I can give him a ring, get you a rate.'

Fox knew her background, that she was a member of the Avery family, but Lara appreciated him not assuming that she could throw money at the problem.

LARA LEFT FOX on the dock speaking on his phone, arranging for the security service. She hadn't liked telling him off – he was off-duty and yet he had come straight over and at the very least, he had taken her seriously.

But she could see there was going to be no heavy police involvement here, no men in white suits dusting for fingerprints. She knew how overstretched the force was, how busy they would be on a hot, busy Friday night. Why would they prioritise her over a stabbing, domestic violence or a drunken assault?

She went up to the top deck of *Misty*, and looked at her phone. She debated whether to call Alex again, but instead, she took a deep breath and rang Stefan.

The ring tone told her he was still overseas, and her heart sank in disappointment.

'Stefan, it's Lara.'

It suddenly seemed reckless to have called him.

'Lara, hi!' She heard genuine pleasure behind the words as well as the sounds of busy city life behind him, traffic, voices in a language she didn't recognise.

'Where are you?'

'Amsterdam. I'm just heading out for dinner with some of the *Telegraaf* team. I have to remind them that I'm still alive… Lara, is something wrong?'

'My place got broken into.'

'Shit. Are you okay? Did they take anything?'

'I'm fine. Just a bit shaken up, I guess.'

Lara wasn't sure why she was telling him all this. Stefan was in Amsterdam, there was nothing he could do to help, but it was just good to hear the concern in his voice, to hear that someone cared.

'Have you called the police?'

'Yes. Someone has just come round.'

'That's good. Look, I won't be back in London until tomorrow afternoon but if you need to stay at my place, my neighbour has a spare key…'

'Don't worry,' Lara said, with a half-smile. The offer was enough, the feeling that if everything fell apart she had somewhere else to go. She lifted her head just a little. 'I'll check into a hotel and sort it out tomorrow.'

'What are you going to do?'

It was a good question. What *was* she going to do?

'I'm going to clear up the boat, I'm going to throw out everything that's broken. And then I'm going to find who did this.'

Lara curled her fingers around the phone, squeezing hard. Even if it hadn't been before, it was personal now.

'I'm going to stop whoever did it, Stefan. And I'm going to make them pay.'

Chapter Thirty

LARA HADN'T BEEN on a date for a long, long time. In different circumstances, she might have felt the usual fizz of anticipation, the rush of excitement when you were about to meet a new lover. But tonight, as much as she wanted to see Stefan, Lara was not in the mood to go out. Fox had been right that she'd feel safe at The Pengelly: perhaps a little too safe. The lifts were operated by residents-only key cards, there were spy-cam intercoms on every hotel suite door and the Head of Security – Fox's friend Mills – had called within ten minutes of Lara's arrival to check everything was to her satisfaction. Mills even gave her his personal mobile number and assured her his team were on call 24/7. It was like having your own bodyguard, although Lara assumed it only applied inside the hotel. Perhaps she was about to find out.

'Have a good evening, Miss Stone.'

Lara nodded to the doorman, a friendly but solid man in a black suit with one of those curly ear-pieces. She hoped he could use it to call in a missile strike if needed.

Stepping out into the street, she tried to breathe in the warm evening air. Stefan had called her the moment he had landed and invited her to Walpole, a romantic bistro on the King's Road only a short stroll from the hotel. Lara was forcing herself to walk partly because it was ridiculous to get a taxi over such a short distance but mainly because she couldn't let 'them' win, whoever they were. That was precisely how terrorism worked: make ordinary people fear for their safety, make them change the way they behave. *Well bugger that*, thought Lara fiercely. Not that she was being silly about it: she was still paying attention to her surroundings.

Across the road she saw a middle-aged man in a casual suit, striding towards the station and a young couple strolling along with their arms hooked together. Nice people, happy people – Lara tried to remind herself that most people were decent and kind.

That morning had been spent sweeping up the glass and cleaning *Misty* with the help of Gustav, the white-haired artist living two berths down who, without saying a word, had just brought his toolbox down and started working on her bookshelves and door.

People *were* good. But still, Lara couldn't help but be on high alert. Hyper-aware, that's what they called it in the army; expecting every face to be hostile, every car to be wired with explosives.

She was still feeling tense as she walked into Walpole. She liked Stefan – and he'd come straight from the airport just to see her. If that wasn't a romantic gesture, she didn't know what was, but it was that very gesture which was making her fret as she gave her name to the maitre'd. Lara wasn't sure if she was ready for a relationship.

But then again… thought Lara, smiling to herself as she saw Stefan already at the table; a flutter in her chest, a catch in her breath. Stefan was smarter than usual, in a crisp blue shirt, his dark blonde hair was pushed back off his face – and those eyes. As he smiled, she wondered if she should just have invited him to the hotel and ordered room service.

'You look great,' he said, standing to kiss her cheek.

She knew he was being kind. The jeans, t-shirt and biker boots were what she always wore. She'd put a dress in her overnight bag but it was still hanging up in her suite. It felt wrong to dress up and look pretty when Dingo was dead and she had failed in her attempts to lay Sandrine to rest. Still, it felt nice to be complimented – and she had to remember to live life, otherwise what was the point?

'You're not too bad yourself,' she smiled, as he pushed her chair in. And good manners too. Aunt Olivia would approve.

The waiter came over and she watched as Stefan charmed and joked, expertly ordering food and wine as the golden lights of Walpole cast a glow over everything. *Relax*, she told herself. *Enjoy.*

'So how are you feeling?' asked Stefan, when they were alone. 'After yesterday.'

'I could have done without it,' she said as casually as she could. 'But checking into the hotel was a good call. There's nothing like crisp hotel sheets to soothe you. I actually had a great night's sleep for once.'

Not entirely true, but she knew she had to put it behind her. She was Lara Stone: tough, capable, resilient. Fake it until you make it, right?

'So what did the police say?'

Lara shrugged. 'Not much. I'm not sure he rates their chances of finding out who did it.'

Stefan nodded sympathetically. Lara was grateful that he wasn't making a big deal about it, wrapping her in cotton wool. Then again, she hadn't exactly told him how unsettled and frightened the break-in had made her.

'You know what we need?' he said, pulling a bottle from an ice bucket. 'We need to get drunk as kippers.'

'Drunk as kippers?'

Stefan frowned.

'Isn't that an English saying?'

She let out a laugh. He was so fluent, sometimes she forgot that English wasn't his first language.

'I don't think so.'

'Really? Oh God, I've been using it for years.'

Lara grinned, feeling a little of the tension subside.

'Well, how about this then,' he said, raising his glass. 'Op één been kun je niet lopen'?

'Sounds good, but what does it mean?'

'You can't walk on one leg. Loosely translated it means 'don't stop at one drink when you can have two.'

Lara sipped the deliciously cold wine as Stefan told her how he had flown from Geneva to Amsterdam, all the mundane details of popping into his apartment – watering the plants, dealing with the bills, how he was thinking of renting it out now the plan was to be in London full-time. It was good to hear about normal life for once. Then he filled her in on the investigation, how Eduardo had visited the Kanjomo mine and put together a small local team to follow the paper-trail of contracts and permits – hopefully – back to the real money men at the top of the chain. Lara sat forward, lowering her voice.

'Stefan, can I be honest? The more I think about it, the more I think the mine is a dead end.'

Stefan frowned. 'What? No, Eduardo is making excellent progress, he said…'

She shook her head. 'That's not what I mean. I'm sure there's a story there about connecting high-level finance to child labour and I don't doubt you'll find it. I just don't think the mine is the real reason why Sandrine was killed.'

She told him about her trip to Edinburgh and Ullapool, about Helen Groves and her friend Rebecca, about Victoria Sachs and the trafficking scandal in Haiti.

'Lara, why didn't you tell me any of this before?'

There was bemusement in his tone, annoyance too.

'Because I only found out on Thursday, then I got back to the houseboat and, well…'

'Have you told Eduardo any of this?'

She shook her head.

'He's back on Monday, right? I figured it could wait.'

The waiter brought over their food. Stefan stared down at it, as if he was thinking. 'But the mine story…

it all fits.'

'It does,' nodded Lara, feeling more energised, more confident as she spoke.

'But Stefan, my boat wasn't just burgled, it was ransacked. They broke my cat's neck.'

'They killed your cat?'

He looked hurt now and Lara didn't blame him. They were romantically involved, and she had kept things from him.

His expression softened.

'You should come and stay with me. I don't want you to be alone.'

His concern squeezed her heart.

'Thank you,' she said, her voice hitching slightly. 'But no. I'm booked into The Pengelly tonight, then I'm going to Oxfordshire, I have a cottage on my uncle's estate.' She pointed to her phone. 'My Aunt Olivia has summoned me.'

Olivia had sent a series of messages saying 'we need a chat', but the tone was clear: Lara's presence was required and she knew from long experience that it was futile to resist.

There was a long, pregnant pause.

'You do know we can quit,' said Stefan.

'Quit the investigation?' said Lara incredulously. 'We – I – need to do this, Stefan. Sandrine would have wanted us to finish the story.'

'Sandrine wouldn't want you to be in any danger.'

His voice was hard and he put down his fork to look at her.

'I do have some experience of this, Lara. Too

much, in fact. I never told you why I became a journalist. It was because my mum's sister Freja disappeared.'

That got Lara's attention.

'Disappeared? What happened?'

'No one knows for sure. Her body was never found, no trace at all in fact. My mum never recovered; it was the not knowing that ate away at her. That was why we moved to the Frisian Islands, so she could try and forget about it. But she never did get over it.'

Lara had liked Stefan from the start. He was passionate, good-looking and smart, but now she felt connected to him on an even deeper level.

She knew only too well what it was like to have questions that couldn't be answered. She could still remember the memorial service for her parents, the quiet of the chapel, the grim faces of their family and friends. There were no coffins, no closure, no gravestone to lay flowers at. Just a big question mark hanging in the air.

'That's what drove me to become a journalist,' continued Stefan. 'My mother was hardly wild about the idea. But when she realised she couldn't stop me, she made me promise that if I ever felt out of my depth, if I knew things were getting dangerous, I had to stop.'

'And would you?'

There was a note of challenge in her voice that Lara immediately regretted.

'I have,' said Stefan. 'I did.'

He looked away, gathering his thoughts.

'I worked in Cologne for a few months. I was investigating an extremist gang and a series of dead bodies I thought were connected. It was a big story. I wanted to prove myself, but I pushed it too far, got myself into a really dangerous situation.'

'What happened?'

'I'd arranged to meet a contact at a biker bar. It was really rough, a really bad part of town – and hey, guess what? It was a trap. I had a knife held to my throat. They told me exactly what they would do if I didn't back off.'

He took an uneven breath, then met her gaze.

'Lara, I was twenty-six years old. I loved my job but I didn't want to die over it. So, yes. I stopped, pulled back – and you know what? I have no regrets. My mum had had enough heartache in her life without losing a son too. And I figured I could do more good alive than dead.'

He looked at her.

'You're judging me.'

Lara shook her head slowly.

'No. I'm thinking I would have done the same thing.'

'So why don't you stop now? If Eduardo wants to carry on, that's his choice, but he's not the one who had his house burgled or his cat murdered. He's not the one looking over his shoulder every two minutes.'

Lara closed her eyes. She had been telling the truth; if she had been in Stefan's shoes, she would have backed off too. But this was different, this wasn't just about a splashy headline or a press award, this was about Sandrine, a woman she had loved as a sister. She wasn't prepared to let someone – anyone – scare her off and she was committed now, all the way. But she loved the way Stefan had opened up to her. And she loved the way he had trusted her because he cared.

'I'll think about it,' she said. 'Tomorrow.'

'Tomorrow?' said Stefan. 'But Lara, this is happening right now. If you're in danger…'

Lara squeezed his hand back.

'Tomorrow,' she whispered. 'Right now I don't want to think about anything else except us. Can we go?'

Stefan searched her face, then nodded and raised his hand to the waitress, quickly pulling his credit card out.

'You get this one,' said Lara, smiling as she stood up. She held her hand out to him. 'And I'll get breakfast at The Pengelly.'

Chapter Thirty-One

LARA LAY ON her back, one leg hooked lazily over Stefan's. What a night. She hoped that Ian Fox's security friend wasn't too rigorous in his surveillance; any CCTV footage covering the approach to Lara's suite when they had arrived back after the restaurant would need an '18' certificate, she thought to herself with a smile. She felt herself glow at the memory and for the first time since Sandrine's death, Lara felt happy. No, it was more than that. Lying naked, barely covered by a crumpled white sheet, she felt alive. It felt so good.

Stefan stirred, turning towards her.

'You're awake,' he said, his voice still groggy.

He leaned across and kissed the curve of her shoulder.

'How do you feel about a late check-out?'

Lara laughed with pleasure.

'Very tempting indeed,' she said. 'But remember I have to go to my Aunt's? Olivia wants to *talk*.' She said the last word in imitation of a disapproving school-mistress, which pretty much summed up their relationship.

'What's so important?' he asked. Lara could hardly

blame Stefan for his disappointment. After all, he had come straight from the airport to see her the evening before and she was rewarding him by kicking him out of bed.

'My cousin Charlie – Olivia's son – is having an affair,' she sighed, not wanting to go into too much detail. 'I kind of put the cat amongst the pigeons. It doesn't sound very pressing, I know, but there's a lot of family politics involved.'

Lara turned on her side, propping herself up with her elbow. She hated to ruin the mood, but something had been nagging at her and she had to get it off her chest.

'Listen, can I ask you something personal?'

He laughed, circling her nipple with his fingertip. 'I think you probably qualify for that.'

'Well… I saw Alex on Friday and he'd heard you were seeking investment for a news project. Is that true?'

She didn't add that Alex had thrown it at her in the middle of a prickly argument with the clear implication that Stefan was not trustworthy.

'He's right, yes. But it was a while ago. I had an idea for a digital news and events business and took a few meetings to see if I could raise some capital, but it didn't come to anything.'

Lara almost sighed with relief. She didn't know why it had become such a big thing in her head, perhaps because Alex had seemed so certain that Stefan was up to something underhand. At the same time, Lara was intrigued.

'Does Eduardo know? I mean, was it something you were doing together?'

'Yes and no. Yes, he knew and no, he wasn't involved.'

He smiled as he saw Lara was keen for a more detailed explanation.

'Look, I love the work we do at the collective and I love Eduardo like a brother, but he's not the easiest man to deal with and as he finances Le Caché personally, it puts him in a powerful position as far as decisions are concerned. A lot of the time it doesn't feel much like a collective.'

'So what happened to your idea, the one you were trying to get funding for?'

Stefan shrugged a shoulder.

'I wasn't having much luck raising the money and then Eduardo decided to open the Shoreditch office, so I put my news empire on hold. I've always wanted to live in London so I see it as a win-win.' He gently pushed a lock of hair away from her face. 'Especially now.'

He turned his face to kiss her, softly at first, then more insistent, pressing his naked body against hers.

Lara groaned and rolled away.

'Down boy, I'm late for Aunt Olivia already. She won't be pleased.'

He muttered something in Dutch which Lara guessed would also displease her aunt. She looked at the bedside clock: she really was late. She reluctantly slid out of bed and went to grab some clean clothes from her bag, while Stefan lay there watching her.

'Are you sure you're happy going all the way to Oxfordshire? I mean, after what happened to your boat?'

'Stefan, I'm a big girl.'

The truth was, Lara was still nervous about it, but she couldn't let it stop her.

'At least let me drive you there,' said Stefan. Lara retrieved a boot from under the bed then looked up.

'I didn't know you had a car.'

'I don't. But we'll work something out.'

Lara laughed and bent to kiss him.

'That's sweet, but I think I'll be fine on the bike. Look, I think Eduardo wanted to meet tomorrow. Why don't you both come to mine? I can cook – sort of, anyway.'

'Are you sure?'

'I want to have people over. I need to fill the boat with some fun and laughter again.'

'Well, if it's fun you're after,' he said, with a wolfish grin, making a grab for her.

'You're going to have to wait for more of that,' she laughed. 'But I'll make it up to you, I promise.'

He raised an eyebrow.

'Promise?'

'You can count on it.'

THE SUNDAY MORNING roads were so quiet it took just over an hour to get to Foxhills on the bike.

Lara lowered her speed to dip between the open

iron gates and roared down the avenue of limes, an arch of vibrant, textured green leaning over the gravel drive. As the house appeared through the trees, Lara finally eased back on the throttle and slowed, a sign of respect for the elegant old house. This was the point in the journey that always made Lara think of the day almost twenty-five years ago when her grandmother, Rose Avery, had brought her back to Foxhills. 'A new life,' Granny had said, meaning it kindly, but Lara had known that it meant her old life – in that rambling Pimlico pile full of her father's curiosities and the unwavering love of her parents – had gone forever.

She could also remember waving David and Ramona Avery off on their annual sailing trip to celebrate their anniversary. It had been the first week of the school holidays, as it always was, and Granny Rose would plan fun things for them to do whilst Lara stayed at the Avery's Holland Park home: an afternoon tea at the Savoy, a West End musical. That year it had been Joseph and his Technicolour Dreamcoat and Lara had waited at the stage door to get her programme signed, but Lara had never got to show her parents.

Lara pulled up at the side of the main entrance, standing the bike up next to Nicholas's vintage Jaguar. He rarely drove the car, but it was kept buffed and polished next to the door, a prop for an imaginary photo-shoot.

Lara pulled off her helmet and looked up at Foxhills' tall windows, almost believing she might be able to see herself as a girl standing there, looking out in vain for her parents' return. She saw nothing of course:

just glass and reflections.

Lara had spent those first horrible few weeks with her grandparents here at the main house, but in accordance with her parents' will, Nicholas was to be her legal guardian and she moved a quarter mile across the estate to Nicholas and Olivia's farmhouse. It was just as well. Within the year, her grandfather Richard had died, by the time Lara got to the sixth form, Granny Rose had gone too – and the big house had passed down to Nicholas.

Lara shook off the memories and walked around the side of the house, slipping off her leather jacket and leaving it draped around a decorative urn: she was well aware how Olivia loathed her motorbike – it wouldn't do to get off to a bad start, it was going to be difficult as it was.

She found Olivia Avery on the sun terrace at the rear of the house, her face hidden by a wide-brimmed hat as she bent to prune a rose bush. Lara would never say it to her face, but she had always admired her Aunt's style. Even in her gardening gear, a crisp white shirt worn underneath a denim pinafore dress, Olivia looked as if she had stepped straight from the pages of a Vogue 'gardens' supplement.

'Oh darling, you came,' said Olivia, sweeping across for a vague embrace. 'I hope your journey wasn't too taxing.'

'Quite the opposite,' said Lara, looking up at the eggshell sky. 'It's a glorious day.'

'It is, isn't it? Actually it's perfect, as I've been desperate to show you the Butterfly Garden. Can you believe it's finally finished?'

Lara didn't know Olivia had been creating a Butterfly Garden, but it didn't surprise her at all. Over the past few years, her aunt had reinvented herself as a horticulturist. *Tatler* had called her 'the new Bunny Mellon', the famed American garden designer and socialite, which Lara was sure would have thrilled her.

'I don't know what keeps you in London in the summer,' said Olivia, leading Lara through the walled garden. 'Especially now you're not working.'

Lara had to admit there was something in what Olivia was saying. There were numerous properties in the grounds of Foxhills and Lara had use of a small cottage, willed to her by her grandmother. It was beautiful, chocolate-box pretty, but it had never really felt like home. She looked out across the lawns and the trees beyond. All of it was so familiar, but all so loaded with baggage. Even now, Lara could remember the smell of fruit trees and tomatoes ripening in the sun and she still had fond memories of the original gardeners, Joan and Graham, an elderly married couple who always seemed to have Sherbet Lemons in their pockets. There had been happy times here too.

'Are you feeling well, my dear? You look tired.'

Lara couldn't help blushing, thinking of her night with Stefan.

'Busy night?'

Olivia said it as if she were reading her mind. Her aunt had always had an unsettling ability to pick up on Lara's mood. She followed Olivia through a doorway in the garden's flint wall and out into an open area. In her childhood, it had always been called 'The Meadow', but rather than a wide field, it had elements of an English country garden with stone-flagged paths criss-crossed by long beds of iris, pansies, tulips and foxgloves. She had learnt the names of these plants trailing after her grandmother on perfect summer days exactly like this. Rose Avery had also been a keen gardener, but Lara could definitely see how Olivia had curated the space and put her own unique mark on it. The brick walls were scrubbed and pointed so they looked like they were laid quite recently rather than 200 years ago, everything just so, every last petal and leaf swept away.

'This is lovely,' said Lara honestly.

Olivia gave a brief smile.

'They say gardening is the pursuit for A-type personalities,' she said. 'It suits the perfectionist in me.' Olivia reached over and dead-headed a purple iris, tucking the bud into her apron. 'But the work is never done; try as you like, nature simply can't be tamed.'

Lara looked curiously at her aunt. You had to know Olivia Avery to know how incongruous that statement was. Aunt Olivia was the epitome of the socialite tastemaker, impeccably turned out, tirelessly controlling every aspect of her environment, forging alliances and ousting enemies. Admitting weakness, even a small one, just wasn't in her vocabulary.

Olivia gestured to the far corner of the garden where a round green table had been set up.

'Let's go and sit under the pergola. I'll have some lemonade brought down.'

Olivia pulled out a phone and gave a few clipped instructions to an unseen lackey, then sat down opposite Lara, giving her the benefit of her cool smile. Olivia's long neck and pale blue eyes gave her an elegance, but rarely warmth. As they waited for the refreshments, Olivia pointed out the various improvements she had made to the garden – the butterfly friendly-flowers and larval food plants she had nurtured: sweet Williams, forget-me-nots and sorrel. A housekeeper bustled over with a jug and poured the drinks into two hi-ball glasses before discreetly withdrawing.

'So,' said Olivia, carefully folding her hands in her lap. 'Charlie told me what happened.'

She was straight to the point as always, but this time Lara refused to be brow-beaten.

'And what did Charlie tell you exactly?'

Lara was pushing back, but she was also curious. Had Charlie really called up Olivia and said, 'Mother, I've been caught shagging the Deputy Editor's girlfriend'?

Olivia pursed her lips.

'He told me that you have been spying on him, Lara. That you had taken *photographs* of him.'

She almost laughed at that: as if the invasion of Charlie's privacy was the biggest issue here.

'Not spying actually. I simply happened to see him when I went to his house to discuss a work issue.'

'Really? It was my understanding you don't actually work at the *Chronicle* at the moment.'

'Does that really matter, Olivia? What matters is

what I saw.'

Olivia raised her eyebrows a fraction.

'What you *thought* you saw. You didn't have the courtesy to actually ask Charlie what was going on, did you?'

'No, but…'

'So instead you decided to start causing trouble.'

'Excuse me? *I'm* the one making trouble here?'

'Don't play games Lara. You ran off and told Alex Ford that Charlie is having an affair with his girlfriend.'

'Alex is my friend and if his girlfriend has been cheating on him, I think he deserves to know.'

Olivia exhaled loudly.

'All very noble and selfless,' she said bitterly. 'And as usual with zero thought for the consequences.'

'I'm sorry?' said Lara frowning. 'Consequences for whom? For Charlie?'

'For the newspaper,' said Olivia impatiently. 'And for your friend Alex.'

'Olivia, I was trying to do the right thing.'

'Right for who? You?'

Olivia shook her head, then looked away across the garden.

'Lara, I am not your mother. I have never tried to replace her, but I do care about your well-being. When you make unwise choices, I feel it's my duty to step in and say something. I've seen how you look at Alex. Lord knows, I don't blame you. He is a smart, good-looking man, but he chose someone else. Don't let your regret ruin other people's lives.'

Lara's anger boiled up.

'Don't make this about me, Olivia,' she snapped. 'So yes, perhaps I should have considered Alex's position a little more, but this all comes down to one thing: Alicia was shagging Charlie behind Alex's back. If Nicholas was having an affair I assume you'd want to know?'

'Don't be so naïve, Lara,' she replied, with a haughty expression. 'You say you're trying to help Alex? He's an ambitious man, highly capable and he's going places. A future editor. Your ill-judged piety may have ruined all that.'

'So you're telling me the Avery board would actually pass over the best man for the job because your son can't keep it in his pants?' Lara barked out a laugh. 'That's a fine way to run a business.'

'Alex is an employee,' said Olivia, steel in her voice. 'Charlie is family. It doesn't matter how good Alex is, he will lose that fight.'

Lara knew that Olivia was only pointing out the obvious, but Lara wasn't going to take it lying down. She owed Alex that much.

'What are you suggesting Olivia? That morals don't matter in this business?'

'I didn't say that...'

'Well let me assure you that morals *do* matter. They matter more than anything else in a newspaper company. We can't hold people to account if our own ethics are questionable and as a shareholder in Avery Media Group, I will do everything in my power to make sure our company adheres to the very highest standards.'

She expected her aunt to fire one of her disapproving looks, but instead Olivia put an elegant hand on Lara's.

'You're just like your father,' she said, with a gentle laugh.

Lara was too stunned to reply.

'Oh, David was just the same. Impulsive, bull-headed, unshakably principled, irritating though that could be. The truth was all that mattered to him, it was as if he believed "the truth" was an absolute thing and he'd do anything to get it. He was utterly fearless that way.' She looked away sadly. 'Perhaps too fearless.'

Lara was completely thrown. She had never heard Olivia talk about her father before – and she certainly hadn't expected to hear her speak so warmly about him. Before she could ask any more questions, Olivia stood and began walking back through the garden. It seemed Olivia's 'talk' was over.

'Come,' she said over her shoulder. 'Shall we see if we can find some butterflies?'

Lara was too exhausted to quarrel. Instead, she followed in her wake, snaking through the shrubs, sending colourful insects fluttering though the air. Lara wasn't an expert but she recognised cabbage whites, red admirals and a painted lady.

'So did you enjoy the *Chronicle* party?' asked Olivia, trailing her fingers along a long-stemmed white flower.

'It was something of a success, wasn't it?'

'Everyone came,' agreed Lara.

Lara gave a half-smile, the sight of the butterflies and the flowers softening her mood.

'Is there anyone you don't know?'

Olivia pretended to think about it and gave a mischievous shrug. 'No, no one worth knowing anyway.'

Lara raised her eyebrows as a sudden thought occurred to her.

'So you know Victoria Sachs?'

'Victoria. Of course.'

'Was she at the party?'

'No. She was invited: I received an invitation to her fundraiser, so I had to ask her. Thankfully she was in New York. The numbers were getting out of hand.'

'What fundraiser was this?'

Olivia waved a hand.

'She's hosting a benefit lunch at Claridge's for her charity ImpactAid. It's tomorrow actually. Victoria's a little too pleased with herself, but it should be fun nevertheless. The auction is always hard-fought.'

A thought started to gain traction.

'Can I come?'

Olivia turned to look at her.

'Really?' said Olivia, surprised. 'I didn't think you were interested in that sort of thing.'

'Not usually, but after the month I've had, I could do with a bit of fun.'

Olivia nodded in agreement. 'I won't argue with you there. As it happens, I think Lavinia Dawson has dropped out, so there will be a place at our table.'

'Do you mind?'

Olivia smiled – a real one this time, or perhaps as

real as Olivia could manage.

'Mind? I'd be delighted. Just two girls together, hmm?'

'My thoughts exactly,' said Lara. But that wasn't all she was thinking. She was planning something much more interesting.

Chapter Thirty-Two

ALEX RAPPED ON the door of the little office.

'Harris, do you have a minute?'

Harris Grant jumped in his seat, looking up with a guilty start. 'Sorry,' he said, wrapping up the sandwich he was eating and pushing it into a drawer. 'Just, you know, taking a break and I'll get right onto the…'

Alex held up a hand to stop the stream of nervous babble from the business editor. The *Chronicle's* business section was run from an office at the far end of the floor and Alex could understand how his unannounced appearance might make Harris anxious: he rarely came down this way especially for a one-to-one.

'Relax, Harris, you're fine,' said Alex, sitting in the chair opposite the man. 'I just need some information about a finance guy. Michael Sachs.'

'You too, huh?' he said, wiping some crumbs off his lip.

'What do you mean?'

'Lara called me on Friday asking the same thing. Are you two working on something together again?'

'I suppose we are.'

It was bending the truth a little, but it was also why

he was here now. Charlie didn't come into the office on weekends, which was a blessing in disguise, given the revelations about his affair with Alicia. It also meant that Alex couldn't make his case for Lara's reinstatement, but he still wanted to make amends with Lara and this was another way he knew he could help.

'Is she coming back into the office?'

The business editor looked hopeful. Alex knew Harris liked Lara – everyone did – but he also knew the question was a loaded one. Alex had heard the word 'redundancies' muttered on more than one occasion since the Tait verdict and if Nicholas Avery was prepared to axe someone as brilliant as Lara, his *niece*, just to shave off a few editorial costs and satisfy the advertisers, then no job was safe.

'Soon,' he said vaguely. 'In the meantime, what did you tell her about Sachs?'

Harris sat back in his seat, pushing it back toward the window.

'In general? Michael Sachs is one of the biggest names in investment, very rich, very connected. Or are you asking about ClearView?'

'ClearView?'

'His monstrosity of a building project in Paddington.'

Harris quickly tapped on his keyboard and turned the screen so Alex could see; a photo of a tall modernist block on the north side of the park still under construction.

'What is it, Sachs's new office?'

'Probably, but this is more about PR. There's an

arts centre and a theatre on the ground floor and a boutique cinema in the basement. It's all going to be free or subsidised.'

Alex frowned. 'I thought Sachs was a ruthless money man.'

'Sure, but this is a fifteen-storey monument to Sachs's ego, setting himself up as a patron of the arts, Mr. Nice Guy giving something back to the people.'

Alex picked up on Harris' sceptical tone.

'So you don't think Sachs is a nice guy?'

Harris raised a brow. 'He's generous with his philanthropy, sure, but you don't get rich running a soup kitchen. Sachs's a tough operator. There are certainly whispers about him being particularly nasty if you cross him, too.'

Alex immediately thought of Lara. That morning, he'd gone round to the houseboat with a bag of croissants as a peace offering, but Lara hadn't been there. He'd assumed she was with Stefan and had kicked himself for speaking out against him. He knew what Lara was like – pig-headed and stubborn. If he voiced his disapproval about Stefan Melberg, it was just like her to go and move in with him, just to prove a point.

But if Lara's love life was her own business, he could still be worried about her and he hated her dropping off the radar like this.

Harris carried on talking.

'Sachs's fund is very successful, but he's pivoting heavily into real estate – lending money on property as well as developing it and investing in it. The big rumour I heard when I asked around is he is actively looking to sell Sachs Capital.'

'Why the shift?'

Harris laced his hands behind his head. 'Who knows? But Sachs has always been a genius at moving with the times. He'll know what he's doing. Besides, a sale of his company will be a major windfall. Maybe he just wants to quit while he's ahead.'

Alex tried to process everything he'd been told.

'Did you tell this to Lara?'

'Not yet. I was going to call her tonight.'

He glanced at his chunky watch.

'Speaking of which… do you mind if I push off?'

'Course not,' he smiled, remembering that Harris had a wife and three teenage boys. Just because Alex didn't mind working on Sundays, it didn't mean that other colleagues with families didn't resent missing pub lunches, five-a-aside matches, park walks with friends and all the other things normal people did at the weekend.

Alex made another pit-stop before he headed back to his office. The picture desk was like the beating heart of the news room. More than ever, pictures generated stories, so this department was one of the busiest, with junior editors scanning the wires looking for images, fielding requests and acting as a conduit for snaps from paparazzi and the eagle-eyed public alike. And right at the centre of it all, like a craggy spider, was Gary McTavish.

He grabbed a couple of coffees from the machine and crossed over to Gary's desk.

‘Urgent job for you,’ he said, handing him a cup.

The *Chronicle*’s Chief Picture Editor was one of Alex’s favourite members of staff. He was pushing sixty, but giving up a chronic addiction to Red Bull and taking up cycling had seen him lose some weight and look ten years younger. As one of the old timers, Gary was used to the right-now-if-not-sooner pace of the newsroom. If there was one person who put in longer hours at the *Chronicle*, it was Gary.

‘Thanks for the rocket fuel,’ he grinned, blowing on the hot liquid.

‘Shoot,’ he said.

‘Michael Sachs, high-finance guy. Currently building a huge development near Hyde Park called ClearView.’

‘What are we looking for?’

‘Not sure,’ said Alex. ‘Parties, charity dos, openings, especially anything in the last year. Make that the last five years. There might not be much, but get me everything.’

Gary nodded, tapped his pencil decisively on the desk. ‘I’ll get on it now. What’s this for by the way?’

‘News piece I’m working on.’

Gary raised an eyebrow.

‘Getting your hands dirty again, eh? Good stuff.’

‘Yeah, it is isn’t it?’ he said, smiling.

BACK IN HIS office, Alex shut the door and dropped into his ergonomic chair, spinning it round until he faced the plate glass window and the city, darkening in the dusk, beyond it. It was true what Gary had said.

Alex had spent the past two years, before, during and after the Felix Tait trail banging on about the vital importance of journalism and a free press and yet when was the last time he'd actually reported on anything? When was the last time he'd actually *written* anything? And it was worse than that, wasn't it? Alex was actually thinking about abandoning the *Chronicle*'s sinking ship to join Dominic's digital project for a life of more of the same – more meetings, staffing issues and glad-handling the advertisers rather than holding them to account. If he really cared about crusading journalism that made a difference, why wasn't he down with the troops, fighting?

Sighing, he tried calling Lara again but when it went straight to message, he flipped through some layouts that had been sent over by the features department, not really concentrating.

'Are pizzas on the way, boss?' asked Steve from the production department. Alex edited the Monday edition every fortnight, and from the start, he'd ordered take-out for the staff who worked long into the evening.

He paid for it out of his own pocket, and at some point, he guessed people had forgotten that and considered it a company perk. He didn't mind. People like Steve had been in since 9am and wouldn't leave until the night-shift team arrived once the first edition had gone off to press.

He gave a thumbs up sign and hopped online to order a dozen Margheritas.

The food had just arrived when Gary walked past

his office slipping on his cycling helmet, his trousers legs already cuffed with clips for his cycle journey home.

'I've got to push off early tonight. Wife's birthday. Pete's in charge of the desk,' he said, name-checking his deputy. 'The stuff you want is on the server,' he said, fiddling with his hat strap.

'That was quick.'

'You know me. I've emailed you a link.'

'Thanks a lot. I appreciate it. Now push off before you're in trouble with the missus for being late. And by the way, that hat makes you look like an alien.'

'State of the art, mate,' he grinned and left Alex to it.

It wasn't early, no matter what Gary said. It was almost ten o'clock and the office had taken on a more muted sound. The night shift was beginning to trickle in, Monday's first edition, had been declared 'off-stone' and sent to print. Although the lights were always on in a daily newspaper, the frenetic energy of the office simmered down to an industrious hum.

'Come on Michael Sachs, let's have a look at you, then,' he muttered, as he clicked on Gary's file.

Whoever said a picture was worth a thousand words had probably been a photographer, but Alex had always known the value of the picture desk with his stories. Back in the day, it had been paparazzi snaps: Britney shaving her head, Nigella's marriage imploding, Sean Penn coming out swinging. But Instagram had stopped all that: celebs could tell their own stories on their feeds, and the big news events were documented by a thousand cameras from a thousand angles courtesy of the general public and their smartphones. The image was still king, but that didn't mean they couldn't be manipulated and controlled.

Just like this, thought Alex, scrolling through hundreds of near-identical shots of Michael Sachs. At art gallery openings, charity dinners and fundraisers, or with happy benefactors of his numerous charitable foundations.

He wasn't sure why he was surprised that there were so many pictures of Sachs. Money men were always out and about on the party circuit flexing their wallets, improving their profile, showing off their Masters of the Universe credentials. And although middle-aged financiers were not of obvious interest to the press, and by extension, the paparazzi, they were often surrounded by beautiful women, which did make them of interest to editors looking to glamorise their pages.

He leant closer to inspect Sachs. He was a good-looking man in the Richard Gere silver fox mode. The cut of his suits said Saville Row, his tan spoke of skiing holidays and winter breaks. Even from these grainy pictures Sachs oozed the sort of self-confidence that Alex had often encountered among the top movers and shakers. If you lived such a charmed life, why wouldn't you feel confident? The wife was also a beauty, hovering around sixty, well-preserved, elegant with a look of Catherine Zeta Jones.

The pictures began to blur before Alex's eyes. The same slightly forced smile, the same suits and dresses, many of the same people appearing next to the Sachses. This was pointless. He didn't know what he had expected to find; a picture of Sachs and Meyer surrounded by teenage prostitutes?

He was just about to switch off his machine when he saw it. David Becker, the investor he'd bonded with at Dom's pitch dinner, standing shoulder to shoulder with Michael Sachs. Looking, it had to be said, like great pals.

Alex glanced at his watch, an idea forming. It was a thin idea, but it was better than no idea at all.

He took out his wallet and pulled out a business card he had put in there three days before.

'David Becker. It's about time we got reacquainted,' he muttered. And made the call.

ALEX HAD THOUGHT his own gym was pretty fancy, with three floors of spinning rooms, fitness studios and lavender-infused towels, but The Mayfair Racquets Club was a whole different world. Hidden away on a discreet mews near Berkeley Square, there was a doorman in tails and a bowler hat and a beautiful redhead on reception who already knew his name and immediately showed him the way to the changing rooms. It was exactly the sort of place that a high-flyer like Jonathon Meyer would be a member of, thought Alex with a slight sense of foreboding as he opened his assigned locker and found the regulation club whites crisply ironed and waiting for him.

Alex had been apprehensive about meeting David Becker here, especially as he hadn't held any kind of racquet in close to a decade, but there hadn't been much choice; Becker's squash partner had dropped out that morning and David was flying out to Frankfurt later in the day. Time was money and all that. He supposed the squash court was a better setting for a private conversation than the bar and an on-court humiliation was a small price to pay if he got the information he wanted.

David was already smashing a ball against the wall when Alex arrived at Court Three.

'Looking good, Alex,' called Becker, as Alex opened the glass door and went inside. 'Let's see what you've got then,' he said, not pausing for small talk.

David hit the wall, a couple of inches above the red service line. Alex retrieved the shot without too much difficulty, moving around the court with more ease than a man who sat behind a desk for fourteen hours a day deserved to.

'Nice shot,' said David. 'I didn't know you played.'

'It's been a while,' he replied, concentrating as he thwacked the ball low and hard. 'Not since school really.'

'Harrow?'

'The other place,' said Alex. It was his standard response to public school old boys; he knew that to them, 'the other place' meant Eton or Harrow, depending on who you spoke to, but technically Kendal Grammar was another place too. He returned

Becker's serve and smiled to himself as he remembered the town's squash club, an old warehouse just off the A6. He'd go with his mates Jacko or Gaz, messing about on the bus journey there but taking the game deadly seriously when they were on court.

Alex was exhausted by the time they'd finished the first game. David had beaten him, but Alex had put up a fair fight: that was all that was required. Becker wiped his face with a towel and squirted some water into his mouth from a bottle with a thick plastic straw.

'So, have you given any thought to Dom's offer yet?'

'Plenty,' said Alex honestly. 'That's why I wanted to talk, actually.'

Becker smiled.

'You know everyone is really keen to get you on board. Ideas you can change, develop or even reverse, but without the right staff to do that, you're screwed.'

'I was just interested to know more about the financial side of things. The backing and so on.'

'Sensible,' said David. He outlined some figures and who they had in mind for next-stage investors.

'We need someone with vision, but they'd also need deep pockets,' said David. 'The problem with too many new media ventures is not having sufficient backing to get through the first few years.'

'You know Michael Sachs right?'

Becker gave him a sideways look.

'A little. Why do you ask?'

Alex knew he had to play it gently. Last night when he'd seen the picture of Becker and Sachs together, he'd been convinced David would be a conduit to insider information, but in the cold light of day, it felt more tenuous. After all, Alex had met all kinds of people at parties, but he didn't know the first thing about their financial dealings.

'We're running a news piece on Sachs's ClearView development,' said Alex casually. 'You know the project's very big on the arts, the creative side, so I thought he might be interested in backing a media venture. Have you tried him?'

'Mike's not usually interested in our sort of stuff,' said David, looking doubtful. 'He does use media people for corporate intelligence work but that's about it.'

'Corporate intelligence?'

Alex knew what it was but he wanted to keep Becker talking; not least because he needed to catch his breath before the next game.

'Corporate intelligence is investigative research into companies you might be interested in buying or sectors or opportunities you have an interest in. One CI start-up a friend of mine backed two years ago has unicorn status already. He's made an absolute *killing*.'

'So why do you think Sachs would be interested in corporate intelligence?'

Becker gave a low laugh.

'Because due diligence is Mike's superpower. You want to know why Michael Sachs is so successful? He researches everything and everyone he invests in and uses what he finds as leverage.'

David paused to wipe the handle of his racket with

a towel. 'In fact I sent your mate Stefan Melberg his way.'

Alex tried not to react.

'Stefan?' he repeated, his heart jumping. 'What for? Investment?'

'No, I didn't think his news idea stacked up, but I thought Stefan was smart and Sachs mentioned he was on the lookout for brilliant researchers, so I recommended him.'

'Wow. I've always got the idea that Stefan was kind of anti-corporate. Did he do it?'

Becker shrugged and tossed Alex the ball. 'No idea. But I do know Michael Sachs pays very, very well. I find that overcomes a lot of principles.'

Yes, thought Alex, throwing up a serve. *I imagine it does.*

Chapter Thirty-Three

'. . . AND THE FINAL lot in the auction, ladies and gentlemen, is the grand prize.' A twitter of excitement ran around the hotel ballroom. 'One week in Penelope and Robert Devaine's villa on Harbour Island!'

There was a ripple of applause and Lara looked over at her Aunt Olivia.

'It's beautiful,' she said. 'Nicholas and I stayed there last New Year.'

Lara had always wondered why anyone would want to come to a society fundraiser. Yes, Claridge's was a beautiful hotel and the lunch had been lavish, but who would pay upwards of a thousand pounds a ticket for the privilege of spending yet more money on auction prizes donated by your friends? But then again, Lara had always wanted to go to the Bahamas. And right now, being 4,000 miles from this spot seemed eminently appealing.

'Who will start me off at a very modest one thousand pounds?' asked the auctioneer.

There was an expectant pause, then a slim arm went up on the next table. An elderly lady in a velvet dress had made a bid.

'That's Elspeth Hart-Daniels,' whispered Olivia, leaning across. 'She'll be hoping that someone outbids her.'

'She doesn't want to win? Why?'

'Ted – her husband – lost a packet in the last crunch. She's still putting on a brave face, but she can't afford to fly to Nassau, let alone stay on the island for a week.'

The one saving grace about this lunch had been having Olivia sitting next to her. Olivia knew everyone in the room and had the inside track on their wealth, politics and social position. It was fascinating, like watching a soap opera with the director giving a running commentary. Lara watched Mrs. Hart-Daniels' face when another bid came in. The old woman tried to look disappointed, but Lara could see the relief.

'You're right,' said Lara and Olivia nodded.

Looking at the lunch through her reporter's eyes, Lara could see that the event was really about power. People flexing their wealth, showing how little money meant to them, creating a league table of who was the most important. Even the seating plan was loaded with meaning. The top players sat at the front, the most visible and the most vocal in the auctions, everyone applauding their bids, but the prime spot was at Victoria Sachs's table slap-bang in the middle of the room, surrounded by admirers, desperate to gain a smile or an acknowledgement from the Queen Bee. The question for Lara was how could she break through that ring and get to Victoria Sachs?

Lara took a sip of wine trying to think it through.

She knew it had been risky coming here today, but what else could she do? She remembered something Alex had once said when he was back in London, heading up the news desk. She'd been having trouble with a story, hitting dead end after dead end.

'Sometimes you've got to shake the tree and see what falls out,' Alex had told her.

'We have a new bid,' said the auctioneer, leaning forward from his podium, shading his eyes to peer into the crowd. 'A generous bid from the lovely Marguerite Hurlingham.' A ripple of applause and a cool smile from Victoria Sachs.

'So who will give me a bid of ten thousand pounds?'

Suddenly Lara knew what she had to do.

'Fifteen thousand!' she shouted.

Olivia's head swivelled towards her, but Lara kept her eyes focused on the auctioneer, who pointed at her with his gavel. 'Fifteen thousand!' he repeated with glee. 'From the young lady at the back. Now who's going to…'

'Sixteen!' came a cry from a table near the middle. A red-faced man with wire-rimmed glasses who had turned to grin at Lara. Perhaps he thought that bidding against her would win her heart. *Au contraire*, she thought. All eyes were now on Lara, including – as she had hoped – those of Victoria Sachs. It was one way to get someone's attention.

'The bid is at sixteen thousand,' said the auctioneer. 'And let's all remember that this is for the ImpactAid charity and all the good work they are doing out in Haiti.'

Lara felt a hand on her knee. 'Lara, what are you *doing*?' murmured Olivia. 'It's not actually that nice a place. You'd be better off staying at The Dunmore.'

'Twenty thousand pounds!' shouted Lara, figuring she might as well throw herself all in. It was reckless and irresponsible – she supposed theoretically she could afford it, but even so, Lara was reminded of the one time she had done a parachute jump. Goaded into it by Alex when he was stationed in South Africa, standing in the doorway of that rickety prop plane, she had felt the same mixture of adrenaline and idiocy.

'Looks like we have someone who loves the Bahamas,' said the auctioneer. 'Is there anyone else who fancies a week in the lap of luxury in Harbour Island?'

There was a tense hush as the auctioneer scanned the audience.

'Anyone?' he asked, 'No?'

Oh God, thought Lara, her euphoria rapidly turning to panic.

The auctioneer raised his gavel with a flourish. 'Going once… going twice.'

The sound of the gavel smashing against the lectern vibrated around the room.

As the crowd burst into applause, Olivia leant in. 'What the hell was all that about?' she whispered.

'Just trying to fit in, Auntie,' she said, finishing off the rest of her wine.

THE MAIN EVENT over, people were beginning to get up and move towards the hotel lobby. Lara followed the flow, accepting the odd arm-squeeze and 'well done' from the society ladies. It was strange: the money being thrown about here was ludicrous, but there was a jolly village fete atmosphere, as if Lara had just won the fruit basket in the raffle.

'Here she is!' said a woman grabbing Lara by the arm.

'Let me introduce you to Penny. She owns the villa.'

Penny was a less slender and stylish version of Olivia. She had a regal bearing, pale blonde hair in a cloud around her head. Her blue blazer had shiny gold buttons with a horse's head stamped onto them.

'It's you, Olivia's niece. Lara, isn't it?'

'That's right.'

'You're going to have a wonderful time. Weather can be a bit hit or miss in September, hurricane season. But of course, you miss the crowds.'

Lara frowned. Had she just paid £20,000 for going out of season? She made a point to check the small print on the auction.

'Have you seen Victoria?'

'She's just had to visit the little girls' room, dear,' said Penny, pointing down the corridor. 'Although she's not the one collecting payment. I think you'll have to speak to Lucinda Dyson for that….'

IGNORING THE WOMAN, Lara followed the corridor that led away from the ballroom. Lara guessed this wasn't the bathroom that the guests were meant to use. It was quiet here, the sound of pots and pans in the distance suggesting they were close to the kitchens.

She pushed down the door handle and went inside. Victoria Sachs was standing by the sinks, leaning into a mirror, applying a vivid red lipstick. She looked up as Lara walked in.

'Ah, our mystery bidder,' said Victoria, bringing the full beam of her smile to bear on Lara. She could immediately see that Victoria Sachs had that charisma that truly successful people were blessed with, a sort of golden glow that invited you in. You felt happy just being in their presence.

'Are you a big fan of Harbour Island?'

'Never been, actually, but it is somewhere I've always dreamed of.'

'Well, you've got yourself a bargain.' She lowered her voice and drew Lara closer. 'Joanna Ashcroft's Bahamas place went for one hundred grand at an event I went to the other week, although Jeffrey Archer was doing the auction, and Joanna's place is a little more luxe than Penny's. Don't tell Penny I said so,' she added.

She turned to look at Lara directly.

'You're Olivia Avery's niece, aren't you?'

'I am. I'm Lara. Lara Stone.'

'The journalist.'

Lara looked at her.

'I make a point of checking out the guest list,' said Victoria.

'Do you know why I'm here?' Lara was genuinely curious.

'I assumed you were here to support ImpactAid,'

she said more crisply.

'I suppose you could say I am.'

Lara's heart was thudding. She wasn't just shaking the tree, she was about to burn it down.

Lara put her hand in the pocket of her silk dress and pulled out a USB memory stick.

'What's this?' said Victoria. The woman's face had been heavily Botoxed but Lara could still see a deep frown appear between her brows.

'Photographs and footage of one of your ImpactAid officials in Haiti involved in illegal trafficking, taken by Helen Groves. You know Helen, of course. She was one of your volunteers in Haiti.'

There was a split-second flash of alarm, then the smooth confidence reappeared. *Oh, you're good*, thought Lara, wondering for one terrible moment if Victoria knew that it was all a bluff. That the memory stick was blank. Rebecca had told them about the existence of the pictures, but the files had disappeared, possibly on Sandrine's missing laptop.

Lara felt her heart hammering, her hands shaking. This was a high-wire walk over a tiger's cage, but it was the only option she had left, to force information out of Victoria Sachs. Victoria took the memory stick and looked at it in the pale palm of her hand.

'And what do you expect me to do with this?'

'I expect you to tell me what happened when Helen Groves showed you these images.'

'Helen…?'

Lara's anger and desperation spilled over.

'Do *not* mess me about, Mrs. Sachs,' she snapped.

'I seriously doubt you've forgotten Helen Groves. She was killed six weeks ago in Port-au-Prince. You met with her at your hotel. She told you what she had seen. How ImpactAid volunteers were identifying Haitian girls for trafficking.'

'I really don't know what you're talking about. Now, if you'll excuse me, I have a car waiting for me. Perhaps I can arrange a black coffee for you to sober up.'

Lara stepped between Victoria and the door.

'Your car can wait,' said Lara, steel in her voice. It was all or nothing now; there was no way back, she had to keep pushing.

'Either you speak to me now or you deal with it when the story comes out.'

She watched Victoria's face harden.

'Are you journalists so desperate for news that you will actually make things up? Of yes. I forgot. You work for the *Chronicle*. You were caught out recently in the High Court with the Felix Tait libel action. Felix is a friend of ours. Perhaps he can give us his lawyer's contact details if you continue with this fantasy.'

'We have lawyers too, Victoria. And journalists. Lots of journalists who are very good at getting to the truth. Journalists who can ruin reputations.'

'You really think you can threaten me, Lara?' she said, putting the memory stick on the vanity unit. 'Do you have any idea who my husband is? I can have this story shut down,' – she clicked her fingers – 'Just like that. We can buy you up wholesale and burn you to the ground. Is that what you want?'

Victoria took a step towards her, until she was so close Lara could see the lines of her face, tiny cracks buried under a pale film of foundation, like fine veins in marble.

'Do you know what sort of work we do at ImpactAid?' asked Victoria, her voice more controlled now. 'We provide clean water, food and education for some of the most deprived people on earth, people who have been to hell and back, people who look to us to make their lives just a little bit better.'

'I don't doubt the good intentions of your charity, Mrs. Sachs,' said Lara. 'But your organisation has abused its position.'

Victoria let out an incredulous laugh.

'Abused? How exactly?'

'You knew that your staff had taken advantage of those very people you were there to help. And you tried to cover it up.'

'There was no cover-up, Miss Stone,' she said firmly.

'Helen Groves disagreed with you.'

'There were a couple of bad apples and they were dealt with. It is all properly documented by the charity's human resources department and I would be happy to give your editor their contact details. Now if that is all...'

She tried to step around Lara, but Lara stood her ground.

'You can walk away, Mrs. Sachs, but the story will still run. We already have witnesses and documents, I am simply giving you the chance to tell me what happened.'

Victoria jabbed a finger at Lara.

'If you print this story, you'll have another very expensive libel suit on your hands,' she growled. 'I've spent twenty years building this charity, we've raised millions of pounds, helped thousands of people. I'm not going to throw all that away because some hysterical gap year student makes accusations.'

Lara raised her eyebrows.

'So you do know Helen Groves.'

'This is ridiculous!' she cried, pushing past Lara, reaching for the door handle. Lara slammed a hand onto the door, making Sachs look at her in alarm.

'No Victoria, it's not ridiculous,' she said. 'A girl is dead.'

'If that is so, then it is tragic and I feel for her friends and relatives.'

Lara saw something in her face. Shame? Victoria *knew* something.

'And Sandrine Legard? A journalist for *Le Figaro*, have you heard of her, Mrs. Sachs?'

'No, why would I?'

'Perhaps she contacted you. Sandrine had also been talking to Helen Groves and was about to file her story when…' – Lara banged the door again, making Victoria flinch – 'She hit the ground. Fatally.'

'Why are you telling me this?' said Victoria quietly.

'I believe that someone murdered Helen Groves and Sandrine Legard, Victoria. I don't believe that person was you. But I think you can help me find the person who did.'

'You are actually delusional,' she snorted.

'Am I?' said Lara, looking at her closely. 'Do you really believe that? And what about Jonathon Meyer? Do you still think his death was a tragic accident too? Because there's an awful lot of accidents going on around your husband.'

'What's my husband got to do with this?'

'He asked Jonathon Meyer to help him clean up the problem in Haiti, Victoria. He asked him to get rid of Helen.'

'And do you really believe all this, this... *bullshit*?' hissed Victoria. 'Do you really think my husband – a respected businessman – has actually been murdering people?'

Lara shook her head.

'I think you panicked when Helen contacted you. I think you asked your husband to help you out. And I think Michael panicked too because any scandal would impact on the sale of Sachs Capital.'

She was grateful for the information that Harris Grant, Business Editor of the *Chronicle* had told her about Michael Sachs, especially when she saw Victoria flinch.

It was speculation what Lara had just said, but now Lara saw that she had guessed correctly. Whatever Michael had done, it all hinged on that sale, so Victoria's reaction meant there was still some humanity in her.

'Please Victoria, co-operate with me, help me get the truth out.'

'Co-operate'?' she sneered. 'In what universe would you believe I'd help you write some deranged story which destroys my husband's reputation? I would call the police on you, but I genuinely think you need psychological help.'

Lara knew she had reached the end of the line. She had only one card left to play. She stepped away from the exit.

'Go if you must,' she said. 'But I'm not so sure your loyalties to Michael are well-placed.'

The woman stopped, one hand on the door knob.

'Michael is having an affair, Victoria,' said Lara.

'What? How on earth could you…'

'Michael's PA, Helen. She told me. Apparently it's been going on a while and it's not the first time.'

It was more conjecture but Lara had nothing to lose.

Victoria's face drained of all colour.

'You poisonous little bitch,' she whispered.

'Maybe,' said Lara. 'But this is about you, not me. You can let Michael betray you over and over, or we can put a stop to this. Work with me, Victoria. I don't believe you wanted anything bad to happen to Helen or Sandrine.'

The defiance returned to Victoria's voice.

'You have no proof of any of this,' she said, opening the door. 'If you had, you would have already printed the story.'

Lara nodded slowly.

'You could be right,' she said. 'But are you prepared to take the risk? If this story is true, it will come out eventually, you know it will.' She nodded towards the memory stick, still sitting by the sink. 'And if you let that happen, Victoria, then those girls' blood will be on *your* hands.'

Chapter Thirty-Four

THE STAKEOUT HAD been less exciting than Stella had imagined. True, she was glad that she hadn't been arrested or shot in the back with a poison dart, but following Michael Sachs had been mundane to the point of being deathly dull.

She'd been watching him all weekend but so far there had been little to report other than his South Kensington house was absolutely lush, and his Mayfair office, a sober townhouse near Shepherd Market, was quite small. If Stella was worth over a billion quid she was quite certain she'd commandeer some penthouse with a slide down to Harrods Food Hall and maybe have an open top Ferrari on call to take her home.

At least the ClearView development showed some imagination when it came to spending his money, she thought, sipping her tepid latte and observing the complex from the window seat of a café a hundred yards away from the site. Harris, the *Chronicle*'s Business Editor, had told Lara that ClearView was Sachs's latest investment, and compared to everything around it, it was huge: towering at least ten stories above the white Georgian apartment blocks either side, it was a sleek fin of silver and glass, sticking out like a modernist thumb.

According to a construction worker Stella had sweet-talked an hour earlier, it was running two months behind schedule. The lower levels were finished, the glass was polished and glinting in the late afternoon sun, but the upper floors were still shrouded in white plastic sheeting.

No wonder Michael Sachs was still inside. She'd seen him step out of a black Mercedes three hours earlier, but had yet to emerge; she could imagine the rollicking the building team were getting.

SHE WAS ABOUT to order another coffee when her phone rang.

'Stella, it's Alex.'

Her heart gave a little flip. She always got nervous talking to Alex Ford. Stella was slightly in awe of the boss. If Hollywood ever decided to do a newsroom drama, she'd always thought they should come and knock on the *Chronicle*'s Deputy Editor's door and just give him the part.

'Hello Alex.'

'Listen, are you with Lara?' he said. He sounded distracted, urgent; not his usual in-control self.

'No, I've been working on my own today. Why, is something wrong?'

'I hope not. Do you know where she is?'

'She's been at her aunt's house in Oxfordshire this weekend. Apparently there was a break-in at her houseboat but she's back in London now.'

'Break-in?'

Stella paused, not sure how much she should tell Alex. After all, he wasn't her boss anymore and Lara had given her the distinct impression that Alex disapproved of the Meyer investigation. Besides, she didn't know much about the burglary. Lara had been vague.

'Stella, please,' said Alex, picking up on her hesitation. 'I'm worried about her. I tried her at the *Misty*, but she's not there and she's not answering her phone. Any idea where else she could be? Could she have met Stefan Melberg?'

Stefan? Did Alex know about him?

Stella wasn't certain that Lara was shagging the handsome Dutch journalist, but Stella considered herself pretty intuitive about these sort of things and she had seen the way Lara and Stefan had looked at each other that morning at the Le Caché office. Perhaps Alex had worked it out too, and perhaps he was jealous, but there was concern in his voice that put her on edge too.

'I do know she was meeting Victoria Sachs today at some fundraiser,' said Stella, looking at her watch again. 'Mind you, that was a lunch thing.'

'Victoria Sachs? Damn.'

This didn't sound good.

'We could always try the Le Caché office. I think Eduardo is back from Africa today and there was some plan to meet him and Stefan.'

'Where is the Le Caché office?' he asked.

'Shoreditch. I haven't got the exact address but if you meet me at Shoreditch High Street tube, I'll take you there.'

ALEX WAS ALREADY waiting on the far side of the barriers under the shadow of the bridge. He was wearing a white shirt with the sleeves rolled up and a deep frown.

'Hi,' said Stella. 'Have you been waiting long? I've been…'

'Which way?' he said, cutting her off.

Stella stopped, then shook her head.

'Not until you tell me what's going on.'

She knew she was being pushy but the truth was, this was more her investigation that his.

Alex had a reputation for being a fair, supportive manager, unlike many senior news executives. Today though, he looked tough, the man who in editorial meetings Stella had seen tear into anyone he thought was giving less than 100%.

'Alex, tell me or I'm not taking another step. Lara's my friend too.'

Stella could barely believe she had just spoken to the great Alex Ford that way, but she was sick of being the last to know everything.

'I think Stefan's been working for Michael Sachs,' he said finally.

'*What?* You're serious?'

She examined his face again.

'You're really worried?'

'Stella, Sachs is the man Lara suspects of…'

'Killing Sandrine?' she said, glancing around. 'You think Lara's in *dange*r?'

‘At the very least Stefan’s been lying to Lara. Right now, I just want to find her.’

Stella wanted to find her friend too. She’d tried Lara’s phone as soon as she’d got off the line from Alex, only to be told, ‘the person you are calling is not available.’

‘Then let’s move,’ she said decisively, heading across the main road and back into the streets of Shoreditch, relying on her memory to lead her to the Le Caché office: being new and being security conscious, there was no address for the collective online.

She found it.

‘This is it?’ said Alex dubiously, looking up at the warehouse conversion Stella had visited with Lara.

‘Expecting something more grand?’

‘This is actually pretty fancy,’ he said and banged on the door. Stella stepped back into the road, trying to see through the upper windows to the mezzanine level.

‘Lights are off,’ she called. ‘Don’t think anyone’s home.’

Alex put his hands on his hips and blew out his cheeks.

‘Dammit.’

‘I think Stefan lives around here,’ said Stella, remembering a conversation from the previous week when she’d been at the Le Caché office. When Stella had brought bagels for the team, Stefan had mentioned that there was an excellent bakery on Redchurch Street, where he lived. If she was right that Lara and Stefan were seeing each other romantically, it was possible, likely, that they'd met at the Le Caché office and then gone back to his place. Lara was a professional but she wasn't a nun.

Stella knew Redchurch Street, a narrow lane filled with boutique shops and art galleries that had somehow become the Carnaby Street of East London. Stefan had also mentioned he lived above a café, but as they turned onto the street, she saw just how many food places there were – Turkish, Lebanese, Sushi, even a pastry shop specialising in cat-shaped cakes.

'Okay,' said Stella. 'I'll take this side, you take that side. Look for buzzers.'

Stella strode off, not looking back to see what Alex's reaction was to being given instructions by a junior member of staff.

If she felt in a hurry, she was. She was as worried about Lara as Alex was. Stefan had been entirely smooth and plausible. If he had been lying to all of them, there was no telling what he was capable of.

The first door was next to a swish patisserie and had four buzzers: Khan, 'Belinda B', Williams and Gerard. No 'Stefan'. *Pass.* As Stella moved down, she glanced back. Alex was talking to a woman standing in an open doorway. Presumably he had pressed all the buttons until he'd got a response. He wasn't letting anything get in his way. Stella knew that Lara had had a lot of heartache in her life – the death of her parents and her best friend – but watching Alex, she couldn't help but feel that Lara was one lucky lady, and that happiness was there if she was prepared to grasp it.

Alex waved at her, pointing meaningfully towards

a door next to a pizzeria.

'Green door, top floor,' he said, running up. Stella saw the bell-push straight away. 'S. Melberg' – she jabbed at it and looked up towards the top window.

'Nothing,' she muttered. No crackling intercom, no door unlocking.

'What about Eduardo Ortega. Do you have his number?'

'He's in the Congo. Due back today.'

'*The Congo?*'

'Long story. But yes, I've got it.'

Stella glanced at her watch: almost five o'clock. She took out her own phone and, pressing her lips together, called Eduardo. She barely knew him, but this was an emergency and if he was back from the Congo, he might be able to locate Stefan.

'This is Eduardo Ortega…'

Damn. Stella left a message and hung up. Alex looked as dejected as she felt.

'Look, why don't we go and wait in that coffee shop across the road? If they've been out, they'll probably come back soon. If not, maybe we can try *Misty* again.'

Alex shrugged. 'Fine.'

The café had a Scandinavian vibe, all cedar-cladded walls and chrome fittings. Stella could picture Stefan coming in here, sitting at a corner table with his laptop and avocado on rye. Yet, despite the area's sheen of artiness, the East End was still fairly gritty, the brickwork caked in decades of grime and graffiti. Back towards Bethnal Green and down to Whitechapel, it was a long run of fried chicken outlets, phone shops and hairdressers specialising in 'realistic' extensions. For a young demographic, it was cool, but it wasn't Knightsbridge, that was for sure. Stella wondered how it made Stefan feel at the end of every working day watching Eduardo leave for his pile in Kensington. Was that why he'd gone over to the dark side?

'What can I get you?'

The pretty barista with a sleeve of tattoos was smiling at Alex. Stella supposed she would be smiling too if she had customers like Alex and Stefan. The best she'd had in Starclucks was the guy from the betting shop and he was fifty if he was a day. The cakes here were definitely better than the muck Uncle Jimmy stocked too. The sticky cinnamon rolls and slabs of Victoria Sponge dripping in buttercream looked delicious.

'Can I have one of each?' said Stella, pointing.

The barista used a pair of tongs to put the cakes on plate.

'Everything alright with you guys?' she asked, nodding towards the street. 'I saw you going from door to door.'

'We were looking for someone,' said Alex. 'He has a flat across the street. Stefan Melberg.'

'The Swedish guy?'

Alex looked up.

'Well, he's Dutch, but yes. Do you know him?'

She gave a sly smile.

'Stefan the writer? Everyone knows him. He's in here all the time.'

Stella could imagine Stefan Melberg catching the

eye of all the locals, which gave her an idea. If she worked here, Stella would know when a handsome man usually came in, definitely. It would be something to look forward to.

'You haven't seen him today, have you?' asked Stella.

The barista shook her head.

'Maybe he's at his girlfriend's. Who knows?'

lex and Stella exchanged a look.

'Girlfriend?'

The barista nodded.

'The lady with the long dark hair.'

Lara. So her boss was seeing Stefan.

'The French girl,' she continued, pointing to their pastry display. 'She loved our madeleines. Said they were better than anything she'd had in Paris.'

Stella's eyes opened wide. *French?*

Alex pulled out his phone and quickly swiped about on the screen, finally holding up a picture of Sandrine.

'That's her,' said the girl, nodding.

Stella felt her pulse start to thud.

'Do you remember when she was in here last?'

The young woman pouted. 'She's only been in once or twice. Last saw her a couple of weeks ago, maybe? Yes, it was that Friday when we had that heavy rainstorm in the morning. She came in with the Swedish, sorry, Dutch guy for breakfast and they were soaked.' She smiled to herself. 'Didn't seem to bother them though. All over each other, they were. Hardly touched their breakfast. She had this fabulous red coat. I must ask her where she got it from next time she comes in…'

Stella saw the shock on Alex's face give way to anger.

'Sandrine,' he muttered, then without another word, pushed out through the door. Stella rushed to follow.

'Hey, don't you want your cake?' shouted the barista.

'Sorry!' Stella shouted over her shoulder. 'Put it on the Swedish guy's bill!'

Alex was walking fast, his head over his phone.

'Alex, wait,' she called, running to catch up. 'Where are we going?'

He put his phone to his ear.

'I'm calling Ian Fox,' he said.

'Detective Fox?'

He nodded. 'If Lara's in danger, I need someone who can find her.'

'But is this…'

She stopped as her phone hummed.

She looked down at the message which had just popped up.

Just landed in Brussels. Supposed to be meeting Lara and Stefan at Lara's houseboat at 6pm but I've just missed my connecting flight to Heathrow so won't be able to make it. Everything ok? Eduardo.

Stella put her hand over Alex's phone and shook her head.

'Grab a cab,' she said. 'We're going to Chelsea.'

Chapter Thirty-Five

LARA GLANCED AT her watch, nerves jangling. It was gone five o'clock and Stefan was due any minute. Well, Stefan and Eduardo: Lara had to remind herself she had invited them both and that, technically, this was a business meeting. Even so, Lara was on edge, dashing around cueing up some Aretha and rearranging the flowers on the table: a jam jar of mustard pansies and pink and lilac stocks, which reminded her of Foxhills. Even so, she looked up through the skylight with foreboding. The bright floral colours were in sharp contrast to the grey sky. It had been muggy all day and rain was already patting against the glass; another thunderstorm was forecast, which put paid to Lara's plan of a romantic evening drinking wine coolers on the deck.

'Calm yourself,' she muttered. 'Business meeting, remember?'

Still, it felt significant that this would be Stefan's first visit to her home. She could admit to herself that she *liked*-liked him. Yes, it had all happened super-fast and no, she didn't really know him and obviously, you shouldn't get involved with people you work with, but then wasn't that how love was supposed to be –

illogical, spontaneous and head-over-heels? *Love.* She was like a ditzy teenager. She'd even put fresh sheets on the bed.

Lara was just checking the chicken in the oven when she heard a tentative knock on the door. A locksmith had reinforced the frame so well it would take a bazooka to get through it now. He had also drilled a peephole and Lara bent to peer through it.

'Stefan!' she smiled, unlocking the door. He looked relieved to see her too, his shoulders hunched against the rain, a neon yellow umbrella keeping the worst off.

'Come in, come in,' she said, greeting him with a kiss.

He stepped inside, looking around with wide eyes.

'This is amazing.'

Lara grinned, uncommonly pleased at his reaction.

'No Eduardo?' she asked, a hint of hope in her voice.

'Didn't he call you? He missed his connection and doesn't think he'll be back in London until around ten.'

Lara pulled a face.

'Oh no: my phone's been off. I switched it to silent for this society auction I went to today. I must have forgotten to switch it back on.'

'That will explain it. I was worried about you,' he said, with a hint of reproach.

She pulled him close.

'That's sweet, but you don't have to be worried.'

They kissed again, more slowly this time. Lara

melted against him, her fingers trailing along his neck.

Stefan stepped away and took a bottle of red wine from his rucksack.

'From my favourite wine shop in Amsterdam. The owner's brother has a vineyard in Provence.'

Lara smiled, then turned to the kitchen drawer to get her corkscrew. For the first time since she had moved into *Misty*, Lara knew exactly where everything was, an unintentional consequence of the break-in: she'd had to put everything back piece by piece. As she opened the wine, she watched Stefan walk slowly around the boat, clearly fascinated by the way she lived.

'An auction?' he said absently. 'Did you win anything?'

'A week in Harbour Island in a posh villa. Shall we go?'

She had meant it as a joke, but once the words were out, Lara realised she longed to do just that. How many years had it been since she had gone anywhere simply for pleasure and especially with someone she just wanted to spend time with? Wasn't that what normal couples did? The thought of walking along a pink sands shore, letting cool, clear water wash against her feet, and doing it with someone like Stefan was something she suddenly couldn't wait for.

As she turned back around holding two glasses of wine, she saw Stefan bent over his phone, quickly tapping out a message.

'Something urgent?' she said.

'I'm telling Eduardo not to bother coming,' he

said, looking up with a half-smile. 'We don't want him to rush, do we?'

'No, we don't.'

Tonight, she wanted Stefan to stay on the boat; she wanted to laugh with him, have lots of sex and sit on the deck watching the sunrise, wrapped in his arms. Most of all, Lara wanted *Misty* to be full of happy memories again and that would be a fine start.

Stefan took his wine and gestured up at the rain, now running across the skylight like silver veins. 'Well, I don't think we're going anywhere.'

'That's exactly how I want it,' said Lara, stepping towards him.

'So where was this auction?' he asked, his tipped glass a barrier between them.

'Claridge's.'

'Fancy.'

'I went with Olivia because I knew Victoria Sachs would be there. Michael Sachs's wife.'

Stefan lowered the glass, his face suddenly serious.

'I know who she is, Lara. The question is, why did you go? What did you hope to achieve?'

Lara put her wine glass down.

'I went because I know what they did to Helen Groves and Sandrine, I just can't prove it. And I wanted to rattle her cage, force an error, get her admit to something.'

'And did she?'

'No, but it was better than doing nothing.'

'Really?' said Stefan, shaking his head in frustration.

'Poking a hornet's nest, especially on your own, is dangerous. I thought we'd talked about this? About taking a step back from the story until we've re-grouped, involved more journalists. Someone trashed your house on Friday. You said it yourself, it was a warning.'

'I need to find out what happened to Sandrine once and for all.'

'Sandrine's dead, Lara! Nothing is going to bring her back.'

Stefan's voice was loud in the empty space.

Lara blinked at him.

'I never said I thought the break-in was a warning.'

She had, but not to Stefan. Why was he being so hardline about this?

'Will you please stop this? For me,' he said, his voice low and controlled. He was beginning to say more when there was a loud bang at the door.

Lara looked up in alarm.

'Lara!' came a muffled voice. 'Let me in!'

'Alex?' she said with relief, recognising his voice instantly.

'I didn't know you were expecting company,' said Stefan, still looking sour.

'I wasn't,' said Lara, crossing to the door.

She peeped through the hole, then quickly opened it. Alex pushed inside, rain dripping from his hair, his shirt soaked through. Stefan immediately stood up, his expression wary.

'Thank God, you're here,' said Alex, out of breath. 'I've been phoning you all day.'

'Look, I'm fine. Alex, what are you doing here? Shouldn't you be at work?'

The penny dropped. He'd been fired. That's why he looked so angry.

Alex glared at Stefan. *If looks could kill*, thought Lara immediately. Wasn't that what someone had said about Jago Bain when he was thrown off *Pandora*?

'Why don't you tell her why I'm here, Stefan?' said Alex.

Stefan frowned. 'Tell her what?'

'Why don't you start with the part about having an affair with Sandrine?'

'*What?*' said Lara. 'Alex, have you gone mad? What the hell are you talking about?'

Alex turned back to Lara.

'I'm sorry Lar, but it's true. Stella and I went to Stefan's flat and we got confirmation: Sandrine had been there.'

'I don't know what you've been smoking, my friend…' began Stefan, but Alex whirled around and took a step towards him, making Stefan jerk back.

'Alex!' shouted Lara, throwing herself in between them. 'What the hell is wrong with you? Is this about Alicia and Charlie? I mean, I understand that you're upset but there's no need to lash out at us.'

'Yeah, it's bullshit,' said Stefan. Alex's head snapped up, his eyes blazing.

'Bullshit?' said Alex, pulling out his phone. He quickly scrolled to a picture and held it up. The breath caught in Lara's throat. It was Sandrine.

'I showed this picture to the barista in the café

opposite Stefan's flat and she immediately identified Sandrine as *Stefan's girlfriend.* She saw them there kissing on the day she died.'

'Lara, it's a lie,' said Stefan. 'That waitress must have got confused. It was someone else. Polly, an art student I met in a club the other week. I'm sorry, I should have told you, but…'

'Don't you dare,' growled Alex, holding up the phone again. 'Are you saying *Polly* also spoke French, also loved madeleines and also wore a red coat? That this fictional woman looked just like Sandrine.'

Lara couldn't breathe. The red coat. She could still picture her friend slipping it on that night as she left the Engineer, she could remember seeing it draped over the back of a chair in that empty Marylebone apartment.

And she could see Sandrine's face on Alex's photo. Beautiful, vibrant Sandrine. *Unmistakable* Sandrine. If the barista had seen her, had spoken to her, she wouldn't forget.

'Stefan?' she said, searching his face. But Stefan couldn't meet her eye. Far off across the river, she heard a grumble of thunder and the light had all but gone from the day.

'Yes, I was seeing Sandrine,' he said defiantly. 'So, what? Eduardo was obsessed with work. It's no wonder she went looking elsewhere for affection.'

'Affection?' Thought Lara, a sickness growing in her stomach.

'*That* was why Sandrine was here,' said Lara, the pieces finally falling into place. 'The night I met

Sandrine at the bar, she was cagey about why she had come to London early, so I assumed she'd come to see Eduardo. But she'd come to see you, hadn't she?'

She watched Stefan's face, still hoping for a denial, but he just stood there, mute.

'Tell her what else you've been up to, Stefan,' said Alex. Lara hardly recognised him, his anger barely contained.

'He's been working for Michael Sachs,' said Alex. 'Spying, essentially.'

'Working for Sachs?' snorted Stefan. 'Don't be ridiculous.'

'You don't think my sources are good?' said Alex, challenging him. Everyone knew Alex Ford's reputation as one of the best journalists in the business.

'I was with David Becker at lunchtime. I know you went to him for finance. I know he recommended you to Michael Sachs for corporate intelligence work. And that's why you went out of your way to get close to Sandrine Legard. Why you seduced her. To find out what she knew.'

Lara felt as though she had been punched.

'Stefan? Is it true?'

'Lara, you have to understand…' he began.

'TELL ME!' Her yell reverberated around the boat and even in the low light she could tell Stefan had paled. He dropped his head, then nodded.

'Becker didn't want to invest in my idea, but a couple of months later he called me and asked if I was interested in some research work for a friend of his. Said it would be well-paid.'

'So much for your principles.'

'Principles?' he snapped. 'I'm not like you or Eduardo, I don't have a big family trust fund. You don't know how it feels to be constantly in debt at the end of every month.'

Lara bristled. Now *that* was bullshit. Stefan worked for some of the biggest newspapers in the world, he wasn't exactly a pauper. But she couldn't allow him to sidetrack her.

'What did Sachs want you to find out?' she asked.

Stefan looked towards the door, but both Alex and Lara were in the way. He sighed in defeat.

'Sachs just wanted to find out how much Sandrine knew about the trafficking scandal connected to ImpactAid. He said Sandrine's story would damage the charity. Simple. Just information, nothing else. No one gets hurt.'

'No one gets hurt?' Lara hissed. 'Sandrine's dead, Stefan! And you set her up to be murdered by Michael Sachs!'

'I didn't know what sort of man he was!' shouted Stefan. 'I didn't *know*!' The last word trailed off into a strangled wail as he slid down into a chair, clasping his hands together on top of his head. 'I didn't know.'

No-one spoke. The only sound was the tip-tap of rain beating down on the roof.

'What information did Sandrine have?' said Alex, after a moment.

Stefan shook his head.

'Enough. Photographs of the traffickers, a video Helen had shot of them taking the girls, Helen's correspondence with Victoria Sachs. Enough to prove what was happening and that ImpactAid had covered it up or at least done nothing about it.'

'She showed you all this?' asked Alex.

Stefan nodded.

'And you sent it all on to Michael Sachs.'

'Look, the charity was doing valuable work,' he said defensively. 'An expose would have ruined them.'

Lara closed her eyes in dismay. Why had Sandrine chosen Stefan to confide in? Why had she trusted this snake over her? *But then I trusted him too.* Did our desires really blind us, did hope strap blinkers to our eyes?

'I didn't know Sachs was dangerous,' said Stefan, his voice barely a whisper now. 'I swear to you.'

Lara tilted her head back, looking up at the pewter sky through wrinkled rain-washed glass.

'Is that why you targeted me too?' she asked. 'Have you been feeding Sachs information on us too?'

'No!' said Stefan. 'After Sandrine I stopped.'

She could believe it, but still, Stefan had seemed a little too eager to persuade her and Eduardo that Jonathon Meyer's inner circle and the Kanjomo Mine were the threads to follow, steering them onto an alternative narrative, trying to deflect attention away from the real one – and from everything he had done.

'So why didn't you tell us, Stefan? After Sandrine died?'

'Because I wanted to believe Helen's death was an accident,' he said, his voice desperate now. 'I wanted to believe Sandrine had depression and had taken her own life.'

Alex glanced at Lara.

'And now?' he asked. 'Is that what you think?'

Stefan hung his head, blond hair falling over his face.

'No,' he said. 'Now I'm scared about what they did to her.'

Lara felt emotions roll over her like waves: relief, anger and finally a terrible ache of sadness. She had been right all along. Sandrine hadn't killed herself, but she hadn't been able to save her friend and that wonderful burning bright life-force was gone forever.

'Why, Stefan?' she asked. 'Why did you do it?'

'A hundred thousand reasons.'

'£100,000?' said Alex. 'That was the price of Sandrine's life?'

'Everyone has a price, Alex. Even you.'

Before Alex could answer Stefan picked up his rucksack. Lara tensed, almost expecting him to pull out a weapon, but instead he opened his laptop and began typing.

'What are you doing?'

'Accessing my files. They're all encrypted – in the cloud.'

Finally, he closed the computer and stood up, holding something out to Lara: a USB flash drive.

'Take it,' he said. 'Put it somewhere safe.' When she failed to move, Stefan took her hand and forced it into her grip. 'Sandrine's files,' he said. 'All of them.'

Lara looked down at the little plastic stick.

'But I thought you gave them to Sachs.'

'I did, but I made copies.'

Stefan's face was pale, but his eyes were still hopeful.

'I never wanted to be the bad guy,' he said in a voice so quiet she could hardly hear it.

'I think you'd better go,' she replied. Only a short time earlier, Lara had longed to be alone with Stefan, had dared to dream about a life together. Now she couldn't bear to be breathing the same air. She had wasted enough time on him already.

Stefan nodded to himself and, hoisting his bag, headed towards the door and was gone.

ALEX CAME OVER and put his arms around her. He held her for a long time. It felt good, his strong arms making Lara feel as if she wasn't alone in the world.

'I'm so sorry,' he whispered and Lara looked up, her damp eyes searching his.

'Don't be sorry,' said Lara. 'Seriously Alex, none of this is your fault. And don't you think I'd rather know?'

'I wasn't sure I'd ever get to tell you. I can't believe you ghosted me for three whole days.'

'I felt bad. I was avoiding you.'

'Yeah,' he said, with a twisted smile. 'I got that message.'

She sighed heavily, thinking about what she'd just heard, thinking about Stefan's betrayal, both of Sandrine and of her.

'I've been so stupid,' she whispered. 'How could I have been taken in by him?'

'We've all had the wool pulled over our eyes at some point.'

Lara squeezed his hand. She thought about Alex, alone in bed, wondering why Alicia had gone looking for the attention of another man. She pictured him there, naked save for a white sheet, then she quickly pulled away from him.

Her hand was still in his.

'Lara, Stella said someone broke into the houseboat.'

Her friend's face was serious. She knew she'd have to tell him the truth, because he looked determined enough to find out anyway.

'I came home on Friday and *Misty* had been trashed.'

'Why didn't you call me?'

'We'd just had a row, I didn't want to bother you....'

She felt herself get emotional again.

'They killed Dingo, Alex.'

His anger had a stillness now, but she could feel its heat.

'We'll find them and we'll bring them down,' he said.

Lara held up the USB stick. 'Then we should go and take a look.'

THEY WENT THROUGH into Lara's study. The walls were now stripped, empty of all those photos, maps, and notes relating to the story. Lara was actually glad; it felt as if they were starting afresh – and now they had real information, not guesses. She pushed the stick into her laptop as Alex bent to look over her shoulder.

'Wow,' he whispered as Lara clicked on each file. It was just as Stefan had said: emails, documents, a transcript of Sandrine's interviews with Helen Groves, even a shaky video of a lawyer offering Helen a bribe to keep quiet.

'We've got them,' said Lara.

'No,' said Alex. 'Not quite.'

'What do you mean? This is evidence.'

'Evidence of a scandal at a small aid agency on the other side of the world. It's barely enough to get half a page in the "World News" section. There's motive here, and it's a PR nightmare, but there's nothing to prove anyone was murdered.'

Lara opened her mouth to object, then stopped herself. Alex was right. Three people were dead and yet at best, they had evidence of an attempted cover-up. They'd come so far and yet they still had so little.

She put her hands behind her head trying to think.

'I'm going to call Stella. She'll be frantic with worry,' said Alex.

He explained how Stella had accompanied him to Stefan's flat and how she had wanted to call in a SWAT team when Eduardo had said that Stefan was heading to Lara's boat.

'It took all my powers of persuasion to make her stand down.'

'I definitely need to give that girl a raise,' smiled

Lara.

'Next, you're coming to stay at mine,' said Alex, straightening up. 'We might not have concrete proof, but *they* don't know that.' He gestured around the boat. 'And they're obviously getting jumpy.'

Lara shook her head decisively. 'No,' she said. 'I appreciate the offer, but I won't be pushed out of my home again.'

He looked at her. 'Lar, I just keeping thinking…'

She stopped him.

'Maybe you could stay here? I mean, the mattress over there has been slashed, but we can probably improvise something.'

Alex smiled.

'I've slept in tougher spots.'

'Is this where you start telling me your war stories again?'

'I would but… Can you smell something burning?'

'Oh crap!' she cried, dashing to the kitchen, yanking the oven open. Smoke poured out, immediately setting off the fire alarm. Lara grabbed a tea towel and waved it in front of the charred bird as Alex ran around opening the door and windows. Finally, the ringing cut off. They both looked at each other and burst out laughing.

'Takeaway?' she asked.

Alex grinned.

'Sushi, maybe?'

'I'll call the restaurant, you call Stella.'

Lara went back to her study and grabbed her phone, but before she could dial, she noticed a blinking message in the centre of the screen. Unknown number:

We need to talk. I have evidence you may want to see.

Victoria.

Lara's heart lurched. Had her plan of confronting Victoria Sachs at the auction actually paid off and made her rethink her position? Or was it a trap? Whichever way, Lara wanted – needed – to know what Victoria Sachs had to say.

She walked back into the living room. 'Bad news,' she said. 'The restaurant can't deliver. Can you go and collect it? It's only on the King's Road. Ten-minute walk, tops.'

Alex peered up at the skylight dubiously.

'Have you seen the weather out there?'

'It's definitely easing off. And you're already damp,' she pulled a goofy smile. 'Or you could stay here and I'll cook.'

'No, no,' laughed Alex, backing towards the door. 'I'll go, I'll go.'

Lara waited until she heard Alex pass through the creaky gate, then counted to twenty, giving him time to turn the corner. Then she grabbed her jacket and helmet. It was time to bring this to an end.

Chapter Thirty-Six

DUSK SETTLED UPON the city. Slate grey clouds pressed low over roads barely lit by streetlamps. The roads had begun to clear of traffic making it easy for Lara's bike to hiss along Sloane Street, whose pavements were all but abandoned of shoppers and tourists.

Lara had called Victoria Sachs before she had left the boatyard, partly to make sure it was her, partly to see if she could second-guess her mood. 'Meet me at ClearView,' she'd said. 'I've found something you need to see. Come alone.' That was the entire conversation, leaving Lara to fill in the blanks.

She had tried to think it all through. At City University, they had been taught Occam's Razor, the principle that the most simple explanation was the most likely. And the most likely outcome of Lara's ambush at Claridge's? That Victoria Sachs would go straight home and tell her husband everything. Assuming that position, Michael's strategy could be any number of things, from calling in the lawyers, to arranging for an 'accident' for Lara Stone, just as he had for Helen and Jonathon and Sandrine.

Then again, Lara had heard something in Victoria

Sachs's voice, even though they had just exchanged a few words. Regret? Shame? Lara could imagine Victoria going to her husband for advice on the potential ImpactAid scandal. She could imagine her handing the problem over to him, and like Stefan, she could easily imagine her ignoring Helen's accident or passing off Meyer's mugging as tragic coincidence. Over her many years as a journalist, Lara had come to realise that good people could be bad, and bad people could be good, but inherently, most, when push came to shove, would do the decent thing. Just like Stefan had, finally.

ClearView was impressive, even in the rain. The elegantly curved façade had the effect of making the building seem to float above the street. Shivering white tarpaulins covered the upper floors, but at street level, it looked polished and sleek, open for business in every sense. Lara pulled the bike into the drive in front of the entrance and kicked it onto its stand. Pushing through the revolving door, she shook off the rain, glad at least to be out of the storm. The cavernous lobby was wide, glossy – and abandoned, no one behind the wide reception desk.

From the moment Victoria had suggested it, Lara had wondered what the significance was of meeting at ClearView. Stella had done her homework; knew that although the development wasn't quite finished, both Michael and Victoria already had offices here.

'Hello?' said Lara, walking over, feeling foolish. She saw a large manila envelope sitting on the desk, her name carelessly scrawled on the front. Glancing around, Lara picked it up and tipped the contents into her hand: a thin plastic card with the Sachs Capital logo and the word 'Visitor' beneath.

Curiouser and curiouser. To the left of the reception, there was a gate with a red panel on the top. Lara tapped the card on it and with a discreet 'beep' the gate slid open. Simultaneously, a lift in the rear wall pinged, the doors revealing a mirrored interior.

Lara had to admit it was slick as she stepped inside, the number '15' lighting up automatically. She rode up, fighting a sense of inevitability, the feeling that someone had mapped all this out for her. As the lift doors opened, Lara took out her phone to text Alex. She knew he'd be back at the houseboat at any moment and see that she wasn't there.

Yes, he'd worry and he'd be right to. Victoria's intentions suddenly felt darker than they had when Lara had spoken to her.

At ClearView, Sachs's new development. Victoria wants to talk. Come in ten minutes if you haven't heard from me.

As she sent the message to Alex, Lara stepped out of the lift and looked around.

Floor fifteen was almost finished. Almost, but not quite. The floors were covered in a fine layer of dust and she could still see steel beams through the open ceiling above her, but everything else looked in place. The desks were still shrouded in plastic, but the computers were linked by multi-coloured snakes of cabling. A bank of chic, sculptured wall-lights were illuminated, but otherwise it was dark. There was even a CCTV camera pointing down, an unblinking red eye observing Lara's arrival.

'Hello?' she said, walking into the wide-open space. Directly in front of her were tall windows, still with arrows indicating which way up the glass should be installed. At the far end, Lara could feel the breeze: no glass, not yet; the holes in the wall were simply covered with the white sheeting she had seen from the street.

'Lara Stone,' said a baritone voice, coming from within the unfurnished space. A figure stepped out of the shadows. Although they had never met, Lara recognised him immediately. Michael Sachs was handsome and tall, his grey hair swept back like he'd just left the stylist's chair. As he strode towards her, Lara tensed until she realised his hand was extended towards her.

'We meet at last,' he said.

Lara felt exposed and off-balance. She looked around.

'Where's Victoria?' she said, trying to keep her voice even.

'Where Victoria usually is, having dinner, having fun with her friends.'

She didn't miss the contempt in Michael's voice. 'I sent her away as I thought it might be more constructive if we spoke privately, man-to-man as it were. But first, let me show you around.'

Before she had time to object, Michael strode off, enthusiastically talking her through the many features of his new office: the Italian design and the state of the art computer brains hidden behind sliding panels.

'And come and see the view,' said Sachs, leading Lara to the far end of the floor where the sheeting was rattling against the scaffold. 'The windows go in last so we could crane everything else up, but they will be seamless, giving a 180 across the park. It was a bugger getting planning permission, but it's magnificent, don't you think?'

As Lara gazed out, all she could see was darkness and the storm whipping the tops of the trees – and all she could hear was the sound of a trap snapping closed. Victoria had set her up, lured her to an empty building. And now Michael had her where he wanted her.

Lara took a breath. She wasn't going to let him intimidate her, however vulnerable she was feeling.

'Well, I'm glad you showed me all this,' she said. 'Because it's really helped me understand your nasty little conjuring trick.'

Sachs looked at her, surprised, but Lara continued.

'From the start, I thought this was about greed. But it isn't, is it? It's about fear.'

'Fear? I think you've lost me.'

'You had to shut down Helen Groves because any scandal regarding the charity would undermine your plan to sell Sachs Capital. If the ImpactAid trafficking story came out, your investors would have pulled their money out of your fund and the sale of the company would be derailed. Investors want to see corporate responsibility in this day and age, not corruption, cover-ups and trafficking.'

Sachs put up a hand, but she kept going.

Lara gestured towards the floor.

'You've sunk all your money into this place, haven't you? My guess is you've over-extended. And if you lose the fund, you'll lose your investment here too. And you'll have nothing left. *That's* why you were so desperate to keep the story quiet.'

Sachs clicked his tongue.

'It's a creative story, Ms. Stone. I can see why you've done so well in journalism.'

'So you're denying it?'

'Denying what? Some fairy tale about a non-existent scandal and disappearing investors?'

'No,' said Lara. 'Denying that you killed Jonathon Meyer.'

He smiled at her and suddenly Lara caught a glimpse of the man behind the carefully-groomed façade. He looked like a wolf sizing up his prey.

'No. I did not kill Jonathon Meyer,' he said. 'Jon died after a particularly brutal street attack. I wasn't even in the country at the time.'

'Let me rephrase,' said Lara. 'Did you arrange to have Jonathon Meyer murdered?'

Sachs remained calm, just a slight irritated shake of the head. 'Murder? Scandal? Do you realise how unlikely all these accusations sound? They might even suggest an unbalanced mind. Suicidal, in fact.'

Lara took a step away, her disquiet growing. She hoped that Alex had read his text.

'And I suppose saying that you had Helen Groves and Sandrine Legard killed would also show that I was slipping into madness?'

'It would,' said Sachs, with a creeping smile. 'In fact, Lara, that's exactly what I will say.'

'Will say?' said Lara, feeling the atmosphere change.

'When your body is found out on the drive.'

Lara immediately turned and strode back to the lift, looking for the 'down' button. But there was no 'down' button. In fact there were no buttons at all. Her panic rising, she pulled out the security pass and waved it in front of the door. Nothing.

Lara whirled around.

'This is what they call a smart building,' said Sachs, raising a finger towards the cameras dotted all around the room. 'The whole thing is wired up for audio visual monitoring, facial recognition, GPS orientation, voice commands: seamless integration between security and data.'

Lara backed away past a line of offices, looking for another corridor or a staircase.

'Only way out,' he said, nodded towards the billowing plastic. The weather outside was deteriorating again; the wind was tugging at the tarpaulins.

Shit.

'Come on Lara,' said Sachs, following her. 'As a writer you must appreciate how elegant the story is. Accosting my wife at her benefit lunch only shows how unhealthy your obsession with me was. So, driven mad by grief, you steal a security pass from your boyfriend, Sachs Capital researcher Stefan Melberg. You violently confront me, and when that doesn't work, you jump to your death in an attempt to frame me. You want to end it all, but at least you'll take me with you.'

She looked down at the laminate. 'This is Stef-an's?'

He shrugged. 'Like I said, elegant.'

Lara threw down the pass and moved away from Sachs, trying every door she came to. All locked. Or maybe they required face recognition or a magic word or something. Sachs followed her, his movements unhurried. He wasn't a particularly big man, but he could certainly overpower Lara.

And then there was nowhere else to go. Sachs was between her and the lift bank, only the open window frames behind her.

'You don't have to do this, Michael,' she said as calmly as she could.

Sachs smiled.

'Correct. Which is why I have a loyal roster of specialist staff.' He glanced at his watch. 'Speaking of which, Mr. Schmitt should be here any time now.'

'Schmitt? Who's Schmitt?'

'I don't know what his real name is, but that's what Jonathon Meyer called him when he introduced us. Schmitt is the man who snips off all my loose ends.'

Sachs picked up an office chair. 'Here, have a seat while we wait.'

'I prefer to stand.'

'SIT DOWN!' he roared, banging the chair down. Lara sat, painfully aware of the open space only a few feet behind her. Lara knew she had to do something –

anything. Ask questions, hope for an opening. Make him think he'd won.

'So this is what it's all about?' she said, as Sachs sat down opposite her. 'A building?'

'Not just "a building", Miss Stone. A legacy. Something that will stand for centuries. Carnegie Hall, the Tate Gallery, the Guggenheim, all owe their existence to the proceeds of industry; steel, sugar, mining, but who remembers that? They just see the art and the music.'

Sachs nodded to himself. 'But you're right, the project was far more expensive than I ever anticipated. So I couldn't let your friends Helen and Sandrine derail my sale of Sachs Capital.'

'What happened?' croaked Lara. She knew it might be the last thing she ever heard, but she desperately wanted to hear it, to know if she had been right.

'I asked Jonathon Meyer if he knew a man who could fix the problem,' said Sachs. 'He did – and it was shockingly easy. I mean, this Helen girl walked around the slums of Haiti with a big camera,' he said incredulously. 'It was almost as if she had a death wish.'

His mouth curled into a sneer.

'And then there was poor Sandrine Legard and her history of mental health problems. A suicide was plausible, which was fortunate for me.'

Lara felt fury flood through her, but she knew she couldn't rise to his bait. Keep him talking.

'But what about Jonathon Meyer? He was your friend.'

'Was, Lara,' snapped Michael. 'Past tense. He tried to blackmail me, said I *owed* him for shutting up that ImpactAid girl, wanted me to bail him out. Now does that sound like a friend?'

Lara pictured *Pandora*, white and glistening in the Côte d'Azur sun, the ultimate status symbol of the super-rich.

'But Meyer was successful,' she frowned. 'I saw his yacht…'

Sachs gave a snort. 'Meyer was operating a Ponzi scheme to plug the black hole in his accounts.'

'A black hole? I thought Jonathon was a financial genius?'

'Well, he doesn't look so clever now,' hissed Sachs, spittle flying towards Lara.

'What did he want from you, Michael?'

He stood up and began to pace around as if he was unravelling it in his own head.

'When Jonathon realised he needed more investors to plump his pot, he figured that the best way to attract them was to go public with his client list. Money follows money. But most of them always wanted anonymity so he begged me not just to invest but be open about our relationship. He knew that my involvement would attract others. When I said no, he used Helen Groves as leverage.'

'Let me guess, you used Schmitt to get rid of Meyer.'

'What goes around comes around,' he said, his voice dripping with menace. 'Besides, Schmitt didn't mind. I pay that psychopath better.'

There was a sound behind them: the ping of the lift arriving.

'Ah, here he comes now…'

Lara's heart was beating hard. There was the sound of footsteps now. Light heels tapping against concrete. Female.

Not how she'd imagined Schmitt. But as she turned she saw Victoria Sachs. Her peacock-green trench coat was belted at the waist, her black umbrella still glistening from the rain. She propped it up against a desk and walked towards them, plucking off her gloves. Concern fluttered across Michael's expression at the sight of his wife.

'What are you doing here?'

'I wanted to see this in person.'

A flash of Michael's wolf-smile again as he checked his watch.

'Oh don't bother, Schmitt won't be coming,' said Victoria briskly. 'Not up here, anyway. In fact, I don't think he'll be going anywhere for a while.'

Lara watched the woman's face. Something was wrong here she thought, hope flowering in her chest.

'What are you talking about?' said Michael. 'We agreed…'

'No, Michael,' she snapped. 'We did not agree. We did not agree to anything. I let Helen Groves down, I admit that. I dealt with it badly. I tried to ignore her allegations and then I panicked and came to you for advice. If you recall, I told you about the problems we were having in Haiti. But I did not ask you to kill anyone. That was all your doing.'

'I see,' he snorted. 'The furious back-pedal. So now you're pretending that you had no idea how I would deal with your problem.'

Victoria shook her head wearily. 'For the record, let me say this, Michael. You're many things, but I never, for one moment, thought you were a murderer.'

'For the record?' repeated Michael, just as Victoria turned and called out: 'Chief Inspector Fox? Would you care to join us?'

Lara gasped as the policeman walked out, accompanied by two uniformed officers. Michael's face was a mask of shock. 'What the hell is this?'

'I told you what Lara had said to me at Claridge's. I suggested we invite her here, because I wanted you to tell her what you've done. Then, I did my homework too, Michael. It was easy to find out who was investigating Sandrine Legard's death and Detective Fox was only too happy to come along as a witness to your confession.' She pointed to one of the cameras. 'And before you think about denying anything, all that smart-tech stuff you like to crow about? It's been recording everything.'

With a roar, Michael lunged at Victoria, but Fox and his two colleagues restrained him easily.

One of the officers wrenched Sachs's arm up behind his back. 'Mr. Sachs,' said Fox. 'I am arresting you on suspicion of murder, you do not have to say anything…'

Michael ignored him and twisted his head towards his wife. 'Victoria!' He yelled. 'What did you *do*?'

'I outplayed you, Michael,' she said calmly.

'You've always been such a bore boasting about your so-called achievements, I knew you wouldn't be able to resist telling Ms. Stone how clever you were. If you can call murder clever.'

As Sachs was hoisted upright, his face turned dark pink with fury.

'It's those bitches' fault. That Scottish one, that French bitch and her,' he said, stabbing his finger towards Lara.

Lara couldn't hold it in any longer. She drew her fist back and punched him full in the face.

Blood running from his nose, Michael twisted to look at Ian Fox.

'You saw that! That was assault. Actual Bodily Harm.'

'Fake news, mate,' said Fox, and bundled him towards the lift.

Epilogue

THE ATMOSPHERE IN the *Chronicle* boardroom was electric. It was standing room only: departments heads, the legal team, even Charlie Avery was there for once. Although they had listened in silence as Alex and Eduardo, assisted by Stella, outlined the investigation into the deaths of Helen Groves, Sandrine Legard, Jonathon Meyer and the scandal of child labour in the Kanjomo mine, there was a palpable hum of energy throughout. Everyone could see this was a sensational story – and for now at least, the *Chronicle* had the exclusive. Part of the appeal of working at a newspaper was knowing what was really going on behind the magic curtain, but this was even better: right now, the people in this crowded room were the only people in the world who knew all this information. In the modern world of instant news, it was rare. No wonder they were sparking.

'Okay, okay,' said Darius as Alex finished. 'So let me get this right: Michael Sachs ordered three murders to protect the sale of his company?' He gave a low whistle. Alex didn't doubt that Darius could smell glory, prizes, perhaps even a prestigious job offer from *The New Yorker* or *The Washington Post*. Or perhaps

Darius had been reminded of the reason he got into journalism in the first place. Perhaps. He could only hope.

'Obviously there's two stories here,' said Alex. 'The investigation into Meyer's death led us to the mines, but what is happening at the Kanjomo mine is a fairly distinct thread.'

Darius turned to Eduardo.

'Look, I know Le Caché shares its stories between various international outlets but we'd like the exclusive on the mines expose.'

Alex raised his eyebrows to Eduardo. It was tricky, but it was really Eduardo's call. Alex had played a part, but this wasn't his story and neither did he expect Eduardo to give much credit to Stefan given he was currently being interviewed by Ian Fox in connection with the death of Sandrine Legard.

'Twenty-four hours exclusivity on the mine story,' said Eduardo, after a moment's thought. 'I have an arrangement with *El Pais* in Madrid and we have Le Caché journalists working on the ground in the DRC, but I can give you "first dibs" on the Kanjomo investigation as long as you credit Le Caché.'

Darius looked as if he was considering it and then said, 'Done.' Alex smiled to himself, knowing that Darius would have already cleared both conditions with Nicholas. Still, it looked decisive in front of the troops. He turned to Frank Benson on the news team.

'The mines angle feels like an extended item for the Saturday edition. Do you agree?'

Frank nodded. 'That would work. In fact we could

do with another 48 hours for photographs and field interviews.'

Darius turned to his deputy.

'Alex. We need to run the Michael Sachs story straight away. The police are involved, so we have to expect leaks. I think we should lead with Jonathon Meyer. It's stronger, sexier, although the French journalist was good-looking, yes?'

'Sandrine,' said Alex. 'Her name was Sandrine Legard.'

Darius bellowed at Gary McTavish who was already halfway out of the door.

'Gary, get more photos of the French bird. And Monaco, we want to see those big fuck-off yachts. The readers love that.'

Darius could be pompous and self-interested, but it was amazing how efficient he could be when his superiors were in the room.

He looked back at Alex.

'I assume you want to write this one?'

The offer actually surprised him. A few days ago, Lara had accused Alex of being jealous of 'proper' journalists like the Le Caché writers who were on the frontline gathering news first-hand. And yes, Alex could admit how much he wanted to run back to his desk, pull together all the facts and file it in time for the first edition going to press. His reporting days had been such a heady, exciting time. The taste of black coffee and lassi at the Press Club in Peshawar, the sweet smell of jasmine outside his apartment window and that buzz of finding and writing stories that mattered, his fingers on the keyboard, tap, tap, tap, racing to meet a deadline for a newspaper six time zones away.

'No, Darius. I won't be writing it,' he said. 'It's not my by-line. It's not my story either.'

Alex waved to Stella, who was waiting by the door. She went out for a few seconds, then returned. There was a pause, then a gasp as Stella led Lara in. There was surprise among the staff, but it was fleeting. No one was really shocked to know that Lara Stone was behind the story. No one except Darius.

'What's going on?' he asked. 'Lara, you're on sabbatical.'

'Officially,' she smiled. 'But you know I can't stay away from you, Darius. What's a girl to do?'

There was laughter and Rob from the news desk gave her a wink. Alex could tell everyone felt the same way: The *Chronicle* was a better place with Lara Stone.

'Lara put everything together on the Meyer story,' said Alex, meeting Lara's eye. 'She chased every lead down, despite no one believing her, including me.'

He saw a tell-tale flush of her cheeks. Despite her talent, Lara was genuinely a team player.

'I was just following Sandrine's tracks. This is her story. Stella helped too.'

Darius waved an impatient hand. 'Christ, put whatever by-line you like on it. Are you going to write this bloody story or not? Because by my calculations you have less than eight hours and we obviously need half of that to run it past legal.'

This part was key: men like Michael Sachs didn't roll over easily and his lawyers would be bullish, murder charge or no murder charge and Alex felt a jab of anxiety. Until the papers were physically in newsagents, no story was a given. He'd seen it happen plenty of times: stories quashed at the final moment by injunctions on a whole host of legal grounds. But this one had to happen. This one was personal: Sachs had murdered Sandrine and threatened Lara, there was no way he would let him get away with that.

As he walked back to his office he saw Charlie hovering by his door.

'Can we have a word?'

Alex nodded.

'Sure.'

It had to happen at some time, he couldn't avoid Charlie forever. Alex had spent days debating how to play it; he knew full well that the situation made Alex's position vulnerable, but he wasn't prepared to make any concessions. If they were going to fire him, he was going down swinging.

Alex gestured to a chair, but Charlie didn't sit, as if he was nervous, ready to make a quick getaway. Shrugging, Alex perched on the edge of his desk.

'Look, I'm sorry,' said Charlie without preamble. 'About Alicia. I never meant it to happen this way. I'll be honest with you Alex, it was a flirtation that got out of hand. And then…'

He winced. Clearly talking about this stuff – feelings, relationships – was difficult for Charlie.

'And then?' prompted Alex.

'…And then it turned out we liked one another.'

Alex was taken aback by his honesty. He hadn't suspected that Charlie Avery, confirmed playboy, was capable of such things. Alex let out a long breath.

'The heart wants what it wants, Charlie, I get that. I just wish there hadn't been the overlap.'

'Yeah, I'm sorry. It took me by surprise. We were wrong, both of us, Alicia and I.'

Charlie sounded genuinely contrite and Alex was even more surprised to find that he wasn't terribly upset. When Alex thought of Alicia, there was annoyance and irritation of course, but beyond that there was a blank. No feelings of sadness or loss. And certainly no sense that he had lost the love of his life. He felt… free.

Impulsively, Alex put out his hand. Charlie looked at it, unsure how to react.

'No hard feelings,' said Alex and Charlie shook it gratefully.

'That's good – great in fact,' he nodded. 'Because I meant what I said in Monaco. You are the editorial future of this company.'

Alex shrugged. He wasn't into games or office power-plays, but he realised that Charlie had just handed him a bargaining chip. In fact, that was the reason he had invited Charlie along to the presentation.

'It's not just me that's the future, Charlie,' he said folding his arms across his chest. 'I think it's time to reinstate the investigations team with Lara back as head of department.'

He felt Charlie's resistance the moment he had said

it.

'Alex, I don't know. My father feels quite strongly about this. He's not convinced that investigations represent value for money.'

'And you know what? I agree with you,' said Alex. 'But here's the thing – so does every other media company. Everyone's closing their investigations departments across the board. Which gives us a huge opportunity.'

'Which is what?'

'We own it, Charlie. We make investigations our bedrock, the thing that sets us apart from everyone else. The *Chronicle*: We Own The Truth.'

Alex waited, watching Charlie turn it over in his mind, trying out the script Alex had just given him, seeing how it sounded coming out of his mouth. He would sound like a visionary – a man with a plan. And most important: Alex knew that Alicia would approve.

'Charlie, you're the managing director of Avery Media Group. *You're* the future here.'

He saw Charlie nod, stand up a little bit straighter in his Tom Ford suit. Why should Nicholas call all the shots, that was what he was thinking.

'You saw the energy in there,' said Alex, pressing his advantage. 'Without stories, real stories, we're nothing. Not serious players anyway. You didn't see people light up like that when Jen-Z from GirlFriday launched her new fragrance, did you?

Charlie laughed. 'Jen-Z has her own fragrance?'

Alex raised his eyebrows. 'Charlie, we put it on the front page.'

'God, did we?'

'I'm afraid so.'

Charlie nodded decisively.

'Leave it with me,' he said. 'I'll see what I can do.'

LARA WAS SITTING alone in the investigations room when Alex found her. Situated in the basement, the room was almost dark, lit only by the screen in front of her. Alex pulled up a chair beside her.

'So what do you think?'

The front page splash was laid out on Lara's screen.

Billionaire Murders Three:
Suspect Charged.

'It's good,' she said. 'As good as I could make it, anyway.'

Alex reached out in the dark and held her hand.

'Lara, it's perfect. Sandrine would be so proud.'

She'd filed the story for the online edition three hours earlier, but had only just put the finishing touches to the version for the print edition. The words had come easily, the whole tragic story pouring out step-by-step. Easy because she had lived it. Easy to describe because she had been there. But at the same time, Lara couldn't remember having felt so much pressure to get a story right. It couldn't just be good. It had to be great. This wasn't just the story of her life, it was the story of her best friend's death.

For the first time for a long time, Lara felt as if she had done something right.

'I've just spoken to Fox,' said Alex. 'They're going to charge Sachs within the hour, so we can name him before the first edition goes off stone.'

Other media outlets had already started to pick up on the story – man arrested in connection with financier murder – but no one had named Sachs. No one knew what had really happened.

'We'll run the version with names and images. Legal have signed off on it. Properly this time.'

Alex squeezed her hand again.

'Now we've got him, Lar,' he said. 'We've got the bastard.'

DARIUS HAD THE biggest office in the building, even larger than the Chairman's office on the top floor. He beckoned Lara in with two fingers.

'Sit.'

It always amazed Lara how much the décor of an office reflected the personality of the owner – and how little they seemed to be aware of it. Nicholas' office was elegant but cold with fake Hepplewhite chairs and a sideboard filled with unused crystal decanters, while Charlie's had slouchy sofas and a huge Warhol print – inevitably from his dollar-sign period. Darius had gone for a portrait of himself by Rankin and endless framed awards and snaps of Darius shaking hands with the likes of Bono and George Bush Jr. No surprise that it was all 'me, me, me' in Darius' playroom.

'So I have some good news,' said Darius. 'Charlie has signed off on reinstating the investigations team. We had to talk Nicholas round but I made him see sense.'

Yeah, right, thought Lara.

'Obviously, I've got to make cuts elsewhere, but I thought you should be the first to know as you will be coming back as head of department.'

He paused, evidently waiting for applause and whooping. When none came, he ploughed on. 'We really need to capitalise on this splash – the Meyer story's going to be big and I'm in talks with your friend Ortega about collaborating more closely with Le Caché. This thing is going to be huge.'

Lara couldn't help smiling. 'So you're saying serious news is the new celebrity gossip right?'

Darius pointed a finger at her. 'Exactly.'

Just as Lara could see the editor's personality laid out in the interior design of his office, she could also see his mind working. Darius liked the idea of the Investigations team returning because of the reflected glory and the credit he could take for the scoops. He had always loved the idea of himself as a political hotshot, a news heavyweight who might be able to sidestep into TV punditry or John Pilger-style analysis. Sir Darius Allen; that would be his ultimate goal.

'So we'll want you back as soon as possible, Lara,' he smiled. 'How does tomorrow sound?'

Lara paused for a moment. She knew she had to keep her resolve, but this was tough. She thought of

Stella who would give her right arm to be back on the beat and she thought of Sandrine who lived – and died – for the newsroom.

'I'm not coming back,' said Lara, trying to keep her voice steady.

Darius looked at her incredulously.

'What? You're kidding, right?'

'No Darius, I'm not.'

Darius began to splutter, falling over his words. It just did not compute for him.

'But why? Do you know how hard I had to push for this?' His eyes opened wide. 'Hang on, you're not going to some digital fucking start-up, are you?'

Lara had to suppress a smile.

'No, not digital. In fact, I'd like to stay at the *Chronicle* if you'll have me, just not full-time.'

Darius sighed deeply, theatrically, spinning his chair to face the window, the picture of a man deep in thought.

'Darius, please,' she said, trying to get him to understand.

'I love the research, I love the reporting part of the job. But being a department head? Being tied to my desk, sending other people out to do the work I love doing? It's just not me, it never was – and having a break from the job made me realise that.

'So what *do* you want?' he said sceptically.

'I want a roving role. Investigations editor-at-large, something like that. You must know that the old team has grown beyond me anyway. Stella Harris is definitely ready to step up to full-time reporter, she did some amazing work on this one.'

He could hardly disagree with that; at Lara's insistence, Alex had given Stella an 'additional reporting by' credit on the story.

'Still, Nicholas isn't going to like this,' said Darius.

Lara smiled.

'I think he'll be glad to see the back of me. Darius, I'm better out in the field. I've brought in two stories in the past fortnight and I was on sabbatical.'

She stood up.

'Imagine what I could do when I really get going.'

IT WAS SEVEN o'clock and Eduardo was sitting in The Mermaid, holding a pint and staring down at his phone. Eduardo was wearing a crisp blue shirt, a wafer-thin gold watch and expensive loafers. Lara thought it was a bit like spotting the Queen in the local chip shop. Eduardo hadn't exactly looked relaxed in Monaco either, but this part of SW1 was definitely out of his comfort zone.

He looked up and smiled at Lara.

'It's excellent work' he said. He had been reading the online version of the Jonathon Meyer story. 'Really, you are a truly gifted writer.'

'Not as good as Sandrine though.'

'Perhaps, perhaps not. But that is the tragedy, isn't it? We'll never know just how good she might have become.'

Eduardo's voice caught and he looked down, pressing a finger against his lips. Lara felt for him.

'You liked her very much didn't you?'

His eyes were sparkling.

'I loved her, Lara. I just didn't know how much until I found out she was gone. And then my heart felt as if it had broken into pieces.'

Lara reached over and touched his hand. 'We can't regret the past.'

'We can regret what we didn't do. I didn't tell Sandrine how I felt. Perhaps if I had told her, none of this would have happened.'

Lara considered it. If Eduardo had declared his love for Sandrine, would she have fallen for Stefan? Maybe. Maybe not. Lara thought about all the decisions that the main players had made and whether different ones would have brought about different outcomes. If Helen Groves hadn't gone out with her camera, would she have discovered the trafficking? If Michael Sachs had simply invested in Jonathon Meyer's fund just because they were friends, then maybe he and Sandrine – and one very loving cat – would still be alive. Shoulda, woulda, coulda; or maybe those things would have happened anyway. Lara wasn't a philosopher, she was a journalist.

Movement to her left caught Lara's eye: Alex coming into the bar, talking on his phone. Lara wondered who he was speaking to. She caught Eduardo watching her, smiling.

'What's so funny?'

'The way you look at him.'

Lara rolled her eyes.

'Not you too. Alex is an old friend, that's all. Besides, he has a terrible reputation with women.'

'I'm sure you'd keep him on his toes.'

'Eduardo, if I ever decide to settle down it will not be with someone like Alex. I need a foil, a partner, not a boss. Alex is one of those people who always thinks he's right.'

Eduardo held up both hands in what Lara assumed was the Spanish version of the Gallic shrug: the Latin shrug perhaps?

'You never answered my question, not really,' he said.

'Which question?'

'How do you feel about joining Le Caché?'

Three weeks previously, Lara wouldn't have given it a second's thought. She would have respectfully declined: she worked at the *Chronicle*, that was what she did, it was who she was. But so much had changed since then. *She* had changed so much since then. She sighed.

'I admire what you do, Eduardo, I really do. But I don't want to be tied down to anyone or anything. In fact, that's exactly what I just said to Darius back at the office.'

Eduardo couldn't hide his surprise.

'You're leaving the *Chronicle*?'

'Something like that. Going solo, setting up my own one-woman Le Caché.'

'Well, we'd be proud to help you out any way we can,' said Eduardo. 'We could make you an honorary member, if you'd prefer that. I think you've earned it.'

'Thank you. I'm touched.'

Lara didn't want to have to mention the elephant in the room; it was painful for both of them, but it had to be tackled.

'And what about Stefan?'

Eduardo gave a sad snort.

'Ah, Stefan. Your friend Chief Inspector Fox said he won't face prosecution. Legally speaking, he didn't really do anything wrong. But we will expel him from Le Caché. I can't tell *De Telegraaf* or any other publication what to do, but once people know what he was involved with and the way he behaved, I imagine Stefan Melberg will struggle to get work even writing for a local paper.'

Lara thought of Stefan's face the previous night, just before he had walked out into the rain, so miserable, so desperate to say he wasn't a bad guy. Despite everything he'd done, she didn't think Stefan was evil, he was just weak. *But you make your bed, you have to lie in it.* Lara supposed that was exactly right in Stefan's case.

Alex approached the table carrying three pints and a packet of crisps between his teeth.

'Drinks,' he grunted.

'Corporate hospitality at its finest,' laughed Lara, taking the crisps away from him.

'At least you know we're not blowing the *Chronicle*'s news budget on champagne,' he said, taking the stool opposite Eduardo. Lara stood up and laid a hand on Alex's shoulder. 'You'll have to drink mine for me. I'm going to leave you two to it.'

Lara was a spare part here anyway: Eduardo and Alex were going to thrash out some sort of information-sharing deal where the *Chronicle* could publish Le Caché stories. All part of Darius's brand new push towards making the paper the home for serious news. Lara wondered how long the idea would survive contact with Nicholas Avery and his bottom line, but she was glad they were trying it at least.

'Where are you going?' asked Alex, looking disappointed.

'Power nap, shower, pot noodle in that order. Then I'll see you back at the office with the party-poppers, I guess.'

'The first edition should be in at elevenish. You'd better be there.'

Lara smiled.

'I wouldn't miss it for the world.'

Eduardo held up his hand as Lara went to leave.

'Will I see you both in Corsica?'

Lara nodded. It was Sandrine's funeral in a week's time.

'I'll be there for a few days beforehand,' said Eduardo. 'Sandrine always used to tell me how clear the water was in the bay where she grew up and I think I want to see it. Sit where she sat, watch the boats go by.'

'We'll be there,' said Lara, meeting Alex's gaze, seeing his nod. 'Although I'm not sure I want to see any yachts for a while.'

Alex walked her out to the street. The sky had gone a deep blue, golden along the horizon, moths fluttering against a sodium lamp illuminating the picnic tables outside the pub. It was warm, but not close; the previous night's tempest seemed to have blown all the cobwebs away for now at least. Alex looked up at the stars just beginning to prick through.

'Are you going to get a cab?'

'No, I think I'll walk.'

'Sure?'

She nodded, squeezing his arm. 'It's over,' she said, taking a deep breath. 'Can't you feel it?'

'Maybe.'

He paused, pushing his hands into his pockets.

'You two looked cosy,' said Alex, nodding back towards the pub.

'Cosy? With Eduardo?' Lara started laughing.

'He's a catch,' insisted Alex, a half-smile on his face. 'If I was a woman, I'd fancy him.'

'Well, even if *I* did, even if he hadn't been seeing my best friend, I'm off relationships. I'm a rotten picker or hadn't you noticed?'

'Was Stefan a relationship?'

'Oh that?' said Lara, with a twinkle in her eye. 'That was just sex.'

Alex laughed, shaking his head.

'You're incredible, you know that?'

Lara felt goosebumps travel up the length of her arm but she tried to ignore them. Instead she tilted her head to one side.

'Is that a compliment, Alex Ford?'

'Might be. Although it's back to subservience when you're back in the office. Remember who's in charge, okay?'

She gave him a friendly tap on the arm, but Alex met her gaze.

'Seriously Lar, I'm sorry if I ever doubted you and your instincts about the story. After all these years, I should have known better. Just so you know, I won't make that mistake again.'

'I'm not coming back to the *Chronicle*,' she said quietly. 'I'm going freelance, going to have a go at doing things my way for a change.'

She had expected surprise, anger, bargaining. Instead Alex just gave her a soft smile.

'Good for you, Lar. That's fantastic.'

She didn't expect him to be so happy for her not coming back onto the team full-time. It disappointed her, but she wasn't quite sure why.

'You'd better get back in,' said Lara, pointing to The Mermaid. 'You're supposed to be wooing Le Caché, not abandoning him with a packet of Frazzles. Eduardo's more of a caviar man.'

'See you back at the office in a couple of hours then?'

'Sure. It's a date.'

Lara stayed there for a moment, watching him go back into the pub, breathing in that warm, sweet-smelling air. Then she turned and began a slow walk home, picking up some food from a deli that was still open on the way – sourdough bread, a wedge of good cheese and a packet of dark chocolate Florentines – before heading down Royal Hospital Road, Burton Court to the right, the Royal Hospital to her left. She smiled at a Chelsea Pensioner in his scarlet coat, and he tipped a finger to his hat.

She heard the car behind her before she saw it, the soft purr of an engine that spoke of expense and precision engineering. She stopped and turned, fighting the urge to run.

The car slid to a stop beside her and the window hummed down to reveal a familiar face. Victoria Sachs. The woman raised an eyebrow. 'Need a lift?'

'Actually, I'm almost home.'

'Then I'll walk with you.'

Victoria climbed out of the car, both feet together in a fluid sideways motion, the sort of thing they used to teach you at finishing school. They strolled along together in silence, the car pacing them at a discreet distance.

'So your story is out tomorrow?' asked Victoria finally.

'Assuming your lawyer isn't about to leap out of the car and serve me with an injunction.'

Victoria smiled.

'I think we've all had enough drama recently.'

'Have you spoken to the police?'

'Yes, I have.'

As they reached the Chelsea Physic Garden, Lara stopped and turned to face the older woman. A gust of wind blew her dark hair away from her face.

'I should say thank you,' said Lara. 'You didn't have to do what you did and I realise that you put yourself on the line. That there still might be consequences for you.'

'Well, I didn't do the right thing for a long time,' said Victoria, looking towards the trees peeking over the brick wall of the garden, their leaves still now after the storm.

'I stayed with a man for money and social position, even when I knew he didn't love me. But then there comes a point when you realise enough is enough.'

She paused before she continued.

'I didn't need you to tell me that Michael was having an affair, Lara. That was just his latest. He was cheating on me all through our marriage. He even has a little flat in St John's Wood – he doesn't think I know about it.' She smiled to herself. Wintry, sad. 'I know about all of it.'

'What happens now?'

'What happens now is that I work with the police and testify against him.'

'You'd do that?'

Victoria's eyes flared.

'Oh yes,' she said, with a cold laugh.

Lara realised at that moment, that Victoria Sachs didn't just want to hurt her husband. She wanted to ruin him.

'You played him, didn't you? You wanted a divorce all along.'

Victoria snorted.

'And he would never have given me one, never. Not easily, anyway, not with all his money tied up with ClearView. It would have been a very, very bitter fight. I'm sure you won't be surprised to hear that Michael Sachs liked control. Where I went, who I spoke to, what money I had access to. But now?' She met Lara's gaze. 'Soon I will be free.'

Had she engineered everything? Lara wondered suddenly. Had this whole thing been a giant game of chess for Victoria Sachs, moving herself, Helen, even Sandrine like pawns to be sacrificed? No. Surely not.

'Did you…?' began Lara, but Victoria stopped her by raising a hand to signal her driver to pull alongside.

'I adapted to the circumstances,' she said. 'And I'll keep doing so. Now I'll have money and the freedom to spend it on the charity.' She opened the door and folded herself elegantly inside. 'And myself of course.'

Lara watched her go, then turned back towards the river. The gate to the wharf still creaked, but perhaps that was a good thing, thought Lara. Not everything needed to change. She stopped by the boatyard office, using her little gold key to open her mailbox. *Bill, bill, junk mail*, she thought, flipping through her post as she walked back to the pier. 'And finally… something for me,' she murmured. It was a letter in an old fashioned, pale blue envelope, handwritten in dark blue, no stamp. She walked up the gangway onto *Misty*, sitting down on the deck to tear it open. Inside was a single sheet of crisp white writing paper, folded in half. Two lines were written down:

Your mother is dead.
Your father is alive.

She re-read it, her fingers gripping the paper until it creased at the edges, and looked around. She was on-edge again. As an investigative journalist, having enemies was an occupational hazard. She'd received various crank calls, threats and letters over the years. Most of them went straight into the bin, some of them went to senior management or the legal team at the *Chronicle*. But this. This felt like something else.

You didn't have to make a threat or throw a punch to hurt someone. Sometimes just a few words were all it took to throw you off your axis and as Lara re-read the letter one more time, she knew that something had changed, possibly forever.

She took a deep breath. There was nothing she could do about it now. Not yet. She would show it to Alex, maybe even Nicholas. She folded the letter in two and slipped it back into the envelope. She would think about it tomorrow.

Coming soon from Tasmina Perry:

A brand new Lara Stone mystery

The Last Supper

Viggo Widlund is the darling of the food world and his remote Swedish estate Kluven houses the most exclusive restaurant in the world. Situated on an isolated peninsula, there is only one communal table for twelve lucky people.

When Lara Stone bags a reservation, it promises to be a night to remember, but someone has very different plans for the evening. Viggo is found dead and everyone at the snowy retreat is a suspect. Can Lara untangle the lies and find the killer before she finds a knife in her own back?

About the Author

Tasmina Perry is the author of the international top ten bestsellers Daddy's Girls, Gold Diggers, Guilty Pleasures, Original Sin, Kiss Heaven Goodbye, Private Lives, Perfect Strangers, The Proposal, Deep Blue Sea, The Last Kiss Goodbye, The House on Sunset Lake, The Pool House and Friend of the Family.

She is a former lawyer and award-winning journalist. She was editing the UK edition of InStyle magazine when her debut novel Daddy's Girls became a top ten bestseller. She has since written fourteen novels, been published in twenty-one countries and sold over two million copies worldwide. She lives in London with her husband and son.

www.tasminaperry.com

Made in United States
North Haven, CT
17 July 2025